To Viv

REVIEWS OF PREVIOUS REDSTONE THRILLERS

KILLING POWER

'Thoroughly enjoyable, a fast and factual thriller interwoven with low politics and the high emotion of a tender love story.' [TB]

'I tentatively started reading and was instantly hooked … I do hope there will be a sequel.' [LH]

'Redolent of that celebrated series of books "Strangers and Brothers" by C P Snow. But better written, far more gripping and you really won't want to put it down.' [CMW]

'Splendid page-turner … excellent! I thoroughly enjoyed it.' [KT]

'Best Story of 2020… held my attention from the first page to the last… story-telling is fast-paced, concise and richly imaginative.' [PY]

'The plot is imaginative and exciting. It reads at a gallop and the characterisation of the main players is very good. The action was good all through … I enjoyed it greatly.' [JF]

'I was immediately hooked on this book and couldn't put it down. I am hoping that there will be a sequel or at least another novel from this fine writer. Highly recommended.' [HS]

'Next month a friend of mine who is coming to Izmir from London will bring me the novel. He said: 'I bought it, came home, just to satisfy my curiosity read a couple of pages, that is that! It was 2 a.m. when I finished it. Very catchy, easy to read, looking forward his next novel.' [OT]

'I really enjoyed it. The characters are all very well drawn. It's a thriller with lots to intrigue the reader leading to some surprising plot twists which will keep you guessing right to the end. Highly recommended.' [MT]

STATE OF RESISTANCE

'Hugely enjoyable, a pacy political/scientific thriller enhanced by sensitive development of Redstone's personal life.' [TDC]

'The author has a knack of producing up to date, relevant and thought-provoking stories. The concept, pace and character development make this a very readable book.' [DR]

'It really is a very good read. Just the right balance of topicality, politics, science and human interest.' [BS]

'So I had to be disciplined and do some other reading before allowing myself to read State of Resistance. But it was worth the wait. The basic plot was ingenious with the outcome far from obvious, and I enjoyed the way the clues were all there, but far too easy to ignore until you realised their significance 100 pages later. However, my biggest surprise was feeling myself within the story in a way I've never experienced before. So a great read. When can we hope for Redstone #3?' [CP]

'A beautifully constructed thriller. I bought the first book, Killing Power, by chance about two years ago, and immediately hooked into it. I could not stop reading until the last page. I was looking forward to a sequel. State of Resistance turned out to be as good. I would like to thank to the writer for the enjoyment I had from these books. I hope there would be some more in the future.' [LU]

'What an excellent novel and just the sort of thing I like to read. Thoroughly enjoyable.' [VG]

'I was very much entertained by State of Resistance - the plot's good and the principal characters are excellent.' [JW]

ALSO BY ELLIOT FINER

Killing Power

State of Resistance

Both novels available on Amazon as paperbacks and ebooks

DEAD PERSONAL

A Redstone thriller

ELLIOT FINER

TUESDAY 27TH JUNE

The packed 16:30 from Bristol Temple Meads was going too fast to allow Ben Ahmed to read the station signs, but he recognized the buildings flashing past. Reading. In another twenty minutes they would arrive at Paddington. He was looking forward to getting home and having dinner with the family. He knew MI5's travel section would pay for an Uber, but it was the tail end of the rush hour, so the Tube would be much faster, albeit unpleasantly crowded.

He closed his laptop and sat back. These new trains weren't any more comfortable than their predecessors, but the engineering was superb. By controlling the tilt of the train on curves, the power drawn by the motors, and the braking, the sophisticated software allowed significantly increased speeds. The journey time from Bristol had been reduced to an hour and twenty minutes. He was proud of his role in influencing the decision to permit the Chinese to supply the trains across the network, but using American rather than Chinese software. MI5 had grown increasingly concerned about the security risk associated with Chinese IT.

He glimpsed attractive half-timbered buildings as the train shot across the Thames at Maidenhead. Seconds later, the train swayed and jolted as it thundered through Slough – lots of bridges, suburban housing, blocks of flats. Not long now. He decided not to get up to collect his bag from the rack over his head until the passengers standing in the crowded aisle had left.

The train flashed through Southall, the domes of the Sikh temple clearly visible, and whipped past a much slower Elizabeth Line train. He loved the clean design and attractive curves of the new Elizabeth Line stations, and regretted that he'd have to take the much older Circle Line at Paddington.

They were well into outer London now, and he was surprised that the train hadn't started to slow down. It couldn't be more than a couple of minutes before the approach to Paddington. The driver was going to have to override the software and brake hard before the final slow entry to the station. What a waste of energy.

The woman sitting next to him touched his shoulder.

'Should we be going so fast here?' she asked.

'I was wondering that myself,' he said.

The train swayed alarmingly. Passengers standing in the aisle stumbled into each other and neighbouring seats. A man called out to pull the emergency handle, but nobody did.

'Maybe the driver has been taken ill,' the woman said. 'But isn't there a safety system? A dead man's handle?'

'There certainly used to be. I imagine it's been replaced by something more modern. I'm sure there are lots of safety systems, and they'll kick in soon.' As an engineer, he knew that there would be multiple backups to stop the train in an emergency.

There was an enormous bang as the swaying train caught some solid object next to the track. A couple of passengers shouted in alarm. A man in front of Ahmed half-stood, reached up and pulled the emergency handle. Nothing happened. Ahmed broke into a cold sweat, the sounds around him fading into his subconscious. Something was seriously wrong. He took a deep breath.

They rattled at tremendous speed past Royal Oak, a Tube station just outside Paddington. There was now no chance they'd be able to stop in time. More passengers were shouting. There was an intermittent unearthly screeching of tortured metal. Ahmed sighed, and leant forward into the brace position he'd seen in airline safety instructions, though with little hope it would help. He felt desperately sad that Anita would have to cope without him, that he wouldn't see the kids grow up. He closed his eyes, tears streaming down his cheeks, and prayed he wouldn't feel too much pain…

WEDNESDAY 28TH JUNE

To Mark Redstone's relief, nobody from London Bio had been on the train or at Paddington. But the latest figures were that almost all the 993 passengers and train crew had been killed – only five were still alive, and they had very serious injuries. A commentator pointed out that the injuries experienced by a passenger of a train hitting the buffers at over a hundred miles an hour would be similar to what would be expected from hitting the ground after jumping out of a high-flying plane. It was amazing that anyone had survived. A further eighty-one fatalities, and many more injuries, had been caused by the derailed train hitting people waiting on the platforms.

In addition, there had been an intense fire. The crash had fractured a gas main running under the shopping centre beyond the end of platform 1, where the train had run out of rail and ploughed through the crowded concourse. The energy released by the crashing train was equivalent to a direct hit by a large World War II bomb. Thirty-seven people had been killed in the fire, while 194 suffered burns, many serious. All London hospitals had been overwhelmed, and fleets of ambulances, aided by the army and the RAF, had ferried the injured to A&E departments all over the south-east of the country.

The prime minister, Michael Jones, had visited the scene of the crash and given a short, moving speech, commiserating with the injured and bereaved, and promising to devote all the resources necessary to tracing the cause and dealing with it. The PM's choice of words didn't escape Redstone's notice. The authorities thought the disaster could be the result of terrorist action, rather than an accident.

The crash had made front page news all over the world. Leaders of most countries had sent messages of shock, sympathy and support. The Americans and the Chinese had offered help in finding out what had happened, given the provenance of the train and the software it used.

Some of the London Bio staff had phoned in to say they'd work from home today. None used Paddington to commute, but a few used one of the other mainline stations. Redstone had walked round the lab that morning talking to those employees who'd come in. Several had said they were worried that the disaster might happen again, at any London terminus, if it had been a result of a design flaw in the trains, which were now in use all across the network. So they had avoided the mainline stations even if their normal commute involved just walking through one of them.

Redstone shared the general fear. His own usual Tube journey terminated at King's Cross. That morning he'd decided to get out at another Tube station, and he'd avoided King's Cross again for his journey home. So had everyone else, it seemed – the streets and Tube stations were far less crowded than usual.

Even suburban streets seemed to be affected. He usually nodded a greeting to a few people on the final leg of his commute, his walk home from his local Tube station, but today the road was deserted.

He walked through the silent house to the garden. He wasn't expecting Laura until much later – she and her MI5 colleagues were working flat out to determine if the Paddington disaster had been the result of a terrorist plot.

He strolled round the garden, his mood gradually being eased by the calm green space in the evening sunshine. Some of the staff at the lab had buried themselves in work, but others hadn't been able to keep away from news feeds on their phones and computers, and had gathered in small groups to talk in hushed tones about the tragedy. He'd become even more upset and anxious as he'd tuned into the horror felt by his colleagues. One of the young scientists had told him this morning that a friend had been coming from Bristol to stay with her. She hadn't heard from the friend, or heard any news of her. She feared the worst. He'd checked with her just before leaving the lab, and she'd still heard nothing.

He sniffed at a velvety dark red rose. Its subtle and sophisticated perfume somehow tickled his brain more pleasurably than that of any other flower.

His black cat, Treacle, bounded across the lawn and stroked his leg with her tail. She led him to the bench in the secluded back corner of the garden. A bird chattered annoyance at the cat's presence. He sat back and inhaled the sweet scent of the honeysuckle, evocative of other warm summer evenings which didn't have today's undercurrent of horror.

Treacle jumped up and nuzzled his arm. He rubbed her between her ears. It was touching that she had sensed his emotional state and was displaying this mixture of care and, well, love. *Oh, get a grip,* he thought. *You haven't a clue what's in a cat's mind. Stop anthropomorphising.*

He decided to call Laura. She picked up immediately.

'Hi. I thought you might not be able to answer. How's it going?'

'It's hard,' she said. 'We've lost one of our own. You can imagine what the mood's like here. We're determined to find out if this is the result of a terror attack.'

'Oh, no. I'm so sorry about your colleague. Anyone you worked with?'

'Yes, Ben Ahmed, our chief engineer. I'm not sure if you ever met him. He was such a nice…' She went silent.

'You all right?'

'Yes, sorry. He was coming back from a meeting at the West Avon power station. Discussing nuclear safety and the like. He had…' She coughed. 'He had a wife and three kids. We know he was on the train, and haven't heard anything from him or about him, so we're pretty sure the worst has happened.'

'I hadn't met him, but of course I understand how you must all be feeling.'

'What about the London Bio crew?' she said. 'All OK?'

'No casualties, but a lot of worry and concern. Any news on whether it was a terrorist attack? Obviously I don't expect you to tell me any state secrets.'

'No news yet. It's doubtful that we'll be able to get much information from what's left of the train, because of the fire as well as the crash, but of course the police forensics officers are working on it. And the fire service experts. And our own.'

'Gavin must be wondering if he did the right thing when he agreed to go back.'

Gavin McKay had been reinstated as Director General of MI5 after having been kicked out the previous year by the cabal who'd been running the government. He'd lost no time in persuading Laura, who'd also been kicked out, to rejoin too.

'I doubt whether he's had any second thoughts,' Laura said. 'He'd have hated being an outsider when something this enormous is going on.'

'I suppose you feel the same.'

'I do.'

'Will you be home for dinner? I'm going to make pasta.'

'Erm… no thanks.' She paused. 'I think I'll stay in my flat tonight. You know, the timing, and…'

'Oh. OK. Speak tomorrow?'

THURSDAY 29TH JUNE

Two groups had claimed responsibility for the crash: one a band of Islamic terrorists based in Yemen, the other British neo-Nazis hitherto known only for their social media ravings. The pundits on TV were discounting both, and speculating it was Russia, or China, or 'just' an accident – in which case, who was to blame? The Chinese manufacturers, or the American software developers who had produced the programs which controlled the train?

The train experts who kept popping up in the media were saying the crash was incomprehensible. They couldn't conceive of a terrorist action or an engineering fault which would allow the train to carry on at top speed, drawing full power from the onboard emergency batteries, after the trackside safety systems had switched off the supply of current to the overhead wires. And even had such a fault occurred, why hadn't the driver been able to stop the train? And if something had happened to the driver, why hadn't the passenger emergency handle worked?

Redstone tore his eyes from his phone as Joanne, his PA, came into his office.

'No need to look guilty,' she said. 'It's natural to want any scrap of news. We're all doing it. I came in to see if you'd like a cuppa.'

'Thanks. Yes please. How are your—'

His phone buzzed. Joanne gestured that he should answer it. He showed her the name of the caller – Michelle Clarke, an IT professor who'd worked with him last year.

'Hello, Michelle,' he said. Joanne waved and walked out. 'It's been a long time.'

'Yes,' Michelle said. 'Mark, I've worked out how the train crash was caused—'

'What!'

'—but I don't know who to tell.'

'Are you sure about what happened?' he said. 'Stupid question. Of course you're sure. This is huge, Michelle.'

'Yes. What I've found is sensitive. I thought you'd know how to get the information to someone in the security services. You're still shacked up with Laura Smith, aren't you? I saw she's back in a senior job at MI5.'

He guessed she'd hacked into some government website to find out about Laura. 'Yes I am still with Laura, and I'm sure she'd want to know what you've worked out. I assume it's to do with IT.'

'Correct. I need to demonstrate what I've worked out, otherwise the… the authorities won't believe me. Can you come up to Cambridge?'

Redstone thought rapidly. If the problem was an IT fault which might affect the whole fleet of trains, the government would want to keep control of the information. Keep it secret.

'The best way is for you to explain it to some people at MI5. In their building.'

'Where's that?'

'It's a big block called Thames House, on the north bank of the Thames at Westminster, just up the river from the Houses of Parliament.'

'Well, I…'

'Michelle,' he said, 'this is urgent. I'll try to arrange a meeting as soon as possible. Could you come today?'

'I can go down to London any time, but Rosie doesn't want me to travel by train in the current circumstances. And I agree. My advice is that you also keep away from trains at the moment.' Rosie, Michelle's daughter, was one of London Bio's young scientists.

'Yes, I am keeping away. My own kids have said the same to me. I'm sure I could get MI5 to provide a car. Leave it with me.

I'll get back to you as soon as I can. Or maybe MI5 will contact you directly.'

'Oh. I wouldn't want to… Um… would you be able to come to the meeting? I'd, well, welcome someone I know, because, well…'

'Of course.'

Immediately after she rang off, he phoned Laura. The call went straight to voicemail. He tried Gavin McKay's office, but was told the Director General was out at meetings with ministers. He asked to be transferred to the Chief Scientist, Jim Clothier, whom he'd worked with three years earlier. To his relief, Clothier answered. Redstone recounted what Michelle had said.

'I've got a lot of respect for Michelle Clarke,' Clothier said. 'As does everyone who knows her work. We'll send a car. Traffic will be awful, for obvious reasons, but at least she'll be coming into London when most people will be going out. Shall we say 5 p.m.?'

*

Redstone and Laura waited in the lobby of Thames House. Marble floor, three lift doors, marble staircases – one up, one down – symmetrically on each side of the lifts.

The revolving door turned, and Michelle entered. Tall, stylish. She peered around nervously and smiled with relief when she saw Redstone.

'Let's go through security,' said Laura, 'and I'll take you up.'

A uniformed officer asked to see the contents of her bag.

'If you'd leave your phone here, you can collect it on your way out,' he said politely.

'No, can't do that,' said Michelle, gripping the phone. 'I need it for the meeting.'

'Sorry, afraid that's the rule.'

'You don't understand. I can't… I need my phone.'

The officer shook his head and held his hand out.

Michelle looked at Redstone and Laura. 'Waste of everyone's time, then.' She pressed a key on the phone and held it to her ear. 'I'll tell Rosie I'm in London and going round to her flat.' She started to walk towards the revolving door.

'Wait,' said Laura, stepping into Michelle's path. 'Are you saying you need the phone as part of the explanation you're going to give us?'

'Of course. Why else would I insist on keeping it?'

Laura turned to the guard. 'Let her keep it. I'll sign whatever you need.'

*

They exited the lift and walked along a lengthy corridor to a grand oak door bearing the sign *Director General.*

'Gavin wanted to hear firsthand what you have to tell us,' Laura said.

They entered a cavernous office, with six windows overlooking the Thames. Gavin McKay jumped up from his corner desk and strode over to greet Michelle, shaking her hand vigorously. She seemed surprised. Jim Clothier walked in and introduced himself to her, saying he'd met her at a conference a few years previously. He warmly greeted Redstone. They congregated round the long meeting table in the centre of the room.

'I need a couple of minutes,' said Michelle, sitting down at one end. She studied her phone, typed rapidly on it, gave a slight smirk, and sat back. 'Ready?'

McKay nodded.

She touched the phone screen. A shrieking alarm went off inside the office, and the same noise reverberated outside in the corridor. The shriek stopped, and a voice said: 'Warning! Black female IT expert in the building!' several times.

There was silence. Michelle beamed at the others.

'Bloody hell,' said McKay. 'You hacked into our Wi-Fi! Us! MI5!'

'Yes. Only your public announcement system, but yes.'

Clothier rushed to the phone on McKay's desk. 'I'll tell the security people it was a trial,' he said.

'So your point is someone could have hacked into the train's software system,' said Redstone.

'Yes,' Michelle said, 'if they knew how to go about it, and had an AI system as good as mine, and they'd trained it by feeding it loads of examples of… never mind. Which I've done. The training, I mean, not… Well, I have done some of the… never mind.'

'You're being a bit too mysterious, Michelle,' McKay said. 'We have no interest in anything you've done that, well, you'd rather we didn't know about. Please be as open as possible. Please explain the process to me, assuming I'm ignorant about IT matters.'

'Sorry. My fault. I did come intending to…' She looked at Redstone, who nodded reassurance.

'So,' she said, 'where to start? I'll tell you what I did here, and then try to explain its relevance to the trains.'

'Excellent,' McKay said. 'Go ahead.'

She stood up, walked across the room and stared up at a small loudspeaker high on the wall. Redstone felt she'd somehow changed – always imposing, but now authoritative and in control. So this was what she was like when she lectured to her students.

'I suppose you realise your PA system has to be maintained by your IT engineers?' she said.

'Er… I haven't thought about it,' McKay said, swivelling his chair to face her, 'and if I had, I wouldn't have realised that IT was involved at all.'

'Oh. Well, obviously all your standard announcements are recorded messages, and can be sent out by someone pressing the right button. That means—'

'Of course. I see.'

‘Good. Well, all IT systems have to be maintained. It’s called digital maintenance.’

‘Why?’ asked Laura. ‘I would have thought that once they were in place…’

‘Because something may need improving, or something has changed. For example, where you want different messages to be heard, if you repurpose an office. Must happen a lot in a building this size.’

Laura nodded. Michelle strode back to the table but remained standing. To Redstone’s astonishment the usually dominant McKay, who was right next to him, was feeling vulnerable and inferior, remembering what it was like when he was an undergraduate, fresh from a rough Glasgow school, listening to a fascinating but difficult physics lecture while a group of posh students behind him were whispering in loud public-school English accents that they’d already done all this in their sixth forms. *I can’t possibly know all that*, he said to himself. *Stop imagining things.*

‘Yesterday,’ Michelle continued, ‘I identified and, well, used one of your technicians who does digital maintenance. Breaches of security systems usually rely on human weakness, so I identified a relevant human.’ She smiled.

‘But our staff lists are confidential,’ Clothier said.

‘The principle of “security by obscurity” has been discredited.’

‘I take it that means keeping things confidential isn’t enough to stop hacking,’ Redstone said.

‘Right. So,’ she said, looking at McKay, ‘first I chose a senior member of your HR department. Then I sent him an email purporting to come from the Cabinet Office. It—’

‘How did you find out his email address?’ asked McKay. ‘Oh, I suppose you easily found out our government email domain.’

‘Yes. So, the email asked him to confirm the Cabinet Office had the details of his name correctly, for their register of government

HR specialists. All he had to do was click on a button. Which he did.'

McKay grimaced. 'Even I know…'

'Right. My system worked out how to get into your staff database, using the spyware he'd unknowingly installed. That's how I identified the right technician.'

'And then you sent him another email?' McKay said.

'Yes. From you, or so he thought. You wanted him to identify dates when he could come up here to a small gathering where you were thanking junior staff for their sterling work.'

'And he clicked on a button.'

'Several, actually. Anyway, one would have been enough to install my spyware. Which allowed me to put a back door in your public announcement system. That means a way I can get in despite you locking the front door.' She grinned.

McKay broke the awkward silence.

'And something like this was done to the trains, you're saying.'

'Yes. My guess is that it was done in America when the original software was developed. Modern trains are stuffed with various IT systems, and it would be impossible for engineers to go out to each train several times a year to maintain them, so the systems have to be accessible using the internet. The engineers have a front door, and the hackers put in a back door, accessible using Wi-Fi.'

'How do you know?' McKay asked.

'You've found it, haven't you,' said Laura.

'Correct. My AI program did, on Cambridge station. The London train.'

'Did you examine the train's code to see how easy it would be to override all the safety systems once you're in?' asked Clothier.

'Briefly. Not straightforward, but not absurdly difficult. Would take a good coder a couple of days, maybe. And then you'd introduce a timing and location trigger so it would happen where and when you planned, while you were some distance away. Maybe in Russia?'

'Could you have downloaded the code itself from inside a train or a station and, well, taken it home, to St Petersburg or wherever, to work on?'

'Yes,' she said. 'You'd need maybe half an hour, but that would be no problem if you were onboard or the train was at a terminus.'

'And to think we insisted the code wasn't developed in China, to ensure security,' said Clothier. 'When the crash happened, we did consider the possibility of hackers, but our experts said it was impossible. The security was too robust.' He gave a weak smile. 'No doubt they would have said that about our PA system in this building. Oh, Michelle – about the back door you created in our system…'

'I'll tell your staff how to restore the system's integrity,' she said. 'Email me a contact.'

'Let's stick to the main issue,' said McKay. 'I suppose the devastation at Paddington means we can't recover enough of the hacked train code to give us a clue about who did it.'

'Afraid that's correct,' said Clothier. 'The train's IT equipment was totally destroyed.'

'If they could do it to the Paddington train, they can do it to others,' said McKay. 'I must tell the PM immediately. Probably means grounding the whole fleet till we've sorted it out. At the very least, it would mean examining the programming of each train to see if it's been tampered with.'

His phone rang – a loud, continuous high-pitched tone. A red light flashed on the handset.

'Hell,' he said, rushing over to his desk. He listened, and slammed the phone down.

'There's been another crash. Manchester Piccadilly. I've got to go over to Number 10. Laura, please get things going here. Sorry, folks, the meeting's over.'

*

Striding up the hill back to his house, Redstone texted the twins, Sophie in Brussels and Graham in California, to reassure them he was all right. They'd already lost one parent to violence, and he was concerned to calm down any fears.

Within an hour of the Manchester crash, the Prime Minister had announced that the whole fleet of the new trains had been taken out of service until the source of the problem had been identified and rectified. He'd made no mention of hacking. Old rolling stock would be brought back into service where possible, but much of it had been scrapped or sold off. The train network was going to be seriously disrupted for weeks, with resultant pressure on the road network. People were asked to avoid travelling if they could, and work from home, as they had during the pandemic.

Redstone wandered round his garden. There was an excellent crop of raspberries this year. He picked some and ate them on the spot – tart and sweet, they gave him an unreasonable amount of pleasure and satisfaction. Must be some atavistic pleasure from growing his own food.

Laura again wasn't going to come home this evening. Of course she was frantically busy, but he worried there was more to it than that. He'd recently sensed that something was bothering her. He wanted to ask her about it, but he was afraid that if she did tell him, he wouldn't like what he heard.

Treacle trotted into the middle of the lawn and rolled onto her back, looking him in the eyes. He bent down to stroke her. She was demonstrating she felt safe with him, and she was seeking affection. *You're doing it again,* he said to himself. *You can't know what the cat is thinking or feeling. Get real.*

FRIDAY 30TH JUNE

The Manchester train had not been as full as the one which crashed in Paddington. Nevertheless, the fatalities totalled a shocking 571, including many hit by the derailed train as its carriages ploughed into people on the platforms. Speculation about terrorism was mounting. Comparisons were drawn with the 9/11 attacks, which had claimed the lives of just under three thousand people. Maybe there had been suicide bombers on the trains? The suspicion that the cause was hacking hadn't yet hit the headlines.

Redstone had encouraged London Bio staff to work from home if they were affected by the withdrawal of the train fleet, or were simply fearful of travelling. They could do more work there than some might expect, since much scientific research involved reading, thinking and writing. It was by no means all practical laboratory-based work. But Joanne told him that the majority had come into the lab this morning.

'People don't work only for the money, you know,' she said. 'Or even for the pleasure of doing science, which you assure me is real, though I have my doubts. They come in for the company. Especially mine.'

'Of course,' he said. 'I know you've designed this place to be a social club with a small amount of science on the side.'

'Surprised you noticed,' she said. 'When are you going to join in?'

He sighed. 'I suppose I have been a bit preoccupied recently.'

'You've been drifting back to the bad habits you had after Kate was…'

'Murdered.'

'Using work as an escape from your problems. Is something wrong?'

He realised his worries about Laura must have been deeper than he'd consciously realised. It wouldn't be right to confide in Joanne.

'I hadn't… maybe it's about Project Smoothaway. The company needs it to succeed, otherwise…'

She looked at him sceptically. It was clear she'd divined there was another problem.

'Things will turn out fine,' she said. 'They have so far. Anyway, talking about Project Smoothaway, how are your own migraines? Had any more recently?'

'Not for some weeks, I'm pleased to say, but…'

'But what?'

'But I keep feeling on the verge. I'm sort of prepared for a big one to hit me. I don't know why – I haven't had this feeling before.'

'Maybe it's fear of it happening.'

'Could be. Wouldn't it be wonderful to know that if a migraine started, I could just pick up a tube of London Bio cream, rub it into my temple, and smooth the migraine away without any side effects? Simply the knowledge of that option would take away all the fear.'

'Of course. You haven't recently been as heavily involved in the project as before. Maybe you could help the staff with the remaining problems. I'd do it myself, but I've got to comb my hair.' She mimicked using a comb. 'Why don't you go round the staff and chat? All the more important while David's on holiday.' David Pepper was the chief scientist.

'Quite right. I'll go now.'

He went downstairs and wandered round the lab and the offices, asking about progress, offering suggestions, and chatting about the train crashes and people's travel arrangements. There was a lot of speculation about whether Russia was to blame. Returning to the top floor, Redstone walked round the big lab, enjoying the chemical smells, the clinking of glassware and the hum of the instruments.

He'd been so familiar with all this when he'd been a practical scientist instead of a manager. He must find time to do some real chemistry.

He stopped at Rosie's bench. She was bent over a computer, staring at an array of figures on the screen. She gave a start when he greeted her.

'Oh, hi,' she said. 'I was absorbed in…' She gestured at the screen. 'I'm pretty sure we've now got the basic chemical model right, but I'm not convinced we've got every biochemical trigger factored in. It's a pity the test tube can't tell us if it's got a headache.'

'A migraine isn't…'

'I know what you're going to say. I was joking. I know it's more than a headache.'

'Sorry. Of course you know. Let's see.' He peered over her shoulder. 'Seems pretty good apart from…' He pointed at the bottom right of the screen.

'That's what I thought. We've been thinking about adding one of the cofactors which help the enzymes get rid of excess neurotransmitters in the nerve fibres.'

'Excellent idea. Did Joanne suggest it?'

She looked at him as though he was mad. 'What? You know Joanne isn't…'

He smiled. 'Just an ongoing joke between me and her. It *is* a good idea. Well done. Delve into it and let me know what you think might do the trick.'

He stared at an automated sampling system clicking round at the far end of the lab, turned to go, then changed his mind.

'I suppose you know I met Michelle yesterday. It was great to see her again. Did she go round to your flat? She said she might.'

'Yes. She stayed the night. She said she'd been with you.'

'I didn't get the chance to chat to her. How's she doing?'

Rosie paused. 'Her business is flourishing, and she seems to be, well, almost worshipped by her students.'

'I sense a "but",' he said.

'Yes.' She lowered her eyes. 'Mum broke up with her partner a couple of months ago. She's on her own again. But now really on her own, since I moved to London. She seems to be coping, but I do worry. She's quite, um, unworldly. As you know.'

'Would it be helpful if I offered to meet up with her from time to time?'

'Might be. Shall I ask her?'

'Why not?'

SATURDAY 1ST JULY

The government declared Saturday a day of national mourning. The king was to lead prayers at Westminster Abbey. The country was asked to respect a two-minute silence at 5:46 p.m., the time of the Paddington disaster. The media contained countless articles speculating about the crashes, with experts still puzzling over the possible cause.

Redstone spent the day at home. Laura was working flat out at Thames House. In the afternoon, running out of things to do, he decided to clean his car.

'Hi Mark,' said a voice as he bent over, trying to clean the wheels, which were encrusted with black grime resistant to the pressure washer jet. He looked up to see Mary, his neighbour, standing in her drive.

'Hi Mary,' he said. 'How's things? And whatever you say next, don't let it be "Will you do my car after you've finished yours?"'

'Wouldn't dream of it,' she said. 'Will you clean my drive after you've finished your car?'

He laughed, felt guilty for laughing at a time of national tragedy, and then told himself nobody would benefit if he tried to be sombre.

'Laura snowed under at work, I suppose, given the circumstances,' said Mary.

Redstone raised an eyebrow. 'Has she told you what she does?' he asked.

'No, but I've put two and two together. If I say she's a senior official in the security services, will you have to get me arrested? Or get her to arrest me?'

He smiled. 'I can't possibly comment, except to confirm you're good at arithmetic. Putting two and two together, for example.'

'On the subject of two, how about two for tea? Fancy coming in for a cuppa?'

He gestured at his boots, wet and dirty jeans, and the pressure washer. 'I…'

'When you've finished, then. I'll give you half an hour, and then I'll put the kettle on.'

*

He sat at Mary's kitchen table.

'It's been ages,' he said. 'I'd forgotten how strange it is to be in a mirror image of my own house.' He looked around the room. 'Well, only the actual building, of course.'

'The girls used to be in and out of the two houses all the time,' Mary said.

'Sophie tells me they've stayed in touch, despite her being in Brussels and Zena in Newcastle.'

'Yes, they've remained good friends, I'm glad to say. Actually Zena was due to come down to visit us today, but the train problem messed that up. She is going to come, but by bus. Be here tomorrow.'

'You said visit us?' Mary lived alone. Prominent on the dresser was a photo of her, at least twenty years younger, with her husband. They were posing outside a restaurant in Dublin. He'd been killed in a car crash.

'Me, my sister and her family, and some of our friends.'

'Ah, of course.' Mary's sister lived nearby, which was why she'd moved here.

'Must be great that Zena's coming. Is she staying long?'

'I am looking forward to having her here. She's decided to try for a job in London. She wants to make a fresh start – she split from her boyfriend up there, and he works in the same company, so it's all a bit tricky.'

'Will she be living here, then?'

'Only at first, while she's job-hunting. She wants a place of her own. Still, I'll be seeing more of her, which'll be welcome.'

Redstone's phone pinged – a text.

'Laura,' he said. 'She's just leaving work.'

'That's nice. I hope the Tube won't be packed.'

'You saw her in action when I was attacked last year. If necessary, she'll chuck some other passengers out of the train to make room.'

*

'I needed to get out of that hothouse atmosphere,' Laura said, putting down her knife and fork. 'Great fish, by the way. Thanks. You can imagine what it's like – huge pressure from within the organisation, but also from the politicians. Can't blame them, I suppose.'

'Are you able to tell me what the current thinking is?' Redstone asked.

'So far, we don't know who's responsible. We're looking into all the terrorist organisations we know of.'

'Must be lots.'

'Yes, but many of them are easy to eliminate because they have nowhere near the level of sophistication they'd need to hack into the train's system in the way Michelle described. Which we now think is right, by the way.'

'Good,' he said. 'On both counts.'

'We've also been looking at the US connection, because the programming was developed there. The code wasn't shared with the Chinese, but there was a lot of interest in it from a number of US groups. Even the White House. It was thought to be a major advance. Anyway, no joy there either, so far. And of course there's always the Russian angle.'

‘What next, then?’

‘We’ll keep plugging away. For example, we’re examining CCTV coverage of train carriages and station platforms to see if we can spot anyone suspicious. And GCHQ have recovered a few lines of code from the train that crashed in Manchester, though no clues from that so far.’ She put her plate on top of his. ‘I suppose the perpetrators will claim responsibility sooner or later.’

He started clearing the table.

‘How have you been?’ she asked.

‘Oh, fine. Missed you, but I understand, of course.’

‘Well, I’m here now. Fancy an early night?’

SUNDAY 2ND JULY

Redstone was woken by a vicious pain jabbing above his right eye, which was swollen and watering. The side of his head felt as though it was being crushed by a huge weight. The patter of rain on the window was unbearably loud. He winced against the brightness of the bedside clock, which showed 1:30 a.m. The smell of soap from the bathroom made him want to vomit, and he was covered in cold sweat. He stumbled out of bed and fell to his knees in front of the toilet bowl, retching, his stomach spasming but producing only a thin, bitter liquid. Laura came in and stroked the back of his head, but he had to push her hand away because the touch was excruciating.

'Migraine,' he whispered. She found his migraine treatment in the cabinet and passed him a tablet. He dissolved it on his tongue, wincing at the taste. After a few minutes, his nausea eased. He lurched to his feet and made his way back to bed. Laura stood gazing at him anxiously, and then returned to her side of the bed.

Twenty minutes later, the symptoms had hardly diminished. He wiped sweat from his forehead and cursed. The medication should have kicked in by now. He turned over, felt intense nausea, and turned back.

'Mark, I'm worried,' Laura said. 'Doesn't seem like one of your usual migraines. I'm wondering if it's connected with that procedure you went through. You know what happened to the others who had it. I know it was some time ago, but maybe… If it doesn't get better in half an hour, I'm going to dial 999.'

He grunted and continued to toss and turn, trying to ease the pain and the nausea.

At 8 a.m. he awoke, feeling exhausted but with no remaining migraine symptoms. Laura rose from the bedroom chair and bent over him. He told her how he felt. She smiled her relief and went downstairs to get him a cup of tea.

He awoke again at noon, feeling almost normal.

'Are you sure it was just a migraine?' asked Laura.

'Felt the same as other migraines I've had for decades, except much more intense.'

'I was frightened. Have you had one that bad before?'

'Don't think so.'

'All the more reason to think it might be a result of the procedure,' she said.

He recollected what had happened after MI5 had modified his brain processes three years earlier. The objective had been to enable him to monitor people without their seeing him, and that had indeed happened for a period. But while carrying out the spying role he'd experienced increasingly frequent migraine-like symptoms. To his relief they had gone after the spying ability had faded away.

'The other guys who had the treatment got brain haemorrhages,' he said. 'Not the same.'

'Even so… I'd like you to have an MRI scan to check everything's all right.'

'I doubt whether it would show anything. I don't want to make a fuss.'

'Oh, for pity's sake,' she said, 'what harm can it do? I'm going to speak to the MI5 medical officer, unless you forbid it. Even if you do, actually.'

'I haven't got the energy to argue,' he said, secretly pleased she was showing such concern.

'Have you got the energy to go out for lunch? Might make you feel better. I'll drive.'

*

They sat in a quiet, half-empty Thai restaurant in the historic part of Hertford, less than an hour's drive from home. Every possible space in the room was richly decorated with Thai carved figures and screens, and yet the restaurant felt calm and peaceful. The waitresses were dressed in traditional slim gowns, with black sashes as a mark of respect for those killed in the crashes.

'Excellent food,' Laura said. 'Especially the banana fritters. And amazing value.'

'Yes,' Redstone said. 'I feel much better. Thanks for bringing me here. Let's go for a walk by the river.'

They strolled down a path alongside a row of elegant narrow Victorian cottages on their left and to the right a chain of houseboats on the River Lea. Past the cottages was a group of allotments. Redstone peered over the fence at the plots of vegetables and the myriad of small sheds. He felt a pang of unrealistic desire for a simpler life, tending an allotment and even living on a houseboat – no, perhaps not the latter, but certainly the former. He knew Laura didn't share this sort of yearning at all. He and she really were different.

They retraced their steps to the town centre, bought ice creams from a van, and took them into the park surrounding Hertford castle. The Union flag above the battlements was flying at half-mast. A noticeboard explained that the castle was originally a Norman fortification which became a Tudor palace and fell into disrepair, before being partially restored in the last century. Redstone didn't feel a sense of history – the town itself, with narrow streets and the mixed architecture typical of many English towns, was far more atmospheric.

'I'm still feeling a bit washed out,' Redstone said. 'OK if we go home and I rest?'

‘Of course. I need to log into the office and do some work anyway.’

*

Later that evening, they were sitting watching television when Treacle came into the room. The cat jumped on Redstone’s lap, looked at Laura and gave a long, piteous-sounding miaow.

‘What’s wrong, darling?’ Laura said to her.

‘Nothing’s wrong,’ said Redstone. She’s just saying hello. She vaguely remembers not seeing you for a few days.’

Laura stared at Redstone. ‘That’s a very precise statement for someone who can’t possibly know whether what he’s saying is true. And who prides himself on being accurate and scientific.’

‘Oh,’ he said, ‘I’m sure what I said was true. Humans are misled by the dying fall in cats’ miaows when they communicate with us.’

‘Maybe so, but you can’t know what Treacle remembers.’

‘I… How odd! Of course you’re right, and I was being ridiculous, and yet I was so sure – and frankly I still am. I seem to know what was in her mind. Impossible, of course. God, Laura, do you think I’m OK?’

‘You seem fine. Maybe it’s an after-effect of the migraine. Do they normally leave you feeling confused, or with odd thoughts, or whatever? After all, it is the brain that’s affected.’

‘It is. And some nerves in the head. But no, I’ve never felt this way.’

‘Maybe it wasn’t a normal migraine, as I said. I’m still concerned it might be a delayed after-effect of that procedure.’

‘I did have after-effects while I was doing the spying, but they stopped when the procedure stopped working.’

‘Mark, those two guys who MI5 treated after you – they got seriously ill. The effects were life-changing. That’s why the programme was stopped. I'm going to make sure you're given a thorough check-up.'

'OK.'

He sat back and turned over in his mind how it had felt when he knew, or thought he knew, what Treacle was thinking. It wasn't as though he understood her miaow, and that she'd been speaking in a language he could understand. It was more like having subconsciously drawn a conclusion. Yes, that was it – he'd been able to draw a conclusion which was obvious to his subconscious self. Like looking around in Hertford and knowing which direction to go to get back to the car.

Which of his senses had he used? Vision, of course: he'd observed the cat's body language; and hearing; but also – also what? Not touch, or taste – but maybe smell? Maybe Treacle had been giving off signals through pheromones? He knew that migraines were often triggered by smell. Was there a connection?

'You all right?' said Laura.

'Yes, fine. Just thinking about what it felt like when I thought I knew what Treacle was, well, thinking.' He dug out his phone and googled pheromones. To his surprise, there were lots of adverts for cat pheromones – chemicals which could be sprayed, or used in a diffuser, to affect cats' behaviour, including calming them. Cats themselves produced these chemicals when they rubbed their chins on objects, and in other situations. He read further: all life forms seemed to communicate with pheromones, certainly insects but even plants. Pheromones were a way of signalling.

But it couldn't be only pheromones. Maybe his brain had drawn together signals from all his senses, and drawn a conclusion from the combination.

'You're obviously thinking something interesting,' said Laura. 'Care to let me in on the secret?'

He explained his idea.

'But aren't pheromones specific to the species producing them? We aren't affected by pheromones from ants, are we? We don't know what ants are signalling to each other.'

'That's true…'

'And we're not affected by those cat sprays you saw advertised, surely? Otherwise, they wouldn't be allowed.'

'I …'

'You're not a cat,' she said. 'Unless the MI5 treatment gave you some feline properties. See if you can jump up about twenty feet into the air.'

'Good point.'

'Anyway, we all draw conclusions about an animal's feelings from what we see and hear. Everyone's brain does that automatically.' She stared at Treacle, who wandered over to the door, delicately pulled it open with a front paw, and disappeared into the hall. 'I accept that some people are better at it than others, maybe because they're more experienced, but that's different from being sure they know what an animal is thinking.'

'You're very persuasive,' he said. 'Maybe because I've been talking rubbish.'

She smiled and touched his hand. 'I know you *felt* you understood what Treacle meant. So something was going on. You need to come up with a better theory for why you were so sure.'

'Maybe the migraine did affect, well, my judgement. Maybe it's done that before, but I didn't realise it.'

'Sounds a more realistic theory to me,' she said. 'And I'm still going to get you examined by the MI5 medical officer. Or I could take you up the road to the vet. Can you get into the cat carrier?'

MONDAY 3RD JULY

They sat side by side on the Tube, which was still less crowded than usual. Laura was reading the *Financial Times*, despite having no particular interest in financial issues – she'd told Redstone it was the paper with the least inaccurate reporting and the least biased opinions. Redstone was tackling the crossword in the *Metro*. The train roared and juddered through the tunnel.

Redstone looked up as an end door of the carriage slammed shut. A grimy young man in an oversized jacket entered the carriage and stood swaying with the motion of the train. He started stumbling down the aisle, going from passenger to passenger, staring at them with bloodshot eyes, holding out a paper cup and asking for money for food. Everyone looked away and either shook their head or just ignored him, except for a young woman, who fished a wrapped sandwich out of her bag and pressed it into the beggar's hand. He glanced at the package, thrust it into his pocket, and lurched further down the aisle. He reached Redstone and asked him for money. Redstone shook his head and the beggar moved on to Laura.

'I'm not going to give you any money,' she said, 'for the reason that's in every other passenger's mind. We're all thinking you'll spend it on drugs. And we all know that companies out there are desperate to recruit people. We think you could earn a decent wage if you got a job, rather than getting money by begging. But you probably need help with the drugs first.'

'Ah, shut up,' the beggar muttered. 'I don't need a lecture from you. I need some money. For food.'

'I'm not giving you a lecture,' Laura said, 'it's advice. I'm trying to help. If you're addicted to some drug, you need professional support. I know it's difficult—'

The beggar raised his voice. 'Mind your own…' As he registered what he saw in Laura's face, his manner changed. He took a step back, clutched his jacket round his torso, and hurried to the door. The train slowed as it entered King's Cross station. Immediately the doors slid open he hurried out of the carriage.

Laura watched him disappear. A woman seated opposite called out 'Well said'. Laura shrugged and gave a wry smile.

'You've done it again,' said Redstone.

'I didn't do anything.'

'No. He's a lucky man.'

'You're not, though. You've missed your stop.'

'Damn. Was that King's Cross? Never mind, I'll get off at Russell Square and walk back, like I did last week. It was worth it to see you in action.'

*

He'd not been at the lab long when an unknown number called his phone. It was the MI5 medical officer, telling him she'd booked Redstone an appointment for an MRI scan at University College Hospital at noon. The hospital was only a few minutes' walk away, so he had plenty of time. Time to become nervous. Nervous about the procedure itself – the prospect of having to lie still in the confining machine – as well as about what it might show.

Joanne came into his office.

'You're a bit pale,' she said. 'Everything OK?'

He told her Laura had arranged an emergency MRI scan because of his migraine.

'But you've always had migraines. Does Laura think it might be something different this time?'

'She wants to make sure there's nothing fundamentally wrong. I don't believe there is. I'm telling myself there's no need to be nervous.'

'One day you'll learn that emotions don't always follow logic,' she said. 'Or maybe you won't. Have a swig of whisky. That'll help.'

*

Redstone lay on the hard bed of the MRI machine in the low-ceilinged basement. He tried to adjust the thin hospital gown to reduce the discomfort of folds under his back, but gave up – it didn't really matter. The whisky was doing its job. He supposed he should mention the whisky to the nurse, who was adjusting a sort of helmet on his head, but somehow the opportunity didn't present itself before the nurse, or maybe she wasn't a nurse, left the room. He'd only drunk two small glasses. Or was it three?

The scanning bed slid into the machine. The equipment made a variety of loud knocking and clicking sounds. He concentrated on the music in the helmet's headphones, and dozed off.

A voice announced there were five more minutes. He grunted and went back to sleep, and the next thing he knew was the nurse gently shaking his shoulder and telling him the scan was completed.

By special arrangement with the MI5 medical officer, a consultant examined the scan immediately it was finished, while Redstone was getting dressed. She invited him into a cramped, untidy office.

'Good news,' she said. 'I can't see any abnormalities. However, I have to warn you that not every brain condition shows up on an MRI scan. If your symptoms persist, we'll need to investigate further.'

As he walked back to the lab, he phoned Laura to tell her the result of the scan. The call went straight to voicemail. He strode on, feeling flat, less relieved than he might have expected. Maybe it was because of the consultant's warning. Or maybe it was because he'd been unable to talk to Laura about it.

*

Later that afternoon, he was in his office reading a new scientific article on migraine when Laura rang.

'Hi,' he said. 'I tried to get you earlier, but—'

'I know. I'll explain in a minute. How did it go?'

'Fine. No abnormalities, but the consultant warned me that MRI doesn't pick up all conditions.'

'That's a relief. I mean that there were no abnormalities.' She sniggered. 'Sorry, I was thinking she must have got it wrong if she said your brain is normal. Seriously, maybe it was just an ordinary migraine, then. Listen, I wanted to bring you up to speed. Restricted information at the moment, but I'm sure it'll soon be in the public domain, because we've had to tell ministers.'

'So cynical, for such an innocent young woman. Right, bring me up to speed.'

'Cynical – I prefer realistic. Innocent – hardly. Young – only compared to you, grandpa.'

He laughed. 'Come on, get on with it.'

'Well, GCHQ have recovered some of the code from the hard drive of the train that crashed in Manchester. Just fragments, because over ninety percent was destroyed, but they found something that struck them as odd – a print instruction. Why would the programming for a train's systems contain an option to print anything?'

'Maybe as part of the testing?'

'Well, they were suspicious, and couldn't make out what was to be printed. Some sort of diagram.'

'Fits in with it being part of the testing regime.'

'Shut up and listen. They activated the instruction. You realise I'm out of my depth, here, by the way, and probably using all the wrong terminology.'

'All sounds meaningful to me,' he said.

'Good. So they connected a printer, or maybe they didn't… anyway, what came out was a sort of banner with Arabic characters. It says, "God is Great" in Arabic.'

'Allahu Akbar.'

'Exactly.'

'I assume that wasn't in the original programming of the train, then.'

'Quite,' she said.

'So is everyone assuming the terrorists are Islamists?'

'Do I detect a note of suspicion?'

'You do. Sounds too obvious. Could have been put there just to send us, I mean you, down a false trail.'

'Well done, that man. Maybe you should become an intelligence officer if you grow up. We agree.'

'Odd that those instructions are amongst the fragments which weren't destroyed. What were the chances?'

'Exactly. So GCHQ examined all the other fragments, and found several more bits of the set of print instructions. In other words, the terrorists had inserted many copies, to increase the chances we'd find one pretty well intact.'

'Well,' he said, 'all that means is that they wanted us to find it. Doesn't say anything about who they were.'

'True. Anyway, presenting this info to the public is fraught with difficulties. If it's not handled right, it could lead to violence against Muslims. Riots, God knows what.'

'Yes, I can see that. Maybe that's what the terrorists want.'

'That was our conclusion, which points in fact to the perpetrators not being Islamic.'

'Good point,' he said. 'All this is pretty subtle stuff. Fortunately, Michael Jones will be able to handle it, I think. He's a very professional politician.'

'We hope so. But he doesn't control the media.'

‘Ah. Maybe the real terrorists will feed hate messages into social media themselves, as soon as the news is leaked.’

‘Or even leak it themselves,’ she said.

‘Bloody hell.’

‘Exactly.’

‘Let’s discuss it more at home later.’

*

Thinking Laura would enjoy a good meal after a stressful day, Redstone carefully prepared a fish curry. He’d serve it with fresh rice almost as soon as she got home. The weather was hot, and the kitchen hotter, so he went into the garden to cool down. He felt a bit guilty that the curry smell had permeated the neighbourhood.

‘Smells delicious,’ called Mary over the fence. ‘How are you?’

‘Fine, thanks. Laura’s been working hard, as you’d expect in the circumstances, so I thought she’d need feeding properly.’

‘Lucky Laura. Have you seen the news? The security people think the train crashes were the result of hacking. And they’ve discovered an Arabic slogan in the Manchester train’s computer system. But the Prime Minister says it was probably put there to cause riots, and we’re all too sensible to be fooled like that. He says.’

‘I hope he’s right. You think he is?’

‘Well, someone did the hacking. I wouldn’t riot as a result of their finding that slogan, but there are loads of idiots out there who would.’

‘That’s the worry,’ he said. ‘Depends on what the media say. Including social media.’

‘Yes. I’m going in to peruse Twitter. Enjoy the dinner.’

He sat on the bench. Treacle jumped up and sat next to him, feeling contented.

His phone pinged – a text from Laura. She wasn't coming home tonight – too busy. He felt upset and disappointed. If any of his friends had lived nearby, he would have called to see if they were free to come round for the dinner which was now going to be wasted. But they all lived a long way away.

How about Mary?

He phoned her. 'Hello neighbour,' he said. 'This might sound rude and insulting, but I hope you won't take it that way. Laura's now not coming home this evening. Might you be free to help me eat that curry I've just made? I'd love your company. Please say if it's not con—'

'How kind!' she said. 'I was wondering what to cook. I'd love to come round. Half an hour?'

*

'That was pretty good,' Mary said. 'Laura missed out. Staying in her flat, I suppose?'

'Yes. It's more convenient for … oh, you know where she works, let's not pretend. For Thames House. They're no doubt under even greater pressure, given the accusations on social media.'

'As far as I've seen, though, it's just the normal bigots and cranks,'

'Does it matter who starts these things? Once the numbers ratchet up, who knows what can happen.'

'Well, let's not waste energy worrying about it. About your curry. Did you know I—'

Redstone's phone chimed. 'Excuse me,' he said. 'Hi, Sophie. How are you?'

Mary gestured at the door.

He shook his head. 'No, please stay,' he said. He switched to loudspeaker. 'I was talking to Mary, who popped round to help me eat dinner. Laura couldn't make it.'

'Hi Mary,' said Sophie. 'Just wanted to check you're OK, Dad. Brussels is full of rumours.'

The phone beeped – Graham, in California.

'Hold on, Sophie,' Redstone said, 'Graham's calling too. I'll patch him in.'

The four of them exchanged greetings.

'What's the inside information, Dad?' Graham asked. 'I assume Laura's keeping you up to speed.'

'Nothing concrete yet. It's true that the investigators discovered Arabic words in the remaining fragments of code, but they could have been put there to mislead everyone.'

'I think it's that,' Mary called out. Redstone gestured that she should join the conversation fully. She moved her chair next to his, and leant towards him and the phone. He liked her subtle perfume.

'Mary, how's Zena? Still in Newcastle?' Graham said.

'She's moving down here in a few days. Wants a job in London.'

'Is her partner coming too?'

'No,' said Mary. 'They've split up. You still with that girl we saw at Christmas?'

'Same, I'm afraid.'

'Pity you're five thousand miles away.'

'Yes. I must get in touch with her.'

'So,' said Redstone, 'as we were saying before we got on to important things, Mary thinks the terrorists aimed to produce civil unrest.'

'Yes,' said Mary. 'That's in line with their overall aim, isn't it? Terrible people. They want to cause as much disruption as possible. Shameful. All those poor people killed and injured. Let's hope the authorities catch them quickly so there are no more tragedies.'

TUESDAY 4TH JULY

'I hate this road,' said Hilda Branch.

'Not as much as I do,' said her husband Joe, slowing their elderly Nissan Micra as the brake lights of the lorry in front glowed in response to a reduction in the speed limit displayed on the overhead gantry. 'But you know it takes ages if we use the back roads.'

Each of the four lanes of the M25 was crowded with head-to-tail traffic, now moving at forty miles an hour. Joe lacked confidence about driving in these conditions, and stayed in the inside lane, almost the only car in a line of lorries and large vans. He and Hilda made the journey every week, to visit Hilda's mother in her nursing home near Waltham Cross. He always got nervous beforehand.

The speed signs suddenly changed back to the national limit. The traffic speeded up. The huge lorry behind him moved so near the Micra that all Joe could see in the mirror was its radiator grille. He put his foot on the accelerator.

The lane signs on the overhead gantry changed yet again, now showing red crosses for the two outside lanes. The information board on the gantry read LANES BLOCKED. Cars swerved to the left to join the two remaining open lanes. Joe was hemmed in by lorries ahead and behind, and a wall of faster-moving lorries, vans and now cars to his right. To his left was the gravelly embankment – the emergency lane had been abolished to allow the number of traffic lanes to be increased to four, as part of the 'smart motorway' system.

Red brake lights suddenly gleamed ahead. A white van swerved into Joe's lane, causing him to jam on his brakes. A long, deep hoot reverberated behind him. A huge jolt shoved them forwards in their seats. A massive bang, and everything went black.

*

The media were reporting several demonstrations and some isolated instances of physical attacks on Muslims, but no one had been seriously hurt. Police stood guard outside many mosques round the country.

It was clear that the train crashes were the work of terrorists, whether Islamic or not, and there was much criticism of the anti-terrorism authorities who had allowed the perpetrators to get through their nets.

Shortly after arriving at the lab, Redstone went downstairs to talk to the two London Bio staff who'd told Joanne they'd received some abuse on their way into work together. An elderly white man had shouted at the two young women, who wore hijabs, but other passengers had told him to shut up.

He went back upstairs and settled at his desk, trying to design an experiment which would help test Rosie's idea about how to improve the performance of the Smoothaway cream. He wanted to do some real chemistry himself. Pity David was on holiday – it would have been good to bounce ideas off him.

Joanne popped her head round the door.

'Huge pile-up on the M25. It's the signs on the overhead gantries. They're giving wrong information, apparently.'

'Oh dear,' said Redstone. 'Some people would say an accident waiting to happen. There's been a lot of criticism of the smart motorways, so-called. Anyone hurt?'

'Eleven killed. A crash, then drivers crashed into the crash, and so on. The motorway's going to be closed for at least a day. I'll let the staff know in case anyone has plans to use it.' She went back into her office.

He finished designing his experiment, walked through Joanne's office into the big lab, and made his way to Rosie's bench.

‘Hi. I want to discuss some ideas,’ he said. ‘I’ve been thinking about how to test your—’

‘Hey!’ A scientist on the other side of the lab called out. ‘There’s chaos on the roads all over the place!’ He waved his phone. Rosie and Redstone looked at their own phones. Much of the motorway network was grinding to a halt. Lane closure signs came on and then went off, speed limits kept changing, and drivers were deciding to ignore all the signs and then finding some of them were because of real incidents, resulting in shunts, some bad crashes, and huge tailbacks.

Redstone’s phone rang. Michelle.

‘I suppose you know how the enemy, or whatever you call them, are messing up the roads?’ she said.

‘Tell me.’

‘They’ve hacked into Highways England's control centres. There are a few around the country, and they’re digitally linked.’

‘I suppose you’ve checked that,’ he said. ‘Of course you have.’

‘I did examine the coding. Briefly. It would be easy to mess up the lane control signs. In fact I—’

‘Don’t tell me. You did it yourself.’

‘I just checked that I could. It’s straightforward to introduce a randomizer and disconnect the links which are used by the human controllers. I didn’t actually—’

‘So you think it’s the same people who tampered with the trains.’

‘Of course. Don’t you?’

‘I do,’ he said. ‘Thanks. I’ll tell MI5 straight away.’

He phoned Laura. The call went straight to her voicemail, so he tried Jim Clothier, who answered immediately. He told Clothier what Michelle had said.

‘Yes, we’ve reached the same conclusion,’ said Clothier. ‘GCHQ were trying to get hold of the code, but it seems the hackers inserted an instruction to make the whole program wipe itself after a certain time. Now nothing's working. No warning signs, no speed limit signs, nothing.'

'Hell. What's the government doing?'

'They're about to announce a thirty miles an hour limit on all motorways, enforced by police using old-fashioned methods.'

'The country's going to grind to a halt. The hackers are achieving their objectives. Assuming that's what they want.'

'Yes,' Clothier said, 'though they still haven't broken cover. No announcements, no threats, no demands. Makes it hard to figure out who they are.'

*

As he sat in the Piccadilly Line train going home, Redstone wondered if the hackers' next target would be the Tube system. It was an obvious way of bringing chaos to the capital. If they were trying to influence the government, London was surely the place to target. Maybe they lived in London and didn't want to be inconvenienced themselves? Or was that too fanciful? He'd put the thought to Laura and see how she reacted.

She rang as he walked into his garden.

'Hi Laura. How are you? Snowed under, I imagine.'

'Yes,' she said. 'Get home all right?'

'I did, thanks.' He told her his idea about the Tube system.

'It's not a silly thought,' she said, 'but not particularly helpful at present. If we had a bunch of plausible suspects and wanted to know where to concentrate our resources, we might look first into those based in London. But we're not at that stage, I'm afraid. That's confidential, of course.'

'Of course.'

'Jim told me you called. I gather your IT genius girlfriend made an input again.'

'Well, she…' He didn't know how to react to Laura's uncharacteristic tone.

'Pity she's not nearer,' Laura said, 'or you could invite *her* to dinner this time. As it is, it'll have to be Mary again. Afraid I won't be going to your house.'

'Oh. I'll miss you.'

'Well, it is Independence Day.' She paused. 'Mark, sorry I'm being bitchy,' she said. 'It's… well, you know.'

He wished he did know.

TWO DAYS LATER – THURSDAY 6TH JULY

There were widespread complaints from industrialists and their representative organisations about the thirty miles an hour speed limit, which was already causing delays in deliveries, congestion in ports, and problems for professional drivers, who had to stop driving once they had clocked up their permitted hours. The media were riddled with forecasts of a steep decline in economic output, of job losses, and of investors moving overseas. The country was going to become poorer and weaker, according to the pundits. Was this the terrorists' aim? Why hadn't they broken cover to reveal their objectives or demands? What was MI5 doing about it? Newspapers that supported opposition parties accused Jones and his ministers of complacency and inaction.

The government said it was doing all it could to restore the smart motorway systems and the train coding, but it had to ensure the replaced software could resist further hacking attempts. The intelligence community was working flat out to identify the terrorists and bring them to justice.

Redstone was interested that the Tube into work was still emptier than usual. Maybe it was simply because some regular commuters used it as the final stage of a journey involving main line trains or motorway journeys. Or maybe it was because many commuters were switching to home working, rather than just those whose travel was specifically affected by the transport problems.

Wearing a lab coat and safety glasses, Redstone stood at the bench next to Rosie's, assembling glass apparatus. Despite the travel difficulties, Rosie and most of the rest of London Bio's staff had turned up. He'd printed out Rosie's notes on how to make the revised formulation of the Smoothaway cream, and had agreed with her what he would contribute and what she and the rest of the team would be doing. He hadn't argued when she'd suggested that their contribution should be rather more than his, given how much lab experience each of them had accumulated during the last year.

As he carefully weighed out the first chemical, he smiled as he recalled how his late wife, Kate, had mocked him for weighing each ingredient while cooking. 'How much is a "pinch" supposed to be?' he would complain. Nowadays he knew, and rarely weighed out anything at home. He glanced at Rosie as she studiously adjusted a glass valve while monitoring the flow of a clear liquid dripping into a round-bottomed flask. *God, this is fun.* Why had he given up bench work for the office? Wanting to be in charge, he supposed. Which also had its benefits.

By 4 p.m., they'd finished the first phase of the preparation.

'Too late to start the next phase,' he said. 'Why don't you knock off early?'

Rosie shook her head. 'Oh, I couldn't do that.'

'Why not?'

'The boss might notice. He's a real tartar. We're all terrified of him.'

He laughed. 'Excellent. I must learn some management skills from him. Go on, bugger off home.'

'Oh,' she said, 'before I, er, go, I did ask Mum if she'd like to meet you socially. She's grateful, but doesn't think you should put yourself out for her.'

'Right.' At least he'd tried to be helpful.

Back in his office, he hung up his lab coat and thumped down in his comfortable chair. He put his feet up on an open drawer and texted Laura to find out if she was going home this evening. She replied immediately – she would go to his house, but not until late, so he should eat without her. He sighed.

*

'Hi Mark,' called Mary over the fence. 'Laura coming back this evening? She must be up to her eyeballs at work.'

'Yes, but not till late, apparently.'

'You eating on your own, then?'

He hesitated. Was she fishing for another invitation?

'Yes, I'll knock up something—'

'How about coming over here, then? I'm making a special meal, to celebrate Zena's return. And there's too much, as usual. We'd love you to join us.'

'Yes, do come,' called a disembodied voice which he recognised as Zena's.

'Oh, hello Zena,' he said. 'Wherever you are. Welcome back! Thanks, Mary. That'll be great. What time?'

*

The table was laid with a white tablecloth, candles, a small arrangement of flowers, shining cutlery and sparkling glassware. The air was suffused with warm smells.

'This is lovely,' he said. 'As are both of you,' he added. He blushed – was that over the top? They did both look glamourous: Mary in a fawn dress with a flimsy reddish scarf thingy round her neck, and Zena in a glittering black top and short skirt. 'Sorry if that sounded a bit…'

'It sounded great,' said Mary. 'I don't normally get such compliments nowadays. But I'm sure Zena does. Don't you, darling.'

'Not really,' Zena said. 'The youth of today have no manners,' she added, in a trembly imitation of an old woman.

He grinned. 'And, as I started to say before your astounding beauty diverted me, the way you've laid the table is wonderful. Like in the best of posh restaurants.'

'Hardly a surprise,' said Zena. 'Considering.'

'Considering what?'

'Don't you know what Mum did in Dublin, before, you know?'

'Er… oh yes, they had a restaurant.'

'Only the poshest restaurant in the city.'

'Well,' said Mary, 'Not *the* poshest. *Amongst* the poshest.'

'Wow!' Redstone said. 'What made you… well, I think I know why you came here, after your husband was…'

'Killed,' said Mary. 'Say it as it is. If you're asking why I took up nursing rather than starting a new restaurant, it's because I was so inspired by the nurses who cared for me after the accident. Well, that was one reason.'

'I didn't realise you were also hurt in the accident,' Redstone said.

'Yes. Head injuries. Made a full recovery, I'm pleased to say. Unlike Patrick. Sorry, didn't mean to put a damper on the atmosphere. Fancy a drink?'

She poured prosecco into three glasses.

'To Zena: to the start of a new phase in your life, my dear,' she said.

'Hear, hear,' said Redstone. They clinked glasses and drank.

As they ate the first course – avocado salad – they chatted about Zena's plans: she was hesitating about whether to pursue her career in theatre management, and thought it wouldn't be difficult to find a job in the West End to help her reach a decision. Mary cleared away the plates.

'Roast beef and Yorkshire pudding next, by any chance?' said Redstone.

'How did you know?' asked Zena.

‘I recognized the smell as soon as I came in. One of my favourite dishes. I don’t often cook it myself, because you need—’

‘—a big joint to make the beef turn out well, ‘said Mary.

‘Exactly,’ he said.

‘We’ll be having roast beef sandwiches over the next few days,’ she said. ‘And I can give you some to take home. It freezes nicely. I’ll be taking some to the church, too.’

He raised his glass of claret.

‘Here’s to roast beef,’ he said.

*

As he entered his house, a bit drunk, he realised that Laura had returned. She wouldn’t have been surprised to find him out because he’d texted her to say where he was going. He tiptoed upstairs. She was in bed – apparently asleep, but he wasn’t sure if it was a pretence. He decided not to test it.

FRIDAY 7TH JULY

Redstone awoke feeling happy. He lay in bed, recalling the previous night's dinner. Excellent food and drink in the company of an attractive and interesting woman and her pleasant daughter. What not to like?

Laura lay next to him, unmoving, breathing evenly. He wasn't sure if she was awake, so he kept quiet and still. He'd better play down the evening when he talked to her about it.

She wanted to leave him. A stable life based in suburbia wasn't for her. She needed excitement, change, challenge. She remained fond of him, and was worried about how to tell him. She wasn't sure what their future relationship would be like.

WHAT? WHERE THE HELL DID THAT COME FROM?

He rushed to the bathroom and sat on the closed WC, sweating, his head in his hands. Had she said all that last night – and he'd forgotten? No, he hadn't been that drunk. He was sure he'd come in and found her asleep, or pretending to be. He hadn't dreamt it – it seemed real, different from a dream. Had he deduced it from her behaviour recently? It was consistent with how she'd been in the last few weeks.

'You OK?' Laura called from outside the bathroom door.

'Yes, thanks,' he said. 'Sorry if I disturbed you. Just had a bad dream, I think.'

'Probably too much rich food last night,' she said. 'I'm going to rush off. I'll have breakfast at work. Lots to do, as you can imagine.'

He pulled himself together, completed his ablutions and went down to breakfast. For once he didn't switch on the news – he wanted to think more about the… the what? The deduction, he decided.

The deduction churned over in his mind through his journey into work. Unfortunately, it made sense. She'd definitely been showing signs of not enjoying coming to the Southgate house, but he was confident that she remained fond of him. And her background – orphaned, care homes, army – would make some people yearn for suburban stability, but had moulded Laura in the opposite way. And there was the fact that she had a failed marriage behind her. It all fitted.

But there was a major flaw in this story, and it was him. Specifically, his ability to divine what was in women's minds. He was bad at it – Kate, Sophie, Laura and others had told him. Not that he hadn't already known. But maybe he was getting better in his old age? Well, middle age.

Time to put all this aside for the moment, and let it mature in his subconscious. He greeted Joanne, walked into his office and donned his lab coat.

'That's disgusting,' she said from the doorway.

'What?'

'It's stained and it's even got holes in it. Heaven's sake, we can afford to give you a new one.'

He glanced down at the lab coat, with its chemical stains and acid burns. 'I like it. It's a, well, sort of badge of honour, and brings back memories. See, this hole—' he stuck his finger through a hole near the hem '—was made by a drop of nitric acid when I was—'

'Never mind. Go and enjoy yourself,' she said.

He walked into the lab.

'Ready for the next phase?' he said to Rosie, who was leaning against the windowsill at the far end of the white-topped bench.

'Sure,' she said, 'but are you? You seem, well, preoccupied. If you don't mind my saying.'

'I'm fine. See, you did that, and I'm not sure I would have.'

'Did what? I didn't do anything!'

'You noticed I'm preoccupied, as you put it.'

'Well, it was obvious,' she said. 'Obvious that something's on your mind. Something worrying, or upsetting, I'd say. Sorry if I'm being intrusive.'

'Not at all. Er… can I do an experiment on you? Actually, it's on me, but I need you to help.'

'What do you mean?'

'Please think about… an object. Or an activity. I want to see if I can figure out what it is.'

'You mean by asking a series of questions?'

'No. Please, just think of something.'

'Really? Um… OK, I'm thinking.'

He looked at her.

'Damn. I haven't got a clue.'

'Of course not. How could you? I was thinking about going for a swim in the sea.'

'Oh. It was a stupid idea. Let's get on with the science.'

A couple of hours later, Rosie's phone clinked. She picked it up.

'You might be interested in this. Mum says she's been asked to advise on the reprogramming of the motorway sign stuff. She wants me to tell you.'

'That's a great move. I bet our friends in influential places were involved.'

'You mean MI5? Laura, and Gavin McKay, and Jim Clothier?'

He raised his eyebrows. 'You know everything?'

'You taught me that no scientist can ever say they know everything. There are always unknown unknowns.' He smiled. 'But Mum has kept me informed,' she continued. 'And something you probably don't realise you don't know is that I've been security vetted.'

'Good heavens! Is that because of Michelle's involvement in, er, government issues?'

'Partly. And I'm sure you know I now live with Lewis.' Lewis Ellington was Laura's assistant.

‘Of course.’ Her phone clinked again.

‘Ah! What Mum calls “the enemy” have surfaced on social media. Seems the main platforms are all carrying the same message.’ She showed him her phone. *Blame Jones. His corrupt and incompetent regime installed the so-called smart motorways and the rightly called stupid trains. What more havoc can he wreak?*

‘Oh dear,’ Redstone said. ‘Michael Jones is going to hate this. It’s rubbish, especially the “corrupt and incompetent” bit, but it’s also true – the motorways were converted and the trains were ordered while he was prime minister. A few years ago, of course, in his previous term of office.’

‘What about that last bit?’ said Rosie. ‘Does it mean the enemy are going to find another way of disrupting the country?’

‘Looks like it. I wonder what they have in mind.’

*

‘Do you want to tell me your problem?’ asked Joanne as he sat at his meeting table eating an avocado and bacon bap.

‘What problem?’

‘The one that’s made you distracted this morning.’

‘But I haven’t been with you this morning. Till now. Do you mean Rosie’s been talking to you?’

‘Look,’ she said, ‘do you really think your life isn’t monitored and controlled by an all-powerful cabal who regularly meet in our secret headquarters, namely the women’s loos?’

‘Well… I’ve got this strong feeling that Laura is fed up with me.’

‘Oh dear. That’s awful. What’s she said?’

‘She hasn’t said anything, but… Oh, I suppose I’ve got to talk to her about it.’

‘Yes.’

‘I’m not sure if she’ll be going to the house this evening,’ he said.

'Better ring her to find out, then.'

'Right.'

'Things will work out,' Joanne said.

She left his office. He phoned Laura, the call went straight to voicemail, and he left a message. Two hours later, as he was standing next to Rosie titrating a solution into a flask, Laura texted saying she'd be back at around 9 p.m.

*

'So what is it you wanted to talk about?' Laura said, sitting opposite Redstone at the kitchen table with her hand round a large gin and tonic.

He took a deep breath. 'It's about our relationship. I realised…' He gulped. 'Well, I suddenly had a feeling that you can't stand living a suburban life anymore, so you want to leave me, and you're searching for a way of telling me without upsetting me too much.' He turned away.

She paled, and drank deeply. 'I…' She gazed at the floor. 'Sorry,' she said, 'it's true.' She looked up. 'But how did you… I mean, it's so…' She stood, paced to the French windows, and stared at the twilit garden.

'Mark,' she said, turning to face him, 'before we get into that, I want to say I'm really fond of you, and it's not your fault. It's to do with my personality. I need excitement, variety—'

'I know,' he said. 'We both like challenges and change, but not of the same sort.'

'That's right. For you it's intellectual, and in your work. For me it's my lifestyle, everyday stuff.'

'Suppose so,' he said. 'So what now? Are we still… together in some way?'

‘I don’t know. You’ve caught me off guard. Actually I’m amazed at how well you’ve read me.’ She drank from her glass. ‘How long has it taken you to work out my feelings and thoughts like that?’

‘I’m not sure,’ he said. ‘I assume it’s been a process, but if so, it’s been subconscious. The whole thing just popped into my mind yesterday, soon after I’d woken up. That’s why I rushed to the bathroom. I was pretty…’ His voice cracked. He cleared his throat. ‘I was shaken.’

‘Are you saying this, well, realisation occurred to you while we were lying next to each other?’

‘Yes. I thought you might be still asleep.’

‘I wasn’t. I was lying there thinking exactly what you’ve described. It’s as though you were reading my thoughts.’

‘No, it wasn’t like that,’ he said. ‘There were no words. I couldn’t hear your voice, or your way of phrasing things.’

‘But you seem to have read my emotions, as it were.’

‘The likely explanation is that I just subconsciously put lots of small clues together,’ he said.

‘Like when you read Treacle’s emotions the other day?’

‘Er… maybe.’

‘What am I thinking, or feeling, now?’ She leant back on the glass of the French windows and gazed at him without expression.

He studied her, but nothing came.

‘I haven’t a clue.’

‘You’re the scientist here. What can we do to sort out how you read my thoughts?’

‘As I said, I didn’t read your thoughts.’

‘I think you’re taking the expression too literally,’ she said. ‘Something happened which resulted in your knowing what I was thinking.’

‘You’ve changed the subject,’ he said. ‘Don’t we need to talk more about, well, us?’

'Sorry. It's... To be honest, I'm not sure there's anything else I can say. I know it must be horrible for you, but I've been here before. In my first marriage. I'm just not the sort of person you need.' She shrugged.

He sighed. 'OK. Let's get back to the non-mind-reading.'

'I was saying you might not like calling it mind-reading, but you suddenly learned what I was thinking. Don't get hung up on the terminology.'

'I suppose that's fair. I can read a newspaper article and tell you what it said without remembering the actual words the writer used. But let's be rational. It can't be that I read your mind.'

'Why not?'

'Nobody can read minds. There's nothing special about me.' As he said this, he realised it might not be true. The way his brain had been irradiated by MI5 three years ago was special. Very special.

'Maybe it's not you. Maybe I'm giving off some signals somehow. No, can't be that. That would have the same logical flaw. There's nothing special about me.'

'Er... I'm now wondering if—'

'Let's be imaginative,' she said. 'Might there not be some physical process which explains it? Don't brains give off electrical currents?'

'There is a lot of electrical activity in the brain. It produces small voltage fluctuations in the scalp. That's how EEG machines work – they detect the voltage changes.'

'Remind me...'

'Electroencephalograms. People use them for brain research. But the electric fields are so minute that you have to have sensors actually on the scalp to detect anything.'

'Nevertheless,' she said, 'they're there. I know because a successful scientist just told me.' He smiled.

‘Right,’ he said. ‘Let’s assume people could read other people’s thoughts by picking up these minute electric field fluctuations. They’d need… Ah!’

He walked over to the French windows, crouched slightly, and put his head very close to hers.

‘What are you doing?’ she said.

‘Bear with me. Think of something.’

‘OK.’

‘Eating a chocolate ice cream,’ he said.

She flung her arms around him. ‘Yes!’

He started to hug her, but she disengaged.

‘Sorry,’ she said, ‘hardly appropriate in the circumstances.’

‘Yes, it was appropriate,’ he said. ‘Shows the underlying feeling, even if you do need to move out.’

She gave a half-shrug. ‘Back to the main event, though. I suppose you came close because the signal is weak?’

‘Exactly. When we were lying in bed our heads were only, what, thirty centimetres apart? The strength of an electric field falls off dramatically as you get further away from the source.’

‘When you worked out what Treacle was thinking the other day she was on your lap, wasn’t she?’

‘Yes. Her head was quite close to mine.’

‘There you are, then,’ she said.

Redstone moistened his lips. ‘I need a G&T too.’ He went to the fridge, busied himself making the drink, and took a mouthful.

‘Well,’ he said, ‘it looks as though my brain can pick up electric fields from yours and Treacle’s. Maybe that’s not so amazing. But the big question remains – how did my brain manage to interpret what it picked up? I’m wondering if it’s to do with the treatment I got at Thames House three years ago.’

‘Ah. And the migraine?’

‘Yes, could well be connected. Seems quite likely. I guess it was a side effect of my brain reorganising itself to pick up thoughts.’

‘But why just me? And Treacle, of course. Have you picked up anyone else’s thoughts?’

‘No. I tried with Rosie at the lab the other day, but got nothing. Mind you, she was a few metres away, so…’

‘Maybe the fact that you know me well has something to do with it. And you know Treacle well.’

‘Could be. We could test the idea by trying it on someone I don’t know so well. How about Mary, next door? I’ll phone her to see if she’s in.’

Laura frowned. ‘No,’ she said, ‘wait.’

‘Why not?’

‘I don’t like the idea of… well, there could be security implications.’

‘What do you mean?’ He wished he was back standing close to Laura so he could understand what was going through her mind, because he suspected he’d pick up a whiff of jealousy. Or was that wishful thinking?

‘If you have this ability as a result of that irradiation, we certainly don’t want anyone to know about it. That project had the very highest classification.’

‘Oh,’ he said. ‘Fair point.’

‘What’s more,’ she said, warming to the subject, ‘the ability might be useful to the security services now.’

‘I don’t see how. I can’t go around touching heads with suspected spies. They might notice.’

‘I don’t know. But I think we should take you and your head to Thames House, as soon as possible, and talk to Jim Clothier.’

‘I suppose you’re right.’

‘Good. I’ll set it up first thing on Monday.’

‘OK,’ he said. ‘But what about tonight? Are you going back to your flat, or do you want to sleep in the spare room, or what?’

She flushed. ‘I feel quite excited by all this. Let’s do some more close-up experiments.’

Reading her mind isn't the same as understanding it, he thought.

MONDAY 10TH JULY

Laura warned Redstone not to tell anyone about his new ability, and then rushed off, saying again she'd have breakfast at work.

He sat at the kitchen table, munching toast and listening to the news. The low motorway speed limits were disrupting goods transport, and shortages were starting to appear in shops. Companies were agitating for the national speed limit on the motorway network to be raised to fifty miles an hour. The opposition parties were saying the PM couldn't deny his leading role in the decisions which allowed the terrorist acts.

Redstone's Tube commute was still not as busy as usual. As he entered Joanne's office, puffing from running up the stairs, Laura rang.

'I've fixed a meeting with Jim Clothier,' she said. '11 a.m. Is that OK?'

'Sure. Do I ask for him when I go in?'

'No. Say you're meeting me.'

He nearly asked her whether she saw him as her personal asset, as the terminology went if what he'd read in spy stories was accurate. But he thought better of it.

*

Exiting Pimlico Tube station, he decided to walk to Thames House via Millbank, because he enjoyed seeing the river. He strode down Vauxhall Bridge Road, a wide dual carriageway clogged with buses and lorries, his eyes watering from the pollution, and veered left onto Millbank. It started to rain heavily, to his relief – his garden needed water. He dodged sideways as a lorry sent a shower of spray onto the pavement as it squished past. The skyline on the other side of the river was crowded with new blocks of high-rise flats, resulting in the majesty of the wide Thames being visually weakened. *Oh well, people have to live somewhere,* he reasoned. Maybe people in Georgian times had complained about the pleasant, stuccoed terrace on his left.

He passed a traditional red phone box, presumably there just for tourists' photos in this age of mobile phones, and glanced at the Tate Britain gallery. He must go there again – it had been some time. But who would he go with? A wave of sadness passed through him. 'Passing Strangers', sung by Sarah Vaughan, started playing in his mind.

There were always strong gusts of wind at the base of Millbank Tower. His umbrella blew inside out, and the rain soaked his face and hair. Maybe he'd made a mistake coming by this route. Anyway, here he was, at Thames House, an imposing pre-war neoclassical pile in grubby grey stone. He trotted up the shallow steps and entered the lobby where he'd met Laura and Michelle eight days ago. It seemed much longer.

He told the receptionist that he was expected. She checked her computer and phoned Laura. He asked for a toilet where he could dry himself, but the receptionist told him he'd have to wait until he'd gone through security.

He sat in an uncomfortable low black padded chair and waited.

Laura stepped out of a lift in the inner lobby and waved at him. A guard took his phone, passed him through a security arch, and opened a gate to let him through to join her.

'I need to use a loo to dry my face and hair,' he said.

'It's only water. You won't melt.'

'Dissolve, not melt. It's uncomfortable. Suppose I'd said I needed to—'

'Very well,' she said. 'Over there, on the corner.'

A couple of minutes later, he rejoined her.

‘Down the stairs to Jim’s territory,’ she said, leading the way. He remembered going down this staircase three years earlier, when he was being prepared for the spying role. Seemed like another life. Interesting how time expanded when a lot was happening.

They descended two flights. She keyed a code by a metal door, which swung open to reveal a cavernous area lit by strip lights. To the right were rooms of various sizes, formed by partitions with glass panels. Some people were sitting in offices and others were working in laboratories and workshops. In the central corridor, waiting for them, was Jim Clothier.

‘A real pleasure to see you again so soon after we met upstairs,’ he said, shaking Redstone’s hand warmly. ‘Laura’s given me hints about something you’ve discovered, and I can’t wait to find out more. Come into my office. Tea?’

They sat in Clothier’s cluttered office, which had an airy feel as a result of the glass panels separating it from the corridor and the adjacent rooms. Redstone recounted his experiences of knowing what Laura was thinking. He added that he thought he’d done the same with his cat, which had however refused to confirm his reading was correct.

‘Exciting!’ said Clothier. ‘Maybe that treatment we gave you… well, let’s see.’ He dug in his desk drawer and brought out a piece of chalk. ‘Let’s do some state-of-the-art science.’ He stood with one heel against the wall, chalked a line on the floor by the toe of that shoe, and chalked six more equally spaced lines in a ladder-like array away from the wall.

‘There’s our measure, using the old-fashioned unit of feet. For youngsters like you, Laura, one foot is 30.48 centimetres.’

‘Explains why I’m paid in groats,’ Laura said, ‘with people like you in charge.’

‘And you’re worth every groat. Now, Mark, stand with your back to the wall.’

Redstone did as he was asked.

'Laura,' Clothier continued, 'stand with your toes on the mark nearest Mark.' He grinned. 'Sorry about the word mark, Mark – quite unintentional. Lucky your surname isn't Chalk.'

'Wrong way round. "Time" has been suggested,' Redstone said.

Laura stood with her toes touching Redstone's, her face level with his chest. He avoided looking down at her.

'Now think of a number between one and a hundred, Laura,' Clothier said.

She nodded.

'She's thinking 30.48,' said Redstone, surprised at his own confidence. He was sure this was right.

'Correct!' said Laura triumphantly.

'I meant a whole number,' said Clothier, 'but even better. Amazing! You can certainly do it at that distance. Laura, go to the next chalk line away from Mark and think of another number.'

She shuffled back.

'48.30,' said Redstone, smiling broadly.

'Yes!' said Laura. 'I like this game.'

Clothier blew out his cheeks. 'I'm… I can't… this is incredible. Next chalk line, Laura.'

She shuffled back.

'Ah,' said Redstone. 'It's a number very near a hundred, but I'm not sure what exactly.'

'It was 99.99,' said Laura.

'Fascinating!' said Clothier. 'Seems that you're not reading Laura's mind visually or aurally, but instead you're picking up the concept.'

'That is more what it feels like.'

'Righto,' said Clothier, 'let's continue. Next line back, please, Laura.'

She shuffled back.

'Are you thinking of a number?' asked Redstone.

'I was,' she said.

'I didn't pick up anything,' Redstone said to Clothier.

'Please stand toe to toe again,' Clothier said. He took a transparent plastic ruler off his desk. 'Your foreheads are about thirty centimetres apart, mainly in the vertical direction. So the effect reduces to zero when the total distance between your heads is about forty or fifty centimetres. The next question is whether it's a result of the close relationship you two have developed.'

Redstone and Laura looked at each other. He blinked away tears and turned away.

Clothier coughed. 'Try it on me,' he said. He stood toe to toe with Redstone. 'Well, Mark?'

'Forty-seven,' he replied, 'but it felt different. Still, well, conceptual, but clearer.'

'Interesting. Forty-seven was correct. Next mark, Mark.' He shuffled back a foot.

'A million and one,' Redstone said. 'You cheated.'

Clothier jigged up and down with a grin on his face. 'Amazing! I'll go another foot. Let's see if the extra clarity compensates for the extra distance.' One more.' He shuffled back a further foot.

'I can't pick up a number,' said Redstone. 'I'm feeling, well, summertime.'

'Right! Seems that Laura and I think in somewhat different ways. That's not surprising – brain scientists know that some of us think using words, others with pictures, others in more abstract ways…'

'Very well,' Redstone said, 'but we haven't addressed how the information gets transferred, have we.'

'No, but it must be by electromagnetic radiation. What else could it be? Let's do another experiment. Bear with me.' He rushed out, and returned minutes later with a roll of aluminium oven foil and a reel of stiff wire.

'Ah,' said Redstone. 'You're going to make me a helmet.'

'Almost right. I'm going to make myself a helmet, in the first instance. Here, help me.' He walked over to the corner of his office, picked up a toolbox, rooted around and brought out a pair of pliers.

'We'll make a frame with the wire, then cover it with foil.'

'Shall I stay?' asked Laura.

'Yes please,' said Clothier. 'We'll need you later.'

Clothier and Redstone sat at the meeting table and bent, cut and twisted the wire until it formed the frame of a helmet. Clothier donned it, and Redstone adjusted it to a reasonable fit. It took just a minute to cover it with foil.

'Now try to read my mind,' Clothier said. 'Get as close as you can without bursting into laughter.'

Redstone sat next to Clothier and they leant their heads together.

'You're thinking we look as though we're posing for a funny greetings card,' said Redstone.

'Interesting,' said Clothier. 'In fact, I was thinking of fish and chips with a pickled cucumber on the side.'

'I didn't get even an inkling of that.'

'No, I imagine what you thought was what you yourself were thinking, if you see what I mean. You'll have to learn to distinguish the two.'

'What do you mean – I'll have to learn?'

'We'll come back to that. Now you put on the helmet.'

Redstone donned the wire and foil contraption, they repeated the test, and again found the signal was blocked by the helmet. Clothier got Laura to wear it, and once more Redstone couldn't pick up any thoughts.

'One last test. Well, last for the time being,' Clothier said. He opened a drawer and produced a black plastic box with a screen, switches and an extending aerial.

'Detects electric fields,' he said.

He adjusted the switches, held the aerial next to Laura's head, peered at the screen, and made a note on a pad. He repeated the process after she'd removed the helmet.

'More evidence,' he said. 'Unsurprisingly, there *is* an electric field that's blocked by our elegant headwear, though it's very weak. Mark, this amazing ability of yours seems very likely to have been brought on by what we did to your brain three years ago. For that reason alone, it's crucial that you don't tell anyone about it. But I'm also thinking we might be able to use it in our work, with your cooperation of course.'

'OK. Laura's already warned me, and she also felt it might be useful to the security services. But I can't see how, as I said to her. I can't wander around putting my head next to people to see if they're thinking dangerous thoughts.'

'"My brain, more busy than the labouring spider, Weaves tedious snares to trap mine enemies",' Clothier said.

'Eh?'

'*Othello*. Seems to me there are two separate issues,' Clothier said. 'Obviously we'd have to have identified an individual whose thoughts we want to tap, before we asked you to use this ability. And the second issue is the range. I need to do some more tests, but I'm already confident I can design a device which will amplify the electric fields you're picking up, so that you can make sense of them from a greater distance.'

'Ah,' Redstone said. He had a vision of walking along the street, wearing a heavy rucksack connected by a cable to a strange hat on his head, being bombarded with thoughts from all and sundry. 'I'm not too keen on that. It would drive me mad.'

'How could we tell?' said Laura.

Redstone grinned.

'Of course we don't want you to be overwhelmed,' said Clothier. 'We'd have to make it directional somehow. I'm warming to this.

We must do some more detailed testing. I need a few hours' preparation. Can you come in tomorrow morning?'

'Well,' said Redstone, 'I'm in the middle of an experiment—' The lights went out, the background hum of air conditioning and instruments stopped. A second later some lamps came on, but the silence remained.

'Damn,' said Clothier. 'Power cut. The emergency system only covers some lighting and the key IT equipment.'

A man shrugging on a red tabard stuck his head round the door and gestured to the exit.

'Right,' said Clothier. 'Everyone upstairs.'

They joined a crowd of men and women, some wearing lab coats, some in T-shirts and jeans, some wearing business attire, filing up the marble staircase. As they reached the lobby, Redstone was surprised to see it was still daylight – in fact bright sunlight. The rain had stopped. People drifted outside, and stood chatting.

A woman came up to Clothier, pulled him aside, and spoke to him in a voice which was too low for Redstone to be able to make out the words. Clothier clapped his hands for attention.

'Listen, everyone. It seems that the power cut is very widespread. Our energy experts are guessing the National Grid has been targeted. We'll know more shortly.'

Minutes later the woman returned to Clothier and muttered to him. He looked round and spoke in a loud voice.

'We now think National Grid's IT system has been hacked. It's telling the system that demand is zero, so all the power stations have switched off or disconnected from the grid.'

A young man appeared from the staircase.

'The DG wants you and Laura in his office, please,' he said to Clothier. 'Now.'

Laura half-waved to Redstone and strode to the stairs.

'I'll be in touch – when I can,' Clothier said to Redstone. He grimaced. 'Now I've got to climb up five flights.'

Redstone left the building. What should he do now? His phone had no signal. He checked with others gathered on the pavement, and theirs were the same. The Tubes would have stopped running, but he could get a bus up to London Bio. If he walked through Parliament Square to Whitehall there would be several possible buses. He set off, but quickly saw that traffic was packed in a stationary mess. Of course – the traffic lights were out, and the junctions had become blocked. Ah well, he'd walk. Should take less than an hour.

This act by the terrorists would be affecting everyone in the country. The public would be baying for blood.

TUESDAY 11TH JULY

Many of the London Bio staff, including Joanne, had decided to go home by bus or on foot. 'I'm too old for camping out,' Joanne had said as she set off. But the rest, including Redstone, chose to spend the night sleeping in the building. Local shops had given away sandwiches and other food which could no longer be kept chilled, but wouldn't sell anything until their electronic tills came back into action.

The atmosphere in the lab had been relaxed and cheerful. Redstone had given a group of young scientists permission to make some dilute hooch in the lab, though he'd insisted on overseeing what they were doing, to ensure nothing dangerous was added or accidentally produced. He admitted that the result was quite acceptable, and they sat round in the conference room toasting London Bio, speculating about who 'the enemy' were and what they wanted, and how long it would take for the power to come back on.

Folded lab coats had served for pillows, cardboard for mattresses. Mains water was only dribbling out of the taps, so once they'd used up their bottled water, they'd drunk distilled water from the lab supplies. Redstone had forgotten how unpleasant pure water tasted – he remembered being surprised the first time he'd drunk some. The minute traces of minerals in natural water made so much difference. He thought he'd slept badly, but when he woke in his office at 7 a.m. he did feel refreshed.

He flicked the light switch, but the light didn't come on. Power hadn't been restored. He walked round to the toilets, tried the tap in the sink, and to his surprise the water spluttered and banged and then flowed out in a steady stream. Power had been restored to the water companies. He washed his face, took a drink, and went downstairs. Staff were sitting around, chatting and drinking tea, which they were making using water boiled over Bunsen burners. He accepted a cup.

'Hey!' said Rosie. 'I've got a signal!' She waved her phone, put it to her ear, walked into a corner, and started speaking. Others picked up their phones and started dialling.

Redstone waved to the group and returned to his office. Who to call first? He tried Laura, but got the unobtainable signal. Maybe Sophie? She might have a better overview from Brussels about what was going on in the UK.

She answered immediately.

'Dad! Are you OK?'

'I'm fine,' he said. He told her how he'd spent the night. 'Tell me what the Brussels media are reporting.'

'It's not just the Brussels media, it's global. I suppose you haven't been able to access the internet. The whole UK was blacked out. Social media are saying it's an astonishing display of incompetence on the part of Jones's government. They should have made the electricity network hacker-proof. It should have been top priority.'

'Difficult to argue with that, I suppose,' said Redstone. 'Have people died? In hospitals and so on?'

'No reports of that. They said hospitals have backup generators. There were a number of road accidents. No streetlights, no traffic lights.'

'Anything from our government?'

'They've had an emergency meeting,' she said. 'In that snake place.'

'Eh? Oh, COBRA. Stands for Cabinet Office Briefing Room A. It's a meeting room. Some genius invented the acronym to make it sound sexy.'

'It may sound sexy, but your government doesn't seem to have come up with anything. Other than the usual platitudes.'

‘I’m glad you’re becoming healthily sceptical,’ Redstone said.

‘Dad, who wouldn’t be sceptical when Britain is going down the tubes and your government seems unable to do anything about it?’

‘I note the way you keep referring to them as *your* government.’

‘Well, Jones is your buddy, isn’t he?’

‘I wouldn’t—’

‘You helped them out of a pickle last year. Haven’t they come begging you to do it again?’

‘It wasn’t me, it was mainly Michelle. And they’ve enlisted her help already.’

‘Really?’ Sophie said. ‘I would have thought they have enough computer experts, in GCHQ.’

‘She is a world-class expert. A leader in her field.’

‘Well, let’s hope she can lead them out of the mucky field they seem to be stuck in at the moment. Anyway, as long as you’re OK. I’ll tell Graham. Laura all right?’

‘I assume so, but I haven’t been able to contact her. Sophie, I need to tell you and Graham that Laura… oh, my phone’s running out of juice. Talk to you when we’ve got power back on.’

*

Redstone decided to go home. He estimated he could walk it in three hours, with a short break en route, and if he was lucky he could take a bus at least part of the way. He’d stick to the main bus routes, in case. He set off walking north, and in under half an hour was in Camden Town, a multicultural area of converted three-storey Victorian houses, interspersed with ugly post-war construction on sites where the original buildings had been destroyed by Second World War bombs, as was true in so much of London. And elsewhere. Including Germany.

There was no sign of buses, just slow-moving lorries, vans and cars. He continued up the road, passing Kentish Town Tube station.

The area felt less confining, the road was a bit wider, and soon the wall-to-wall shops had given way to terraced houses. He wondered about the social history of Camden Town and Kentish Town when the houses were built. What sort of people lived there?

Navigating through the packed traffic across the complicated road junction at Archway, he eyed the steep hill ahead of him, and then realised there were buses parked a short distance ahead. He jogged up to the first one, hopped on, and collapsed with relief into the one remaining empty seat, next to an elderly woman. She shrank to her left. *Afraid this big man would jog her right arm, which was hurting after a fall she'd had last week.*

'Don't worry,' Redstone said. 'I know how…' He stopped. He'd been about to tell her he knew how painful it could be, and commiserate with her. 'You seem concerned I'll push into you. I'll be careful.'

'You're very perceptive. Thanks.'

The bus started with a jerk. Redstone thought about what had nearly happened. Was this new ability a curse or a blessing? Would he have been better off if he hadn't read Laura's mind about wanting to leave him?

Oh well, it is what it is. He hated that phrase, with its implied stoicism and acceptance of inability to influence one's own life, but sometimes it was appropriate.

Half an hour later the bus was crawling through Muswell Hill. He changed buses, and another half-hour later was walking through his leafy suburb to his house.

*

The power came back on soon after 6 p.m. The TV news said that National Grid had sorted out the software problem, with help from GCHQ, who were treating it as another terrorist act.

He needed to tell the twins about the split with Laura. He set up a Zoom call – fortunately both Sophie and Graham were available.

'It's a real shame, Dad,' said Sophie, 'but I can't say I'm totally surprised.'

'For once I agree with my beloved sister,' said Graham. 'You and Laura are very different people, with very different backgrounds.'

'I hope you'll be able to keep friendly relations with her,' said Sophie.

'So do I,' said Redstone, 'but at the moment I have no idea how it's going to end up.'

'Well, you'll just have to get back in the market,' said Graham, 'like me. Have you thought of internet dating?'

'That's not very romantic,' said Sophie.

'Maybe not,' Graham said, 'but it works. Lots of my friends have got hooked up through the internet.'

'Give me a chance, kids,' said Redstone. 'Laura hasn't even moved her stuff out yet.'

'Dad,' Sophie said, 'we deserted you when Mum died, and we're not going to do it again.'

'Correct,' said Graham.

'You didn't desert me,' said Redstone. 'I wanted you to escape and get on with your lives, not live here bogged down by memories and worrying about me. If you remember, I helped you find places in Brussels and California.'

'Doesn't stop us feeling we deserted you,' said Sophie.

'Anyway,' said Graham, 'the point is that we're going to try to look after you, one way or another. I mean your emotional state. Everyone needs support. We both feel you need a partner. Despite what we said a minute ago, I'm disappointed that Laura is leaving – you are very different from each other, but in some ways, you were a good fit. Still, it is what it is, and we'll do whatever we can to make sure you find someone.'

'Wow,' said Sophie. 'For once Graham has hit the emotional nail on the head. Must be the effect of California.'

WEDNESDAY 12TH JULY

Redstone looked up from his desk in London Bio as Rosie slipped round the door.

'Can I bother you for a moment?'

'Of course.' He stepped over to the meeting table.

'It's Mum,' she said, sitting down at right angles to him. 'She's very worked up. She's been asked to go to a meeting with the Prime Minister at Number 10, to talk about the hacking.'

'No need for her to be worried,' Redstone said. 'She'll know more about the subject than anyone else in the room, I imagine. Certainly more than Michael Jones.'

'She doesn't get worried about *that* sort of thing. It's the thought of going to Number 10. Very important place, strange people round the table…'

'But she knows Michael Jones well. From when she helped him last year.'

'He wasn't PM then, and they used to meet in an ordinary office. Anyway, it's not rational. The point is she wants me to ask if you would accompany her.'

'But I haven't been invited,' he said. 'I can't just turn up to a meeting at Number 10.'

'Can't you get yourself invited?'

'Rosie, I'm not some ultra-VIP who can get into meetings in Number 10 whenever he wants to.'

'But you're part of Michael Jones's inner circle, aren't you?'

'I suppose I was last year, when he was out in the cold, but not now. He's surrounded by Cabinet colleagues, civil servants, special advisers… I'm not even in his outer circle.'

Rosie's shoulders drooped.

'Er... well, I'll try,' he said. 'Maybe if I phone and explain. I'll have a go, but don't hold your breath.'

*

'Good news,' Redstone said to Rosie an hour later. 'I explained to the Number 10 private secretary that Michelle was uncomfortable in that sort of environment, and she'd be happier if I could accompany her. He said... Anyway, eventually he agreed to ask the PM. He's just rung back. To my surprise, the PM would welcome my presence, as a companion to Michelle, but also... well, never mind.'

'Don't say "never mind". Tell me.'

'I didn't want to sound... Michael Jones has asked me more than once to be one of his special advisers. I've always said no, but he's remained keen.'

'So does that mean you'll be helping him on this hacking stuff? He certainly needs help, given the abuse he's getting.'

'To be honest, Rosie, I can't see what I have to offer. I'm no expert in that sort of thing, or anything political. I can't understand why he'd want my advice.'

'Maybe he wants to hear from someone he trusts,' she said. 'You do tend to say it as you see it.' She blushed. 'Oh, sorry, that was rude. I didn't mean—'

'I'm not in the slightest offended. You're far from the first person to say that. Kate used to say it regularly.' He smiled. 'Maybe you're right. Prime ministers can get surrounded by advisers who tell them only things they think they'll want to hear. True of all leaders, I suppose. Including CEOs of biotechnology companies.'

'Does that mean I can tell you what I really think of Project Smoothaway?' she said with a straight face.

'Oh. Does that mean you've found a flaw in my—'

'It's the title. It's so corny!'

He burst out laughing. 'I know,' he said. 'It was meant to be a joke, but it somehow stuck. Should we change it?'

'Absolutely not,' she said. 'We all love its corniness.'

'Good. So, back to the PM, you'll tell Michelle, will you? I don't know who else will be there, but I'll look after her if she needs me to.'

As she left his office, Laura rang.

'Sorry I haven't been in touch,' she said. 'Snowed under. Anyway, Gavin's just informed me you'll be at the meeting with Michelle and the PM. He asked me to tell you it's a good decision. The PM needs help right now, as you'll have picked up.'

'Oh, that's kind of Gavin,' Redstone said. 'Laura, are you coming home—'

'Sorry, have to go.' She rang off. He wished her head was close to his so he could know if her work was the real reason she hadn't been in touch. But he knew the answer even without fancy mind-reading.

Joanne came in. She stood with her arms akimbo.

'I'm afraid you've just got to accept it, and move on,' she said. 'Lots of couples break up. The trick is not to let it get acrimonious.'

'But I didn't say anything about—'

'You're an open book, dear,' she said. 'Anyway, it seems you've got an event coming up to take your mind off your personal life. Number 10 called. The meeting with the Prime Minister is tomorrow at 8 a.m.'

'Oh God. Why did I agree to get involved?'

'Because you wanted to help Michelle. And why wouldn't you want to go? Other people would jump at the chance to attend a meeting with the prime minister.'

'Yes, but—'

'He's just a man, like everyone else. Except women. He might be nervous of you and Michelle. I bet he is, especially if there are technical issues to discuss. And if you're nervous, imagine all the men except you are sitting there with no clothes on. But not the women, of course.'

'If I do remember your sage advice, I'll start sniggering while he's talking about something awful, like the number of people killed.'

'Turn it into a cough,' she said with a grin.

'That's sorted, then,' he said. 'So, 8 a.m. That's early. It's all very well for him, living over the shop, but the rest of us have to commute. Poor Michelle will have to travel in all the way from Cambridge. She's invited too, by the way.'

'Yes, I know she's invited, and I know that's why you're going. She'll be staying at Rosie's overnight.'

'Oh, I forgot about your mafia. What else can you tell me?'

'The motorway sign stuff is sorted out,' she said. 'The PM is going to make an announcement in the next few minutes.'

'How on earth did you… oh, Michelle told Rosie, I suppose.'

'Correct.'

'Something you don't know – I've got to go to MI5 this afternoon. Not sure how long I'll be. And I'm not allowed to tell you why.'

'I did know you're going there, as it happens,' she said. 'And don't worry – I'll find out why sooner or later. Probably sooner.'

'Heavens, Joanne, are you in touch with Laura too? Even though…'

'I couldn't possibly reveal my sources. Or Laura would kill me.'

*

Clothier checked his notes. 'That's all the tests,' he said. 'Well done.'

'Thank goodness for that,' said Redstone. 'It was more tiring than I expected.'

‘I need a day or two to process the results,’ Clothier said, turning to his screen.

‘Any immediate reactions?’

‘I’m sure it’s as we expected, electromagnetic radiation. We’ve now got data about the frequency distribution, and the location of the receptors in your skull.’

‘You said you’d design a device which could amplify the signal. Can it also block the signal? I don’t want to pick up thoughts unless I want to, if you see what I mean.’

‘Understood. Shouldn’t be a problem. I’ll be in touch.’ He twiddled his pen. ‘Mark, this ability you’ve developed is amazing, astounding, unique. In other circumstances I’d be pressing you to offer your services to some academic researchers so that they could find out more. They’d no doubt want to do loads of MRI scans, test the limits of your ability more precisely, test you with different subjects – I mean people whose thoughts you would be reading, such as some with brain injuries, some with… I don’t know, maybe dementia, epilepsy… you could be the subject of hundreds of studies. You could find yourself under pressure to devote most of your time to being examined and tested. It would open up a whole new field of brain science. Could lead to all sorts of breakthroughs, including treatments for brain disorders.’

‘Oh, God,’ Redstone said. ‘I know it’s selfish of me, but it sounds a nightmare. I couldn’t stand—’

‘Don’t worry. I’m going to keep knowledge of this strictly limited. For MI5’s reasons, as well as yours. And we need to ensure none of us does anything accidentally to make people wonder about you.’

‘Couldn’t agree more,’ said Redstone. ‘Maybe in the long term…’

‘Maybe,’ Clothier said. ‘The very long term.’

*

Redstone trudged up the hill to his house.

He drenched the flowers in the tubs, while Treacle attacked the hose, pretending it was a snake. Zena popped her head over the greenery topping the fence.

'Hi, Mark. How's things?'

'Oh, you know. Not so bad,' he said. 'How are you? And Mary?'

'We're fine. Mum's at work. Laura coming home this evening?'

'Afraid not. It seems we've broken up.'

'Oh, Mark, I'm so sorry,' she said. 'I hope you're OK. Is it her dumping you, or you kicking her out?'

'Blimey, Zena, you don't beat around the bush, do you? It's complicated. I'm certainly not kicking her out. We're just very different people.'

'Yes, I'd noticed. She's a woman and you're a man.'

'You know very well what I mean,' he said. 'We've got different needs, and—'

'Yes. She's a woman, and you're a man. Sorry, I'm being facetious, but you expect your partner to be different from you. It'd be pretty boring otherwise.'

He turned off the hose. 'There are degrees of difference, Zena. Think of the boys you know. I'm sure there are some who are so different from you that you couldn't envisage living with them.'

'I'm not interested in boys at all.' He started to apologise but she interrupted him with a laugh. 'It's men that I fancy,' she said.

'Sorry.'

'You're forgiven. Fancy coming over for a drink?'

'Oh, I… I was going to start cooking.'

'Come round and we'll get a takeaway. I don't want you to be lonely there, on your own again.'

'Well, I… oh, why not! Thanks. Good idea. I'll be round shortly.'

*

They sat in Mary's garden eating pizza and drinking red wine. The setting sun cast a rosy glow.

'Sorry to hear you broke up with your boyfriend,' Redstone said.

She shrugged. 'It was never going to last. He was pretty immature. Pity it took me so long to work that out.' She sipped her wine. 'Any advice on how to find a better man?'

'You're hardly asking the right person. Not least because I'm a man myself. But anyway, my current situation isn't exactly…'

'You and Kate had the most wonderful relationship. I don't suppose you could ever repeat it. And I guess you don't want to.'

'Doesn't mean I want to be alone, though,' he said. 'If I knew what to do about it, I'd do it.'

'Sorry. I was just asking your advice without thinking. Like I used to when I was growing up.'

Redstone nodded. Zena and Sophie had been very close as teenagers, and to some extent he'd acted as a sort of father figure to Zena when needed.

'Let's move on. Tell me more about your new theatre company.'

They chatted, he drank more wine.

'Tell you what,' she said after a while, 'let's go inside and listen to some music. Mum's got a mix you'll enjoy – you're a jazz fan, aren't you. I used to hear it when I was in your house with Sophie. Mum's playlist isn't pure jazz, but I bet you'll like it.'

Indoors, he slumped onto a sofa and half-closed his eyes while Zena fiddled with a hi-fi system and her phone.

'Ah. Found it,' she said.

The room filled with the sound of Humphrey Lyttleton's 'Bad Penny Blues'. The fast rhythm of the piano, the muted trumpet – he perked up and couldn't stop his foot tapping. Zena started dancing in the middle of the room, and beckoned him to join her. He shook his head firmly. She carried on dancing in front of him.

The track finished. She stood poised, waiting for the next one: Bill Withers, singing 'Ain't no sunshine when she's gone'. She started dancing slowly to the singer's plaintive voice and the simple guitar chords. As the backing strings came in, Redstone burst into tears. He sat sobbing. Zena stopped dancing and stood staring. The door opened, and Mary came in.

'What's going on?' she said to Zena.

'I was playing your jazz mix, and this song upset Mark. He's broken up with Laura.'

Mary strode to the hi-fi and switched it off. The sudden silence shocked Redstone. He took a deep breath and stopped weeping. Mary sat on the sofa beside him and put her arm round his shoulders.

'Go and make a cup of tea,' she said to Zena, who rushed out.

'I'm sorry about you and Laura,' she said to Redstone. 'You must be feeling awful. That song is truly haunting. Maybe the lyrics…'

'Yes. Amazing, for such simple words.'

'And the tune. And his voice… it's a great piece of music. Great music arouses emotions.' She rubbed his shoulder. 'OK now?'

'Yes,' he said. 'Thanks, Mary. Where's that tea?' He smiled weakly.

She hugged him. Her head was right next to his, but he didn't have a clue about what she was thinking.

*

Redstone washed his face in cold water. He'd made a fool of himself – he needed to apologise to Mary. 10 p.m. – was it too late to phone? He'd risk it.

'Hi. Sorry it's late. Is it all right to talk briefly?'

'Of course,' she said. 'You OK now?'

'Yes, but I want to say I'm sorry for being so—'

'Don't be silly. I understand. That song is very… your reaction was understandable. Healthy, even.'

'I just felt terribly alone. So separate from everyone else. I don't understand why—'

'It's called the human condition. We can talk about it sometime. You should feel free to ring or come in whenever…'

'Thanks,' he said. 'I'd like that. Oh, and I do like that song, by the way.'

'Yes, it's one of my favourites too. He's a great blues singer.'

'Which reminds me. Do you like sick jokes?'

'I'm an NHS nurse. Of course I like sick jokes.'

He smiled. 'Right, then. How do you make a canary into a great blues singer?'

'I don't know. How do you make a canary into a great blues singer?'

'Put it in a microwave, then its bill withers.'

She chuckled. 'That's awful,' she said. 'Here's one for you. A woman's lying on the bed of an MRI machine, shaking with fear. The radiologist says "Right, Mrs Bloomsbury, we'll slide your head into this tunnel, scan your brain for half an hour, and see if we can find out why you suffer from this awful claustrophobia."'

He laughed out loud. 'That sounds like a real NHS joke. Quite close to home, actually.'

'Oh, I'm sorry, do you—'

'No, it's a great joke. I'll explain what I meant next time we meet.'

'Make that soon. I'm not far away.'

THURSDAY 13TH JULY

Michelle stared around the Number 10 Cabinet Room. She was standing next to Redstone, directly across the famous long, boat-shaped table from the one seat with arms, that of the Prime Minister. Redstone himself felt nervous and out of place, even though he'd worked in Number 10 three years earlier.

Other attendees were drifting into the room. Redstone scanned the name plates in front of each of the seats clustered round the centre of the table: Prime Minister, Cabinet Secretary, Director General of MI5, Home Secretary, Secretary of State for Transport, Director of GCHQ. And he and Michelle, described simply as Dr Mark Redstone and Professor Michelle Clarke.

Michael Jones marched in, followed by Roger Feast, the Cabinet Secretary. Jones looked pale and tense.

He called the meeting to order and made introductions. He glanced at his notes.

'I've got one objective for this meeting' he said. 'To get ideas for how to identify the terrorists who seem intent on causing death and destruction and wrecking our economy. And how to stop them, of course.'

Michelle scribbled on the pad in front of her. *Two objectives.* Redstone kept a straight face.

'I'll ask Gavin McKay to summarise what we know so far,' Jones continued. 'Gavin?'

McKay cleared his throat. He seemed uncharacteristically nervous and harassed.

'The first question has been whether the enemy, as we're calling them,' he nodded to Michelle, 'is a state actor or non-state – some rogue group. We haven't been able to pick up any signs that it's one of the traditional antagonistic states that support cyber warfare, of which China and Russia are of course leading contenders. Both of those governments have gone to great lengths to assure us they're not involved. Of course we can't take their word at face value, but our experts are inclined to believe them.'

'That's correct,' the GCHQ director said, adjusting her horn-rimmed glasses. 'The coding used by the enemy has none of the hallmarks, the signatures if you like, we associate with China or Russia. The abuse and blame directed at us on social media is misplaced. We haven't been lax in protecting the UK against those countries.'

'But China and Russia know we'll retaliate if we think it is them,' the Home Secretary said. 'Doesn't it follow that they would mask their identity?' She squared her shoulders, her slight double chin making her seem pleased with her remark.

'They'd certainly try,' said the GCHQ director. 'But they'd fail.'

'Moving on,' said McKay, 'the same applies to all the other states we've considered. Of course we've also employed traditional, non-cyber methods of gathering information, using MI6's assets, but the answer is zilch.'

'Are you now sure the Arabic slogans recovered from the Manchester train were a hoax?' Jones said.

'We regard that as highly probable, Prime Minister. Designed to foment civil unrest. So we're down to non-state actors. It's most likely a group, such as a right-wing terror organisation, rather than an individual.'

'Why?' said Michelle.

'Because the resources needed to achieve what they've done would be beyond the capacity of any individual hacker.'

'Incorrect,' said Michelle.

'Let me guess,' said Jones. 'You're implying you could have done it yourself, alone.'

Michelle flashed him a look of approval. 'Exactly.'

'That's a very bold statement,' said the Home Secretary.

'I believe her,' said the Prime Minister. 'I have personal experience of Michelle's, well, genius.'

The Home Secretary flushed. 'It's lovely that Michelle is a genius. But how many others like her are there?'

'Maybe not many as talented as Michelle,' said the GCHQ director, 'but you'd be surprised at the number of highly proficient hackers we have to deal with.'

'Have you looked into all those you know about?' asked the Home Secretary.

'Of course. No evidence linking any of them with the attacks we've suffered.'

Jones cleared his throat. 'So the question remains – how do we identify this enemy?

The GCHQ director leant forward. 'I wish I could come up with—'

'I'll tell you,' said Michelle. 'We identify their next targets and put in place tracers to find out where any hacking comes from.'

'Can we do that?' asked Jones.

'It wouldn't be easy,' said the GCHQ director, 'because the hackers would ensure—'

'We could do it,' said Michelle. 'But it would require a huge amount of computing power, dedicated to that task.'

'So that means we've got to be clever in guessing the next target,' said McKay, 'because we couldn't monitor more than one or two possibilities at the same time.'

'Probably just one,' said Michelle.

'Good. We're developing a plan,' said Jones. 'Let's hear suggestions for the next target.'

'My area, I suppose,' said the Secretary of State for Transport. 'Could be airports, or container terminals, or the Tube…'

'Seems to me they're keen on targets which have maximum and immediate impact on ordinary people,' said McKay. 'So I'd favour the Tube out of that list.'

'No good,' said Michelle. 'A hacker might be able to mess up the signalling on one line at a time, but not the whole network. Doesn't meet your criteria.'

'How about the NHS?' said Jones.

'Frankly, Prime Minister,' said the GCHQ director, 'their IT is such a complicated, decentralised and antiquated mess that a hacker wouldn't be able to wreak widespread damage.' Michelle nodded.

'Water supply?' said Jones.

'Not much IT involved in the main job of pumping the stuff around. They could target the drinking water treatment plants, but again only one at a time, I'd think.'

'Anyway,' said Redstone, 'in a sense they've already targeted water. For many of us it stopped running out of our taps when the power went off.'

'Well, gas? Oil? Petrol?'

Michelle shook her head.

'Banks?'

'The systems for paying by credit card would be a juicy target,' said the GCHQ director, 'but we've done a great deal of work with them recently. We're confident they're now impregnable.'

Michelle started to speak, but stopped as the Home Secretary said that given the GCHQ assessment the government shouldn't waste resources on monitoring the credit card systems.

'Prime Minister,' said Feast, 'I suggest we ask colleagues here to go away and think of vulnerable areas we haven't covered, let me know their ideas, and I'll liaise with Michelle and GCHQ to take the best one forward.'

'Agreed,' said Jones. He thanked the attendees, reminded them of the need for absolute secrecy, and asked them to put their thinking caps on and contact the Cabinet Secretary with ideas. He stood up and walked out. The others collected their papers, and some drifted towards Michelle, who appeared surprised at the attention but stood up to talk to them.

Feast came over to Redstone and shook his hand.

'Great to see you and Michelle again. How are you? How's London Bio doing? Must be a year since we all met.'

'Yes, it—'

An aide touched Redstone's arm. 'The Prime Minister would like a chat with you in his study, if you're free.'

'I assume that last bit is just you being polite,' Redstone said.

The aide looked puzzled.

'About my being free, I mean.'

'Oh no, if you're not free you don't have to come,' the aide said. 'Of course, the Prime Minister would have you killed, but our press office would deny all knowledge. As they often do when bad things happen.' He almost succeeded in keeping a straight face.

Redstone chuckled. 'Lead the way, then.'

He said goodbye to Feast and followed the aide through corridors to a room about the size of Redstone's sitting room at home, although with a much higher ceiling. There was a big screen on one wall, bookcases with diagonal wire mesh instead of glass in their doors, and a large circular wooden table with a polished slice of a tree trunk in its centre.

'Thanks for coming round,' said Jones. 'It's great to be working with you again. Take a seat. I wanted a private chat, off the record.'

'Of course,' said Redstone.

'As you know,' Jones said, 'I've been relentlessly attacked on social media for the things that the hackers have done. Politicians are used to being vilified, but this feels somehow different. Horribly personal.'

'Yes, I can see why you'd feel that,' said Redstone. 'Maybe it *is* personal. Maybe the hackers have something against you as an individual, rather than against the government or the country.'

'Exactly. So you don't think I'm being paranoid?'

'No, I don't. Doesn't mean it really is personal, though.'

'I know. But if it is, the question I have to ask myself is whether the country would be better off if I resigned, and so gave the hackers what it seems they want.'

Redstone sat back in his chair, shocked.

'Prime Min—'

'Michael.'

'Michael, I can't advise you on—'

'If not you, who? I know and trust you. You were a tremendous help in getting me back into power last year, and there was your brave work three years ago—'

'But there are people much better placed—'

'I disagree. I can't ask my colleagues, my special advisers, or my top civil servants. Well, I could ask them, but I'd have to use a filter when judging their replies. They've all got irons in the fire, one way or another. You haven't. I want advice from someone who isn't personally involved, and has shown good judgment in the past.'

'Well, I—'

'What's more,' Jones said, 'if I ask colleagues here there's always the risk that my actual asking will be leaked. That would weaken my position as prime minister. And encourage the terrorists. I'm sure I can trust you to keep this discussion secret. So what's your advice? What are your thoughts? Come on, cough up.'

'Very well,' Redstone said. 'My advice is to wait till the next attack by the enemy. The three so far aren't enough to reveal a convincing pattern. I know the social media attacks add weight to your theory that it's about you personally, but it's all far from conclusive.'

'I don't find that very persuasive, Mark. Doing nothing, waiting, is a positive act.'

‘I’d agree if we hadn’t decided on a new approach at the meeting we’ve just come from. But if Michelle’s idea works out, waiting for the next attack could allow us to track down the enemy.’

‘True. Good point.’ He got up and paced along the wall containing the tall windows. ‘I don’t like this room,’ he said. ‘This table is a fine piece of workmanship, but it’s too big for a study. I can’t walk around easily. I like to move around while I’m thinking.’

‘So get rid of the table,’ said Redstone. ‘You’re in charge.’

‘Trouble is it’s got special significance. It was made for—’

‘Get it moved somewhere prestigious where more people can see it. Maybe the V&A would like it.’

‘Excellent advice! I knew it was right to ask you to come here today.’

Redstone reflected he hadn’t been asked – he himself had requested if he could attend. He kept silent.

‘OK,’ said Jones, ‘I agree both about the table and on not resigning at the moment. In that order of certainty.’

*

Back at his office, Redstone phoned Clothier.

‘Jim, something’s happened which makes me wonder if the mind-reading ability has disappeared. I had my head right next to someone yesterday evening, and I couldn’t pick up a trace of what she was thinking. And then this morning I was sitting next to someone, and the same thing.’

‘Hmm,’ Clothier said. ‘This morning, were you sitting in, let’s say, a normal configuration? Like at a meeting table?’

‘Exactly that.’

‘I suspect your neighbour was simply out of range. Were your shoulders touching?’

‘No. Not even nearly.’

‘There you go, then.’

'I did consider that. But what about yesterday?'

'One swallow doesn't make a summer,' Clothier said. 'Could have been to do with her rather than you. Was she wearing a hat?'

'No.'

'Any source of interfering electromagnetic radiation nearby?'

'Er… not that I can think of.'

'Maybe she just doesn't emit radiation in the same way as the people you've, er, read so far. Interesting. Let's not get ahead of ourselves – let's see if your ability has changed when you next come in, and if it hasn't, we'll think more about your friend.'

'OK. When do you want me to come in?'

'Thursday, if that's convenient. Listen, do you ever wear a hat?'

'Eh?' Redstone said. 'Er… yes, I wear a baseball cap if the weather's hot. Or cold.'

'Any particular colour?'

'I suppose you're going to make me one with equipment stuffed inside. Make it navy blue with the MI5 logo on the front and the word "spy" embroidered on the peak.'

'Just what I had in mind.'

Redstone pocketed the phone and wandered along to the big lab.

'Hi Rosie. How are you, and how's Smoothaway going?'

'Not bad,' she said, swinging round on her chair. 'The new formulation seems promising. Well, let's say we haven't encountered the same problem as with the previous one.'

'Excellent.' He peered at her screen. 'Still a long way to go, but we may be heading in the right direction.' He stood back and stretched. 'Heard from Mum since the meeting at Number 10? She played a blinder. Star of the meeting, I'd say.'

'Wow! She told me she thought it'd gone fine, and it wasn't as scary as she'd feared. Thanks very much for going with her.'

'No big deal. Let's hope Michelle's expertise won't be needed again soon.'

FRIDAY 14TH JULY

The morning news had once again been dominated by the terrorists' attacks. Commentators were speculating. What was next? Should Jones resign, and if he did, would it make any difference? Above all, who was responsible for the attacks, and why hadn't the police and MI5 tracked them down?

Redstone wanted to discuss it with someone involved. He rang Michelle.

'Any thoughts on what the enemy might target next?' he asked. 'Roger Feast's office has told me nobody's come up with any new ideas.'

'No. Not my area. If you can come up with some possibilities, I'll tell you if they're plausible from the hacking point of view.'

'The way I see it, they're targeting Michael Jones himself, so their next attack has to fit with that motive. Doesn't have to affect everyone in the country – just produce the result that Michael's reputation is further damaged. He's now being blamed for not doing enough to prepare against terrorist attacks.'

'Maybe they won't do any more terrorism, but step up their social media campaigning instead. Seen today's?'

'No.'

'Rosie sent me an example. Manufactured picture of Jones in a pile of dung. I've forgotten the exact words. Something about the stench of incompetence and corruption.'

'Oh dear. He was feeling bad enough already.'

After a few minutes musing but still failing to come up with an idea for the next target, he decided to give up and walk around the lab. He trotted down the stairs. As he approached the floor below, an initially weak but foul smell, like rotten eggs, grew stronger. He rushed into the downstairs lab to discover a group of staff frantically busy round a sink at the end of the nearest bench.

'What's going on?' he asked. 'Smells like hydrogen sulphide.'

'Yes, we think it is,' a young man said. 'Some chemicals have reacted in the drain. From when we were washing—'

'You should be wearing respirators, then. H_2S is very poisonous.' He was sure that David would have had them wearing respirators by now.

'Sorry,' the young scientist said. He went to a cupboard and pulled out some black full-face respirators, offering one to Redstone and doling out the others to his colleagues. Redstone felt like a character in a science fiction movie.

'Good,' he said, his voice sounding strained and echoey in his own ears. 'Well, it's probably not too dangerous, because humans can smell an incredibly small amount. And several of you seem to be still alive.' They chuckled dutifully. 'We need lots of water with some sodium bicarbonate dissolved in it. Spray it in the air and pour it down the drain.'

He stood to the side and watched as they followed his instructions. After a few minutes he removed his respirator.

'Seems to have gone,' he said. 'I suppose I should have a written report on the incident, for the record.'

'I'll do it,' said the young man.

Redstone went back upstairs and told Joanne to expect the report.

'So it's dangerous, this stuff, is it?' she said. 'You chemists…'

'It is dangerous in theory,' he said, 'but in practice it's got such a strong and horrible smell that people usually detect it and take action before it reaches poisonous levels. It's the smell of rotten eggs.'

Joanne wrinkled her nose.

'And drains smell of it too, in some cases,' Redstone added. 'I imagine it contributed to the famous Great Stink in Victorian times.

Which led…' He stopped. 'Sorry, I've had an idea.' He rushed into his office, pulling his phone from his pocket as he went.

'Hi Michelle. Me again. Listen, have you read about the vast, expensive new sewage system that's recently been opened in London?'

'No,' she said.

'Oh. Well, perhaps you could google it. And when you have, could you tell me whether a hacker might be able to divert untreated sewage into the Thames upstream of Westminster?'

'Ah,' she said, 'I see where you're coming from. I'll get back to you.'

*

Two hours later, Michelle rang back.

'The answer is yes,' she said. 'It would be quite complicated, but doable. You'd have to bypass the equipment that cleans out the worst pollution, and then open an emergency route into the Thames. There are a couple of possibilities not far from Westminster, but if it were me, I'd go for the major works a bit further out. Quite a way upstream, but it would mean the stink would affect a lot of west London as it travels through to Westminster.'

'Yes! Including some very posh bits of London. And presumably it would then affect the City and beyond, where loads of wealthy people work. OK with you if I put this idea to Roger Feast?'

'Of course.'

Minutes later, he was speaking to Feast.

'Hmm,' Feast said. 'It wouldn't cause the death and destruction that the terrorists seem to want to wreak on us.'

'No, but politically it would be very smart. It would cause the government a lot of trouble.'

'True, but it doesn't fit with what they've done so far. I suspect you're thinking of what you yourself would do rather than what someone driven by hatred and callousness might be plotting. You're being too civilised.'

'Oh. I take your point.'

'However,' Feast said, 'the truth is I haven't received any better proposed targets, or in fact any that sounded remotely plausible. I'll come back to you.'

He rang back half an hour later.

'Colleagues thought it worth pursuing, since we haven't got any other ideas,' he said. 'I've asked GCHQ to liaise with Michelle.'

SATURDAY 15TH JULY

Redstone was sitting in his garden with a glass of wine. Treacle was lying next to him on the bench. He'd been trying to give up thinking about the terror attacks, and get on with his normal life.

The garden was too dry – there had been only a couple of short spells of rain in the last few weeks, nowhere near enough to keep the plants healthy. He must do a lot of watering this evening.

Sophie rang.

'Dad, you OK?'

'You sound worried,' he said. 'Yes, I'm fine. How are you? I was just thinking we need some more rain.'

'I suppose you've got no one to talk to about that sort of thing, now Laura's gone. You can always ring me, you know. Must be difficult on your own.'

'Thanks, Sophie. Very thoughtful. But is there some specific reason you're concerned?

'Dad. Can't I simply be acting as a loving daughter?'

'Sorry. Maybe being on my own is making me a cynic.'

'I hope not. Um, you know I keep in touch with Zena?'

'Sort of. I can't say I'd thought about it. Of course, you were very close when you were teenagers.'

'Yes. Well, we do keep in touch. WhatsApp, phone, you know.'

What had Zena been saying to Sophie? He waited for Sophie to say more.

'You still there?' she said.

'Sure. Waiting for you to tell me what Zena's said to you.'

'Oh. Well, she said you'd burst into tears while you were round at their house having a pizza, and Mary had to comfort you.'

‘Oh,’ he said. ‘Every word of that is true, but the whole story is a lot more complex.’ He outlined what had happened.

‘I’m so sorry you had that… that attack of loneliness,’ Sophie said. ‘You should call me if you feel that way again.’

‘Thanks, darling.’ He smiled to himself. ‘I’ve got to get used to the fact that you’re now caring for me.’

‘I’m sure you still also care for me,’ she said.

‘Of course.’

‘Dad, can I get a bit more personal?’

‘What do you mean?’

‘You know that Graham and I don’t want you to build an emotional shrine to Mum, don’t you? We want you to be happy. Mum would want you to be happy. Having a relationship with another woman wouldn’t be being unfaithful to Mum’s memory.’

‘Wow,’ he said. ‘That’s… thanks, Sophie. But I’m not sure where it leaves me, now that Laura’s gone.’

‘We want you to search for a new relationship. Doesn’t have to be the love of your life. I suppose Mum was that.’

‘Yes. Sophie, darling, I know I can’t have everything in a relationship. No one can. But there has to be some spark. I thought there was with Laura.’ His voice cracked.

‘Dad, I’m so sorry. I didn’t mean to upset you. Let’s drop the subject.’

‘That would be a relief.’

‘Have you considered asking Mary out?’ she asked.

‘I thought we were dropping the subject.’

‘We have. What’s wrong with asking Mary to go for a drink?’

‘Nothing, I suppose. She’s a very kind woman.’

‘And good looking. And bright. And…’

‘OK, OK. I get the point,’ he said. ‘What with you and Joanne…’

‘So are you going to ask her out? You need a… a romantic companion. Those years when you were on your own didn’t do you any good.’

‘You’ve said all that already.’

‘Sorry,’ she said, not sounding sorry at all.

‘Mary has her own rich social life. She’s got lots of friends and relatives. And I’ve got a lot going on at the moment.’ He wished he could tell Sophie about the mind-reading, but knew he shouldn’t. ‘Did you know I’ve been to a meeting with the PM?’

‘Of course. If it wasn’t for Joanne, I’d never know anything.’

MONDAY 17TH JULY

‘Here it is,’ said Clothier, handing Redstone a worn navy-blue baseball cap. Redstone examined it, turning it over in his hands.

‘Looks old and well-used,’ he said.

‘I take that as a compliment,’ said Clothier.

‘Quite natty, actually,’ Redstone said. ‘Can I try it on?’

‘Sure. There’s a mirror over there.’

Redstone donned the cap and adjusted it in front of the mirror.

‘So how does it connect to the amplifying equipment?’ he asked. He took it off and examined it. ‘Is there an aerial built into the peak?’

‘O ye of little faith,’ said Clothier. ‘Everything’s built in, including the battery. The switch is in the buckle at the back here, where you adjust the strap to fit your head. Look, I’ll show you how to switch it on.’ Redstone passed him the cap, and watched him manipulate the pin in the buckle.

‘And if you do this’ – Clothier squeezed a cloth-covered button at the side of the buckle – ‘it becomes a signal blocker as opposed to an amplifier. Now let’s try it.’ Redstone took it and gingerly placed it on his head.

It’s quite robust, Clothier thought, *so you don’t have to treat it as though it’s fragile.*

‘Good,’ Redstone said, tugging the peak down.

‘Good what?’ said Clothier.

‘Good it’s not fragile, of course. Oh! You didn’t say anything!’

‘That’s right. Stay there, and I’ll move back. Let’s see what the range is.’

‘“Uneasy is the head that wears a crown”,’ Redstone said.

‘Right.’

They gradually moved further apart, and figured out the range was about three metres.

'Now turn sideways,' said Clothier. 'I'll move much closer.'

Redstone did as he was told, and realised the cap was directional. He picked up Clothier's thoughts only when the cap's peak was pointing towards him.

'One last test,' said Clothier. 'Switch it to blocking mode.' Redstone did so, and found he couldn't detect Clothier's thoughts even when they stood toe to toe. He took off the cap.

'You're a genius,' he said, grabbing Clothier's hand and shaking it vigorously. Clothier bobbed his head and smiled.

'One last thing,' Clothier said. 'If you lift the lining here, you'll see a USB socket, like in your phone. You should recharge it using a normal phone charger. Obviously somewhere private.'

Redstone looked at the socket. 'So what now?' he said. 'When are you going to ask me to use it?'

'Not up to me. I'll tell Laura it works, and then it's in the hands of her lot.'

'Who keeps it now?'

'I don't see why you shouldn't. Nobody who took it to pieces would be able to figure out what it's for, unless they already knew someone with your ability. There's nothing secret in the technology itself. You might as well take it and have fun with it.'

Redstone thought Clothier sounded rather wistful – as though he wished he had this new-found ability. Maybe anyone would want it. Maybe he could have some fun with it.

He pondered this as he strode through the quiet back streets towards Pimlico Tube station. Would he wear the cap in the lab, for example? It would seem like spying on his friends. He decided to use it only with strangers. Or in some situation where knowing what someone was thinking would be truly useful.

He donned the cap as he entered the station, and instead of walking down the escalator as usual, he stood behind a middle-aged woman as the escalator trundled down.

She was concerned she would feel too hot on the train.

This is mundane rubbish, and not fair even on strangers, he said to himself. He removed the cap, switched it off, and put it in his bag.

Five minutes later he was sitting on a train reflecting that the woman had been right. It was too hot. Why was the Victoria Line always so warm? He looked at the diagrammatic map of the line above the opposite windows, and realised that the whole line was underground. The Piccadilly Line, the one he usually used, had quite a lot of its route above ground. That would give the heat generated by the motors a chance to escape. *Bloody scientist,* he could imagine Laura saying. *Not worth worrying about if you can't do anything to change it.* Just one example of how different they were. She'd probably hunt down the engineer who designed the system and kill him.

'You look unusually pensive,' Joanne said as he walked into her office.

'Yes, well observed,' he said. 'I was thinking about stuff I normally let slide by – you know, relationships, and life, and stuff like that. Where your expertise lies.'

'Oh dear,' she said. 'Must be serious. Worrying about life post-Laura?'

'Got it in one.'

'Something will turn up. You've got to be open to opportunities as they arise. In fact, create opportunities. You need to expand your social life.'

'As you've been saying for years.'

'Maybe you're seeing the truth of it, at last?' she said.

'Hmm. Any news? Has the company collapsed while I've been out?'

‘Not quite. Young Rosie’s chirpy – seems your pet project’s going well.’

‘Excellent. I’ll go and… no, I won’t keep looking over her shoulder. Not good for her.’

His phone buzzed – Michelle. He waved at Joanne, walked into his office and closed the door.

‘Have you seen the latest social media campaign?’ Michelle asked.

‘No. Tell me.’

‘It’s using the word *stink* again. His policies stink, his personality stinks, his colleagues can’t bear the stink – he should resign. Or words to that effect.’

‘Oh dear. Not exactly subtle.’

‘Social media campaigns don’t have to be subtle to be effective, according to Rosie. Anyway, the point is it seems increasingly likely that your guess about the next target is going to prove right. GCHQ have been rather good, I must say. We’re ready to trace the hackers if they do target the new sewage system.’

*

That evening, as Redstone arrived home and opened his front door, Laura rang.

‘You OK?’ she said. ‘Mark, I’m sorry to have been so, well, distant recently. Work’s been overwhelming, as you can imagine, but I’ve got to confess it wasn’t just that.’

‘You needn’t—’

‘I didn’t know how to… I want us to stay on good terms. I hope you don’t feel bitter about my behaviour.’

‘Laura,’ he said, ‘nothing could be further from my mind. I was only today reflecting I too want to stay on good terms. I… I know you can’t read my mind like I read yours that time, but I want you to know I feel fond of you as well.’

‘My word,’ she said. ‘That’s unusually – that’s very open of you. It’s great. Thanks. What a relief.’

‘So what next?’

‘Ah. I need to go round to your house to collect my stuff. Would tomorrow evening be all right?’

‘Sure.’

‘And I know about the cap Jim’s made for you, of course. Could I ask you not to wear it with me?’

‘I won’t. I’ve already worked out that I shouldn’t wear it with people I know. Don’t worry. Your thoughts are safe from me.’

*

A mixture of emotions churned inside Redstone – relief and pleasure that he and Laura were going to stay on good terms, sadness that their liaison was over, fear of a new period of loneliness, and, to his surprise, a strand of optimism and even excitement that a new phase of his life could be opening. He strongly wanted to talk this through with someone. Face to face. Mary would be convenient, and would no doubt say she was happy to chat, but she might in truth not want to get involved. Or she might have better things to do, like watch TV. But she was inherently kind. Most people were.

*

‘Natty cap,’ Mary said, ‘but it’s not cold in here.’

‘Oh, sorry,’ Redstone said. ‘Do you mind if I keep it on for the moment? I, er, my hair’s a bit grotty.’

‘Of course not. I’ll make a drink, and then you can tell me all.’

They sat opposite each other at the small kitchen table. He couldn’t pick up the slightest hint of what she was thinking. Maybe the cap wasn’t working?

Zena burst into the room.

'Mark!' she said. 'Lovely to see you! Are you well? Private chat with Mum?'

'Well, in a way,' he said. 'I need to talk something through…' *Zena was thinking about a young man she'd chatted to earlier today.*

He whipped off the cap, flushing. He shouldn't be listening in to that.

'You OK?' said Mary, leaning over and touching his hand.

'Yes, sorry,' he said. 'I shouldn't have been wearing the cap. Too hot. As I was saying, Zena, yes, I do need a private chat with Mary, if you wouldn't mind.'

'OK,' she said. 'I'll go and….' She stepped out of the door, leant back in, gave a little wave and disappeared.

Redstone told Mary about his soup of emotions.

'I'm impressed that you can analyse yourself like that,' she said. 'Most people don't even try.'

'Now you mention it, I'm surprised myself,' he said. 'I've never been one for self-analysis. Probably because I'm no good at analysing emotions in other people.'

'Or maybe your lack of interest in self-analysis has hampered your understanding of others.'

'Maybe,' he said. 'I suppose events have forced me to pay more attention to what people are thinking and feeling.'

'What do you mean?'

'I… oh, Laura, and…' He wished he hadn't said that. It was his mind-reading, of course, but he couldn't even hint at that to Mary. 'No, not events,' he said. 'Just the way my life is going at the moment. With Laura.'

'And maybe it's also accumulating experience. Ageing has its benefits.'

He smiled at her. He would have liked to tell her how much he enjoyed talking to her, but it didn't seem quite right.

‘Talking about it has been very helpful,’ he said. ‘Many thanks. I should go now.’

‘I don’t think I contributed much,’ she said, standing up. ‘But sometimes we just need someone to talk to.’ They walked together to her front door.

‘Maybe you’d like to come round again for a meal?’ he said.

‘Lovely,’ she said. She stood on tiptoe, kissed his cheek, and opened the door.

TUESDAY 18TH JULY

Laura phoned while Redstone was at his desk agonising about whether to go round to Rosie and ask about progress on Project Smoothaway.

'Seen the news?' she said.

'No. A new attack?'

'Yes. Your guess turned out to be spot on. Reports of a strong smell of drains from west London along the river to Westminster, and as far as Docklands. It's bad here, in Thames House. Very unpleasant. And lots of social media posts about Jones's stinking leadership, saying he has to go. People are blaming the terrorists but also saying Jones should have been spending more on counterterrorism. You know, more police, and more pay for me.'

'You wish. What are Thames Water saying?'

'They've confirmed they've been hacked. It's very strange. It doesn't fit in with the other attacks. Nobody's been hurt, there's been no real damage. Some colleagues are speculating it might not be the same terrorists. Maybe there are two groups, they're saying. Maybe a second team has jumped on the bandwagon, people who are less vicious but also want Jones to go.'

'The way you say, "some colleagues" implies you think differently.'

'I do. I suspect there are two factions within the terrorist organisation. The brutal faction took the lead for the train crashes – the road signs were some sort of compromise – and the power cuts and now the sewage hack were led by the non-brutal faction.'

'Makes sense to me,' Redstone said. 'But they must both have the same overall objective.'

‘I suppose so, but that also puzzles us. What is it? It seems to be aimed at Michael Jones himself, but that’s too personal to make sense.’

‘Maybe one of the leaders, or the overall leader, has some sort of personal grudge against him. Maybe Michael did something to some guy which left him seething with anger and wanting revenge.’

‘Yes,’ she said, ‘but it must have been quite recently, otherwise the guy would have done all this before. And Michael was out of power last year.’

‘Maybe the guy has recently got out of prison.’

‘We’re looking into that possibility, but haven’t come up with any convincing suspects so far.’

‘I don’t envy you your job,’ Redstone said. ‘I suppose your priority has to be to keep on trying to track them down.’

‘Right. GCHQ are working on the sewage case, and expect to have the tracing information shortly.’

‘Good.’ He paused. ‘Laura, I worked with Michelle on trying to predict what the enemy would do next. It was a joint effort. Anyone told her?’

‘I’m not her case officer.’

‘Yes, but—’

‘I expect GCHQ will have kept her in the loop. They’ve been working closely with her.’

‘Maybe I’ll… Will you tell me if you locate the hackers from the tracing?’

‘We make these decisions on the basis of the situation as we find it.’

‘Blimey, Laura, you sound like… never mind. See you later at home?’

‘Yes,’ she said. ‘Late. After you’ve had your dinner.’

When she’d rung off, he phoned Michelle. She already knew about the hacking.

‘How’s the tracing going?’ he said.

‘No idea. They’ve shut me out. They seemed to react badly to some of the points I was making about how they’re going about it.’

‘Oh dear. Are you concerned that they won’t get it right?’

‘Depends on how skilled the hackers turn out to be. I have a suspicion they’re far more sophisticated than GCHQ give them credit for. The code I’ve seen…’

‘Are they going to tell you how it pans out?’

‘I suspect not. They keep quoting national security at me.’

‘I think I’m in the same situation,’ he said.

‘Really? Aren’t you and Laura close?’

‘We were, but we’ve broken up.’

‘Sorry to hear that. Sorry for you, I mean. I know how it feels. Anyway, must go. Bye.’

Redstone sat at his desk, feeling hard done by. There was nobody he could talk to about it without breaking the Official Secrets Act, which he’d last signed three years ago when he’d been based in Number 10. Oh, yes there was – Jim Clothier, and he needed to talk to him anyway.

He got through straight away, and told Clothier about not being able to read Mary’s thoughts the previous evening.

‘Though the thoughts of another person in the room came across very clearly,’ he said.

‘This woman Mary – it must be something about *her*,’ Clothier said. ‘I’d love to be able to find out more, but I can’t see how we could do it without letting her in on what you can do with other people. She’s not on our system, by any chance, is she?’

‘Do you mean has she been vetted for some reason?’

‘Yes.’

‘Very unlikely. She works for the NHS, and before that she ran a restaurant. Too normal for the likes of MI5.’

‘You’d be surprised, but I admit it doesn’t sound promising. How would you feel about telling me who she is?’

‘Oh.’ *What harm could it do?* ‘Very well. She’s my next-door neighbour.’ He gave Clothier Mary’s details.

‘Actually, we might have looked into her in the past,’ Clothier said, ‘when we were checking your own security. We do occasionally check people’s neighbours. Don’t worry. It’s not intrusive. She won’t know, unless you tell her, and you mustn’t do that unless we let her into the magic circle.’

‘It would be rather nice for me if we did let her in, as you put it,’ Redstone said. ‘Someone I could talk to about what’s going on. I suppose you know Laura and I have broken up.’

‘Yes, I was told,’ Clothier said. ‘Sorry. I know it can be lonely and frustrating sometimes when you’re loaded with some information you’d love to discuss with someone.’

‘Or suddenly not told information when you were closely involved.’

‘That sounds a bit specific. Something current?’

‘Yes. I know GCHQ are trying to trace the people who hacked into the sewage system, but I’d like to know if they’re succeeding.’

‘I can certainly keep you up to speed on that,’ Clothier said, ‘not least because we’re likely to want to use your mind-reading if we trace these people. The latest is that GCHQ have homed in on a building in a business park off the North Circular Road, in Tottenham. The guy who rents it runs an IT business, managing companies’ websites and the like. The right sort of person to have lots of appropriate hardware.’

‘That’s it, then!’

‘We’ll see. Special Branch and our people are raiding it as we speak. Which is a relief, given the huge political pressure we’re experiencing. All those posh rich people unable to smell their money.’

‘You sound uncharacteristically bitter, Jim.’

‘Sorry. Put it down to lack of sleep. Anyway, if all goes to plan, we’ll be interrogating the Tottenham guy tomorrow, and I imagine you’ll be asked to sit in.’

‘Oh. I’m a bit nervous, but it should be OK.’

‘I’m quite excited,’ said Clothier. ‘I want to see if your skill works in that situation. I can’t see why it wouldn’t, unless we come across another Mary.’

‘Can’t rule that out, I suppose. Er, Jim – is someone in MI5 my case officer? Is that how it works? Is it Laura?’

‘Ah,’ Clothier said. ‘We don’t have iron-clad rules about how we liaise with outsiders, but I can see why it might be awkward if it were Laura managing you. I’ll try to arrange that it’s me. I’ll point out that your services will likely be used on lots of quite different cases, so you’re a technical asset.’

‘Like a camera hidden in a lapel badge.’

‘Exactly, though not as sophisticated.’

*

Number 10 issued a defiant message. The Prime Minister categorically rejected the smears and lies being propagated by the terrorists who, in their evil attempt to change the government by force had killed and injured thousands of British citizens, and caused huge fear and massive time-wasting disruption for millions more. These anonymous enemies of the state didn’t have the guts to try to achieve their ends through the ballot box. The British people had the intelligence to see through the terrorists’ malign propaganda, and would be delighted to hear that the security forces were closing in on the ruthless murderers.

Redstone was pleased that Jones was standing firm. He donned his cap, sat on the garden bench, and told Treacle so. She assumed he was greeting her, and said hello, which came out as a plaintive-sounding miaow.

After dinner, he sat listening to a podcast while waiting for Laura. He looked out of the front window and was annoyed to see a big black BMW SUV parked across his drive, its windows open and angry rap music thumping out. Laura would want to park in the drive to load her stuff into her car. He opened the front door to ask the driver to move, but before he had a chance Laura drew up behind the BMW. Her battered old Land Rover was an ex-army vehicle, more powerful and indeed better armoured than it appeared.

She got out, walked over to the BMW and spoke to the driver, a young man with a shaven head. Redstone couldn't hear the conversation, but the car didn't move. Laura took a step back, gestured at her Land Rover, and spoke to the driver again. She stood upright, relaxed, perfectly still, looking at him. He started to get out of the car, paused and stared at her. He then made a big show of consulting his heavy gold watch, sat back behind the wheel and slammed his door shut. The BMW accelerated away. Laura got back into the Land Rover and drove it into the drive.

'How did you persuade him to go?' Redstone said.

'I told him I'd use my vehicle to shove his out of the way, if he didn't move.'

'As simple as that.'

'Well, I told him my thoughts on why he was there.'

'Which were?'

'He was a drug dealer who'd arrived to hand out supplies to his subordinates and receive their cash. Your road makes a good rendezvous because it's easy to park here, and there's no police activity. He parked across your drive as a display of his power. Rules and common decency are for lesser beings than him.'

She took a couple of big empty canvas holdalls out of the Land Rover.

'How on earth did you know all that about him?' Redstone asked. 'All your stuff is in the bedroom and the bathroom. You don't seem to have left anything anywhere else.' *She stayed here rather than lived here.*

'Yes, thanks. I deduced it from his manner, his car, his age, and my knowledge of how drug dealers work.'

'And he didn't threaten you?'

'He seemed to believe it wouldn't be worth it. Maybe he thought I was a big drug lord. Or lady.' She ran up the stairs.

'Need any help?' Redstone called.

'No, I'm fine, thanks.'

'Cup of tea?'

'Sorry. No time.'

He sat in the kitchen, waiting for Laura to finish, turning over the incident outside. What would she have done to the guy if he'd got out of his car? He was lucky he hadn't tried. She must have given him that look – the one Redstone had first seen three years ago, when Laura had caused a top civil servant called Valerie Hitchcock to stumble out of a meeting simply by staring at her.

God, he'd miss Laura.

WEDNESDAY 19TH JULY

'Can you come in this morning?' Clothier said on the phone. 'As I forecast, we've got someone in custody, and want to interrogate him in your presence. I'll send a driver.'

An hour later Redstone got out of the car, in front of Thames House. He wrinkled his nose at the sulphurous putrid smell of the sewage-infested river. No surprise that many well-heeled residents of the wealthy riverside areas were using their money and influence to make the government's life difficult.

He was shown into a small room on the fourth floor. Jim Clothier sprang up and shook his hand.

'Glad you didn't forget the cap,' he said. 'I assume it's switched off at present.'

'Yes.'

Redstone sniffed.

'Not too bad in here,' Clothier said, 'but it's worse down in my empire in the basement. "It smells to heaven," as the bard said. I assume the smelly gases are heavier than air. You're the chemist – you tell me.'

Redstone did a rapid calculation in his head. 'A bit for the hydrogen sulphide,' he said, 'but more so for the other odorants.'

'Anyway, Thames Water are close to resuming normal service,' said Clothier. 'The smell won't be here much longer.' He poured Redstone a coffee. 'Let's talk about our detainee. His name is Donald Quart. As I told you, he's an IT expert. We've also discovered he's a member of a couple of extremist right-wing organisations, and has all sorts of unpleasant stuff on one of his computer drives. He hasn't yet been told why we've detained him.'

'How are we going to play the interrogation?' said Redstone.

'You'll sit next to the interrogator, and write anything you pick up, that you think might be relevant, on the pad between you. So that she can read it.'

'What if Quart or his solicitor can read upside-down?'

'We've put a low screen across the table to prevent that. About a foot high, and slanted towards you and the interrogator. Who, by the way, has asked that you don't sit close to her, and that you make every effort not to read her mind.'

'Fair enough,' Redstone said. 'Are you going to introduce us before the interrogation?'

'No need.'

'Oh. It's Laura.'

'Yes, we want to keep knowledge of your ability very tightly controlled. I know it might be awkward for you both, but there you are.'

'Understood. Will you be monitoring proceedings from outside the room?'

'Yes. And I'll have a camera trained on your notepad, and will be able to speak to Laura through her earpiece if necessary.'

'OK. Ready when you are.'

They walked down the corridor to a door guarded by a uniformed officer. Clothier told Redstone to go in. He would be in the neighbouring room.

'Quart has a duty solicitor with him,' said Clothier.

The room contained a metal table, with the black plastic screen Clothier had described, and four plastic chairs. A young man was seated next to the solicitor, a grey-haired woman, on one side of the table. Laura sat opposite, and gestured to Redstone to sit next to her.

'Mr Quart has been formally cautioned,' Laura said, 'so let's start. Mr Quart – were you paid for the hacking?'

Quart was surprised and relieved. 'What? I—'

The solicitor interrupted. 'I've advised Mr Quart that he needn't answer any questions.'

'And he knows that we and a jury can draw inferences from any refusal,' said Laura.

Redstone scribbled *He expected to be interrogated about something else* on the pad. Laura glanced at it.

'What was the purpose of your hacking?'

Quart turned to the solicitor, who shook her head.

'No comment,' he said. *He has done some hacking,* Redstone wrote.

'Listen,' Laura said, 'we know you've been hacking. If you refuse to say anything about it, it will be obvious that you did it with intent to cause harm.'

'I didn't harm anyone,' he said. *He believes that*, Redstone scribbled.

'You can't be serious,' Laura said. 'What about all the people who were killed?'

Quart looked at her blankly. Redstone wrote *He doesn't know what you're talking about.*

'Let's take a step back,' said Laura. 'How much were you paid for the hacking?'

'£480,' Quart said. 'Wasn't pay – just expenses. I needed to build an extra piece of kit.' *All true.*

'Are you skilled at building computer kit?' asked Laura.

'I'm pretty good. I've built all my own stuff. I could do a lot more if I could get funding, if the government would help us entrepreneurs instead of doling out cash to immigrants and—'

The solicitor put her hand on his arm, and he stopped.

'Would you say your software skills match your hardware expertise?' asked Laura.

'I'm good, but I could be even better if I could get on one of those courses reserved for rich gender-bending Muslims—'

The solicitor stopped him again.

'What was your objective when you did that hacking?'

'No comment,' Quart said. *To get names and addresses, of course.*

'So your paymasters—'

'They weren't bloody paymasters, you stupid… I'm part of the top team. We work together.' He shrugged off the solicitor's hand. 'Unlike you lot in government. The ruling bloody classes. We can see how they're taking over. *Our* lives matter as much as theirs. More – we're English.'

Redstone scribbled *He hacked a Black Lives Matter group.*

'And what did you and your white supremacist colleagues do with the names and addresses you got through your hacking?'

'No comment.' *Surprised at how much you know. Posted shit through letter boxes.*

'We'll leave you to stew in your own excreta for now,' Laura said. 'Interview suspended.' She nodded to Redstone, got up and marched out, Redstone on her heels.

They met Clothier back in the first room. Redstone removed his cap.

'What a triumph!' Clothier said. 'This is an astounding breakthrough in interrogation. And you worked together beautifully.'

Laura flushed slightly. 'Yes,' she said, 'the interrogation went well, but it's clear that we got the wrong man. GCHQ cocked it up.'

Clothier shrugged. 'Not the first time this sort of thing's happened. I assume you'll tell GCHQ.'

'Yes. I don't know what they'll do next.'

'I think Michelle expected that you'd find GCHQ had the wrong person,' Redstone said. 'She told me the hackers are more sophisticated than GCHQ realise, or words to that effect. I wonder if she herself could trace them from the data GCHQ harvested when the sewage works were hacked.'

'Interesting idea,' said Clothier. 'If anyone could, she could. Laura, will you put this to them when you phone?'

‘Not my place to interfere in the way they work,’ Laura said.

Redstone stared at her. If he’d been wearing the cap, he was sure he’d have picked up thoughts of jealousy. She’d normally do anything necessary to achieve her goals.

‘I’ll do it, if I’m allowed to,’ he said.

‘I think that’s beyond your role here,’ Laura said.

‘Come on,’ Clothier said. ‘We have a shared goal, and if there’s a chance Michelle can help us achieve it, we should seize it with both hands. If you can seize a goal with both hands. *I’ll* speak to GCHQ.’

Redstone nodded.

‘I’ll leave you two to it,’ Laura said, and walked out.

Clothier looked at Redstone, who was embarrassed but couldn’t see what he’d done to be embarrassed about. He shrugged.

‘Let’s go down to my smelly office,’ Clothier said, ‘have a drink to celebrate the success of the mind-reading, and talk to GCHQ.’

THURSDAY 20TH JULY

'Can we meet?' asked Michelle on the phone. 'I want to discuss the hacking stuff with someone, and I suppose you've got the right security clearance.'

'Sure,' said Redstone, closing his office door. 'Where would you like—'

'In my lab in Cambridge. It's easier for me to show you what I think is going on. Shall we say two o'clock?'

'But it's already five past eleven. I've got to… oh, fine. I'll do my best.'

'Good.'

Redstone told Joanne what he'd arranged.

'Plenty of time,' she said. 'I'll send you an eTicket.'

Two hours later he was at King's Cross station boarding the train, an older model than the ones which had been hacked. He settled into a window seat. Soon the parched golden brown Hertfordshire fields were flashing by. He opened his bag to pull out his laptop, and came across his cap. Should he wear it when he met Michelle? Maybe at the beginning, to set the scene.

A taxi took him from Cambridge station to the university's computer science centre, a modern brick and glass building with an oversized flat roof supported at the edges on slender metal pillars. He collected a security badge from the receptionist, and walked down a corridor to Michelle's lab. She was sitting staring at a screen and typing. The room hadn't changed since he was there the year before – spacious, square, lots of exposed brick, and two small windows in one wall, just below the ceiling. The back wall was taken up with a row of glass-doored cabinets containing grey computer equipment. Bunches of cables led from the tops of the cabinets to metal ducts attached to the ceiling. Other cables, stuck down with yellow safety tape, snaked across the tiled floor to tables on which stood screens and keyboards.

'Ah,' she said, 'there you are. Pull up a chair.' He sat next to her. *She hadn't noticed his cap, and was thinking about how to present a complex technical issue to this man – him – whose IT knowledge was pretty limited.*

'Nice to see you,' he said. 'You're looking well.' *She barely registered his remark, dismissed it as irrelevant, but knew societal norms required her to acknowledge it.*

'And you,' she mumbled. She pressed some keys and gestured to her screen.

'This diagram shows a snapshot in time of the path the enemy followed to hack Thames Water,' she said. 'By "path", I mean path in cyberspace.'

Redstone found it was confusing to read her thoughts while listening to her voice, so he removed his cap. The screen showed what resembled a complex asymmetrical spider's web with a pulsing red spot in the middle, a blue spot halfway out on the left, and a yellow spot on the top edge.

'Is the red spot Thames Water's IT setup?' he said.

'Yes.'

'And the other two?'

'Now watch,' she said, ignoring his question. She pressed a key, and the web changed shape, and kept changing, with the exception of the three spots.

'That's a slowed-down version of what was happening. Now I'll speed it up to about a thousandth of its real speed.'

The web kept changing so fast that Redstone could only just make out the lines joining the blue and red spots, while the yellow spot had disappeared.

'So GCHQ were fooled into thinking they'd solved the puzzle once they'd spotted the links to the blue spot. Which is the address of the guy they arrested. But the path from him to the actual hackers, who are the yellow spot, was changing too fast for their equipment to notice it existed at all. With the way they'd set up their kit.'

'But you got the yellow spot.'

'Yes,' she said. 'Here, I've printed out details. Including the physical address. It's in a block of flats in Pimlico,'

'Oddly, not that far from MI5.' *And Laura's flat.* 'So they set up that racist idiot to be a fall guy, a decoy.'

'Yes. Quite easy to find someone like that. Doesn't need much research. I've tried it.'

'Blimey.' He unfolded the sheet of paper Michelle handed him, containing the address, and took a photo of it on his phone.

'These hackers are extremely good,' she said. 'I haven't seen anything as impressive as this since last year, when we were dealing with those American people. It's reminiscent of what Cardew did over there. But he's dead, of course.' President Cardew had set up an artificial intelligence program which had in effect run the USA while fooling everyone into thinking the presidency was governing as normal.

'Yes, he's gone.' Redstone put his cap on. 'Right, I'd better get this information to MI5 as soon as possible.'

'Good,' she said. *She started to think about her next project, which was to adjust her stock market forecasting program to take better account of exceptional major events.*

'I'll say goodbye, then,' he said.

'Bye,' she said, barely registering his words.

He went into the corridor and sent Clothier the photo of the information Michelle had printed, and then called him.

'I've just sent you some information using WhatsApp, which I'm told means it can't be hacked,' he said.

'That's right. What is it?'

Redstone explained.

'Good grief!' Clothier said. 'GCHQ aren't going to like this. Right, I'll get it acted on straight away. I expect we'll be asking you to come in again, once we've got the hacker or hackers in custody.'

*

Redstone sat back in the train seat, reviewing what he'd learnt from Michelle and wondering where it would lead. His phone rang as his train reached the outer London suburbs.

'The hackers have gone,' Clothier said. 'The cupboard's bare. All the hardware stripped out, though it had been there. Either someone tipped them off, or they anticipated the trace.'

'Do you honestly think someone might have tipped them off?' Redstone said. 'You're talking about a traitor at the heart of government. Or me or Michelle, I suppose.'

'Highly unlikely, but you can't rule it out. No, my money's on them being bright enough to realise we'd trace the hack sooner or later. In this case it was later – too late. If we'd used Michelle's expertise sooner… oh well, water under the bridge. No, sewage under the bridge.'

'What do you think they'll try next?'

'Who knows? Maybe we can get a clue from the wording of their next Twitter campaign against the PM.'

'Maybe,' Redstone said. 'Would it be OK if I discussed this with Michelle?'

'Yes, go ahead,' Clothier said. 'She's the one who's got it right so far.'

*

As Redstone was leaving his local Tube station, he took out his phone and scrolled through what he still thought of as Twitter. The latest abuse aimed at Michael Jones focused on a report by the

House of Commons Public Accounts Committee, the most powerful committee of Parliament. The committee's role was to hold the government to account on public spending. Their new report attacked wasted expenditure by the Ministry of Defence's procurement arm.

Old news, Redstone thought, as he walked through the park at the bottom of his road. It had been a theme for decades, maybe centuries. Weapons costing more than budgeted... maybe he should have been in the weapons business rather than pharmaceuticals.

He read further. The posts were blaming Jones personally. He'd appointed the relevant ministers, he was responsible. 'Jones wastes billions on dud guns but won't help hungry kids,' one post said, with a cartoon showing an *Oliver Twist* scenario – Jones sending a starving boy away with one hand while with the other behind his back, passing a wodge of money to a fat man holding a broken rifle.

Redstone hoped Jones wouldn't be too depressed by this utter rubbish.

'Penny for them,' said Zena, panting. 'God, you walk fast.'

'Oh!' Redstone said. 'Hi.' She was going to walk home with him, and he didn't want to read her mind. He adjusted his cap to shielding mode.

'I was on the same Tube,' she said. 'Came up the stairs a few people behind you. Good day?

'I've come straight from King's Cross. I was in Cambridge. Didn't seem worth going back to the lab.'

'Have a good time there?'

'I wouldn't exactly describe it as a good time. It was work. It was very interesting and...' He decided not to tell her any more. 'How about you? How was your day?'

'Yes, the play's coming on well. We open later this week. Would you like to come to the first night? Lots of important people there.'

‘That’s very kind of you, but it’s not going to be the sort of… actually, I haven’t a clue what play you’re doing. I’m assuming it’s chosen to appeal to, well, your age group, but maybe that’s rubbish.’

‘I’m not sure what age group the playwright had in mind,’ she said with a faint smirk. ‘It seems to appeal to a wide range. You may have heard of it. *Julius Caesar*. The playwright’s name is—’

‘All right, you got me there. Maybe I will come. Can you text me the details? When and where.’

‘Sure,’ she said. ‘It’s near Tower Bridge. I can show you around backstage afterwards.’

They walked on.

‘Would you like to bring a companion?’ she said. ‘Let me know, and I’ll try to wangle two tickets for you.’

‘Er… yes, thanks. I don’t like going to the theatre on my own.’

‘Of course not. Leave it with me.’

They reached his house.

‘Bye, then,’ she said.

‘Bye,’ he said. ‘Give my love to Mary.’

*

After he’d eaten, he phoned Michelle and told her what MI5 and Special Branch had found when they’d raided the address she’d supplied.

‘Not surprising,’ she said. ‘Your lot gave them a ridiculous amount of time. And warning. They probably had a sort of tripwire arrangement to tell them if GCHQ traced the Tottenham guy. That’s what I would have done.’

‘What would you target next if you were in their shoes?’ he asked, ignoring her reference to ‘your lot’.

‘The credit card systems,’ she said immediately. ‘Would cause tremendous inconvenience to loads of people.’

‘But GCHQ said in the meeting at Number 10—’

'Arrogant, unimaginative... Of course the systems aren't impregnable.'

'Ah. So if you were in charge of tracing a hacking attack on the credit card systems, could you find the hackers?'

'Yes, and do it quickly if I had access to GCHQ's kit.'

'Hmm,' he said. 'Your guess for the next target may be right. The hackers' social media messaging is now alleging financial mismanagement. Sort of fits.' He paused. 'Leave it to me. I've got to think through how to handle this.'

He sat at his desk and pulled a notebook towards him. Objective: to get Michelle put in charge of how GCHQ handles the next hacking attempt. Obstacles: GCHQ director, and at her urging the Home Secretary, and possibly Laura because of her antipathy towards Michelle. Allies: Clothier, McKay, probably Roger Feast – and almost certainly Michael Jones.

Could he ring the PM himself? Redstone could probably get through the cordon of private secretaries, given his relationship with the PM. But Jones would seek advice from McKay and Feast before committing himself, and they'd be less helpful if they'd been left out of the loop. So there were just two people Redstone had to convince – McKay and Feast. He could go direct to McKay, but it would be tactically better to get Clothier to persuade him. He looked at the clock – 8:45 p.m. Worth a try. The matter was urgent – the hackers could be doing their thing tomorrow, or even now.

His call to Clothier went through to a duty officer, who promised to try to contact Clothier on his private number and ask him to phone Redstone urgently. The Cabinet Office put Redstone on hold, and then Feast came on the line. Still at the office. Redstone explained what Michelle had said. Feast agreed that Michelle should be given urgent access to GCHQ's relevant equipment, and promised to advise the PM accordingly as soon as he could get hold of him. As he rang off, Clothier came through. He agreed with Redstone, and said he'd speak to McKay immediately.

Redstone poured himself a whisky. For the moment he'd done all he could to save the country from further disaster, so he was free to turn his attention to his much more difficult problem – who to take to Zena's play. None of his friends now lived in or near London – one was in Philadelphia, one in Zurich, one in Oslo… the nearest was in Cheshire, and he wouldn't come down for a play, especially if his wife wasn't invited too. In fact, all his friends were paired off. He felt a wave of self-pity and took a slug of the whisky. Sophie and Graham were also too far away. He didn't think any of his London Bio colleagues would be keen – they too had partners. Michelle would almost certainly decline.

That left Laura. A few weeks ago, she would have been keen to go. Maybe she still would. He'd ask her. The worst that could happen was that she'd refuse. And leave him feeling even worse. What if she had a new, er, friend? God, he hadn't thought of that. No, it wasn't love for someone else which made her want to break it off with Redstone – he'd had the amazing luxury of having been able to read her emotions. However, time had passed since then… He told himself to get a grip. He phoned her. To his surprise, she answered immediately.

'You remember Zena next door?' he said.

'Well, I met her once, at that party Mary threw.'

'Right. She's working in a theatre near Tower Bridge, and has invited me and a companion to go to the opening night of *Julius Caesar* later this week. Would you like to come? I know you like Shakespeare.'

'When is it exactly?'

'Ah, sorry, I'm waiting for Zena to text me.'

'Well, diary permitting, I'll accept your invitation,' she said. 'Could be fun, in all sorts of ways. As long as it's just—'

'Yes, I'm not trying to change anything between us. Just to see the play.'

'Would you be wearing your cap?'

‘Yes, in blocking mode. I’ve found it’s very confusing to be picking up people’s thoughts while trying to listen to something.’

‘Good. Fine, then.’

FRIDAY 21ST JULY

Redstone smiled at the four younger scientists seated round the meeting table in his office.

'You're doing a great job,' he said. 'David will be proud when he gets back. As I am. Anything more you want to discuss, except for the name, which is going to remain Project Smoothaway?'

The oldest of the group flung up his arms and said, 'Oh, no!' in mock horror. The others grinned.

'In your experience,' Rosie said to Redstone, 'how much longer before it can be tried on a human?'

'Difficult to say. Could be as little as six months, if everything goes well. The safety testing above all, of course.'

'Will we be using Star Boston Pharma for the next phases? Clinical trials and so on?' asked another researcher. Star Boston was the big pharmaceutical company that had partnered London Bio for previous products.

'Yes. They've proved good to work with.'

Joanne came into the office.

'Michelle rang,' she said. 'I told her you'd ring back.'

'Thanks.' Redstone closed the meeting, and called Michelle on his mobile.

'Thought I should tell you,' she said. 'Whatever it was you did after our conversation yesterday paid off. I'm now in Cheltenham, at GCHQ. We're working with the banks to be ready if the enemy tries to hack the credit card systems.'

'Excellent.'

'And there have been more social media messages today which point to our guess being right. The latest says, er…' Redstone heard someone call out. 'Thanks. It says, *You can't credit Jones's incompetence.*'

'Yes, that does suggest we were right. Good luck with the tracing.'

'Not a matter of luck,' she said.

*

Two hours later, Clothier phoned.

'Got the location,' he said. 'It's an office in a small industrial estate in St Albans. The police are raiding it now. What's more, Michelle and GCHQ were able to foil the hacking. The credit card systems are still working.'

'Brilliant!'

'They're bringing someone in. Don't know much about him yet. The office has the top-end computer equipment you'd expect of a sophisticated hacker. He was living on site.'

'I'm confident they've got the right person this time,' said Redstone, 'because of Michelle's involvement. I imagine you'll be wanting me to sit in the interrogation as before?'

'Yes please. I'll send a car.'

*

'We're not sure of this man's nationality,' Clothier said to Redstone, as they sat side by side in Thames House. In front of them was a screen showing the suspect: a young man with a short black beard, sitting next to the same solicitor as before. 'We haven't got anything on him in our files. His biometrics don't match any in the immigration database. He claims not to speak English. I'm concerned you won't understand his thoughts if they're in a foreign language you don't speak.'

'My only other language is French,' said Redstone. 'But the process isn't like reading words. After all, I understand what my cat is feeling, and I don't speak miaow.'

'Yes, but with due respect to your cat, people's thoughts are more complex.'

'If you say so,' Redstone said. 'Have we got time to do an experiment? Can you produce a member of staff who can think in a different language?'

'Funny you should say that,' said Clothier. 'She's sitting next door waiting. She's one of my technicians. I've warned her not to breathe a word of what happens, and I trust her. She can think in another language. I won't tell you what it is. I'll bring her in.'

He left the room, and reappeared with a young woman Redstone remembered seeing near Clothier's office. He introduced her, calling her "Ms X", and asked her to sit opposite him and Redstone.

'Put your cap on, Mark, and let's try,' Clothier said. 'Now, Ms X, where was your mother born?'

Ms X shuffled a little in her chair.

'Interesting,' said Redstone. 'I'm getting a jumble of images and, well, feelings, about a city I'm pretty sure is Stockholm.' Ms X gave a broad smile. 'But it's not a fair trial,' he continued, 'because I know Stockholm. I might have got it right only because I recognized the… the pictures. What if Ms X had thought of some small place in Siberia, for example?'

'OK,' said Clothier, 'Ms X – think of a small town you like. Anywhere in the world.'

Ms X scrunched up her eyes.

'Bodrum, in Turkey,' said Redstone. Ms X gaped at him. 'She thought of its name.'

'Ms X,' said Clothier, 'think of your favourite piece of music.' She sat for a few seconds and then nodded.

'Excellent taste, though again you thought of its name,' said Redstone. 'I love the bit after the first section, where the drums play and then he crashes in with the organ, don't you? Jimmy Smith, "Walk on the Wild Side".'

She clapped.

'Who introduced you to that piece?' Redstone asked. 'Think the answer, don't speak.'

She nodded.

'It was your father.' She gave the thumbs up.

'Why did you hack the GCHQ computer?' said Redstone. Ms X sat back with a startled look.

'She was initially shocked, and was about to deny it, before realising it was a dummy question. That's good, because no pictures or names were involved.'

She nodded.

'One more,' Clothier said. 'What's your favourite pudding?'

'Ah,' Redstone said. 'I got a word in a language which I don't think was Swedish. So I don't know it from its name. The pudding is a milk – no, a rice pudding, with, ah, rose water? Maybe you're thinking in a Middle Eastern language. Arabic? No, you just rejected that. Ah, Turkish. Of course.'

'You can speak now, Ms X, or Suna as we can now call you,' said Clothier. 'You've done brilliantly. Many thanks for your help.'

'Yes,' said Redstone, 'and congratulations on your excellent taste in music and pudding!'

'It's been a real pleasure,' she said. 'Incredible! Fascinating! Don't worry, I won't breathe a word to anyone. Seems to me the interrogation should go well, wherever the suspect comes from.'

'I agree,' said Clothier.

After Suna had left the room, Clothier asked Redstone how her thoughts had been formulated.

'A combination of pictures and words, I suppose,' Redstone said, 'with, above all… I'm not sure how to express it. Concepts.'

'Interesting. Academics would die to get their hands on you. How people think is a hot topic. Too bad.'

Redstone asked Clothier whether it wouldn't have been wise for Laura to have been in the room, so that she could see how it went. He assumed Laura was going to do the interrogating again.

'She didn't want to join us. As it turned out, I don't think it would have changed how she's going to conduct the interrogation. I'll pop round and tell her it should work as before, but that she should allow you to intercede if you think it would help.'

Five minutes later, Redstone was seated next to Laura at the table with the low slanted screen. The suspect was massaging his face.

'Good morning,' said Laura. 'I've been informed you don't want to reveal your name, but please tell me how you'd like me to address you.'

The suspect kept still and silent.

'OK, I'll call you Mr Pussy,' said Laura. The suspect blinked.

He knows what that means.

'I'm not happy with that,' said the solicitor. 'Insulting and bullying.'

'What would your client prefer?' Laura asked. The suspect stayed silent. She turned back to the young man.

'Where was your mother born?'

The suspect stared at the ceiling.

A big hospital. Could be America.

'And where did you grow up?'

The suspect snorted.

Looks like a big city – Boston?

'Let's talk about the girl you took to the prom at your high school. Why did she hate you?'

The suspect jolted upright. 'That's a fucking lie!' he said in an American accent.

The solicitor put her hand on his arm, and asked Laura for a break so that she could confer with her client. A guard led them out. Clothier came in a minute later.

'Well done!' he said. 'An American! Who'd have predicted that!'

'Yes,' Laura said, 'I thought I'd surprise him with a personal question based on Mark's feeling that it was the US… and it paid off.'

'My guess is he'll now give us his name and demand to see someone from the US embassy,' said Clothier. 'Are we obliged to agree?'

'Not sure. We need to ask one of our lawyers. Can you do that and let me know through the earpiece? And contact the FBI with his biometrics to see if they've got him on record. I'm sure they'll play ball, given the circumstances. Meanwhile I think we should get him back in, to keep up the momentum. Our objective is to confirm he's the hacker, or at least was involved in the hacking, and find out who's behind it.'

Clothier left, and a guard escorted the suspect and his solicitor back in.

'My client wants to make a statement,' the solicitor said. Laura nodded. The suspect took a deep breath.

'I'm an American citizen,' he said. 'You can't hold me here like this. And I want an American lawyer instead of this Brit.' He gestured to the solicitor and shuffled in his chair.

'We certainly can hold you here,' Laura said. 'And we will, till you've answered my questions. We've hardly got started.'

'I know important people. I need to send a private email.'

Fleeting image of an older woman, Redstone wrote.

'We'll see how co-operative you are,' Laura said, 'and then decide what privileges you're allowed.'

'I'm not telling you anything. What are you going to do, torture me? Is that what your silent friend is here for?' *Scared.*

Redstone stared at the suspect and massaged his right fist.

'My colleague is an expert in finding out what people know,' said Laura. 'Do you really want to put him to the test?'

'You can't touch me without causing a diplomatic incident,' the suspect said. *Images of prisoners being hit. From films.*

'Of course we can,' Laura said. 'What embassy is going to help some guy who claims to be one of their citizens, when he won't give his name? When the whole country's baying for the terrorists' blood? Get real.'

The suspect turned to his solicitor, who shrugged.

'I've been told not to reveal anything,' he said, avoiding Redstone's eyes. 'I'm staying shtum.'

Scared of the elderly woman.

'You know that if you refuse to answer a question, your refusal may be taken into account later,' Laura said. 'So I'm going to continue to ask questions, and you can decide whether to answer or to keep adding to the refusals. Why did you do the hacking?'

The suspect kept his lips tightly closed.

Dollars, Redstone scribbled.

Laura glanced at the pad.

'Who paid you to do the hacking?'

Lips remained tightly closed. *Only an initial payment. Not yet fully paid.*

'My guess,' Laura said, 'is that when we look into your financial affairs, we'll find you've been cheated by the man who's conned you into doing his dirty work.'

Triumphant sneer.

'Or, of course,' Redstone interjected, 'it could have been a woman.' The suspect clenched his jaw and stared at Redstone. *Elderly woman.*

'Let's take a short break,' said Laura.

A guard escorted the suspect and his solicitor out of the room, and Clothier came in almost immediately.

'I want to show him some pictures of elderly women,' Laura said. 'Different types of face. Of course we can't make it a real virtual lineup, because we haven't got any suspects for the elderly woman person, but I'm hoping that he'll react in a way which will give Mark information on the woman's appearance.'

'Good idea,' said Clothier. 'Give me a few minutes.' He rushed out.

Ten minutes later, Laura, Redstone, the suspect and the solicitor were back in the interrogation room. Laura gestured to a big screen on the wall behind him and her.

'I'm going to show you some faces,' she said. 'We'd like you to tell us if you recognize any of them.'

The suspect snorted and said nothing.

Laura clicked a remote control.

Redstone glanced over his shoulder, to see a picture of the queen.

'Yeah, you got it,' the suspect said with a smirk. 'Def. Can I go now?'

Laura clicked again. Nicole Kidman.

'Hey, I know her. Can't recall her name. Yes, she's in the gang too.' *Too young.*

Another click: Helen Mirren.

'What the fuck are you playing at?' *Right sort of age.*

Another picture: Susan Sarandon. The suspect folded his arms and gave an artificial yawn.

I don't think he ever saw her face. Redstone recalled that Clothier, in another room, was reading what he was writing via a camera trained on the pad. *Jim, can you doctor the Helen Mirren picture so she's wearing a mask?*

Laura nodded to Redstone.

'One last picture,' she said. 'A slight technical hitch – we'll have it in a minute.' She touched her earpiece. 'Ah.' She clicked the remote control. The suspect's eyes widened.

That's it.

'Did this woman mastermind communicate with you only by video calls?' she asked.

The suspect shrugged.

Yes.

'And the calls were from where?'

He shrugged again.

He doesn't know.

'Did you receive the calls during the day or at night?'

He gazed at the ceiling.

At 8pm every third day.

'And was it light or dark where she was calling from?'

He didn't notice. Ah, same as in his room.

'Let's take another break,' Laura said.

The suspect and his solicitor both gave Redstone a puzzled stare as they left the room.

Clothier came in. 'Clever last question,' he said. 'So the woman was more or less in our time zone. Not in America, anyway.'

'Well, we got quite a lot there,' said Laura. 'We now need to slog through the files to see if we can find any elderly women who might have hired him.'

'We don't know if the IT mastermind was the woman or if it was this young guy,' said Redstone. 'Shouldn't assume it was him.'

'Good point,' Laura said.

'We could ask him a highly technical question about a detailed hacking issue, and Mark can see if he understands it,' Clothier said.

'Or the other way round,' Laura said. 'I could make up some gobbledygook and see if he recognizes it for rubbish.'

'Great idea,' said Clothier, 'and more fun. Let's get them back in.'

Five minutes later the four were again sitting in the interrogation room.

'When you were overcoming the raid filters using that clever dyke-breaching technique, which was of course copied from the Dutch,' Laura said, 'how did you ensure the automatic Fortran defence protocols wouldn't kick in?'

The suspect stared at her in silence. *It's gibberish to him, but he thinks it's because he doesn't understand.*

'Are you a famous hacker?' she asked.

Sneer. Obvious we don't realise why he was hired.

'What piece of IT gear would you most like to own?'

He has a list. High-end virtual reality gaming equipment. Some technical details.

'Have you ever worked for a company that writes games?'

More important than that.

'Would you say the hacking you did was a technical triumph?'

Got it right at last. Proud to be a key part of the team.

Laura touched her earpiece.

'Ah,' she said, 'the FBI has a file on you, Tyler Lynch.'

Shit.

Laura picked up her tablet. 'We're going to adjourn for now. You'll be held overnight. At least.'

*

Laura, Redstone and Clothier sat round a table in Clothier's basement office. Redstone wasn't sure if he could smell drains or if it was in his imagination. Laura and Clothier had read on their tablets the FBI's file on Lynch, and then Clothier had passed his tablet to Redstone so he could read it, despite Laura's look of disapproval. She interlaced her fingers.

'So this is how it seems to me,' she said. 'First, the facts. Lynch has been employed by a number of clients, including federal offices, in New England. He's a freelance high-end expert at procuring, assembling and getting the best out of IT equipment. He's a hardware specialist, not programming. The FBI has a file on him because he was used in some sensitive areas. They're not sure how trustworthy he is.'

'And Lynch lives alone. No close social contacts,' said Clothier.

‘Yes,’ she said. ‘I think that was a key reason why some organisation hired him to do the hacking. Or maybe they hired him simply to set up the equipment to do the hacking. Odd that they used an elderly woman as their interface with Lynch. Maybe she’s a relative of the big boss, like his mother or aunt.’

‘I assume they’re based in New England,’ said Redstone. ‘That’s how they got to know him.’

‘Or they’ve got a branch there,’ Laura said. ‘I’m now considering whether it might be some major organised crime group.’

‘That makes sense,’ said Clothier. ‘Otherwise, how did they get him into the UK without passing through immigration? They must have a people-smuggling setup.’

‘Unfortunately, it’s not that hard,’ said Laura. ‘Lots of undocumented immigrants here. Still, it does all fit.’

‘But why go to the trouble of bringing him over here?’ asked Redstone. ‘There are lots of excellent IT technicians in the UK.’

‘Because it was for illegal work,’ said Laura. ‘He knows no one here, so he’s unlikely to blab. And they may not know of anyone here with his talents who would be willing to do something which risks a long prison sentence.’

‘Presumably they paid him some money in advance,’ said Clothier, ‘smuggled him into the country, and promised to smuggle him back and pay the rest when the job was finished.’

‘And knew they wouldn’t have to complete their side of the bargain,’ she said. ‘That’s one reason they didn’t let him know who they were. They used this woman as their go-between, and even then contacted him only electronically and with her wearing a mask in video calls.’

‘But why would an organised crime gang do all that hacking?’ said Redstone. ‘They haven’t made any financial demands. It’s all been political – seemingly aimed at getting Michael Jones out of office, though it might in fact be to get the whole government out, or to damage the country. Anyway, it certainly seems political, rather than ordinarily criminal. If you see what I mean.'

'Ah. Good point,' said Laura. 'The campaign does seem more like the actions of an enemy state. I know GCHQ ruled that out earlier, but maybe they were mistaken. Or maybe an enemy state hired an organised crime group to work on their behalf. That's far from unknown. We'll have to investigate these possibilities.'

They stood up.

'Before you go, Mark,' said Laura, 'when's *Julius Caesar*? My diary's getting full. I could make it on Saturday, but otherwise I'm out, I'm afraid.'

'Good question,' Redstone said. 'I haven't heard from Zena. I'll pop into Mary's when I get home. I'll let you know, but my guess is she's forgotten.'

Clothier looked at them with raised eyebrows.

'I thought you two… oh, none of my business,' he said.

'It's complicated,' said Laura. Redstone nodded sadly.

MONDAY 24TH JULY

'The Home Secretary's office rang,' said Joanne. 'She wants to see you. Shall I make an appointment?'

'Eh? What's it about?'

'They wouldn't say.'

'I don't understand it,' said Redstone. 'Our work here has no relevance to the Home Office. And I've never met her, except that she was at that meeting I went to at Number 10.'

'What about that secret stuff you do with your MI5 friends? You know, the things I'm not supposed to know about. MI5 reports to her, doesn't it?'

'Yes, but why would she… oh, there's no use speculating. I need to ask someone.'

'Which could have been your first thought,' Joanne said. 'Men.' She gave a theatrical sigh. 'How about Sir Gavin McKay? He's one of your buddies from that little team last year. He should know.'

'Good idea.'

*

'I haven't a clue why she'd want to see you,' McKay said. 'I haven't mentioned you to her.'

'It must be about the terrorist attacks. Surely they're at the top of her agenda.'

'Maybe, but I don't see why she'd want to talk to you about them. Or ask your advice.'

'Would I be right in assuming you don't tell ministers details of individuals who help you, or what they do for you?' Redstone asked.

'You would. She won't know how you're helping us now, if that's what you mean. Go and see her, but be careful. And don't wear your cap.'

'What do you mean about being careful?'

'Octavia Pitt is a politician,' McKay said, 'with her own ambitions. She no doubt has some agenda that may not be obvious to you when you're with her.'

'I'm not entirely—'

'Just reminding you that not everyone's an uncomplicated scientist.'

'Hmm,' Redstone said. 'I'm beginning to realise that.'

'Well, there you go, then.'

*

Later that afternoon he found himself standing outside the Home Office building in Marsham Street, admiring the coloured glass panels in the overhanging part of the roof. The wide modern block was a good example of imaginative recent design, but he wondered how many years would pass before it seemed out of date and perhaps trying too hard.

He was shown into the inner ministerial office by a private secretary who seemed taken aback when the Home Secretary, a dark-haired woman in her late forties, asked him to leave.

'Dr Redstone, many thanks for coming in so quickly,' she said.

'Pleasure, Home Sec—'

'Call me Tavia.'

'Er… well, Tavia, it's no problem for me to come here, but—'

'But you want to know why I asked you.' She smiled.

'To be honest, yes,' he said.

'Ah, we should always be honest. Please take a seat.' She gestured to a sofa, and sat in an armchair at right angles to Redstone. 'It's very simple – I just wanted to get to know you. We were briefly introduced at that meeting at Number 10 where your friend Professor Clarke dazzled us all, but as I recall we didn't speak to each other.'

'No, we didn't. I suppose the occasion didn't arise.'

'You mean there was no need. It was a business meeting, not a social gathering. I understand that.'

'Well, here I am,' he said.

'Tell me about yourself. I know you run a successful biotechnology company. I'm full of admiration.'

'Thanks. Yes, London Bio. We specialise in medication to do with the skin. Our best-selling invention is a method of delivering drugs through the skin without an injection.'

'Yes,' she said. 'I know about that. My dentist used it on me last month. To deliver the local anaesthetic. Brilliant.'

'And recently,' Redstone said, 'we've patented a treatment for a common form of skin cancer. BCCs – basal cell carcinomas.'

'Yes, so I read. Should be a great success. It's wonderful we have British companies like yours. So it's all science, is it?'

'What do you mean?'

'Well, you must have other strings to your bow. I know Michael values your advice, and I don't think he's terribly interested in scientific matters.'

'I first got to know him when there was an issue about our nuclear electricity programme. My background as a scientist, and having worked on nuclear reactor policy in the Department of Energy—'

'So you acted as an adviser to him?'

'Well, not a political adviser. I was also working with some Home Office staff.'

'You mean MI5.'

'I did some work which is covered by the Official Secrets Act.'

'I understand. Sorry, I didn't mean to make you feel uncomfortable.'

'Quite all right. I also know Michael from having been part of the little group who helped get rid of the rogue administration last year. You may know that those b... that they had targeted London Bio.'

'Yes, my briefing mentioned it, but it wasn't clear why that bunch of traitors targeted your company. Do you know the reason?'

'Well... it was down to Valerie Hitchcock, who was then the Cabinet Secretary. She ran that force of mercenaries during the... the bad period. She hated me. Anyway, she's gone now.'

Tavia looked at him oddly. He wished he was wearing his cap.

'On the personal stuff,' she said, 'if I may, how do you know Professor Clarke?'

He smiled. 'Her daughter works for London Bio, and I got to know Michelle when she did some consultancy work which helped us complete the skin cancer project. She's an absolute star on AI.'

'So I gathered.' She smiled wryly. 'Not exactly my bag. I read PPE at Oxford.'

He resisted expressing a lack of surprise.

'So, on the hacking,' she continued. 'We've got the hacker, but not yet the group behind him. I suppose you know that. Any thoughts?'

Why was she asking him about the hacking? She wasn't supposed to know he'd been involved. 'I've been told they've got the source of the hacking,' he said. 'I don't know anything about who's behind it.'

'So Professor Clarke hasn't told you anything more about that.'

'I doubt whether she'd know. She's an IT specialist, not an expert in terrorists.'

'Of course not.'

He waited for her to say more.

'Well,' she said, 'I've got another meeting, I'm afraid. Many thanks for coming in. Oh, I'm having a small social gathering next week. I'd be honoured if you'd come.'

He blinked.

'Oh, the honour would be mine.'

'Do you have anyone you'd like to bring?'

'That's very kind, but there isn't anyone at the moment.'

'I know the feeling.'

*

'Maybe her purpose in summoning you was related to the fact that the PM seems to like you, for some obscure reason,' McKay said. They were speaking via WhatsApp to ensure security.

'That's right,' Redstone said. 'Although his reason's obvious when you consider the quality of his top intelligence adviser.'

'Ho, ho.'

'Oh, another thing. She reacted a bit oddly when I mentioned Hitchcock. She hasn't got any way of knowing what you and Laura did, has she?'

'Impossible. No witnesses, and we've said absolutely zero. Our involvement was off the books, as you know. In fact, we were private citizens at the time.'

'I recall noticing that I never saw any reference to her death,' said Redstone. 'In the papers or on the news. She had been a public figure, after all. I assumed you'd got it hushed up.'

'No, we didn't get involved in any way. As I just tried to explain. Sorry I was too subtle for you.'

'So, with your immense knowledge of the subtleties of keeping things quiet, what's your explanation? Why wasn't it in the news?'

'No idea,' said McKay. 'Maybe some praiseworthy police officer got suspicious about the manner of her death, knew she deserved to be got rid of, and he or she decided to hush the whole thing up.'

'Surely that would be impossible, with coroners and—'

'Don't be so bloody naïve.'

'My naivety seems to be a theme recently,' Redstone said. 'Changing the subject, any developments on who employed Tyler Lynch?'

'No, except we've eliminated a number of possibilities. But these things often take time. Something happens, and we get a clue. We'll get them in the end. Sooner rather than later, I hope.'

'Is Michelle in the loop? Can I talk to her about it?'

'She's been kept informed by GCHQ. Go ahead. Don't tell her about your cap, of course.' He sniggered. 'Don't talk cap or crap.'

'Ho, ho to you,' said Redstone. 'Frankly, my joke was better.'

*

'How are you?' Redstone asked Michelle.

'OK. Why are you calling?'

'I wanted to discuss where things are on the hacking. I'm up to date on the interrogation of the guy they arrested. Have you been kept in the loop?'

'Yes,' she said.

'Good. Any thoughts on what organisation might be behind the hacking?'

'Why do you say it's an organisation?'

'Well, the guy they arrested told MI5 that his link with the programming experts was an elderly woman, and—'

'So you're assuming an elderly woman couldn't be an expert programmer?' she said.

'Oh. I suppose we—'

'What about middle-aged black women?'

'Of course not. Obviously. Sorry, Michelle – point taken. Well, do you know of any elderly women capable of doing the sort of hacking the enemy did?'

'Wrong way to tackle it,' she said. 'I've been thinking about what other programming I've come across which bears some resemblance to what the hackers have been using. And there has been one set of examples: the programming we dealt with last year. I mentioned it before.'

'You mean the American stuff?'

'Yes. I'm finding more and more similarities with some of the methods the American coder used to produce their superb AI system. Which in effect ran America, if you recall.'

'Of course I recall. But that system was created by President Cardew, and he's been dead for some time,' said Redstone. 'As you know.'

'I know Cardew's dead, but I don't know he did the programming.'

'But all the evidence… oh. Maybe it was someone in his team. Though they would have had to have been working with him for ages, not just in recent years. Much of Cardew's rise to fame and power depended on his early adoption of IT.'

'He did have a woman with him all that time,' she said. 'She'd now be elderly, as you put it.'

'Who? Oh, his mother. You can't mean… you mean Clodagh McCarthy was the IT mastermind behind Cardew's rise?'

'Do you have any evidence against that?'

'Let me think,' Redstone said. 'Give me a moment.' He got up and walked to the window and squinted against the sun beating on the white building on the other side of the road. The street was deserted.

'You there?' Michelle said. 'I've got things to do. I'll leave you to—'

'No, don't go. Michelle, I can't think of any argument against it being Clodagh. In fact, it all fits. She hated Britain, and no doubt hated Michael Jones specifically for his role in exposing her as the convicted terrorist she was.'

'Why do you refer to her in the past tense? Do you know she's now dead?'

‘It was because I was remembering… no, I don’t have any reason to believe she’s not alive. We thought she’d fled back to the States, and I haven’t heard anything about her since.’

‘Well, there you are then,’ Michelle said. ‘I’m going to ring off now.’

‘I’ll ask Gavin McKay if he knows what happened to her. Good Lord, she could still be here in the UK. I’ll let you know what he says.’ When there was no response, he realised he’d said his last couple of sentences to a dead phone.

Excited, he rang McKay, but was told the Director General was in a meeting and would ring back. He went back to the window and stared out. He should be getting on with London Bio business, but he couldn’t let go of the thought that Clodagh McCarthy might be behind the hacking. She had the motive. She was a convicted IRA killer who’d escaped from British custody in 1972 and fled to the USA. There, under a new identity, she had spent decades getting her son into the presidency, and ended up controlling the country. From that position she’d managed to get control of the UK too, with the aim of causing Britain serious economic damage. She’d been exposed by the resistance group led by Michael Jones, and thus gone from the most powerful woman in America to a hunted criminal.

If Michelle was right, Clodagh had both motive and means. And when it came to IT matters, Michelle was very unlikely to be wrong. Maybe he’d try the idea on Laura, see what she thought of it. As he reached for his phone, it rang – McKay.

‘I’m told you wanted to speak urgently,’ McKay said.

Redstone told him of Michelle’s conclusion.

‘But Clodagh… Oh.’ There was a sound of McKay shuffling around. ‘Hell, I suspect Michelle’s come up trumps again. As you say, it all fits. After all, Clodagh was a seasoned terrorist in her first incarnation. And when she was the president’s mother she worked from her house in New England, which is where that guy Lynch, the hardware specialist, operated. And the train software was American – she could have got hold of it there. Yes, it all fits.'

'Even more than I'd realised.'

'I'll make some enquiries,' McKay said, 'and come back to you.'

Ten minutes later McKay rang again.

'There's been no sign of Clodagh in the US since she left for her public trip here last year. For all we know, she might have remained in the UK, hiding out somewhere. Or just living quietly. Hardly anyone would recognize her. I'll take steps to see if we can find her, though I don't hold out a lot of hope for a quick result.'

'I suppose elderly women don't figure high in the public's list of suspicious characters,' said Redstone.

'That's right. And she's undoubtedly got forged credentials. If anyone can get those, an IT genius can.'

'Meanwhile, she's probably planning another attack.'

'Yes,' said McKay, 'but that's true whether or not it's Clodagh. Whoever it is, they won't have stopped now. Why would they? So we've been thinking about possible future targets. Our big worry is that the enemy might switch tactics from hacking to something totally different.'

'Why would they do that?'

'Well, their last hack failed. And we've taken their IT kit. They'd have to restock, and find someone to replace young Tyler Lynch.'

'If it is Clodagh, she'd be able to make bombs. Remember her history – she was an active Irish terrorist.'

'Lots of terrorist groups know how to make bombs, and would be keen to do so. Their problem is getting hold of the materials. They're hard to steal nowadays.'

Redstone thought about the chemistry of explosives. Some were simple to make, but a terrorist would need a large quantity to cause significant damage, and amassing so much would attract attention. Others were much more deadly, but making them was a difficult and hazardous operation, requiring specialised equipment and knowledge. He wouldn't want to have to make dynamite, for example. Its Swedish inventor, Alfred Nobel, had made his fortune from the famous explosive, but its key ingredient was nitroglycerin, an unstable chemical which had killed many people in accidental explosions.

'If not explosives or hacking, what else?' he said.

'The main alternative used by terrorists worldwide has been aircraft or other large speeding vehicles, preferably full of fuel. That would require suicide bombers, which rules out a lot of terrorists.'

'What about chemical weapons?'

'Yes, that's also a strong possibility. Maybe stronger. MI5 and the police are always fearing a chemical weapons attack.'

'God.' Redstone didn't know offhand the detailed chemistry, but suspected that any competent chemist with a well-equipped lab could make enough nerve agent or other chemical weapon to wreak havoc. Though they'd have to be able to procure the ingredients, which would be hard for a rogue lab.

'Well, all I can say is good luck,' he said. 'I'm at your disposal if you need some thoughts read.'

*

Later that evening, Sophie rang from Brussels.

'Zena's been in touch,' she said. 'I gather she messed up her kind offer to take you behind the scenes at her theatre and seduce you.'

'For goodness' sake, Sophie, it wasn't—'

'Of course it wasn't. I was joking. She just wanted to be nice. She's always looked up to you since we were kids. She was mortified that she'd forgotten to get you the tickets.'

'Well, it didn't really matter,' he said.

'Any, er, mature women in your life since we last spoke? How are you getting on with Mary?'

'I've hardly seen her,' he said.

He heard her pouring a drink. 'You need another woman in your life, Dad,' she said. 'Met anyone through work recently?'

'No. Unless you count the Home Secretary. Is that Belgian beer you're drinking? I'm jealous.'

'No, it's English tea. What's that about the Home Secretary? Tell me more.'

'She invited me to meet her, so I went into the Home Office this morning. We chatted, but at the end of it I was none the wiser about why she'd wanted to see me. She invited me to a reception next week.'

'Maybe she fancies you.'

'Don't be ridiculous. We'd never met. Well, except for sitting round the same table in a meeting last week.'

'There you go, then. Instant attraction. Ah, here we are… I've googled her. Octavia Pitt.'

'She told me to call her Tavia.'

'Aha! Not bad looking. Divorced four years ago. What's she like?'

'All right, I suppose. She studied PPE at Oxford.'

'So you're prejudiced against her because she fits the mould of British politicians.'

'She seemed happy to say she didn't understand technology.'

'Dad, please. Everyone says that, unless they actually do understand it. It's a sort of defence mechanism. People feel bewildered and intimidated by what's happening around them. Especially oldsters of your generation.'

'I don't feel—'

'Except you, of course. Promise me you'll give this Tavia a chance at her party next week.'

'Reception, I imagine, not a party. Unlikely to be loud music, wild dancing, drugs, all the stuff you're used to in that den of iniquity you work in.'

‘Yes, Euro Enviro Concern is well known as a centre of multinational orgies. Speaking of which, I’ve been chatting with my lovely brother in California. We’ve agreed we’re going to make a joint visit to our aged father in the near future. Any dates we should avoid?’

‘Not that I can think of. But you know the terrorist attacks are likely to continue?’

‘Suppose so. We’ll keep an eye on the news. Be careful, won’t you.’

ONE YEAR EARLIER

As soon as she heard the front door close, Clodagh wriggled out from under the bed, spitting fluff from her mouth. She heaved herself to her feet and rushed onto the landing. Valerie was dangling from an electrical extension cord tied in a noose round her neck and secured to the iron railing which ran along the landing. Clodagh gave a sharp scream and clawed at the cord, breaking a fingernail but not loosening the cable. She ran back into the bedroom, grabbed a pair of nail clippers from a drawer, and rushed back to the railing, grunting as she fell to her knees.

'Short snips,' she muttered, as she dug into the cord.

The strands suddenly gave way, letting Valerie thump to the floor below. Clodagh rushed down the staircase and yanked the noose wide. Valerie wasn't breathing. Clodagh put one hand on top of the other, interlaced her fingers, pushed down with all her weight on Valerie's chest, and released the pressure. And again, and again, and again, rapidly. After about thirty compressions, Valerie gave a sharp intake of breath and started breathing normally. Clodagh collapsed back on her haunches and wiped away tears with the back of her hand.

Valerie's eyelids fluttered, and then her eyes opened wide.

'Hello,' she said weakly. 'What's going on?'

Clodagh grasped her hand.

'You tell me,' she said. 'I heard the front door opening and a woman call out to you, and—'

'Yes. It was that thug Laura Smith. She must have got a key somehow.'

'And then she was talking to you, but I couldn't make out what—'

'She threatened me and forced me…' Valerie started coughing and choking. Clodagh helped her sit up.

'Stay still,' Clodagh said. 'I'll get you some water.' She went into the kitchen, returned with a glass, and held it to Valerie's lips.

'I can't swallow,' Valerie gasped.

'Take very small sips,' Clodagh said, putting her arm round Valerie's shoulders.

*

An hour later, Valerie was lying in bed, Clodagh sitting next to her, holding her hand.

'Ready to tell me more?' Clodagh said.

'Yes. So Smith forced me to write a grovelling apology about the two women who were, you know, when we bombed Jones's cosy little gathering. It's probably over there, on the desk. I now realise it's meant to look like a suicide note. As I was finishing, I felt a pressure on the side of my neck, here, and that's the last I knew.' She struggled upright and sipped more water.

'Sounds like she anaesthetised you,' Clodagh said. She peered at Valerie's neck. 'Can't see any needle mark.'

'Ah. Proves Redstone was involved. He's an expert at getting drugs through the skin without a needle.'

'It fits. I heard a man's voice. It needed two of them to make it look as though you'd taken your own life. By manoeuvring you into that awful…'

'Yes, must have been him. The pompous shit was acting as Smith's lickspittle. Not for the first time.'

'And Jones will have been behind it,' Clodagh said. 'Smith and Redstone were his hangers-on. Don't worry, they'll get what they deserve. I'll make sure.'

Valerie gave a weak nod. 'We need to get out of here.'

‘I know. You rest, my dear. I’ll find us a new apartment. Somewhere no one will recognize us, while we regroup.’

PRESENT DAY: TUESDAY 25TH JULY

David Pepper would have preferred to be back in the lab after his holiday in Switzerland, but Poppy had pleaded for one last day in London.

At first, he'd demurred – the holiday had left him feeling refreshed and energetic, which made him all the keener to return to work. In his lengthy career he'd never felt as comfortable and fulfilled as he did at London Bio. But a day in London with Poppy would be a good way to end the holiday, and he'd take pleasure in her enjoyment of the shopping expedition. They both needed clothes, she'd said. She'd left home first thing, headed for Oxford Street; he was to join her in Chinatown for lunch before heading for a menswear shop off Regent Street.

He finished tidying the garden and then took the train to Paddington. The damage from the crash three weeks earlier was greater than he'd realised. He followed the signs along a circuitous route, through boarded-up parts of the station, to the Bakerloo Line underground station, where he took the Tube to Piccadilly Circus.

He made his way up Shaftesbury Avenue and turned right into Chinatown. Rows of bright red Chinese lanterns were strung across the road. He pushed his way through the crowds in a pedestrianised street, found the restaurant which Poppy had specified, and joined her at her table.

After a tasty lunch they made their way to the menswear shop, where Poppy persuaded him to buy a suit. They walked back to Piccadilly Circus, carrying four shopping bags between them, to get the Tube to Paddington.

A large tanker lorry was parked near the station entrance nearest to Shaftesbury Avenue. Two workmen, dressed in orange suits with reflective stripes, were working on a pump on the ground near the back of the tanker. A large-diameter ribbed pipe snaked from the tank down through a manhole next to the entrance, which was blocked off by red plastic barriers.

'Not seen that before,' David said. 'Either they're piping something down into the station, or something's being pumped up for them to cart off.'

'No markings on the lorry,' said Poppy. 'Maybe that means it's sewage.'

'Could be. Hope they aren't pumping sewage down rather than up!'

They crossed Regent Street and walked down the stairs of another entrance. As they went round the circular hall to the ticket barriers, David started to feel uneasy. He ushered Poppy ahead of him, followed her through the barrier, and stopped. He put his hand on her shoulder.

'It's bromine. I'm sure of it,' he said.

'What are you talking about?'

'The smell. That acrid smell. Can't you—'

'I can't smell anything. Well, perhaps a little… it's central London.'

'I don't like it,' he said. He looked round for a Transport for London official, but the only one he could see was on the other side of the hall, surrounded by a group of tourists. He took out his phone, but there was no signal.

'Let's go upstairs, out of the station. I'm going to ring someone.'

'Oh, don't make a fuss,' Poppy said. 'Let's just go home. They'll sort it out if there's a real problem.'

'That tanker in the road,' David said. 'It… come on, let's get out of here fast. I'm going to call the police.' He grabbed her arm, pulled her to the barriers, and pushed her hand, which was still holding her payment card, down on the reader. The gate opened and he pushed her through. The barrier slammed shut after her. He banged his own ticket on the reader and shoved through the gate.

Poppy dropped her shopping bag. She stooped to pick it up.

'Leave it!' he said. 'Run!'

'You're scaring me,' she said, but started an awkward jog, angling away from the crowd at the gates.

'No, straight ahead,' David said. 'Furthest away from the tanker.'

They ran into a passage which veered to the right. People coming round the bend into the station stared at them.

'Go back,' David shouted. 'Gas!'

He and Poppy reached the stairs at the end of the passage. Other people were now hot on their heels. There was a scream from behind, in the ticket hall.

As soon as he reached the top of the stairs, he told Poppy to go along Piccadilly while he dialled 999.

'Police. Emergency,' he said between deep breaths. He was put through immediately.

'I think there's a terror attack just starting at Piccadilly Circus Tube station,' he panted. 'Bromine's being pumped down into the station from a tanker parked up near Boots.'

'What's being pumped, did you say?' the operator said.

'Bromine. It's a highly toxic and corrosive gas. Well, liquid.'

'And what makes you think it's this gas or liquid, sir?'

'I know the smell. I work in a lab.'

'Your name, please?'

'David Pepper. Dr David Pepper. I'm a scientist. I know what I'm talking about. I noticed the tanker was unmarked, as though its identification had been painted over. There were—'

'Hold on a minute, please. I'm contacting officers in the area.' David heard some background chatter, and then from his left the howl of a police siren and the sight of flashing blue lights as a police car came tearing up Lower Regent Street.

'Thank God,' he said.

'Please tell me more,' said the operator.

'There were two men dressed in orange suits, you know, the sort workmen wear, operating a pump. The way you get bromine out of a tanker is to pump air in to push the bromine out. There's a thick pipe connected to the tanker and going down through a manhole. As the liquid sprays out at the bottom it'll evaporate into a poisonous gas. It's horrible stuff – causes horrendous burns. You need to evacuate the station.'

'We're on it. Were the two men wearing appropriate protective clothing?'

'Er… no. Not at all. But that doesn't mean—'

'I know, sir. Don't worry, we're taking this seriously. Could you please hold up your hand? An officer will be with you very quickly. Stay on the line.'

David raised his right arm. A slim middle-aged man in plain clothes jogged over.

'Dr Pepper, I'm Detective Sergeant Oliver,' he said. 'Could you please show me some ID?'

David dug out a London Bio business card identifying him as the chief scientist.

'This gentleman is what he said he is, and more,' the detective said into his phone. 'Hell, I can now smell the gas. Or liquid, whatever. It's a bit like bleach?' He glanced at David, who nodded. 'But different. More pungent. God, my eyes are watering, and we're standing out in the open air. For Christ's sake continue with the full emergency procedure.'

David looked round to see people pouring out of the station, many of them coughing, tears rolling down their faces. More police cars were arriving. Two ambulances appeared. Across the traffic jamming the complicated road junction he could make out a lot of activity around the tanker.

'The Fire Brigade specialists are on their way, sir,' the phone operator said to David. 'Have you got any advice before they take over?'

'Get everyone away from here,' David said. 'Bromine is very heavy, so it'll sink – keep as high as possible. If anyone has got any on their skin, wash with loads of water. Same for eyes. It's important to avoid contact, because it's absorbed through the skin. Er… I can't think of anything else.'

'My hero,' said Poppy, taking his arm. He hadn't noticed her making her way to his side. She stared at the three bags of clothes David had put on the pavement and sighed. 'I lost my bag in the station. Ah well, as long as people are safe.'

'I'm afraid they won't all be safe, dear,' said David.

*

Redstone noted that Laura had placed herself at the far end of the meeting table in his office, even though he was not wearing his cap.

'I thought it would be convenient to meet here,' Laura said. 'Welcome back from holiday, David. Not how you expected your first day to go, I imagine.'

'Actually, tomorrow is supposed to be my first day,' David said.

'You did a wonderful thing today,' she said. 'You saved lives. But there are still some horrible casualties, I'm afraid. Number not clear, but likely to grow.'

'Wicked, evil people,' said David. 'Any idea who's behind it?'

'We're treating it as the latest attack by the terrorist group who were responsible for the train crashes and the rest. We have some ideas on who they are, but nothing definite yet.'

‘I’m afraid it will turn out to have been a highly effective act of terror,’ Redstone said. ‘Just once, at just one station, but the fear of it happening again will have a major impact.’

‘I agree,’ said David. ‘Many people don’t like the Tube anyway, but force themselves to use it because it’s so convenient. Loads of them will now take to the roads instead. Or just not come into London.’

‘Yes,’ said Laura, ‘the masterminds behind this atrocity knew what they were doing. Let me bring you up to speed. We’ve arrested the two orange-suited men. They both have criminal records, so we know a fair bit about them. No terrorist links in their backgrounds. We’ll find out more when we interrogate them properly.’ She glanced at Redstone, who gave a minute nod. ‘So far, they’re not talking.’

‘I’m surprised that ordinary criminals know how to handle a tanker of bromine,’ David said.

‘So are we. We’ve identified the tanker, and believe they hijacked it at a service station. We think they must have kidnapped the driver and got him to train them in the basics. Our first task in the interrogation will be to find out where he is.’

‘Another thing,’ said Redstone. ‘Aren’t tankers of nasty stuff like bromine tagged and tracked by their parent company?’

‘That’s right,’ she said. ‘The hijackers removed the transmitting device and somehow sent signals to the parent company which seemed to indicate the tanker was where it was supposed to be.’

‘Ah,’ said Redstone. ‘IT expertise. Points to it being the same people as the hacking.’

‘Exactly,’ said Laura. ‘The experts are seeing if they can deduce anything about the whereabouts of the hackers.’

‘Any chance they’ll ask Michelle? She’s been on top of this from the start.’

David looked up. ‘Our Michelle? Rosie’s mum?’

'Yes,' said Redstone. 'You know how great she is at IT stuff. She's been lending a hand.'

'Excellent.'

'I don't know if they've involved Michelle,' Laura said. 'IT is outside my remit.'

'Where were they pumping the bromine?' David asked. 'I mean, where did the manhole lead to?'

'It led to an inspection chamber in a big shaft carrying signalling cables, phone lines and the like. Lots of branches off to different parts of the station. Bromine was seeping out all over the place. They knew the weak spot. Someone had planned it very carefully.'

'Maybe CCTV will have captured someone scoping it out?' Redstone said.

'Yes, that's one of our lines of enquiry,' Laura said expressionlessly.

'Sorry,' he said. 'Teaching grandmother to—'

'David,' Laura said, 'thanks again for your fantastic work today. No doubt you'll get some official recognition in due course. Mark, if we could…'

'I'll go, then,' said David, getting up. 'Back to discuss with Poppy how to replace the things she bought and lost this morning. See you tomorrow, Mark.'

When the door had closed Redstone asked Laura how she was.

'Fine. How about you?'

'Well. I'm not using the mind-reading except for MI5. I now wear the cap in shielding mode if I know my head will get close to others.'

'Good. But we'll be asking you to use it to help us interrogate the two orange-suited men. Tomorrow morning work for you? We'll send you a car, in the circumstances.'

'OK. Any news on the hunt for Clodagh?'

‘No. We’ve given her photo to all police forces, but she’s probably keeping low. We’re hoping we can extract some useful information from…’

‘I know you don’t want to keep calling them “the orange-suited men”,’ Redstone said. ‘How about Jaffa and Juice?’

She smiled. ‘I sometimes almost miss you. And then I remember your jokes.’

WEDNESDAY 26TH JULY

The bromine attack had left seventy-eight people in hospital with bad burns and damaged lungs. Two people had died. The physiological effects of bromine – deep skin wounds, damage to respiratory tissues and the central nervous system – had resulted in widespread fear and horror, and increased pressure on the government and the security services to catch the terrorists.

'Is the setup the same as before?' Redstone said to Clothier.

'Yes. We'll interrogate them one at a time, starting with Dick Krantz. He's a petty criminal from Lincoln, some thieving, some bad violence, no history of terrorism or anything political. Short term in jail. The only link we can find to the other orange-suited guy, Sylas Connart, is through their girlfriends. Both were in Holloway prison at the same time a few years ago.'

The mention of Holloway prison rang a bell for Redstone, but he couldn't put his finger on why it seemed significant.

'Why was Connart on your database?' he said.

'Not ours, the police's. Petty fraud. Fined. Nothing remotely like what they did at Piccadilly Circus.'

'OK. I'm ready for Mr Krantz.' He donned his cap.

In the interrogation room, now familiar territory, Laura was sitting opposite a burly man with a shaven head and a black eye. Next to him was Krantz's solicitor, a woman in her forties with curly brown hair.

Krantz stared at Redstone. He felt uneasy. As he sat down in the seat he'd occupied before, he noticed that Krantz was in handcuffs.

'Mr Krantz,' said Laura, 'we assume your solicitor has made you familiar with your rights.' The solicitor nodded. Krantz continued to stare at Redstone.

‘So let’s start at the beginning. Tell us who inspired you to hijack the tanker.’

Krantz stayed silent, but carried on glaring at Redstone, who started to sweat.

Need to speak in their absence, Redstone wrote on the pad.

‘I’ll give you a moment to think about the consequences of not answering,’ Laura said. She gestured to Redstone and stood. He followed her out. They went down the corridor to the briefing room, where Clothier joined them. Redstone removed his cap and wiped his forehead with his hand.

‘Something wrong?’ Laura said. ‘You look disturbed.’

‘I can’t pick up anything useful from Krantz. I’m of no value to you in there.’

‘Why?’ Clothier asked. ‘Isn’t the cap working with him?’

‘No, it’s not that at all. Quite the reverse. I’m getting overwhelming thoughts and images of, well, other things.’

‘Come on,’ said Laura. ‘What?’

Redstone took a deep breath. ‘Krantz is full of hate and anger, and barely suppressed violence. It dominated everything I was picking up from him. He was envisaging attacking me and you if he could get out of the handcuffs. Envisaging it in graphic detail.’

‘Ah,’ said Laura. ‘He’d already had an altercation with our people, as I expect you guessed from the state of his face. I should have told you, but it didn’t occur to me that it was relevant.’

‘Well, now we know. That was a horrible experience. I’ve never…’

She put her hand on his arm. ‘I can imagine. Well, I can’t, but I understand. I’m so sorry.’

‘So, I can’t help you with him,’ Redstone said. ‘What about the other guy, Connart? Is he violent?’

‘No. You should be all right with him. Let’s move on to him now, if you’re up for it. If there is a problem, walk out immediately.’

‘Yes, I’m up for it,’ Redstone said.

‘I’ll get someone to tell Krantz we’re now interrogating Connart,’ Laura said. ‘And that Connart’s going to give us his no doubt one-sided take on who did what. So let’s get Krantz back to his holding cell and Connart into the interrogation room.’

‘Will Connart have the same solicitor?’ Redstone asked.

‘No, that wouldn’t be right. It’ll be the duty solicitor who represented Quart and Lynch when you were here before. Why do you ask?’

Redstone shook his head. ‘Never mind.’

She stared at him. ‘She wasn’t having violent thoughts too, was she?’

‘Not at all. Quite the opposite. Though I caught only a fleeting whiff of it before the Krantz stuff overwhelmed me.’

‘What do you mean? Are you saying she fancied you?’

Redstone stared at his knees and breathed out heavily.

‘No,’ he said. He looked up at her. ‘Laura, many people spend a lot of their time thinking about sex. You’re an attractive woman. Very attractive. Don’t you think that some people might have sexual thoughts about you?’

‘What? In the interview room?’ She looked shocked, something he hadn’t seen before. ‘You didn’t say anything!’

‘Didn’t seem relevant. And it might have thrown you off your stride.’

‘Well, in future… no, maybe you’re right. Don’t write anything on the pad about sexual thoughts concerning me. Unless you think it’s impeding the interrogation in some way.’

‘Understood.’

‘I need a break,’ she said, standing up. ‘Shall we start on Connart in, say, an hour?’

When she’d left the room, Clothier put his hand on Redstone’s shoulder. ‘Not an unalloyed benefit, then, this thought reading.’

‘No. Absolutely not. I now use the cap’s shielding mode whenever I’m on public transport and in similar situations. Without it I'd be driven mad. It was mainly banal rubbish flooding at me, including a surprisingly high number of superficial thoughts – well, I was surprised – about the appearance of other people, often with a sexual overtone. Sometimes I got embarrassing or unpleasant or quite upsetting feelings and thoughts. More people than you might expect are suffering pain or low-level unhappiness, or feel angry or irritated. Occasionally I got a burst of happiness, but not often enough to make the thought-reading worthwhile. Or even tolerable.'

'Wow! Maybe that explains why we haven't evolved to have the ability innately. At first sight you might think it would be an invaluable aid to survival. But not if it drives you mad.'

'Maybe some animals do have the ability,' Redstone said. 'Maybe humans are the exception. How would we know?'

'Hmm. Interesting idea. I wish we could pursue it with academic researchers. But we can't, while we're keeping your ability top secret.'

'Anyway, it might not have given much of an evolutionary advantage. When the mind-reading is unaided by your cap it works at such a short range that it wouldn't warn me about the impending charge of an enraged dinosaur.'

'Don't talk about our parliamentarians in that way,' Clothier said. 'It's disrespectful.'

Redstone smiled. 'I'm going to take a short walk up to the workplace of same wonderful parliamentarians, admire the renovations, and come back invigorated for the next interrogation.'

Out in the street, he walked across Victoria Tower Gardens to the wall bordering the Thames. He leant over and studied the patterns in the water. It was comfortably cool here in the shade of the plane trees. Nobody was sitting on any of the benches along the edge of the gardens. It would be busier during the working week, when the offices around the area were full of people working for the government, against the government, or producing commentary on the government.

He strolled to the Rodin statue of the Burghers of Calais. It was about freedom from oppression. It wasn't only a state – your own, or another – who could oppress you. You could be oppressed by terrorists, like the bastards who'd pumped bromine down the Tube.

He walked out of the gardens and looked up at Big Ben. The renovation of the clock faces was now complete, and the ornate stonework and paintwork gleamed in the sunshine.

Time to go back. Within five minutes he was back in the interrogation room. The grey-haired solicitor nodded to him. Connart, a small man with receding hair, stared at him with trepidation as he settled down.

'Well, Mr Connart,' Laura said, 'you were caught red-handed. Several people have been killed in a horrible way. Why were you pumping bromine into the Tube station?'

'She told us it would just make the atmosphere down there unpleasant, and cause some panic. She said the shaft we were pumping it into led to equipment, not to the platforms.'

'Who's this "she"?'

'Don't know anything about her. It was all done on WhatsApp.'

He's telling the truth, but not the whole truth, Redstone wrote.

'We'll come back to that,' Laura said. 'First, tell us how you hijacked the tanker.'

'She told us how to do it. We went into the Keele motorway service station on the M6. It was late, dark, no one around in the lorry park. The tanker driver was resting in his cab. I gestured to him that there was something wrong at the back of the tanker. He got out, and Dick hit him from behind. We tied him up and put him in the boot of our car. Dick got into the cab of the tanker and drove it off.'

'Where did he go?'

‘An industrial building in the Wirral. Deserted. Had been some sort of factory.’

‘And you went to the same place in the car, with the tanker driver in the boot?’

‘Yeah. He started banging and thumping. I was shitting myself that I’d be stopped by the cops for something, but I wasn’t.’

‘Listen,’ Laura said, ‘our top priority is to find the driver. Where is he now, and is he OK?’

‘Well, Dick had a go at him. Don’t understand why.’

‘What do you mean by “had a go”?’

Connart shrugged. Redstone wrote on the pad. *Beat him up, badly. Connart’s upset about it. Couldn’t stop Krantz.*

‘He’s locked in an office in the building,’ Connart said. ‘I left him some water and chocolate bars.’

‘Address?’

‘Er… don’t know. I just followed the satnav in the car. Dick had put in the postcode.’

‘Where’s the car now?’

‘At the building.’

Laura grimaced, and gestured to Redstone.

‘Can you visualise the route you took from Keele?’ Redstone asked.

‘What do you mean?’ Connart said.

‘Well, you’re driving down the M6. In your mind’s eye, can you remember where you turned off?’

‘Yeah.’

‘Let me guess. M56?’

‘That’s right. Good guess.’

‘Now you’re driving on the M56. Where did you turn off that?’

‘Er… not sure.’

‘Can you remember the voice of the satnav man saying anything?’

'It was a woman. Yeah, it's coming back. She said take the exit onto M53 North.'

'You're doing well,' Redstone said. 'What next?'

'Can't remember.'

'Well, what was the building like? Can you picture it? How did it feel?'

'Horrible. Deserted, dark. Rubbish on the ground.'

'Dark brown bricks, almost black?' Redstone asked.

'Exactly. Lots of windows, filthy. Some broken.'

'When you drove in, was there a gate? Like chain fencing fixed to scaffolding poles?'

'Got it again. You're good at this.'

'Any signs saying what it used to be?'

'Not sure.'

Redstone scribbled on the pad. *Big faded brown sign on the building. Single line of lettering.* He glanced at Laura, and wrote *I think that's as much as we'll get. Is it enough for the local police to find it?*

She touched her earpiece, and nodded to Redstone.

'Let's move on,' she said to Connart. 'Tell us how you knew how to operate the tanker. How to discharge its contents.'

'The woman gave us instructions, and Dick... well, persuaded the tanker guy to go through it with us.'

'Did the driver tell you how dangerous the cargo was?'

'He kept on about it. I sort of believed him, but Dick said it was a trick to scare us.'

'How long did it take you to respray the tanker?'

'Only a day. The woman had left the paint and stuff there, ready for us.'

'How do you know Dick?'

'I don't really know him.'

True but not the whole truth, Redstone wrote.

'Do your wives know each other?' Laura said.

That's it.

Connart reddened. 'Not married.'

'OK, girlfriends,' Laura said.

'You know the answer, don't you? Why are you messing me around?'

'They shared a cell in Holloway, didn't they.'

'You know they did.'

'When did your girlfriend –' she glanced down at her notes, '– Cindy introduce you to Dick Krantz?'

'She didn't. Her friend Evie did. About three weeks ago. Evie is Dick's girlfriend.'

'And when did Cindy or Evie meet this mysterious woman who was telling you what to do?'

'No idea. Been trying to work it out.'

'Does Cindy have any idea who the woman is?' Laura asked.

Connart shrugged. 'Not a clue. Nor does Evie.'

'You weren't fussy about pumping that awful chemical down into Piccadilly Circus Tube station, were you? You knew how terrible it was, didn't you? You knew what it was going to do to the people down there.'

Connart turned to his solicitor, who shrugged.

'I told you, I didn't know. I'm not a fucking scientist.'

He didn't know, but he strongly suspected. The money overwhelmed what few scruples he had.

'How much did she pay you?' Laura asked.

'No comment.'

Five thousand in advance, with a promise of another twenty after.

'Let's come back to the WhatsApp messages,' she said. 'How did the woman get your contact details?'

'How would I know? All you need is someone's phone number, don't you?'

'How do you know it's a woman?'

'We worked it out. Must have been another con in Holloway when Cindy and Evie were there.'

'No pictures or other evidence?'

'Nah. Clever, that one.'

*

Clothier pushed aside a clutter of small tools, bits of circuit board and tiny black electronic components scattered on the table in his basement office. Redstone sat on his left, and Laura at the far end.

'Well done, you two,' he said. 'Went well. Some promising lines of enquiry to pursue.'

'Yes,' said Laura. 'I've got the Merseyside police searching for the building where the tanker driver's locked in. They're confident they'll locate him by the end of the day. And we've got the phones the WhatsApp group used. It's clear the mystery woman, if indeed it is a woman, had done her homework well. All the instructions are carefully thought through, and must have been based on a lot of research.'

'I guess the woman hacked Cindy's phone, or Evie's, or both, to get the contact details of the two men,' said Redstone.

'She's a powerful foe,' Laura said. 'It fits with it being Clodagh, except for the Holloway connection.'

'Ah!' Redstone said. 'Holloway! I knew there was something – I've just remembered. Valerie Hitchcock was a prison visitor there at one stage. Before she made her comeback as Cabinet Secretary. She made a big thing of it, trying to show how she was on the side of the angels.'

'But it couldn't be her, of course,' Laura said. She glanced at Clothier.

'It's OK,' Clothier said gently. 'I know what you and Gavin did. Totally merited. Equivalent to killing an enemy soldier in a shooting war.'

‘Well,’ said Redstone, ‘maybe Connart was right. Maybe the mystery woman was a fellow convict, in Holloway at the same time as Evie and Cindy.’

‘Or she could have been a prison officer. Or one of the other prison visitors. Or some other person who got involved with prisoners.’

‘Like the chaplain, you mean,’ said Redstone. The other two stared at him. ‘Oh, I didn’t mean…’

‘Stranger things have happened,’ said Laura. ‘Can’t rule anyone out till we’ve looked into them. I’ve got a team doing that – going through the details of everyone who might have got to know Evie and Cindy well enough to think it worthwhile contacting their boyfriends. I’m going to be talking to both women to see if they can think of anyone particular who fits the bill. I won’t be going easy on them. And I’m going to have another go at Krantz. I’ll be even less easy on him, the sadistic murderer.’

‘I suppose your team are looking for any possible connection between the two girlfriends and Clodagh,’ Redstone said.

‘Of course. And so will I in the interviews.’

‘And no news about Clodagh herself?’

‘Afraid not. But it’s just a matter of time.’

*

He stepped out of the government car and walked up his drive. Mary was tipping weeds into a wheelie bin at the edge of her own drive.

‘Hi,’ she said. ‘Avoiding the Tube?’

‘Yes. I don’t suppose the terrorists will strike in the same way again, but…’

‘That’s what a lot of people at the hospital are thinking. I saw on TV that the Tubes are almost empty. A choking gas down there, no way of escaping – I’m frightening myself just talking about it.’

‘It *is* frightening. Even more so to a chemist like me.’

'It was lucky your man Dr Pepper was there when it happened,' she said.

'Eh? Has David been in the news, then?'

'Yes, didn't you see?'

'I've been tied up today. Hold on.' He pulled out his phone. Nine unread messages. He scanned them – from David, Joanne, Sophie, Rosie, David again…

'I missed a lot, apparently. David's being treated as a sort of hero, which he deserves. BBC TV London want to do a background piece on him and the lab.'

'Good. I look forward to seeing it. Oh… you OK for food this evening? Like to pop round? Zena's let me down at the last minute. Sorry, that sounded…'

'That would be lovely.'

*

Redstone settled back on Mary's sofa, a glass of wine in his hand.

'That was a great meal,' he said. 'And the way you arranged the table, the flowers, and everything – delightful. I can't tell you how much better I feel.' He raised his glass. 'Many thanks.'

She raised hers, and sat next to him. 'Here's to more meals together. If you'd like that, of course.'

'In your professional medical opinion, am I mad? Of course I'd like it. My turn to cook, next time.'

'In my professional opinion as an A&E nurse, I've seen madder people. And not all of them are my colleagues. In my professional opinion as an ex-restauranteur, you'd be mad to cook for me when I love cooking. And I'm good at it, if I say so myself.'

'Well, I can't just keep on accepting your generosity,' he said. 'I've got to return it somehow. How about…' What could he offer? 'How about my driving us out on a day trip somewhere nice?'

'Sounds lovely.'

He tilted his head back so it was resting on the top of the sofa, stared sightlessly at the ceiling, and realised he hadn't a clue what Mary was thinking, despite her being so close. What was the explanation?

TWO DAYS LATER – FRIDAY 28TH JULY

The BBC London interviewer seemed genuinely interested in London Bio, its beginnings, and the way the team had overcome financial and scientific problems to achieve their successes. Staff were filmed working with glass apparatus, automated sampling systems, and anything which involved liquid nitrogen and its associated clouds of condensation.

The director and camera crew seemed particularly taken with Rosie. Redstone realised she was very photogenic. When David and Rosie described Project Smoothaway, the interviewer became excited, confessing that she herself was a migraine sufferer.

'When will it be broadcast?' Redstone asked the director.

'Tomorrow, I hope, while David's intervention at Piccadilly Circus is fresh in viewers' memories. Don't expect a lengthy piece. By the time the producer and the editors have had their way, it'll probably be just a couple of minutes long.'

Once the film crew had left, the lab staff gathered in the meeting room. Joanne produced some bottles of prosecco and a pack of plastic wine glasses, and the staff toasted David.

'And here's to our new film star, Rosie Clarke,' David said, raising his glass. Rosie bowed, while the rest of the staff applauded.

'You might be able to get commissions to be interviewed when the TV people want someone to talk about a development in the pharma industry,' Redstone said. 'We'd be happy to give you the time and support. The media are always on the lookout for experts.'

'Hey,' Joanne said, 'what about me? You could train me to know which end of a round-bottomed flask goes in that grippy thingy. I've always wanted to talk about round-bottomed flasks ever since I heard you scientists going on about them. For obvious reasons.'

*

Back home, Redstone called Michelle, and told her that the terrorists had falsified the transmitted position of the bromine tanker.

'If you had access to what they sent, do you think you could glean anything useful about who sent it or where they sent it from?'

'Not sure,' she said. 'Sounds an interesting little project.'

He told her he'd try to get the information sent to her, and then left a message on Clothier's phone asking if he could arrange that.

'If GCHQ seem reluctant, threaten them with the PM,' he added.

MONDAY 31ST JULY

The afternoon sun was heating up Redstone's office. He pulled down the blind.

Michelle rang. 'It's the same people or person who did the previous hacking,' she said. 'Several characteristic elements of the programming. Not surprising, I suppose. They were very ingenious in the way they arranged false GPS locations to be transmitted. I enjoyed seeing how they did it. Or should I say how she, Clodagh did it? I'm now convinced it's the programmer we dealt with last year.'

'My guess is you're right about it being Clodagh, but the security people haven't yet traced her, as far as I know. Did you get any clues as to where she might be? If it is her.'

'Oh yes, I forgot to mention that. Southern Hertfordshire. The area round Watford. Can't say I know it myself. She herself might not be there, of course, but that's where the GPS manipulation program seems to have been centred. Couldn't narrow it any further than that, because of the way she—'

'Wow! Well done, Michelle. Have you told GCHQ?'

'Er… no. I sort of assumed they'd already… well, I haven't told anyone except you, now.'

'Right. I'll tell MI5.'

He phoned Clothier, and outlined what Michelle had said.

'Great!' Clothier said. 'The Watford area includes a lot of people and buildings, but it's far smaller than the whole of the UK, which is what the search area's been up to now. I'll tell our people and the police immediately.'

Redstone strolled through to Joanne's desk.

'Some of the staff are leaving early so they can get home in time for the BBC London News,' she said. 'You doing the same?'

'Yes,' he said, 'I should. Are we recording it for posterity?'

'We are – and for the staff who live outside London. It's actually London and the South East, so most of our people can get the programme at home.'

'Good. I'll pack up and—'

'Before you go,' she said, have you seen the latest posts on social media? About your friend the Prime Minister?'

'Oh, God. What now? Tell me.'

She picked up her phone and donned thick glasses. 'Here's a good example: "Jones's poisonous government is exposing us all to deadly attacks. He should do the decent thing and go." And that post has attracted lots of likes.' She removed her glasses and waved them at Redstone. 'People know he's not personally responsible for the terror attacks, but they're getting scared. They're grasping for anything which might make them feel safe.'

'Poor man. He's in a very difficult position. Do *you* think he should resign?'

She carefully put her glasses on her desk, and stared at them for a second. 'I honestly can't make up my mind,' she said. 'He can't be seen to be giving in to terrorist blackmail. But on the other hand, his fellow citizens are being killed. Is there some middle way, some temporary deal?'

'The right way would be to catch the murderous vermin,' Redstone said. 'As to a middle way, some sort of compromise, I can't think of one offhand.'

'Nor can I,' she admitted. 'You going to take the Tube home?'

'Yes, I am,' he said. 'I've decided I mustn't give in to the terrorists. Though that's a trivial gesture compared with what Michael Jones is being asked for. What about you?'

'Yes. To be honest, using other ways of getting home is too much hassle. I'm not as principled as you.'

'But you're more honest. I can't deny that's a factor for me too.'

*

At 6:30 he settled down in front of his TV, glass of wine in hand. The London news started. The first item was about a troupe of dancers who'd won an award, the second a lengthy set of interviews with some film stars on the red carpet in front of a cinema in Leicester Square, the third… his eyelids drooped.

He jerked upright. Only three minutes until the end of the programme. Maybe he'd missed the article on London Bio – but surely it would have jogged him out of his reverie?

And there was a familiar face – David Pepper. The presenter was talking about how David, the hero of the Piccadilly Circus Tube attack, was the Chief Scientist of an exciting young London company which was now developing a revolutionary cure for migraines. The scene switched to the big lab outside Redstone's office. The camera panned across the lab, briefly showing David, Redstone and some of the other researchers, and zoomed in on Rosie, who explained the goal of Project Smoothaway. The interviewer turned to the camera and said all migraine sufferers were waiting with bated breath for the project to succeed. The presenter in the studio wished the company luck, and turned to the weather forecaster.

Not too bad, Redstone thought. No mention of the company's successful inventions already in use, but that didn't matter. And even if Project Smoothaway didn't in the end succeed, which was always a possible outcome in the pharmaceutical business – no, probable outcome – nobody would remember this programme.

His phone rang – Mary.

'I've just watched the news article on your company. Very interesting.'

'So you thought it was OK,' he said.

‘It was great. And your young woman came across well.’

‘Rosie. Yes, she seems to have it all. She’s a good scientist, and the camera likes her. I’ve told her she might have a second career as a TV pundit on pharmaceutical issues.’

‘Good for you. Well, I’m looking forward to our trip out together. Have you decided where?’

‘Er… How about St Albans? Do you know it?’

‘I’ve been there a couple of times,’ she said, ‘but ages ago. Great idea.’

*

‘You’re literally grinding your teeth, darling,’ said Clodagh. ‘It’s only a TV programme.’

‘It’s that self-promoting sanctimonious shit Redstone,’ said Valerie. ‘He drives me up the wall. He ruins me, tries to murder me and then he and his politically correct crew are treated as national heroes and saviours. I’ve got to get rid of him. And Smith, of course.’

‘I know, I know. But let’s not get diverted from the main programme. I sense we’re getting close, but we still haven’t got Pitt into Number 10.’

‘Reminds me,’ Valerie said. ‘I must call her tomorrow.’

TUESDAY 1ST AUGUST

'Number 10 called,' Joanne said as Redstone entered the office. 'Can you go to see the Prime Minister at eleven o'clock?'

'What about?'

'A personal matter, apparently.'

'Oh. I take it you said yes.'

'No, I said why can't the lazy so-and-so come here for a change. It's not as if he's got any real problems on his plate.'

'Sarcasm doesn't suit you, Joanne. You know, I think that he might have agreed to come if you'd really said that. I bet he's fed up with being a sort of prisoner in his own home and office.'

'If he's that fed up, he could go to Chequers, couldn't he?'

'No doubt he does, from time to time. Anyway, back to the invitation. Obviously I'll have to go, but I'm not looking forward to it. Every visitor to Number 10 will now have to run the gauntlet of the press parked on the other side of Downing Street. And the reporters will be trying to pick up any hint about how he's reacting to the social media attacks, and about whether the counter-terrorism work is getting anywhere. Oh, well…'

'Can't you go in the back entrance?'

'Not without a staff pass, usually. I suppose they could make an exception. Could you please ask?'

'OK. Shall I order a taxi?'

'No thanks, I prefer to go by…' He stopped and walked to the window. 'Maybe the prime minister *would* in fact like to come here. Depends on how crowded his diary is, I suppose. I'm sure he'd like to see the lab. And the round-bottomed flasks, of course. Politicians like being pictured going round labs. Be more good publicity for London Bio.'

She smiled. 'We won't know if we don't ask. Shall I put it to the flunky who phoned?'

'Why not?'

He went to his desk. He feared Jones would again seek his advice on resigning. He sat turning over and rejecting every possibility that occurred to him.

Joanne rushed in.

'The private secretary asked the PM while I was hanging on,' she said, 'and the answer is yes! He'll be here at 11:15. There'll be him, a couple of aides and security people, and the photographer. They'll stay for no longer than thirty minutes.'

'That gives us just under two hours to prepare. Quite good that it's so short. He'll get us warts and all, and we won't be wasting a lot of time polishing the test tubes.'

*

'Very impressive,' said Jones, walking into Redstone's office. 'You've got some great people here. It's ages since I visited a lab. Too long. There's a buzz, something in the atmosphere you don't get elsewhere.'

'It's the alcohol we use as a solvent,' Redstone said. 'Actually, I know what you mean. I think it comes from the fact that science is a team effort. Virtually everything we do is as part of a team. And it's creative, as well.'

'The opposite of politics, you mean,' said Jones. He turned to his private secretary. 'If you could give me and Mark a few minutes…'

Redstone shut the door and gestured to the meeting table. Jones sat at the side, letting Redstone take the seat at the head of the table. Redstone was pleased and embarrassed by this gesture.

Jones appeared even more drawn than when Redstone had last seen him. And he'd lost weight.

‘I’ll be quick,’ he said. ‘First, I expect you’ve been worrying about what to say if I sought your advice again about whether I should resign. Well, I’m not going to. Seek your advice, I mean. It wouldn’t be fair.’

‘Thanks. I must admit—’

‘And I’m not going to resign. Our policy of never giving in to blackmailers and terrorists is right. It trumps what damage the swine might do, even if they kill more of our innocent citizens. We can’t trust such people not to carry on with their awful deeds even if we give them what they ask for. And we mustn’t set a bad precedent which would encourage other terrorists.’ He brought his fist down on the table. ‘I’m going to trust our police and security services to catch them and put a stop to these atrocious acts. And I’m going to issue a statement saying all that, and do some interviews as well.’

He raised a questioning eyebrow.

‘If you want to know my reaction,’ Redstone said, ‘I was agonizing about what to say if you asked, but now I’ve heard you I’m convinced you’ve made the right decision. Most of the public’s anger is against the terrorists, not you.’

‘I hope that’s true. It should be. Now, let’s get on to the real reason why I wanted to talk to you. It’s about my daughter, Rhiannon. I don’t believe you’ve ever met her.’

‘No, don’t think so.’

‘She likes to keep out of the public eye, and out of politics. She’s now twenty-six, and she’s been offered a good job in Brussels. Working for the federation of European chemical trade associations. She’s a communications expert.’

‘Good for her,’ Redstone said. ‘My own—’

‘I believe you have a daughter of similar age working in Brussels.’

‘Yes, I was going to say. Sophie. She’s been there six years now.’

‘So, the thing is Rhiannon doesn’t know anyone there, and I thought it might be helpful to her if she could talk to Sophie before making a final decision on the job offer. Do you think Sophie could have a chat with Rhiannon?'

'Of course. I'll ring her. She's coming over soon. When does Rhiannon have to decide?'

'She's got some time, because of the holiday season. Couple of weeks, I think. If Sophie isn't coming over by then, maybe they could talk on the phone or by Zoom?'

'Why don't I suggest to Sophie they do that anyway, and then the two young women can take it from there. That might be enough, or they might want to meet. Either here or in Brussels, I suppose.'

'Great. Many thanks. I'll get Rhiannon to send you her details. You know, it would be nice if the two daughters hit it off. I'm afraid my career has had a dampening effect on Rhiannon's social life. You can imagine how people react to becoming close friends with the PM's daughter. The best ones seem to be frightened off, which leaves the worst.'

'Sophie's very sociable – gets it from her mother. And she wouldn't be scared off. I'll let you know her reactions.'

*

The meeting room was packed, as photos of the Prime Minister taken by members of the staff were shown one after the other on the big screen on the front wall.

'A big thank you to our IT colleagues for getting all your photos into one file,' Redstone said. 'Any comments on the visit, before we get back to work?'

'Seems a nice guy,' someone called from the back.

'He seemed interested in what we're doing,' another voice called.

'But is he going to resign to stop further terrorist attacks?' said Joanne. 'If he does, his visit here might turn out to be his last act as Prime Minister.' People murmured agreement.

'You must have seen the arguments for and against his resigning,' said Redstone. 'Giving in to terrorists encourages more terrorism, and in any case the current murderous bunch might just go on to make further demands. Terrorists aren't the most trustworthy of people. But resigning might stop further attacks and loss of life, which he and of course the country would have to live with if they happened. What do you think he should do?'

There was a buzz of conversation. After a couple of minutes, it was clear that most of the staff thought Jones should not resign, but that extra resources should be put into finding the terrorists.

'Mark, do you know what he's going to do?' asked David. 'You and he seem to be, well, buddies.'

'Er… I do know he's going to make a statement in the near future.'

'A very political answer,' said David with a smile. 'If he does stay on, we should find a way to use his visit to the company's advantage.'

'We can use it on those occasions when raising our profile might be useful,' Redstone said. 'Like when we seek more finance, or want to hire better scientists than you lot.'

He grinned at the general booing.

'Anyway, it was a good break from our routine. Something to tell your loved ones, or failing that, your families. I hope you enjoyed it.'

*

Back in his office, he called Sophie and told her about Rhiannon. Sophie was enthusiastic. They'd have to talk by Zoom initially, because she and Graham were having difficulty finding dates when they could both visit London together. But she assured Redstone they'd come soon.

‘And it seems you’ve started a relationship with Mary, Zena tells me,’ she added. ‘Well done!’

‘I wouldn’t say… I didn’t… She cooked me a nice meal, and I’m taking her out as a thank-you.’

‘Of course,’ Sophie said.

*

Redstone walked into his garden. The evening sun was still bright and hot. The shadowed parts of the flower beds were much darker than the sunlit areas.

Treacle bounded down the lawn to greet him. She led him to the bench, jumped up, padded onto his lap as soon as he sat down, turned round once and settled down. She was pleased to be with him, felt safe, and was happy that he was with her in her territory – the garden. Redstone mused that for once he felt thankful for being able to read thoughts and feelings. Maybe being able to do that with his pet was the only unalloyed benefit of this ability.

WEDNESDAY 2ND AUGUST

As Redstone was getting ready to take Mary to St Albans, Laura's assistant, Lewis, rang.

'Mark, some bad news. I thought you should know. Laura's been suspended.'

'What?' Redstone said. 'What do you mean? What's she done?'

'As she was going into the block of flats where she lives, two men attacked her. One had a knife, and the other a baseball bat. You can guess—'

'Is Laura all right?'

'She's got a cut on one arm, not serious, and a painful bruise on the other, nothing broken.'

'I suppose the attackers are in hospital.'

'Worse, I'm afraid. Or maybe worse is the wrong word. The baseball bat man is indeed in hospital, but the knifeman is dead.'

'Why's she been suspended? It's obvious she had to defend herself. MI5 know her capabilities. In fact they recruited her because of her army background.'

'True,' Lewis said. 'All our colleagues are backing her. But the police had to consult the Crown Prosecution Service – after all, someone's dead. They've got to decide if it was unlawful killing. So meanwhile she's on suspension – fully paid, I'm pleased to say. I don't think Gavin McKay had any real choice.'

'Any idea how long it'll be for?'

'Maybe a couple of weeks.'

'How's Laura taking it?' Redstone asked.

'She's furious, not with the Service or the police but with whoever sent the assailants. I wouldn't want to be in their shoes. It's a sort of cold, controlled fury. She's already starting to investigate. On her own time, of course, though she's getting a lot of unofficial help from her colleagues.'

'Lewis,' Redstone said, 'am I supposed to know this? Can I phone her to sympathise?'

'I'm not sure. My guess is it'll soon be an open secret, if it isn't already. So many people in the Service and the police already know. And she's a bit of a heroine. I bet the press get hold of it.'

'Yes. She might make the front pages. I'll ring her straight away. Thanks for telling me.'

Before he could dial Laura's number the phone rang again – Clothier. He told Clothier what Lewis had said.

'News travels fast,' said Clothier.

'Any information on the assailants?'

'Yes. They're both on our databases. Ex-military types, one from Russia and one from South Africa. Both were mercenaries in that awful force Hitchcock ran when she was in power. Both here illegally, having outstayed their visas.'

'Well, they got what they deserved. You want me to sit in on an interrogation?'

'The one who's still alive is in no state to talk, I'm afraid.'

Redstone walked to the window and stared across the street. 'Jim, this isn't the first hint of... of I'm not sure what, but it concerns Valerie Hitchcock. There was the fact that she'd been a prison visitor when those two thugs' girlfriends were in Holloway. And now this mercenary connection. Oh, and the Home Secretary reacted oddly when Hitchcock's name came up in a recent meeting.'

'"Golden lads and girls all must as chimney sweepers come to dust",' Clothier recited.

'What?'

'Shakespeare. She's dead. Gone. Dust.'

'But are we sure she's dust, as you put it? We know Laura and Gavin left her for dead, but maybe something went wrong. Gavin's told me in no uncertain terms that your lot didn't check, because he and Laura were private citizens at the time. I know nothing's been heard or seen of Hitchcock since, but…'

'I'll ask Lewis to do some digging.'

Redstone dialled Laura's number again, but the call went straight to voicemail. He left a message saying he'd heard her news and would like to tell her something relevant, so could she call back.

*

Redstone and Mary left the multistorey car park and walked through a modern precinct of small shops and cafes, in narrow lanes.

'Ages since I've been here,' she said. 'I used to come with Kate now and then. It was nice. But I haven't been since she…'

'Was murdered,' Redstone said. 'It's OK to mention it.'

'That's a healthy attitude. I know you don't stop missing a spouse, but you have to come to terms with it. Though every now and then something happens…' She looked away. 'Yesterday, I had to treat a woman who'd received a bad head injury in a car accident. Just like I got in the accident which killed Patrick.' She dabbed at an eye.

'Oh, I hadn't realised you were injured too,' he said.

'Yes. That's what inspired me to work in A&E.' She tapped her head. 'I'm now the bionic woman – metal plate here.'

'Ah – that explains… never mind.'

'What?' she said. 'What does it explain?'

What the hell should I say? he thought. *I can't tell her it explains why I can't read her mind.*

'Sorry, I got mixed up. Forget what I said.'

She raised an eyebrow, but said nothing.

They crossed the road.

'Let's go down to the Abbey,' Redstone said. 'Unless you want to browse in the market first. It's a real market – not tourist tat.'

'I know,' said Mary, pausing by a greengrocer's stall and fingering a tomato. 'Some good produce here. But let's leave the Abbey for another day. I need some new shoes and some other odds and ends. Can you amuse yourself for about an hour?'

'Of course. There's a hardware shop I enjoy going round, and then I can get a coffee and wait for you.'

'And you can scout out somewhere for us to have lunch.'

'Fine. Ring me when you've finished shopping and I'll tell you where I am.'

Half an hour later, Redstone was sitting sipping a coffee outside a café in a narrow, cobbled pedestrian street lined with old buildings in a mixture of English styles. His phone rang – Laura.

'So news of my battle with the forces of evil has travelled far already,' she said.

'Indeed. How are you feeling?'

'Physically I'm fine. Pissed off at being suspended, but I understand why Gavin had to do it. Every cloud has a silver lining – I'm now able to spend all my waking hours trying to trace the bastards who set those thugs on me.'

'Yes,' he said, 'on that…' He told her what he'd discussed with Clothier about Hitchcock.

'I suppose she was still alive when we left her flat that day. We got out pretty fast after rigging up the hanging. She was unconscious, of course, thanks to the anaesthetic patch you made for us.'

'Could she have escaped from the noose if the anaesthetic had worn off almost immediately after you left?'

'I can't see how. Her weight was keeping it tight. To get out of it she'd have needed someone to help her.'

He sipped his coffee. 'Maybe someone else had a key, and went in afterwards?'

'Would have to have been almost immediately. We would have seen them.'

'You sure there was no one else hiding in the flat itself?'

'We didn't conduct a search,' she said. 'Nobody else appeared when we went in, or made any sound while we were there, so I guess we assumed… Damn, maybe you're right. We didn't do the job properly. Maybe there was someone else there, keeping out of the way for some reason. We should have searched the flat.'

'Though that would have taken longer. As you said, you wanted to get in and out as quickly as possible.'

'Nevertheless,' she said, 'I'm ashamed of myself. I bet she *was* rescued by someone. It all fits.'

He fell silent. The prospect of Hitchcock alive and out for revenge was appalling. He himself would be near the top of her list of people to attack, and if she was alive, it seemed she'd already had a go at Laura.

'So if your theory's right,' Laura continued, 'we need to trace Hitchcock. I'll have to think where to start.'

'She must be in league with the terrorists, if the bromine girlfriend connection is right.'

'True.'

'Well, the hacker's in the Watford area, if Michelle is to be believed. Do you think it likely that Hitchcock would be near the hacker?'

'People in a plot do tend to group together,' Laura said. 'Makes their lives easier.'

'Funnily enough,' he said, 'I'm sitting having coffee in what you might describe as the Watford area. I'm in St Albans.'

'Nice. Yes, that is in what you might call Greater Watford. Look around and tell me if Hitchcock is strolling past.'

'Ho, ho.' He found himself scanning the pedestrians walking along the street. 'Can't see her at the moment.'

'Actually, it *is* the sort of place she might have chosen to hide out. Put yourself in her shoes. Outside London but convenient for it. Near the motorway network. And I bet there are expensive houses and flats up for rent there. We know she's got a taste for the good life.'

'So are you going to search for her in this area?' he asked.

'I'll think about how to narrow down possibilities. I certainly want to get her. Enjoy St Albans. Bye.'

He finished his coffee, stretched, and walked down the main street to the hardware shop. As he made his way up the wooden stairs to the tools section, Laura rang.

'I've had a further thought,' she said. 'Your IT genius friend suspects it's Clodagh behind the hacking, doesn't she.'

'Yes.'

'Suppose she's right, and it *is* Clodagh. We always believed Clodagh and Hitchcock colluded in last year's awful events. What if Clodagh deliberately left a false trail leading us to think she'd gone back to the States, but in reality went to live with Hitchcock? Hid out in Hitchcock's posh flat. Nobody's found any trace of her back in the States.'

Redstone was excited. He loved it when disparate facts came together to form a coherent explanation of something. It was one of the reasons he'd become a scientist.

'If she *was* there,' he said, 'she would have kept out of sight when you and Gavin went in. Hidden, especially if she saw what you were doing. And then she would have released Hitchcock from the noose as soon as you'd gone.'

'Lots of speculation there,' Laura said. 'But it does all hang together. Pun unintended.'

'Did you know that Lewis has been tasked with seeing if there's any evidence that Hitchcock did die?'

'Yes, he told me. No evidence so far. No records of a funeral, no death certificate issued, nobody called the police.'

'So maybe someone will find evidence she's alive. Maybe Hitchcock and Clodagh are holed up together here, in some posh house round the corner. I'll probably spot them buying apples in the market when we go for lunch shortly.'

'Ho, ho. Who's "we"?'

'I've brought Mary here. She's shopping for shoes at the moment.'

'You never took me shoe shopping.'

'I didn't realise I was taking Mary shoe shopping, till she informed me when we were here.'

Laura snorted. 'Didn't read her mind, then?' she said.

'I told you – I don't read minds anymore, unless I have to. Which means for your lot. Except Treacle's – I had a lovely session with her yesterday. She sat on my lap in the garden, and—'

'So you're still a big softie, then. As well as a Dr Dolittle.'

'I admit to being a big softie, I suppose, but Dr Dolittle spoke to animals, didn't he? It was two-way communication. I can't do that.'

'Just as well. Treacle might be embarrassed.'

*

Redstone and Mary sat eating lunch in a spacious barn-like restaurant that was largely constructed of dark wood. He hoped he'd made the right noises about the shoes she'd shown him. She'd smiled at the drill bits he'd bought.

'The Prime Minister's statement was good,' she said. 'Well judged.' She sawed at the pizza on her plate. 'The poor man's in an awful position, but I think he made the right decision.'

'I agree,' Redstone said.

'Have you seen the latest headlines?' She waved her phone and read from it. '*Thugs attack wrong victim. Mystery woman kills one, injures other.* It goes on to say the woman is thought to work for the security services. Excellent pizza, by the way.' She took a forkful of food. 'I can't help wondering if it's someone we know.'

'What do you mean?' he asked, knowing perfectly well what she meant.

'Mark, I know that Laura works for MI5. I also know she used to be in the army, and I saw her in action when you were attacked at home last year. There's something about her – I wouldn't want to try to harm her.'

'I don't know what to say. I can't…'

'Is Laura all right? You can tell me that.'

'Yes. I suppose I can tell you she's got a couple of minor injuries, not serious. You can make your own assumptions about how she got them.'

Mary nodded. 'Glad she's OK. Do they know why she was attacked? Is it anything to do with the terrorists? She must have been working flat out trying to track down those awful people.'

'Sorry, Mary, I can't talk about Laura's work.'

'I understand,' she said. He guessed she understood more than his reticence. And if she'd been able to work out elements of what was going on, no doubt so could others.

*

'I'm getting more and more worried that Redstone and his coterie are on our track,' Valerie Hitchcock said to Clodagh McCarthy.

'What makes you think that?'

'Not sure. Instinct. They're not stupid, and they'll have been putting a lot of effort into piecing together small bits of information.'

'Right. Let's step up our precautions. Your plan for giving him and Smith their just deserts – put it on ice for a while. She's obviously a tough cookie, tougher than your ex-mercenaries.'

'Or luckier,' Valerie said. 'But she has to be lucky every time. We have to be lucky only once.'

‘Even so, we must keep our eyes on the bigger picture, the longer-term goal.’

‘I’m not arguing with that, but I’m not going to let either of them get away with what they did to me.’

‘Of course not,’ said Clodagh. ‘Maybe your Russian friend can help us with a different approach.’

‘Maybe. I’ll have a word. Anyway, I think we need more information on what Redstone’s group are up to.’

‘Any ideas on how to get it?’

THURSDAY 3RD AUGUST

David and Rosie sat down with Redstone at his meeting table.

'You don't seem happy,' Redstone said. 'What's the bad news?'

'The latest Smoothaway formulation,' David said. 'It's having a side effect. Some component is affecting the myelin in the sheaths of the mouse nerves we're using in our migraine models.'

Rosie had tears in her eyes. 'I don't understand it,' she said, her voice breaking. She cleared her throat. 'I checked very carefully. Every ingredient has been passed as safe. None of them interacts with myelin. I looked for contamination, but can't find any. All that work…' She wiped her eyes.

'We've considered whether it's the combination of chemicals rather than any individual ingredient,' David said, 'but we can't find anything in the literature which would support that idea.'

'Damn,' Redstone said. 'You've done what I would have done. What a bloody shame.'

Rosie smiled weakly. 'So what do we do?'

'Hmm. Maybe we should do some analysis of the affected myelin to see if we can get any clues. Is that possible, David?'

'Sure,' David said. 'We'll have to go outside to get help. We haven't got all the right equipment, or the expertise. I'll ask friends in Oxford.'

'Do you want to be involved in that work?' Redstone asked Rosie.

'Yes please, if that's OK with David.'

'Of course,' David said. 'Good for your development.'

'I'm optimistic that the results will point us in the right direction,' Redstone said.

As soon as David and Rosie had left, Redstone slumped in his chair, elbows on the table, head in hands. He hoped he'd put on a good show for David and, especially, Rosie, but he felt despondent. This was a big setback in his pet project. He was responsible, because he'd been overseeing the work while David had been on holiday. He should have foreseen this problem. He'd taken his eye off the ball because of the pressure of the MI5 work. No, it was more than the MI5 stuff – it was the breakup with Laura, and the mind-reading. Too much was happening in his life. He'd forgotten to prioritise. He should put his kids first, his colleagues second, London Bio third, and only then see if he had time for MI5, the Prime Minister, and the other junk he seemed to have accumulated. Which reminded him – there was the Home Secretary's bloody reception this evening. Should he cry off? But he was curious about what lay behind her invitation. No, he'd go, but be more careful about accepting new commitments.

He could hear in his mind's ear Sophie telling him he must make time for himself and take care of his emotional health – a constant theme since Kate's murder. He phoned her.

'Hello darling,' he said. 'I wanted to see how you are, and find out if you've been in touch with Rhiannon yet.'

'What's the matter?' she asked. 'You sound low. Something wrong?'

He told her about Project Smoothaway.

'You've often told me that most pharmaceutical research ends in failure. Sorry, Dad, but you can't put all your emotional eggs in the science basket.'

'You're right, of course. Tell me about you and Oskar. Done anything interesting recently?'

She described a party they'd been to, where she'd been introduced to the Norwegian Foreign Secretary. 'How about your social life?' she said. 'How did it go with Mary?'

'Oh, fine. We had a good time together, I think. She seemed happy when we got home. I felt relaxed with her.'

'So far so good, then. It's early days.'

'Sophie, you're creating a romantic story where there isn't one in reality. We're, well, neighbours who get on.'

'We'll see,' she said.

'So, what about Rhiannon?'

'Yes, she seems very nice. Wants to do everything she can to make her own life away from the shadow of her father, or maybe away from the spotlight on him would be a better way of putting it. Anyway, we've arranged to meet. I was going to tell you – I've given up trying to find a date this month when Graham and I can visit London together. It's not going to happen till maybe September. So I'll be over in the next week or so. I'll let you know exactly when.'

'Fine. I assume you'll be staying with your aged father?'

'Of course I'm going to inflict myself on you. I want to see Treacle.'

*

The Home Secretary's reception was held in a spacious, bland room on the top floor of the Home Office building. As Redstone entered, he felt feelings familiar to him in such situations – being an outsider, of no interest to anyone present. Why the hell had he come? He absently picked a glass of white wine from a tray held by a uniformed woman, took a large gulp, and scanned the room. He recognized no one. He couldn't even spot the Home Secretary. He'd hoped to find Gavin McKay here, since MI5 was technically under the Home Secretary's wing, but no.

He wandered over to a plate-glass window and looked out at the view of rooftops, chimneys, and the upper floors of high buildings. Over to the left he could see Westminster Abbey, and beyond that the elaborate and impressive Victoria Tower of the Houses of Parliament, with Big Ben further back. Victorian Gothic, he thought, and smiled at the realisation that it was unsurprising that the Victoria Tower was Victorian. While Westminster Abbey was truly Gothic. Which was originally a term of abuse, but turned out to be a highly successful architectural style.

'What's so amusing?' asked a voice to his left. He turned to see a slim woman he thought to be a bit younger than himself.

'Oh, nothing. I was thinking about the origins of the words describing some of the architecture over there.'

'Like "mock Gothic", meaning make fun of goths? Apologies for that weak joke. Not good for someone who makes her living making fun of politicians. Hi, I'm Sue Abercrombie, journalist.'

'Mark Redstone, scientist.'

They shook hands.

'I wondered if you were an architect,' she said, 'given your interest in the buildings.'

'No, I haven't got the artistic streak that good architects need. Though I've always been interested in buildings. When I was a kid, I used to make model buildings for our train set. Mine and Dad's. You know, draw and colour bits of card and then fold them and glue the tabs. Don't suppose kids do that anymore. Mine didn't.'

'You look wistful.'

'Do I? Well, everything's simpler when you're young, isn't it. If you're lucky enough to have the right home.' He realised the conversation had been one-sided. 'Sue, we're just talking about me. Tell me about yourself. Who do you write for?'

'I'm a blogger. Political commentator. I take it you're not one of my followers.'

'No, sorry. I don't follow any blogs. Actually, that's not quite true – there's a chemistry one… I can see your eyes glazing over.'

‘That’s unfair, and in fact wrong.’ She smiled. ‘I’m interested in how science and technology influence society.’ She took a gulp of wine. ‘May I ask why you were invited to this thrash?’

‘Good question. Perhaps you can tell me. I barely know the Home Sec – met her only twice. What is this reception for, anyway?’

‘It’s to celebrate the start of the holiday period, apparently. She does it every year. Good that she hasn’t let the terrorists stop this year’s.’ She scanned the room. ‘Some MPs, some senior civil servants, a few fairly sympathetic journalists like me, some party donors, some international terrorists – no, maybe not the last group. You fit into any of those categories?’

‘No. I run a small biotechnology company.’

‘Have I heard of it?’

‘I doubt it. London Bio.’

‘You’re joking,’ she said. ‘I thought you looked familiar. Your company featured on London TV the other day, didn’t it. And your guy was the hero of the bromide attack.’

‘Bromine, not bromide,’ he said. ‘A bromide attack would just reduce people’s sex drive.’ He wished he’d bitten his tongue.

She laughed. ‘Sorry. Is that true? Does bromide do that? I know the term is used that way, but…’

‘I haven’t a clue, and don’t intend to do any experiments to find out,’ he said. He blushed.

‘Me too,’ she said. She beckoned a waiter and exchanged her empty glass for a full one. Redstone followed suit, and looked round to see if there was any food available.

Sue drank deeply from her glass.

‘Anyway,’ she said, ‘we’ve solved the puzzle of why you were invited. Politicians love to be associated with successful entrepreneurs who’ve been in the news, and you tick all the boxes.’

‘But she invited me before the bromine incident. Is there any food anywhere?’

'Over there, on that table. Where Tavia's standing.'

Redstone looked where Sue was pointing, and the Home Secretary caught his eye. She waved and beckoned him over. He told Sue it had been a pleasure chatting to her, but he ought to go to their host, and weaved through groups of loud people to the food table. All the food was beige.

'Hello Mark,' Tavia said. 'Been enjoying the view?'

He wasn't sure if she meant the view from the window or was being sarcastic about his chatting to Sue, who was rather attractive. He wished he had his cap on, though he knew it would look ridiculous in this setting. He should act like a politician, not answering the question.

'Hello, Home Sec…Tavia,' he said. 'Thanks for inviting me. I was just eyeing your food.'

'Can I help you?' she said. She handed him a paper plate. 'These sausage rolls aren't too bad.'

'Thanks. Are you enjoying your party? I mean this event, not the political party.'

'The political party is great. And it's lovely to see a group of people chatting and getting on.' She smiled. 'Your company's been in the news since we last met. Impressive. Tell me how you got into biotechnology. Last time we met, I recall you told me you'd been in the Department of Energy before you founded London Bio.'

'Yes,' he said. 'I was there for several years, after leaving science. I'd worked for a French skincare company before becoming a civil servant.'

'What made you leave Energy and go back to science?'

'I was booted out. It was rather unpleasant. I discovered some corruption, and some people didn't like the fact that I'd done that. Anyway, all in the past now.'

'Very sorry to hear that. How unfair.' She took a sip of wine. 'I know, I mean *knew* someone who was in the Department of Energy. Valerie Hitchcock, who later became Cabinet Secretary. You mentioned her when we met last week. You said she hated you. Was that connected with the corruption you uncovered?'

He stared at her. This couldn't be a coincidence. Hitchcock had been at the very centre of the corruption. He carefully put his plate on the table.

'Are you telling me you know what happened between me and her?' he said.

She took a step back.

'No. Have I said something offensive?'

'Not offensive, but very apropos. It was Valerie who…' He took a sip of wine. 'We were colleagues. I knew her quite well, or so I thought. But then I found out… never mind. As I said. it's all in the past.'

'Yes,' she said. 'You said she tried to destroy your company while she was Cabinet Secretary, so I was just putting two and two together.'

'Well, you were right.'

'How awful. What would you say drives her? I mean drove her?'

'I'd say she wanted status and money,' Redstone said, 'like many people. But she was prepared to, well, do anything to get them.'

'You might think I'd be familiar with that sort of behaviour, being a politician, but I've not encountered any colleague who behaves in such an evil way as… as I assume you're implying. I'm really sorry you had to deal with someone like that. I… I can imagine what it must have been like.'

'Thanks.' He could see she was agitated, but he wasn't near enough to pick up her thoughts.

'Have you seen her since then?' she said.

'Why are you asking that? What's going on?' He moved his head closer to hers to read her thoughts, but she went pale and jerked back. He detected fear and something to do with sex.

'I wish... It's...' She choked on her words, and seemed to shrink. 'Excuse me,' she mumbled, marched to the nearest door and disappeared.

Redstone stood there, stunned. Sue appeared in front of him.

'What on earth did you say to Tavia?' she said. 'She acted as though you'd punched her.'

'It wasn't what I said to her, it was... Sue, I'm conscious you're a journalist, so sorry, I can't say any more to you. I don't want to read about this in the media tomorrow. No offence.'

'I give you my word that anything you tell me is off the record,' she said.

'That means you wouldn't attribute it to me. But you could still use it.'

'No, it means I couldn't publish it at all. It would remain confidential, between you and me. And whoever else you choose to tell, of course.'

He looked at her.

'I can see you don't trust me,' she said. 'I admit I might use the non-information you're not giving me to do some investigating. But I swear that's as far as I'd go.'

'What if you discovered something, and let's say it was very interesting, as a result?'

'I'd publish. I admit it.'

'As I thought. Sue, I admire your honesty and I'm grateful for it, but I mustn't tell you what happened.'

She smiled. 'Oh well, win some lose some. No hard feelings.' She scanned the food. 'Unappetising, isn't it? Fancy going out to a restaurant to get a decent meal?'

'Good idea. Anywhere in particular?'

'There's a great Turkish place in Pimlico. About ten minutes' walk. Sound OK?'

FRIDAY 4TH AUGUST

'How did it go last night?' asked Joanne. 'I suspect you had rather a good time.'

'If you mean I'm a bit hungover, you're right. The reception was… interesting. And I think I got picked up by a journalist.'

'What does that mean?'

'She and I got chatting, I refused to tell her something I didn't want published, and we ended up eating a rather good Turkish meal in Pimlico.'

'And drinking Turkish wine?'

'Yes, as it happens.'

'What did you refuse to tell her?'

'Sorry, Joanne. It's to do with the stuff I've been doing with MI5.'

'Understood. What's this woman's name?'

He told her. She turned to her PC and googled.

'Ah. Good looking. Political blogger. You going to see her again?'

'No,' he said. 'My life's complicated enough as it is.'

'Pity about the professional clash. You might get on well with someone like that.'

'For goodness' sake, what with you and Sophie… by the way, Sophie's coming over in a week or so.'

'That'll be nice. What about the Home Secretary? Did you chat to her? Did you find out why she invited you?'

'We did speak briefly. Sue Abercrombie said I'd been invited because politicians like to be seen associating with science entrepreneurs.'

'I suppose that's just about possible. I'll get you a cuppa for your hangover.'

Redstone sat at his desk. He wished he hadn't felt obliged to mislead Joanne. He didn't like misleading anybody, even by *not* saying something – by being 'economical with the truth', as a cabinet secretary had once famously put it. He wouldn't make a good professional spy.

He should tell someone in MI5 about the incident with the Home Secretary last night. It had to be Gavin McKay, Laura, or Jim Clothier. Maybe McKay would be best, since it was about the Home Secretary herself. He picked up his phone.

'Hello, Mark,' McKay said. 'Calling to tell me what you were up to with Tavia last night?'

'Blimey,' said Redstone. 'Anyone would think you were the head of an intelligence organisation. So you had someone there?'

'I have people everywhere. Get on with it.'

Redstone recounted the conversation and what he'd picked up from Tavia's thoughts.

'So what do you make of it?' McKay said.

'She seemed to be interrogating me about my relationship with Hitchcock, and I picked up a… an implication that Hitchcock's alive. Tavia might have been trying to find out why Hitchcock has it in for me.'

'Good God!'

'And there's more. I picked up that Tavia was afraid of something, and it was to do with sex in some way.'

'And?'

'You remember Hitchcock's speciality.'

'Stop talking in riddles,' McKay said.

'Her record of using sexual blackmail.'

'Ah. Are you speculating that Hitchcock is not only alive, but up to her old tricks, blackmailing the Home Secretary? Bit of a jump, isn't it? To put it mildly.'

'I suppose it is. Sorry. I was suspecting that Hitchcock had forced Tavia to try to extract information from me about how our investigation's going. Which she failed to do, by the way. Maybe I'm being paranoid.'

'The fact that you're paranoid doesn't mean they're not out to get you,' McKay said. 'I've commissioned investigations on the basis of weaker evidence than what you've just recounted. I hate to say it, but your speculations make sense. At the least, your observations reinforce our suspicion that Hitchcock's alive, which is to my regret and shame. I didn't do the job properly. I'm to blame, not Laura. I was leading the operation.'

'What now, then?' asked Redstone.

'I'll now further investigate the Tavia-Hitchcock relationship. I would be obliged to do that for any minister who might be compromised, but given it's the Home Secretary…'

'Oh, there was a journalist who saw a little of what happened, though she didn't hear it. I don't know if that affects—'

'I know. Sue Abercrombie.'

Redstone had a flash of insight.

'She's on your payroll, isn't she?'

'Mark, even if she were, which of course I deny, you mustn't share any information with her. Our informants are paid to inform us, not the other way round. Though we may feed helpful journalists some scraps of information now and then, carefully curated.'

'Can such people get information your officers can't?'

'Sometimes. You'd be surprised how careless some politicians can be when talking to journalists, especially if they think it might help their image. Happy for you to keep in touch with Sue, if you want. Good-looking woman, intelligent, interesting…'

'For Christ's sake, Gavin, you sound like my daughter. And my PA.'

'We all love you, Mark. Some more than others, of course.'

Redstone sat back, sipped his tea, and wondered about Sue. Had MI5 tasked her with finding out why Tavia had wanted to speak to him? Was that why she'd started chatting to him in the first place? Damn. It had been too good to be true. Oh well, that was the end of that relationship. Not that it had ever really got started.

He walked out into the big lab to talk about Project Smoothaway.

*

Later that afternoon he received a WhatsApp call from McKay.

'I've got a plan, and you're part of it,' McKay said. 'We're going to turn Octavia Pitt. Assuming your guess about Hitchcock is right, we're going to get Octavia to switch from Hitchcock's side to ours – we're going to use her to feed Hitchcock false information, and with luck help us locate that vicious woman. That way Octavia can stay as Home Secretary without a stain on her character and in the knowledge that she's actively helping the country. If she helps us locate the terrorists, she can present herself as a public heroine.'

'Aren't you basing rather a lot on my guess?'

'Yes,' said McKay, 'but that's how intelligence organisations work. We rarely have hard facts till late in an investigation. Not like you scientists, who lead such an easy life.'

'Huh. Well, your objective of using Tavia sounds good, but how are you going to achieve it?'

'A combination of guile and threat. We need to meet her somewhere she won't be seen by journalists or others who might recognize her, and where you can wear your cap without looking ridiculous. I thought a park bench, outside central London but easy for her to get to. She lives in Islington. Any ideas?'

'How about Kenwood?' said Redstone. 'Stately home on Hampstead Heath.'

'Yes, I know it. Good idea. They have an outdoor café – we could meet there.'

'OK. When do you have in mind?'

'The sooner the better. Can you make tomorrow?'

'It's a Saturday,' Redstone said.

'All to the good – she won't have to invent explanations for her staff. I'll text you the details.'

SATURDAY 5TH AUGUST

The outdoor seating at Kenwood was situated next to a small colonnade, alongside the plain room where the food and drink were served. Redstone and McKay sat at right angles on uncomfortable chairs by a small, rickety table. McKay had outlined what they were going to tell Tavia Pitt, and they were now discussing how Redstone should alert McKay if he picked up anything of interest in Tavia's thoughts.

'You'll have to drop things into the conversation,' McKay said, 'since we can't use written notes or anything else that would arouse her suspicion. And don't point that bloody cap at me.'

'Righto. How did you persuade her to come? Assuming she does come,' said Redstone, sipping his coffee.

'Oh, she'll come,' said McKay. 'I sent a car for her.'

'Answer the question.'

McKay smiled. 'I told her it was the only way she could stay as Home Secretary, and we knew everything, though I didn't define "everything". And I told her she should bring her burner phone.'

'How do you know she has one? Supplied by Hitchcock, you think?'

'I surmised it. We investigated the calls made on her usual phone, and they were all legitimate, so if she had been in contact with Hitchcock that would be the obvious method. She didn't deny having one.'

Redstone looked around. Although it was just mid-morning, the café was already crowded. Many of the other tables were occupied by families with young children and the occasional dog. Beyond the shrubs bordering the café area, groups of people were strolling amongst the trees and on the browned grass. Would anyone recognize the Home Secretary when she appeared?

A small woman in a wide-brimmed hat scraped back the vacant chair opposite Redstone and sat down.

'Well,' Redstone said, 'you've answered the question in my mind – nobody would recognize you. I hardly did myself. Hello.' He adjusted his cap.

Tavia gripped the edge of the table. 'Hello Mark, hello Gavin.'

'Greetings,' McKay said. 'Used your experience in amateur dramatics?'

'Yes, it helped me change my appearance. Actually it's helped me in my political career, when I appear in public. Much of politics is presentation.' She gave a wry smile. 'I see you're familiar with my time as a student.'

'I'm familiar with a lot about you. Would you like a drink before we start?'

'A Diet Coke would be nice.' She looked round. 'It's self-service. Shall I go and get one?' Redstone picked up that she was nervous, embarrassed, and afraid of what Hitchcock would do if she learned of this meeting. *So it was Hitchcock. He'd been right.*

'No, don't get up,' said McKay to Tavia. He flicked his head to his left. Suna, Clothier's assistant, was leaving a table and heading for the doorway leading to the counter.

'God, Gavin, how many people have you got here?' she said. 'And does that mean you're recording this?'

'Let's concentrate on why we're here. Tell us about the blackmail.'

'Oh, Christ.' She eyed Redstone. 'Do I have to explain in front of…'

'Yes,' said McKay.

'I have good knowledge of Hitchcock's nasty, devious tricks,' Redstone said. McKay gave him an almost imperceptible signal that he had got the message that it was Hitchcock.

'And it's important that you're in a position to tell Hitchcock anything she asks about Mark's mannerisms or whatever,' McKay said to Tavia. 'For reasons I'll explain.'

'So you know it was Valerie Hitchcock,' she said.

'Yes.'

'If I could add a word,' Redstone said, 'we're not here to judge your sexual morals.'

'Bizarrely,' she said, 'I don't believe I was immoral.' She sat up straight. 'It was after I'd been through my divorce, which had received a lot of press coverage. As you'll recall.'

Redstone didn't recall it at all, but didn't comment.

'I was still a backbench MP,' she continued. 'I met Valerie Hitchcock at a reception in the Commons. It was about a study we'd published on energy efficiency in pre-war housing. She was the Energy Permanent Secretary. She was charming, sympathetic, and seemed anxious to be helpful.' Tavia stopped, looked round, and cleared her throat.

'Go on,' said McKay.

'It's embarrassing.' Tavia adjusted her hat to shield her face. 'Very well. She invited me for a drink the following week. We both got a bit tipsy and let our hair down. At least, I thought she did. I certainly did. I told her how much I missed, well, male company. She said she knew of an organisation which helped people in my position. A respectable, discreet dating agency for, as she put it, people at the top. She'd give me details.'

She swallowed and played with a ring on her finger. McKay drummed his fingers on the table. Tavia opened her mouth to speak, but stopped as Suna appeared with her drink.

Tavia waited until Suna had walked off, and then took a gulp of the Coke.

'To cut a long story short,' she said, 'I met this charming man. We went out together a few times – theatre, galleries, dinner. We became close, and… and eventually he took me to a posh flat near Tate Modern.'

'And there?' McKay said.

She stared over McKay's shoulder. 'I found out later – much later – we were filmed. You know. Doing things.'

Redstone picked up her mental pictures of the escort, what she had done, and the interior of the flat. He felt embarrassed and sorry for her.

'And the flat was owned by Hitchcock,' he said.

'I suppose so. Anyway, after our… after the, er, encounter in the flat, the man broke off our relationship, and I heard no more until I became Home Secretary last year, when Michael got back in. Then a smartphone was posted through my letterbox. On the padded envelope was a printed message saying "texts". I switched on the phone and read the first text, which said I should look at the Gallery app. And there was the video.' She exhaled deeply. Redstone turned away so he wasn't picking up her memory of watching the film.

'We don't need to know the details,' said McKay. 'Anything else?'

'Yes, another text saying I should have the phone on at seven every morning. I guessed it was Hitchcock, and recognized her voice when she called the first time. She didn't deny it was her. It's been so wearing, I can't tell you. I keep hoping she won't phone, and when she doesn't, I'm sort of left on edge, and when she does, I feel – dirty.'

'How many times has she rung?' asked McKay.

'Five. The last twice were to instruct me to get information about you, Mark. I don't understand why. I had to find out if you were searching for her, or were interested in her.'

Tavia dug into her handbag and pulled out a phone.

'Here it is, Gavin. But I can't give it to you unless you can return it before tomorrow morning. I don't dare miss a call. I can't face that video going viral. I'd die of shame.'

'Understood.' McKay took the phone from her hand. 'I'll get it copied and back to you by early this afternoon.' He turned to Redstone.

'Tavia, I'm afraid the situation is much more serious than you've realised,' Redstone said.

Tavia jerked upright and gripped her hands together.

'One of the reasons I'm in Hitchcock's sights,' he said, 'is that I'm involved in the hunt for the terrorists. As you know, from that meeting with the PM and Michelle Clarke in Number Ten. And it seems that Hitchcock is part of the plot.'

'What! What!' She collapsed back in her chair. 'Oh, I've been complicit in…'

'You weren't to know,' McKay said. 'As a rule we don't tell ministers about operational matters. But now you can help us by feeding information to Hitchcock. And when I say information, I'm using the term loosely.'

'Of course. But, with respect to Mark here, what's his role in this?'

'I initially got involved because Michelle wanted me as a sort of go-between with the government,' Redstone said. 'You'll have noticed she's, well, a bit unworldly. And it developed from there.'

'You'd be surprised at the contribution Mark is able to make,' said McKay. Redstone nodded acknowledgement of the way McKay had got past the fact that his role was mind-reading.

'I've worked with Michael Jones and MI5 on a couple of other issues,' Redstone continued. 'In both cases we found that Hitchcock was acting against the national interest and using sexual blackmail to achieve her ends. We exposed her. As a result, she went from holding the government's highest official office to being a despised criminal. More reasons why she has it in for me.'

A new worry struck him. He turned to McKay. 'I assume Hitchcock got Tavia to contact me in the first place because she's looking for information to help her plan revenge. Do you think I need some sort of protection? I was pretty safe while Laura was living with me, but now…'

'Let's discuss that later,' said McKay. 'So, Tavia, are you in?'

'Seems I'm part of a pattern. Of course I'll help. But I'm scared it'll lead to Hitchcock leaking that video. What can you do to stop her?'

'Neutralise her. You're going to help us do that,' said McKay. 'As soon as we've arrested her, we'll grab her phone and delete the video.'

She grimaced. 'That's all I can hope for, I suppose,' she said. 'What do you want me to do?'

'First,' said Redstone, 'tell Hitchcock that you've now spoken to me three times, and I've shown no interest in her except a hint that there'd been history between us. You can say it's as though I believe she's now dead.'

'Yes, I can do that.'

'Second, tell her in passing that I mentioned that the hunt for the terrorists is now centred on Ilford. You can say I assumed you'd know anyway, since you're the Home Secretary.'

'Ilford. How do you know the terrorists are there?'

'If it seems appropriate, you can let it slip that it's through some complex work that Michelle did.'

'OK.'

'But you mustn't let her think we're associating her with the terrorism.'

'Understood. But why am I telling her about the Ilford angle?'

'We want it to get back to the terrorist group, to put them off guard. Because it isn't true. If they think MI5 are hunting in the wrong place they'll relax, which should help the hunt. Which is of course centred on the right place.'

'Makes sense. I won't ask where the right place is.'

'Good judgment,' said McKay. 'But there's a further thing we'd like you to try.'

'Well?'

'See if you can persuade Hitchcock to meet you in person.'

'Oh,' she said. 'I really don't want to—'

'It's important,' said McKay. 'Our aim is to find out where she is, and arrest her. It's in your own interest. She'll have that hold over you till we've got her.'

'So you'd have me followed, I suppose. Not sure I like that.'

'You won't know,' McKay said. 'Nor will the terrorists. We're not amateurs.'

'I'll do my best, but I doubt she'll agree. Why should she?'

'Evil people like to gloat over their victims. Listen, it's worth a try, and if she won't do it, we will locate her eventually by some other method. Starting with whatever information we can get from this.' He waved the smartphone he'd taken from her.

*

After Tavia had left, Redstone confirmed he'd picked up no thoughts which contradicted what she'd said.

He mentioned again his concern that Hitchcock would try to attack him. 'Like she did when she got those two thugs to attack Laura, and for the same reason. Revenge. That's what the whole thing seems to be about – Clodagh for Michael Jones's role in exposing her as an ex-terrorist and ruining her life, and Hitchcock for how Laura and I exposed her corruption and how Laura tried to execute her.'

'Remember, Clodagh was already using terrorist tactics against the British state, right from when she was a young woman,' McKay said. 'For her, at least, it must go further than revenge. Her whole life's been dominated by hatred of Britain.'

'So both of them are highly motivated and highly dangerous. And I'm no Laura. I can't defend myself like she did.'

‘Nor could most of us. OK, you make a good point. I’ll make sure you’re protected. You won’t notice the people we put on the job.’ He frowned. ‘Now you mention it, Hitchcock might want to have a go at me too. After all, I was with Laura when we tried to execute her. I’ll increase my own security.’

He stood up.

‘The sooner we can get them, the better. Especially because they’re presumably planning another atrocity.’

MONDAY 7TH AUGUST

Laura phoned as Redstone was at his desk taking a big bite from a bap he'd bought from the Italian sandwich bar round the corner.

'Thought I'd bring you up to speed,' she said. 'We're closing in on them. That phone Hitchcock gave the Home Sec had been rung by what we assume was Hitchcock's burner phone, and the mast it had used is in St Albans.'

'Wow! That's great. Carry on.'

'What are you eating?'

'Avocado and bacon bap.'

'Sounds delicious. I don't mean the sound of you eating it, of course. Back to Hitchcock. We've already collected a list of possible addresses. We got local estate agents to identify furnished upmarket properties which had been let over the last nine months. We eliminated those which are nearer another phone mast, and that narrowed the possibilities to about thirty.'

'Still a lot.'

'Yes, but we're correlating the list with other information. We're now down to a first-priority list of about twenty properties. We're looking into them one at a time.'

'How are you doing that? Just knocking on the door?'

'Not initially. We'd want to be armed and go in mob-handed if we think we've got the right place. We park near the property in a surveillance van, and monitor who comes and goes. That's already eliminated a dozen or so, for example if there are kids being taken on the school run. And one of our colleagues knocks on doors of neighbouring properties, posing as an Amazon delivery driver with a package with a fictitious name. When the occupants say it's not them, he asks if it could be the neighbour, and notes what they say.'

Redstone said, 'Isn't doing all this tricky while you're suspended?

'Oh, didn't anyone tell you? The suspension was lifted. Gavin pressed the CPS to make a rapid decision, and they decided there was no chance of a successful prosecution, to use the official jargon. In other words, the thugs who attacked me got what they deserved.'

'No, nobody did tell me – including you. Congratulations. You must be relieved.'

'Sorry, I should have… I assumed that now we're not together, you wouldn't find my employment status of much interest.'

'Are you barmy?' he said.

'I thought your attention would now be focused on Mary.'

'For goodness' sake, everyone seems to think she and I are spending every moment in each other's arms. It isn't like that. We're just two neighbours, enjoying some friendship. I'm one of her many friends.'

'Oh. Well, how are you?'

'I'm fine, thanks. A problem with our migraine cream project, but I expect we'll overcome it.'

'I suppose that's got you down a bit. I know how important the Smoothaway project is to you.'

'You're right, but drug development is never plain sailing. I'll get over it.'

'Well, best of luck.' Silence, and then she said, 'Mark, does your mind-reading make you feel less alone?'

'Interesting question.' He pondered. 'No, if anything I'd say it makes me feel more alone.'

'Why on earth is that?'

'It reinforces how other people's concerns aren't the same as mine. How we're all different.'

'Interesting,' she said. 'Do you think everyone feels alone?'

'I'm going to annoy you by giving a scientist's answer. Actually, a mathematician's. Do you know what a Venn diagram is?'

'Is it that thing with overlapping circles?'

'Yes. Each circle is a set of members with some common characteristic. So you might have one circle representing all MI5 officers, another representing all highly attractive women, and where they overlapped you'd find Laura Smith.'

'Flattery will get you everywhere, but what's your point?'

'I think each of us is a member of lots of different sets, but there's just one person where all those sets overlap. For example, I'm a man, a chemist, an entrepreneur, an ex-Department of Energy civil servant… and I bet I'm the only person who's in all those sets. So I'm alone as well as not being alone. True of all of us.' *If you add mind-reader, I'm definitely alone*, he thought.

'Very rational,' she said, 'but you've omitted the emotion. What a surprise.'

'No I haven't. I'm saying we can feel alone because in the end we all are. Even if we're members of lots of groups.'

'God, you can be exasperating. Do you feel more alone now I'm no longer, er, with you?'

'Oh.' *Was she fishing? What should he say?* 'Yes. Certainly. And I don't like it. What about you?'

'I'll let you use your scientific intelligence to work that out.'

'I… let's get onto safer ground. Back to your reinstatement.'

'Yes,' she said. 'I wasn't too worried, but it's good to be back. I need to be working in a team for this sort of operation. And to feel less alone.'

*

'Definitely time we moved on,' Clodagh said to Valerie.

'You know it's in hand. We'll be out in a couple of days.'

'Any chance of speeding it up? I'm getting nervous. I've seen a van parked down the road. Was there for hours, and I'm pretty sure there was someone in the back from the way it moved on its springs now and then.'

'Is that all?'

'No. I've seen an Amazon driver going round the area knocking on doors, and it was always the same guy. You rarely see a particular Amazon driver more than once.'

'But how would they have traced us to this area?' Valerie said.

'Good question. Any hints from your pet Home Secretary?'

'Last time I spoke to her, she said the security services had no idea where what they call "the terrorists" are hiding out.'

'She could be lying. I hope every time you've called her you've destroyed the phone you used. And that you've been using a different phone to talk to your Russian friend.'

'Of course,' said Valerie. 'You sure they can't trace us from the computer things you've been doing?'

'Certain. You want me to explain the methods I used to hide our location?'

'No, I believe you. So they couldn't have traced us, then.'

'In any case,' said Clodagh, 'we'll soon need a house with a basement.'

'I know, I know. We've discussed all this. Don't get your knickers in a twist. We'll be in the Barnet house on Wednesday. We can't get in there sooner.'

'My knickers, as you call them, aren't in a twist, but you can't ignore evidence. I wish we had a better handle on how close the MI5 people are to locating us. Are you sure Pitt doesn't know more than she was letting on?'

'I strongly doubt MI5 would have kept her in the loop. The opposite, in fact – the security chiefs keep UK ministers in the dark about so-called operational matters, which basically means anything of interest. They're typical arrogant self-important products of the British public school system.'

Clodagh flushed. 'I know exactly what you mean.'

Valerie stared at her, but Clodagh didn't elaborate.

'Well,' Valerie said, 'I suppose Pitt might know something, even if they didn't tell her. It's hard to keep secrets in Whitehall.'

'You should contact her again, then. Say, how about meeting her face to face? Give you a much better chance of prying the truth from her, and making sure she stays under our control.'

'Good idea. But suppose she's being monitored. Watched by the security services. Might be risky.'

'I'm sure we can work out a way of solving that problem.'

'OK,' Valerie said. 'I'll call her tomorrow morning.'

*

That evening, Sophie rang Redstone.

'I've managed to fix a date with Rhiannon,' she said. 'I'm going to be in England for a week – a sort of summer break. I'll be home to see you on Wednesday, stay a day or two, and then Rhiannon's invited me to stay in her flat for a couple of days. We're going to do some shopping.'

'It'll be great to see you. I'll tell Treacle to expect you. And I've got a personal issue I need to discuss with you – I need your advice.'

'Is it about your women?'

'I haven't got any women, as you put it. That's part of… let's discuss it when you come.'

'What about Mary?'

'For goodness' sake, I keep explaining… as it happens, I'm going into her house now. For a companiable dinner, and that's all.'

'Time will tell,' she said.

*

'Delicious,' Redstone said, wiping his lips on the white napkin. 'How do you get it to taste so good?'

'I add a tiny amount of caster sugar to some savoury dishes, like tonight's,' Mary said. 'Amazing what a difference it makes.'

'Ah. I'll try that.' He drank some wine. 'Mary, can I ask you a personal question? Sparked by something someone said to me today.'

'Depends how personal.'

'Fair enough. Tell me if it's too much. Would you say you feel alone?'

'Do you mean lonely? I don't. I've got lots of friends, my sister's family, the church… and anyway I like a bit of independence.'

'Ah,' he said. 'I suppose I do as well. But I didn't exactly mean that. More that there's no one else who feels the same feelings as you, has the same views…'

'Everyone must feel like that, surely. But it is nice to be able to chat to people about your feelings. You know, a problem shared…' She squinted at him. 'You sure the person who mentioned that wasn't actually asking about how you're getting on without Laura?' She sipped the wine Redstone had brought and nodded appreciatively.

'I do miss… never mind.'

'Do you miss her or, well, someone, anyone, to chat to over breakfast or… Oh, I shouldn't pry.'

'No, it's fine,' he said. 'Both.'

TUESDAY 8TH AUGUST

Clodagh sat outside a café in the underground shopping precinct at Canary Wharf, a shopping bag on her lap. She was wearing a headscarf and a long, flowered dress. A walking stick rested on the side of the chair.

'She's just gone past,' she said into her phone. 'Walking slowly, and dressed in a burka, as you told her. Two guys and a woman following at the same pace.' She looked down at a printed plan of the precinct. 'Call her and tell her to take the second corridor on the right, and then go into the ladies' restroom and wait in a cubicle for your next call. I'll drift along behind them.'

Three minutes later she phoned again.

'The female agent followed her in. Call Pitt and tell her to stay in a cubicle till you call again, and to deny that she's got anyone outside waiting for her.'

Clodagh waited a couple of minutes and then shuffled into the toilets, back bent. She nodded to the MI5 agent, who was washing her hands, and hobbled into a cubicle. Five minutes later she emerged. The agent was leaning on the wall by the washbasins.

'You still here?' Clodagh said in an Eastern European accent. 'Why you waiting? You up to no good?'

'Don't worry, madam,' the agent said. 'I'm waiting for my friend in that cubicle.' She pointed at a locked cubicle door.

'Or you one of those perverts,' Clodagh said. 'Hey, you in there – you got a friend out here waiting for you?'

'No,' said Tavia's voice, muffled by the cubicle door.

'I call police,' Clodagh said, taking out her phone.

The agent sighed. 'I *am*…' She shrugged, straightened up and walked out of the toilets. Clodagh followed her, found her lounging outside, and stared meaningfully. The agent muttered and disappeared round a corner. Clodagh went back into the toilets, and called Hitchcock again.

'Now tell her to come out, collect the bag, and go back in. She should take off the burka, put it in the bag, and put on the wig and the dress that are in the bag. Then she should leave the bag, walk out of the toilets like a disabled old woman, and turn left. You can then meet her and disappear inside that big store at the end.'

Five minutes later, Clodagh exited the toilets wearing the burka. She turned right and stopped to look in the window of a shop selling expensive watches. One of the male agents sauntered past, glancing at her. Clodagh walked into the shop. A couple of minutes later the agent also entered. Clodagh told the shop assistant in a Middle Eastern accent she wanted to browse, and the assistant should serve the agent first. The agent studied her carefully, told the assistant he'd changed his mind, and walked out.

Clodagh spent fifty minutes in the shop, eventually buying a Rolex with cash which she pulled out from under her burka. When she emerged from the shop there was no sign of any of the agents. She pulled out her phone.

'All OK?'

'Yes,' said Hitchcock.

'Good, See you back at the house. Oh, I've bought you a nice gift.'

*

'She was pretty scathing about the professionalism of our agents,' McKay said on the phone to Redstone, 'and I don't blame her. I've given them a good bollocking. Of course, they weren't helped by the way she enthusiastically acceded to Hitchcock's orders. I got the impression she enjoyed the acting role, despite everything.'

'And it's a bit of a coincidence that Hitchcock wanted to meet her just when we wanted her to meet Hitchcock,' Redstone said. 'Too much of a coincidence? Do you think Tavia could be playing us?'

'Can't rule it out. She is a politician, after all. But what she said ties in with my agents' reports. My instinct is she's telling us the truth, more or less.'

'I suppose the other woman, the one who took the burka, was Clodagh,' said Redstone.

'Yes, that's my guess. Another reason the agents deserved a good bollocking. We could have got both of them if they'd done their job properly. I've instigated a review of our training for that sort of operation. I'm ashamed.'

'Oh well, spilt milk and all that. How did Hitchcock react when Tavia told her about my lack of interest in her?'

'Pleased, but suspicious.'

'And the Ilford lead?'

'Octavia said she seemed mildly interested. It might keep them off guard.'

*

The Smoothaway team sat round Redstone's table.

'The analysis hasn't come up with any obvious cause for the problem,' David said. 'The nerve membrane seems to have lost its normal structure, but none of the chemicals we included in the Smoothaway cream is interacting with the membrane. It's a mystery.'

'That's why we're here,' said Rosie. 'For you to solve the mystery.' She gave a weak smile.

'No pressure, then,' Redstone said. 'Let's give it a go. We'll start by listing all the chemicals in the membrane and in the Smoothaway cream. Rosie – could you write up everything on the whiteboard?'

Rosie wrote up two lists, one of the chemicals in the Smoothaway formulation and one listing the components of the nerve membrane. The rest of the group stared at them.

'And that's the lot,' Redstone said. 'You're sure?'

She looked at her colleagues, who mumbled agreement.

'I can't see it,' Redstone said. There's nothing here that would disrupt the normal structure of the nerve membrane. And yet there must be.' He picked up a glass of water and drank deeply. He'd been feeling dehydrated after drinking too much wine the previous evening. He stared at the glass and jerked upright.

'Ah!' he said. 'You've left out an important component of the membrane!'

'I don't think so,' said David. 'We're used to dealing with these materials.'

Redstone grinned. 'You've omitted the simplest component because it's everywhere, and it's everywhere for good reason.'

'You mean water?' Rosie said.

'Exactly. It's not some inert solvent. It's essential for giving the membrane components their structure. It's bound to several of the components. Without it the membrane would fall to bits.'

'But we're not removing water,' said Rosie.

'In a sense we are,' said David. 'Mark's right. These two chemicals are hydrophilic.' He pointed to the third and fifth chemicals on Rosie's list. 'They love water. Maybe in combination they're sucking some away from the membrane molecules.'

'Exactly,' said Redstone. 'Can you devise some experiments to test that idea? Might be rubbish, of course, but if it's right, we'll need to work out what to do about it.'

'No problem,' said David, and simultaneously Rosie said, 'Of course.'

*

'One of your many admirers on the line,' said Joanne. 'Sue Abercrombie.'

'Oh,' said Redstone. 'Does she know I'm here?'

'Yes. I didn't know you—'

'Never mind. Put her through.'

'Hello,' Sue said. 'This is a personal call, but I had to go through your company because I didn't have your mobile number.'

So she wants me to give it to her. 'That's OK,' he said. 'What can I do for you?'

'Well, it was good chatting to you the other evening, and I wondered if you'd like to repeat the experience. There's a new restaurant in Battersea. Would you like to join me for a meal some time? My treat.'

'Do you mean you'll claim it on expenses from MI5?'

'Eh?' she said. 'Sorry, I don't get the joke.'

'Not really a joke. I found out you work for MI5, and I assume that's why you chatted to me at Tavia's do. Keeping an eye on me for them, were you?'

She spoke in a strained voice.

'Someone's been feeding you a pack of lies. If you don't want to talk to me, just say so.'

God, maybe I got it all wrong. 'Sue, I'm truly sorry if I… I don't know what to say. I was told that you work for MI5, and you reported what happened when I spoke to Tavia.'

'I don't work for MI5, as you put it. I sometimes pass them information I think they might find useful, in exchange for insights on political issues. I thought odd behaviour by the Home Secretary was something they might want to know. They *are* responsible for our security.'

'Oh. I owe you a deep apology,' he said. 'I'm very sorry to have been so rude. Are you free to meet for a drink this evening so I can apologise in person?'

'No, let's forget it.' Silence. 'Oh, all right.'

‘Thanks.’ *Must be somewhere I can wear my cap.* ‘How about the Albert in Victoria Street? Is that convenient?

‘Very. 6:30?’

*

Redstone walked down Victoria Street, passing Westminster Cathedral. So different from Westminster Abbey further down the road, both in its construction and its relatively young age. He liked the complex design, with its strong horizontal cream lines in the terracotta-coloured, slightly exotic brickwork.

A few hundred yards, and there was the Albert pub – a narrow building, four storeys high, with an elaborate cornice at the edge of the roof. Each upper storey had overflowing floral displays in window boxes. The backdrop of much taller, ultra-modern office blocks made it look even more attractive than it would have seemed before the new buildings were erected.

He switched on his cap, opened the dark wooden door, and was greeted by a smell of beer and an ocean of noise from the crowds of drinkers crammed together. He stepped inside and recoiled in horror at the cacophony of thoughts and emotions. He ripped off the cap, switched it to shielding mode, and jammed it back on his head. He hadn’t been in a big dense crowd since he’d developed the thought-reading ability, and wondered what it would be like without the cap at all – but he was scared to try. So much for the best-laid plans.

He pushed through the crowd, scanning the room, but couldn’t spot her. He recalled there were a couple of smaller rooms behind the bar, and manoeuvred through the shouting drinkers blocking the doorway, walked through the narrow passage, and found to his relief a calmer atmosphere – but still no Sue.

He looked at his watch. She should be here by now. He found a side exit, went out, and scanned the groups of drinkers standing on the pavement, also shouting at each other – but no Sue.

He pushed past the groups in the alley and went to the front of the pub. He'd wait a few minutes and then give up. Maybe Sue was so angry about his MI5 accusations that she'd changed her mind about the meeting.

After another quarter of an hour, he decided to give up and go home. Rather than get jammed in the crowds in Victoria station, he'd enjoy a pleasant walk through the quiet back streets to Pimlico, a much more civilised way of getting out of the area. He passed the Home Office and stopped at a busy junction for the lights to change.

Someone was shouting behind him, but the sound failed to reach his conscious mind. Running footsteps thumped behind him, and someone hit him on the shoulder. He whirled round, expecting a confrontation, but found Sue, panting hard. She tried to speak, but failed. She pointed back at the Home Office, and bent double, still panting. He didn't know what she meant.

'Take it easy,' he said. 'I can wait till you've recovered your breath.' He looked round for somewhere to sit. 'Ah, there's a coffee bar over there with seating outside. Why don't we grab a table, and I'll get you some water.'

They crossed the road and she collapsed into a plastic chair. 'Must do more exercise,' she gasped. 'Water would be great.'

He went inside, switched his cap back on, and returned with two bottles of water. Sue drank deeply.

'Thanks,' she said. 'I needed that. I'm sorry I didn't make it to the pub in time. I didn't have your number to warn you.'

'My fault,' he said. 'Must rectify that.'

She drank some more water. 'I need to explain why I was detained.'

She's genuinely upset that she couldn't make it in time.

'I got a strange phone call from your friend the Home Secretary,' she continued, 'as I was about to leave for the pub. She wanted to speak to me urgently and in the strictest confidence. Well, I'm a political journalist. What's a girl to do in that situation?'

'Go on.'

'My office is just over there,' she gestured to the back of the coffee bar, 'so it was easy for me to come across to the Home Office. We sat in her office, no civil servants. She was nervous. She said she wanted my advice about a very sensitive issue.'

'Do ministers often tell you sensitive things?'

'No, not really. They sometimes pretend things are sensitive, to make themselves seem important, but it's normally stuff I already know. And it's usually the men who do that rather than the women.'

'Before you go any further,' he said, 'you're not about to reveal some state secret to me, are you?'

'No, certainly not. Anyway, I suspect you know more state secrets than I do, with your record of working with MI5 and the Prime Minister.'

She's proud she's done her homework, and hopes I'm impressed.

'I couldn't possibly comment,' he said, with a smiled acknowledgment of her research.

She smiled back. 'The next thing Tavia said was that it was highly personal. She wanted to know… well, now I think I shouldn't tell you anything more. Sorry.'

Tavia was worried about sexual pictures of her appearing in the media. Wanted Sue's advice.

'Was she asking you in your capacity as a journalist?' Redstone said.

'Yes. Of course, she knows several journalists, so I'm not sure why she asked me.'

'Maybe you've shown yourself to be trustworthy.'

'I'd like to think so.'

'Good for you,' he said. 'If she asked you about a highly personal issue in your capacity as a journalist, I guess it was about a fear of the issue appearing in the media. Something embarrassing.'

'Wow. Maybe you should have been a detective. Certainly in the right ball park.'

‘OK, I’m not asking you to tell me any more about what the issue is, but what was your advice?’

‘I said these things always come out in the end. And since the possibility of it coming out was bothering her, she’d do better by controlling the release herself. I tried to persuade her it wasn’t all that bad. In fact, in some ways she could use it to her advantage – stress her human side, present herself as a victim deserving sympathy. I offered to help.’

‘How did she react?’

‘I’m not sure. She said she was very grateful, but she seemed unconvinced. I guess she’ll go away and think it through.’

‘Are you going to tell MI5?’he said.

‘Why, do you think I should?’

‘Well, you haven’t told me enough to allow me an informed view, but if the Home Secretary is in a position to be blackmailed, for example, someone should make sure the security service knows, don’t you think?’

‘Oh. You’re right, of course. Damn, that puts me in an awkward position.’

‘You could tell them what you told me. I don’t think you broke any confidences.’

‘Yes, I’ll do that. Thanks. I’ll ring them tomorrow.’

A waiter appeared, coughed politely, and removed the empty water bottles.

‘He wants us to go, so he can close up,’ said Redstone.

‘Mind-reader, are you?’

‘Certainly.’

‘Righto. Shall we adjourn to that restaurant?’ She pointed to an Italian restaurant two doors down the road.

‘Yes, good idea. Let’s see if they’ve got a table.’

‘It’s quite upmarket,’ she said, ‘so…’ She gestured with her chin to his cap. He gave a sheepish grin and removed it.

After they'd ordered, she toyed with her bracelet and then looked him in the eye.

'Can I talk to you about when we met at Tavia's do?'

'Of course,' he said, 'but there's no need to explain further – I apologise again for getting the wrong end of the stick.'

'Please bear with me – I've rehearsed this in my mind, and I want to… well, first, what do you think I saw when I noticed you by the windows?'

'I don't understand. You saw me standing there.'

'Yes, but what do you think went through my mind?'

'Er… tall man, dark greying hair, back to the room. Is that what you mean?'

'You're getting there.'

'Maybe a bit of a loner? Not one of the main crowd? Someone you didn't recognize?'

'Good. And you had a slight smile on your face.'

'Oh yes, I think I was amused by how Victoria appeared in the name of everything I was looking at.'

'And what do you think an unattached female investigative journalist would do in that situation? Me, for example?'

'Investigate, I suppose,' he said, flattered. 'Go over, find out more about me. Chat. But I was also told afterwards that you were on MI5's payroll. At least, that's what I thought I was told. Turns out I was wrong, but—'

'Yes, you were wrong. I'm not on their payroll. I'm just someone on their list of contacts, someone who can feed them snippets I pick up. They don't tell me secrets, of course, but in exchange they do give me useful pointers to stories, now and then. That's how it works with several journos.'

'Sue, I believe you totally. I apologise again. Can we put it behind us?'

'Of course,' she said, reaching over and touching his hand. 'Let's talk about something completely different. Tell me about your travels, as a scientist. You must have been to some interesting places.'

WEDNESDAY 9TH AUGUST

'You been plotting with Sue Abercrombie?' asked McKay on the phone.

'Quite the contrary,' Redstone said, giving a thumbs up to Joanne as she made a sign offering a cup of tea. 'I assume you're talking about Tavia revealing all. Oh, unfortunate choice of phrase. You know what I mean.'

'Yes. First I get called in by our esteemed Home Secretary, but maybe not so esteemed for much longer, to tell me she's decided to tell the press about the video. And then I'm told by one of my people that Sue thinks Tavia might be open to blackmail, but can't say any more.'

Redstone recounted his discussion with Sue the previous evening. 'Did you try to persuade Tavia not to tell all?' he asked McKay.

'I did, but to no avail. God knows what's going to happen now. I'm seeing the Prime Minister shortly.'

'What's Tavia going to do? Just recount what happened, or publish the video too?'

'Seems she's putting herself in Sue's hands on the strategy. I'm guessing Sue will advise getting the video out immediately, to avoid prurient speculation about what it might contain.'

'Is Tavia going to name Hitchcock?'

'She says she didn't tell Sue who was behind it, so I don't think so. I advised her not to. I said she should just say the police and security services are aware of what happened, are tracking down the blackmailer, and are confident there's no threat to national security, thanks to Tavia's brave decision to go public.'

'Think the PM will sack her?' Redstone asked.

'No. I've already had a word with Roger Feast, and his view is that sacking her would send a signal to anyone else in that sort of position that they should keep shtum. And the PM will judge that the optics with the general public would be better if he kept her in post.'

'Good. My guess is that the Opposition wouldn't use it against her either, for similar reasons.'

'Agreed.'

'I bet Hitchcock will react violently, perhaps physically, but certainly on social media.'

'Yes,' said McKay, 'we think so too. We're upping Tavia's security, but I think you can help on the social media side. I'd like to turn a threat into an opportunity.'

'What on earth can I do?' Redstone asked. 'I'm the last person to be able to help on social media.'

'You have a special relationship with Michelle Clarke,' said McKay, 'and she's proved herself the best at tracing where the terrorists send their messages from. I'm pretty sure Hitchcock will get Clodagh to send out posts about Tavia. If Michelle is prepared for that, she might be able to trace the source of the posts. GCHQ say it's impossible, but your Cambridge friend might know a way. Could you ask her?'

'Sure. What am I allowed to tell her?'

'She's proved herself trustworthy. Tell her anything you like.'

*

Redstone stepped down from the air-conditioned train and winced at the heat. The forecasters had said it would be the hottest day of the year so far, and it certainly felt like it. He'd come to Cambridge for old times' sake. Had he made the right decision? Maybe he should have just phoned.

He hastened into the shade. At the station exit, he considered abandoning his plan to retrace the steps he'd made so often as a student all those years ago. The scorching sun would make the walk less pleasant than he'd hoped. But he decided to stick to plan A and walk to Michelle's college, St Catharine's. He pulled down the brim of his cap and set off. When he'd been a student at Cambridge, the station area had been unattractive and rundown, as in so many places throughout the world. But now it was being modernised, with new office blocks, a complex one-way road system, and a scattering of coffee shops. He approved.

He made his way down Station Road, past building works, to Hills Road. The heat was getting worse. No shade on the pavement. Sweating heavily, he was starting to regret not taking a cab. Walking in the glare and sun's rays reminded him of travels in Greece and Turkey during summer vacations while he was a research student. That was where he'd met Kate. They'd ended up holding hands everywhere, and had been so happy back at Cambridge.

He turned into Lensfield Road. Ah, the chemistry department. He recalled the smell of the organic chemistry labs, the thrill he'd experienced when first seeing a pure colour through a spectrometer, the pride when he'd held aloft a round-bottomed flask containing beautiful crystals of caffeine he'd isolated from tea.

He turned into Trumpington Street. Not far now, thank God. He'd made a big mistake in not getting a taxi. The sun was glaring straight down on him, and walking was becoming an effort.

Five more minutes and he reached the unpretentious mellow brick buildings of St Catharine's, unique in Cambridge with its main court open to the road. The burly man behind the counter in the porters' lodge eyed him suspiciously.

'Would you like me to direct you to some washrooms before you go to Dr Clarke?' he said. 'If I may say so, sir, you're looking rather… hot.'

Redstone realised he was covered in sweat, and his shirt was dripping wet.

'You wouldn't have a shirt I could borrow? he said.

'I can sell you a college T-shirt,' the porter said. 'XL, I suppose.'

*

Redstone sat opposite Michelle in an armchair in her room, which overlooked an attractive small courtyard. She'd made no comment about his appearance.

'I don't see how it can be done,' she said. 'Messages which appear on social media platforms are on the websites of the social media companies. Only the platforms themselves could track who posts messages. Maybe I could do it if I hacked into the social media systems, but that would be difficult, if not impossible. They have highly sophisticated protection.'

She stopped, and sat gazing at the wall. He waited patiently. She turned back to him.

'What about this video that's at the heart of the blackmail?' she said. 'Is the Home Secretary going to publish it?'

'I don't think she's decided yet,' Redstone said.

'If she doesn't, will the enemy?'

'Probably.'

'I wonder how they'd do it. If it's a big file, as videos often are, they might have to post a link to it.'

'Yes, I've seen that done.'

'So the file itself would be on some other system,' she said. 'There's a slight possibility that I could extract some relevant information from it.'

'Ah. Given the nature of the file, it wouldn't be on a common platform like YouTube. Where would they put a, well, pornographic file?'

'There's a big choice for legitimate porn, but for a file like that it would be some small host somewhere. Increases my chance of getting information from it.'

'Great,' he said. 'I'll feed what you've said back to Gavin McKay, and see if he wants to try to persuade the Home Secretary not to publish it herself.'

*

Redstone trudged up the road from his local Tube station. The heat was now less intense, and the temperature was pleasant in the long shadows. He opened his front door. The house felt less stuffy than he'd expected – Sophie must have arrived and opened the windows. He perked up and hastened through to the back garden, to find Sophie and Zena sitting on the lawn in the shade of the cherry tree, wine glasses in hand and a plate of fruit between them.

'Dad!' Sophie cried. 'You're early!' She scrambled to her feet, rushed over to Redstone and enveloped him in a fierce hug. He kissed her hair. He sensed unconditional love, and feelings of wanting to protect him while wanting to be protected by him – his best experience since being able to read thoughts.

He beamed. 'I've come straight from a meeting in Cambridge,' he said. 'Lovely to see you, darling.'

She released him and stood back. 'Is that why you're wearing that strange outfit?' She gestured at his T-shirt.

'Yes. I got too hot and had to… I must go upstairs and get showered and changed. You look really well. Everything OK?'

'Can I have a hug too?' Zena said, coming up to Redstone. She was wearing a cropped halter top and very short shorts.

'No, Zena,' he said. 'Not dressed like that.'

'Oh, sorry, I—'

'Zena,' said Sophie, 'I need to spend some quality time alone with Dad. So if you could…'

‘Sure. See you later.’ Zena picked up a bag and walked back into the house.

Redstone slumped down on the grass, and Sophie arranged herself beside him. He asked her about her journey, Oskar, her social life, her work.

‘And I wanted to talk to you about Laura,’ he said. He recounted the conversation he’d had with Laura about being alone.

‘Oh, Dad,’ Sophie said. ‘I can’t read her mind. Do you want her to come back?’

‘I was much happier when she was here,’ he said.

‘Not quite a straight answer, Dr Redstone. Do you mean you could be as happy with any woman?’

‘No, of course not. I… I just don’t want Laura to come back and be unhappy again. Wouldn’t be good for either of us.’

‘Well, you know what I’m going to advise, don’t you?’

‘Er… talk to her?’

‘Got it in one.’

‘I don’t want to do that. Doesn’t seem right.’

‘But—’

‘Sophie, Laura left here for a good reason, and it was only three weeks ago. I’m not going to put her under any pressure.’

‘Up to you.’ She glanced at the fence. ‘I gather you don’t see a future with Mary.’

‘I know it sounds like a cliché, but she and I are just good friends.’

‘In your eyes, maybe. What does she think?’

‘I don’t know what other people are thinking. Nobody can.’ *Liar. But what else can I say?*

‘You don’t believe that,’ she said. ‘Most of us get an idea of what others are thinking. You’re not totally incompetent at it. Despite the image you like to project.’

‘Ouch. Well, I think Mary feels the same as I do.’

‘You mentioned this woman Sue the other day. There’s also the Home Secretary, who seems to have an interest in you. What about them?’

‘You can write off the Home Secretary. That turned out to be… well, it wasn’t about, er, an attraction.’

‘And Sue?’

‘I’ve only met her twice. Be reasonable.’

‘In your mind’s eye, which could you envisage living here with you – Sue or Laura?’

‘This conversation is getting ridiculous,’ he said. He tugged at his T-shirt. ‘I’m going to get washed and changed. I’ll be back in fifteen minutes, and you can tell me your news while I drink a nice glass of cold wine. And we can discuss what to do about food this evening, and your plans with Rhiannon. And we won’t talk about my love life.’

*

Later that evening, Redstone’s phone rang.

‘It’s Laura,’ he said to Sophie.

‘Can I speak to her?’ Sophie said.

‘Yes, but—’

Sophie grabbed the phone from Redstone’s hand. ‘Hi Laura. It’s Sophie. Just visiting the old man. How are you?’

Redstone couldn’t make out Laura’s response.

‘Well,’ Sophie said, ‘that’s good, but not good enough. Missing Dad at all? Doesn’t feel right without you here. Treacle misses you, and so does someone else who lives here.’ She listened and turned to Redstone. ‘She says nobody can foresee the future, and you have your good points. She wants to talk to you in private. I’ll disappear.’ She handed over the phone and walked out of the kitchen.

‘Sorry about that,’ Redstone said, ‘but you know what she’s like. Got some news?’

‘Yes, but it’s not great,’ said Laura. ‘We’ve found where Hitchcock and Clodagh were staying, but they’ve gone, with no evidence where to. We’re now certain it’s Hitchcock – they cleaned the place thoroughly, but you can’t get rid of every trace, and we found a hair with DNA that matches traces we found in Hitchcock’s old flat.’

‘How do you know it wasn’t Clodagh’s hair?’ he said. ‘We speculated she’d been staying in Hitchcock’s flat too.’

‘Er… we assumed it was her because the hair was dyed black, which we know Hitchcock does, but I suppose Clodagh might dye hers too. Good point, but it doesn’t matter – it’s the same duo.’

‘Maybe you can get your American cousins to get hold of Clodagh’s DNA somewhere. Should be easy.’

‘Good idea. Anyway, the trouble is we don’t know where they are now. I know you told Gavin this afternoon that Michelle might be able to trace them if they release the sex video, rather than Octavia Pitt herself doing it, so we’re hoping Octavia agrees. Currently that’s our best hope. If I were in Octavia’s shoes, I’d not release it myself. If it’s just on some porn website it’s more difficult for the media to republish extracts of it without looking total shits.’

‘Any idea when she’s going to tell the world?’ he said.

‘Probably tomorrow, Gavin said. It’s being handled by a journalist Octavia knows. Sue Abercrombie. I suppose it’s not the sort of thing you can get your usual press office to handle.’

‘Yes, I’ve met Sue. She told me Tavia had contacted her, though she didn’t tell me any details. She didn’t know I already knew it all.’

‘Oh, you’ve met her, have you?’ Laura said. ‘Get on well?’

‘Yes, actually. Do you know her? She told me she has dealings with MI5 sometimes.’

‘I can’t tell you operational information. I assume you’re not giving away any secrets to her. Learning any from her? Any juicy thoughts?’

‘I told you, I’m not using the cap for anything personal.’

‘You don’t have to use the cap if your head’s close to the other person’s, as I know only too well. So I repeat – any juicy thoughts?’

‘Laura…’

‘Sorry. Shouldn’t have said that. I’ve been working flat out, and I’m pretty tired.’

‘Give yourself a break. Take a day off. How about going to the seaside tomorrow?’

‘You mean with you?’

‘Yes,’ he said. ‘We could drive out to the Essex coast, or take the train down to Brighton, for example.’

‘Er… I’m not sure that would be a good idea.’

‘Why not?’

‘Well, either we’re together, or we’re not. And we’re not.’

‘I don’t see why it has to be so black and white,’ he said. ‘Please think about it.’

THURSDAY 10TH AUGUST

'I had no idea Essex could be like this,' Laura said. They stood outside a small Gothic-style church with a stubby square tower surmounted by a pyramidal steeple. The church was set in small well-tended gardens. All the four benches at the front of the gardens were occupied by elderly people basking in the morning sun. It all seemed a long way from the world of terrorist attacks.

'The water is that way,' he said, pointing down the hill. 'It's not quite the seaside I promised you – the town's on the Blackwater estuary, and the actual sea is a mile or two further east. But it's so attractive, and pretty unspoilt.'

'Good choice. Should we go down to the water?'

'Definitely.'

They strolled down Maldon's narrow main street. Most of the shops and pubs were small two-storey buildings of varying ages, faced in white or cream render.

'Weather's a bit different from yesterday's,' Redstone said. 'The temperature's perfect.'

'Yes. Let's find somewhere to have a coffee outside.'

They nabbed a table in an irregularly shaped pub garden and Redstone went inside to order the drinks.

'They'll bring them,' he said as he sat down opposite Laura.

'That cap is switched off, isn't it?' she said.

'Yes, I'm wearing it because of the sun, not to read your thoughts. What *are* your thoughts?'

'That's a novel way of finding out,' she said. 'I'm feeling more relaxed than I have for ages. Thanks for bringing me out here.'

'It's doing me good too. Things have been piling up. The migraine project, the terrorist stuff, the mind-reading, being…

Anyway, it's been great to see Sophie, and to be able to take a day off here. With you, if I'm allowed to say that.'

She frowned. 'Mark, I enjoy your company, but this mind-reading has got under my skin. I'm a pretty private person, I suppose.'

'I understand. Can we agree to stay friends, at least, so we can spend days like this together now and then?'

'That's all very well,' she said, 'but what happens when you get a new partner?'

A waitress appeared with their drinks, smiled at them and walked off.

'No sign of that happening,' he said. 'Getting a new partner. Not sure I want one, anyway.'

'You could have made a date with that woman. She fancied you. You need to be more… oh, I don't know.' She looked away.

'That's not me,' he said, 'and you know it. How would you have reacted if she'd been a man smiling at you?'

'I'm not in the market. I'm enjoying the freedom of being on my own. For now, anyway. Aren't you?'

'Alone but not lonely, you mean?'

'I suppose so,' she said.

'No, I can't say I am enjoying it. I know I'm a nerd, but I like to be able to chat to someone about my problems, or about something good I've seen or experienced… don't you feel the same?'

'There's no ideal life,' she said.

'I couldn't agree more. Let's go down to the estuary.'

*

Laura put down her cutlery and gazed at the row of Thames barges – big old wooden boats with tall masts, which were lined up on the quayside outside the pub window.

‘Can’t beat fish and chips,’ she said. ‘Poor you, having to stay off the beer. I…’ Her phone rang.

She listened.

‘The Home Secretary has put out her statement. Without the video, as we hoped.’

‘Has Michelle been told?’

‘Yes. She’s working with GCHQ to trace the video if it comes out.’

‘Won’t take long for the press to react,’ he said. ‘I suppose Hitchcock won’t find out till she reads about it, like the rest of us.’

Laura studied her phone. ‘Nothing in the media yet,’ she said. ‘I think we’d better go home. You can drop me at a Tube station. I may be needed at Thames House soon – with a bit of luck.’

*

Redstone glanced at a white van parked outside Mary’s house, opened his front door and heard the TV. Sophie was watching a news channel.

‘Hi Dad,’ she said, kissing his cheek. ‘How’d you get on? Have a good day?’

‘Yes, thanks. Something in the news?’

‘Heaven’s sake, I want to know how you got on with Laura. Is she moving back in?’

‘We had a good time together, but she’s not changed her mind about moving back. I’d say she’s conflicted, but that might be wishful thinking.’ He saw a picture of Tavia on the TV. ‘Ah, can I listen to this?’

The Home Secretary’s statement said that after her divorce three years ago, and before becoming a minister, she’d had a brief liaison with a man to whom she’d been introduced. Their personal encounters were covertly filmed by the person who’d made the introduction, who turned out to be a blackmailer. Subsequently the blackmailer had threatened to release the video online unless the Home Secretary provided information about a certain individual. That person was not a public figure, not in the government and did not work for it.

She did provide innocuous information once, but when pressed for more, she had informed the security service, who told her the blackmailer was a suspect in the recent spate of terrorist attacks. She had then actively co-operated with the security service in an attempt to trace the whereabouts of the suspect, but the operation had failed. After discussion with the security service, she'd decided to issue this statement, thus removing the leverage over her the suspect might believe they had. She recognized that the suspect might now release the video, but it was a price she was prepared to pay. She asked the public to recognize that she had done nothing immoral or against the public interest, had the full support of the security services and the Prime Minister, and intended to continue to work assiduously to keep the country safe.

The Prime Minister had in parallel issued a statement praising Octavia Pitt for her courage and honesty, and affirming she had his full confidence and would continue in the office of Home Secretary.

The immediate reactions of the press were of support for Octavia, but intense interest in who the blackmailing terrorist and the 'mystery individual' might be. So far there was no indication that the video had been published.

Redstone sat down heavily.

'Dad, you've gone pale,' Sophie said. 'What's the matter? You feeling ill?'

'No, it's – nobody warned me. I… I need to take advice, I suppose.'

'What are you talking about? Why should they have warned… oh. Are you saying you're the mystery individual?' She sat down opposite him.

'Yes. Sophie, I'll tell you some of what's going on, but you have to keep it to yourself. OK?'

'I promise,' she said, leaning over the table and pressing his hand.

'You remember I had a series of, let's say, bad interactions with a woman called Valerie Hitchcock?'

'I do. Did she not go to jail and then get out and become Cabinet Secretary for a short period?'

'No, she didn't go to jail. Something went wrong with the judicial system. And yes, she did become Cabinet Secretary, till she was exposed as having risen to high places through repeated use of sexual blackmail. That's not a secret. Certainly not a state secret.'

'Ah, let me guess,' Sophie said excitedly. 'The thing that went wrong with the judicial system was that she blackmailed key people. A judge? A prosecutor? A juror?'

'I'm not telling you any more, because it didn't come out.'

'Damn. Very well, guessing further – when you said she was exposed, it was you who did the exposing.'

'Not me personally, but I was part of the group who were involved.'

'It's no secret that you were part of the group working behind the scenes. So was Laura, wasn't she?'

'You know I can't tell you about Laura's work, Sophie.'

'I'll take that as a yes. So are you saying Valerie Hitchcock is who the Home Secretary described as the suspect for the terrorist attacks, and is the person who's been blackmailing her? And it was for information on you?'

'Yes. And that's certainly confidential. MI5 don't know what Hitchcock does or doesn't know we know, if you follow, and they want to keep her in the dark as much as possible. I'm telling you only because it links back to me being the so-called mystery person.'

'But I was under the impression – not sure why – I thought Hitchcock had died last year.'

'You're not alone,' he said. 'But apparently she didn't.'

'Why would she want to know things about you? And if she did, why ask the Home Secretary, of all people? Ah, that's why the Home Secretary got in touch with you, isn't it. It wasn't your magnetic personality and incredibly good looks, both of which I've inherited, of course, though in a feminine version.'

'You have indeed inherited those qualities. From your mother. Yes, that was why Tavia got in contact with me, to enable her to answer Hitchcock's questions about me.'

'But you haven't said why Hitchcock would have any interest in you.'

'I'm not in her head. You'd have to ask her, though I sincerely hope you're never in a position to do that.'

'Oh, come on, Dad. If you don't tell me, I'm just going to guess.'

'Sophie, you know there's a limit on what I can say.'

'Only if you're involved in something secret. So I deduce you are.'

'No comment.'

'Blimey,' she said. 'You're at it again. In with the secret crowd, I mean. Did Laura get you involved?'

'No comment.'

'Was Hitchcock behind the attack on Laura? The one that nearly got Laura prosecuted for murder?'

'How did you know about the attack?' Redstone asked. 'And Laura wasn't nearly prosecuted. Far from it.'

'Dad, you know there's a grapevine of the women in your life – me, Laura, Rosie, Joanne. Well, was Hitchcock behind the attack?'

'I don't really know.'

'But you sort of know. So Hitchcock is the terrorist, and is after you and Laura, and you're part of the anti-terrorist team for some obscure reason. Why on earth did Laura drag you into that?'

'Sophie, you've shown yourself to be very intelligent, not that it comes as a surprise. You've worked out a lot. But I'm not going to tell you anything more, and it's vital that you keep out of this. These terrorists have already killed and maimed many innocent people. They wouldn't hesitate to do the same to you if you get in their way.'

'Understood, Dad. But what about you? Aren't you at risk?'

'The security services are protecting me.'

'I haven't seen anyone,' she said, looking around.

'No, I was promised we wouldn't see them. But I did notice a parked van outside when I came in.'

'Oh yes. Now you mention it, I did wonder why it was there. I assumed Mary was having work done. Well, that's good. I suppose. Be careful, won't you.'

'Now that I might be in the limelight, I suppose I'd better double-check,' he said. 'I'm going to talk to someone I know about the press aspects, and then someone else about the security angle.'

He picked up his phone to call Sue, but realised they'd still not exchanged numbers. Perhaps he could find hers on the internet. A quick search, and there was her personal website, with a contact number.

'Hi,' he said. 'It's Mark Redstone.'

'Thank heavens!' she said. 'I didn't have your…we forgot—'

'I know.'

'I tried to contact you this morning. When I realised I didn't have your mobile number I called your company. A woman told me you were out, and asked if she could help. Naturally she wouldn't give me your number. I decided it was too sensitive for me to leave a message, so I didn't.'

'I assume you're talking about the reference to me in Tavia's statement,' he said.

'Yes. She insisted on giving what she described as the full picture. She claimed she didn't want anything to come out later which could allow people to say she'd kept something back, though I felt there might be some other reason too. Maybe she doesn't like the way you spoke to her at your party. If it's any consolation, you're not the only one who's peeved. I assume you are peeved?'

'More than peeved. Who else is upset?'

'MI5. Maybe she has it in for Gavin McKay as well. They're pretty unhappy that their operation to trace the blackmailer is described as a failure. Or described at all, actually.'

'Not surprising. But reporters will dig around to find out who the mystery individual is, and work out it's me.'

'Yes, I warned Tavia. But she was adamant.'

'What's more, there's one person who knows who it was and would be very happy to tell the media if doing so would cause me trouble. That's the blackmailer.'

'Ah. She didn't think of that, and nor did I. Does that mean you know who the blackmailer is?'

'Er… I'm afraid I can't answer that.'

'So you do know,' she said. 'I suppose it must be someone you've crossed swords with in the past. I should be able to work it out with a bit of research. In fact, I should have thought of that before.'

'You're very professional, Sue,' he said. 'Pity I'm on the wrong side of your investigative skills.'

'You're not on the wrong side. It's the blackmailer who's my target, not you. Please don't—'

'OK, fair enough. Well, we are where we are. My name is bound to come out sooner or later. Probably sooner. What should I do, in your professional opinion? Should I issue a statement?'

'Let me think about it. Tell you what, how about we meet and draft one together, see what it looks like, and then decide?'

He felt a frisson of pleasure at the prospect of meeting her again.

'Good idea,' he said. 'Thanks. Where and when?'

‘How would you feel about coming to my flat in Westminster tomorrow? I could knock up a light lunch.’

‘Lovely.’

‘I’ll text you details.’

‘Just to check,’ he said, ‘you’ve now got my number, and I’ve got yours. OK?’

‘Yes, at last,’ she said with a chuckle.

Next, he rang Gavin McKay, and was unsurprised to be told by the duty officer that McKay was unavailable. He left a message that he was now more concerned about his safety in the light of the Home Secretary’s statement and a certain person’s likely reaction, and could Gavin get back to him.

He went back down to sit with Sophie, and told her what he’d arranged.

‘You’ve now got me even more worried,’ she said. ‘How about I postpone staying with Rhiannon, and instead you go with me back to Brussels? I don’t suppose Hitchcock’s mob could track you down there.’

‘I don’t think that’s correct. They’ve shown themselves to be experts at using the internet and related technologies. At least here I’m protected by our security people.’

‘Well maybe I should stay with you here, then.’

‘That would be worse,’ he said. ‘You can’t protect me, and I’d have to worry about you. At least you should be out of harm’s way when you stay with Rhiannon. When were you thinking of going?’

‘Tomorrow.’

‘Good. Lovely though it is to have you here, at least I’ll know you’re safe.’

FRIDAY 11TH AUGUST

Sue Abercrombie lived in a 1990s red-brick block of flats near the Home Office, not far from where they'd met earlier in the week.

Redstone checked his appearance in the lift's mirror, exited into a carpeted corridor, and found Sue's flat.

'Welcome!' she said. She was even more attractive than he'd remembered. She showed him into a modern sitting/dining room with a picture window at one end.

'Nice flat,' he said. 'Been here long?'

'Six years, now. My work here in Westminster involves loads of evening functions. I got fed up with commuting every day and getting back late at night. This is so convenient.'

He reflected that he'd find living here claustrophobic, with no garden, people packed together in one building, no obvious way of getting to know the neighbours. Lonely without the benefits of being alone. But then he realised she might have a partner here. Idiot –why didn't he think of that before? He looked at the bookshelves.

'These all yours?' he said.

'Of course. Who else's would they be?' She smiled. 'Do you think I steal books from the local library?'

'Sorry, I'm being stupid. Shall we get down to it?'

She smirked. 'My word, you're a quick worker.'

He burst into laughter.

'I… God, I can't think of anything to say which wouldn't sound even more like…'

'I know what you meant. Just teasing. Yes, let's get down to it. You sit next to me while I type on the laptop.'

He pulled up a chair and leant close to her so that he could see the screen. He could smell her perfume, *and she could smell his aftershave*. He quickly moved away.

'You all right?' she said. 'You won't be able to see the screen if you sit like that.'

'A sudden twinge,' he said, moving back close.

She wondered whether he was telling the truth. Did she smell?

'I think I pulled something in my neck,' he said, 'but it's gone now.'

Relief. She liked his being close to her.

'Let's think about what you'd like to achieve if you issued a statement, and work back from there,' she said.

He eased his chair away, leant back and linked his fingers behind his neck.

'OK. Let's talk about it before you start typing, then you have a go at a draft, and then we can look at the draft together.'

Ten minutes later he was back close to her, studying the screen.

She was thinking about the text.

'I like what you've written,' he said, 'but if you were a journalist coming across this release, wouldn't you want to know more? It doesn't really explain why the blackmailing terrorist was seeking information about me. In truth, it doesn't explain anything. It's just clever words. Sorry if that's insulting – it's a compliment, I suppose.'

'You're right,' she said. 'There is a big hole in the draft. Frankly, unless you can say more, I'm not sure there's much point in issuing a statement.'

He thought rapidly. Would giving her more details end up helping Hitchcock and Clodagh in some way? After all, Sue was a journalist, and her every instinct must be to publish information, especially if she could claim a scoop. If Hitchcock read confirmation that he was involved in trying to track her down, he would be even more at risk of being attacked by her thugs.

'Sue,' he said, 'I'd love to tell you more, but I can't. Not at this stage. I think we should scrap the idea of a statement, and let your journalist colleagues emulate you in trying to find out what they can.'

'Oh well. I'm professionally disappointed, but I assume there's a good reason for what you say. Let's forget the statement. I'm always available if there's some development that makes you change your mind.'

'Thanks,' he said, standing up. 'I'm very grateful for your time.'

'Do you have to rush away? I've put a couple of salads together. Stay for lunch?'

*

Over what turned out to be rather more than a couple of salads, with quite a lot of wine, Redstone asked Sue to tell him about herself. Wealthy parents, read English at Bristol, journalist for a regional paper, period as a ministerial special adviser, failed political consultancy, and now successful political blogger. Series of romantic relationships.

'Just like me, except for everything,' he said, conscious that his voice was slurred.

'Yes, in some ways we are opposites. And you know what they say about opposites…'

'But it isn't true, is it? Human beings are much more complex than magnetic poles. People need to have quite a lot in common to be able to get on.' He was proud of having got this out without stumbling over the words. How many glasses had he consumed?

'Of course they do,' she said. 'But you're concentrating on the differences. We have similar levels of education, we're both single, both intelligent, both interested in politics, both… I'm sure we could come up with a good list if we put our heads together. More wine? Let's go and sit on the couch.'

*

He was woken by his phone ringing in his ear. He rejected the call. Disoriented, he took a moment to work out where he was – Sue's bed. Her side was empty. He had a headache and a dry mouth.

He gathered his thoughts as he gingerly got dressed. He stepped into the living room to find Sue at her computer. She smiled at him.

'Have a good rest? I didn't want to disturb you.'

'Thanks. I…'

'It was very nice, wasn't it?' she said. 'Must do it again sometime. If you'd like to, of course.'

'It was very nice,' he said. 'More than nice. Er…'

'You're not used to casual flings.'

'Ah.' He breathed a sigh of relief. 'No, I'm not. Sorry if that makes me seem a staid nerd. It's because I *am* a staid nerd.'

'Well, maybe I can persuade you to drop some of the nerdiness. Or staidness.'

'Maybe you can.'

'Neither of us is attached, no one got hurt, it was fun, did us both good.' She gestured to the remains of the lunch. 'Fancy a bit more food before you go?'

'It was delicious, but no, thanks. I ought to be getting back.'

'Glad you enjoyed it. They say a good meal is the way to a man's heart, though it wasn't your heart I was aiming for.'

He grinned. 'Sue, it's been delightful. If, well, circumstances work out that way, I'd love to… meet up again.'

*

As he sat on the Tube he reflected on what had happened. He felt guilty, though he couldn't pin down why. He'd been lonely and drunk, and Sue had seduced him. But that wasn't the whole story by any means. He hadn't been unwilling. Far from it. Had it been a mistake? It felt so, but why? She obviously took such encounters lightly. He couldn't.

He thought about what he'd learnt while they'd been in bed together. There hadn't been a lot of thinking going on, but what he had picked up was the huge differences between their attitudes to life. She didn't seek security or stability, but rather wanted change and adventure. He didn't know anyone else like that. Even Laura liked some stability.

He checked his phone. Missed calls from Laura and Sophie. He'd call once he was home.

At his front door, he inserted his key into the mortice lock, but it wouldn't turn. He realised the door was unlocked – what was going on? He felt a frisson of fear. Maybe Sophie had forgotten to lock it when she left? He opened the door and walked in. There was a breeze from the French windows at the back – was Sophie still here? He hurried through into the garden, to find Laura sitting on the bench, stroking Treacle.

'Stop gaping,' she said. 'It's not what you think. Gavin asked me if I'd stay here with you to protect you against all evil. I couldn't get you on the phone. Sophie answered here, so I came over before she left to go to her friend. Hope that's acceptable.'

'More than acceptable. It's great to see you. And I already feel safer.'

'You OK? You seem a bit – strained. And have you been drinking?'

'A bit. I had a boozy lunch. I'm fine. You?'

'Fine too. Sophie helped me change the bedding in what used to be her room. I'll be sleeping there.'

'Of course. Any news about Hitchcock and Clodagh?'

'Not yet, but I'm sure it's just a matter of time.'

SATURDAY 12TH AUGUST

'I was mistaken when I said it was a flat,' said Sophie on the phone. 'It's a small Victorian terraced house. She's done it up beautifully. Open plan downstairs, and two bedrooms upstairs. Tiny garden.'

'I don't know those parts of London,' Redstone said. 'South of the river might as well be Mars, as far as I'm concerned. No security issues? Rhiannon is the Prime Minister's daughter, after all.'

'Yes, Dad, she knows that. She uses her mother's maiden name – Thomas, not Jones – and hardly uses social media. I'm glad I haven't got a public figure for a father.'

'Me too. Well, enjoy your time with her. You coming back here before returning to Brussels?'

'Yes, I'll pop back to cuddle Treacle,' she said. 'I'll keep in touch. Love you.'

Laura came in.

'News,' she said. 'The Home Secretary's home video is out. Doesn't seem to have been widely spotted as yet, but GCHQ have found it on an obscure porn website based in Russia. They say it'll soon be found by others, and then copied widely. Michelle's on the case, but she hasn't come up with anything so far.'

'What a shame,' Redstone said. 'Hitchcock is a nasty piece of work. She's got no benefit from publishing it – it's just an act of hatred.'

'Nothing new there. She wouldn't have got any benefit if her goons had succeeded in killing me. She didn't get any benefit when her guy attacked Michael Jones and instead killed those two lovely women. She just creates misery. Damn, I'm so cross and sorry that Gavin and I failed when we tried to get rid of her last year.'

'Getting Michael Jones out of office won't personally benefit Clodagh either, and yet she's killed and maimed hundreds, thousands, in her campaign against him.'

'Not to mention the killing and maiming she did as a young terrorist all those years ago. I suppose she's got some deep motive which makes twisted sense to her. What a fine pair. Made for each other.'

Laura's phone rang. While she was answering, a thought occurred to Redstone about what they'd just been discussing. What if the terrorists' motivation wasn't limited to revenge? He waited for her to finish the call.

'It was the office,' she said to Redstone. 'They say Michelle's found something, but not very much. She believes the video was posted from somewhere in outer north London, although she's not a hundred percent sure. Doesn't take us very far, I'm afraid.'

'Damn. Does that mean we have to wait for a further atrocity before we have a chance of tracing Hitchcock and Clodagh?'

'Either that, or hope something turns up. Like a police officer spotting one of them. That's often the way these cases proceed.'

'Right,' he said. He gazed out of the window at the bright sunlit garden. 'I had a thought just now that I was going to put to you, but it's gone.'

'It'll come back if you don't think about it.'

'Hope so. I was going to do some work today, catching up, but it's too nice out there. Fancy going out somewhere?'

*

They walked towards the woods, across the fields which were rippling with waves of tall dry grass. Redstone was sweating in the strong sunshine, although dressed only in T-shirt and shorts. And his cap, switched to blocking mode.

‘Aren’t you boiling?’ he said to Laura, who was wearing a light blue jacket over a cream skirt. ‘Why don’t you take off your jacket?’

‘Look,’ she said, opening her jacket wide to reveal a black nylon shoulder holster weighed down by a big pistol. ‘We’ve decided the risk level is now so high that I need to be armed at all times.’

‘Christ, I had no idea.’

They walked on. The sun seemed even hotter. Redstone wondered whether he should be more worried about his safety than in fact he was. He decided his faith in Laura’s ability to protect him was justified.

‘That gun looked uncomfortably heavy,’ he said. ‘Couldn’t you have brought one smaller and lighter?’

‘I like this one,’ she said, patting the bulge under her jacket. ‘It’s a Glock 19, if you’re interested. The body is made of polymer, so it’s not too heavy.’

‘Nineteen. Does that mean they produce lots of different models?’

‘The number is how many rounds it carries.’

‘Oh.’

They reached the woods.

‘What a relief,’ Laura said, fanning her face. ‘Amazing how much difference the shade makes.’

‘Yes, and it’s not just the fact that the direct sunshine is blocked. The trees absorb some of the sun’s energy as well, for photosynthesis. Not a large proportion, but every little helps.’

She smiled at him. ‘I’d like to be irritated that you come out with stuff like that, but unfortunately I quite enjoy it.’

‘I’ll see what other scientific gems I can produce.’ He wiped his forehead. ‘About half a mile, and then we come out onto a road next to the pub.’

Twenty minutes later, they were in the pub’s garden, seated at a picnic table with their backs to an old brick wall. They were shaded by a big oak. The pub was a low, white-walled rambling building, parts of which were clearly hundreds of years old. Near their table, some young children were playing on the equipment in a playground surrounded by a low white fence. Most of the other tables were occupied by families.

Redstone started to order food and drink, using an app on his phone. He looked up as three black cars, with noisy exhausts and loud music blaring, braked to a halt on the verge outside the pub gate, scattering gravel. Six men piled out of the cars, shouting and laughing, and jostled into the pub garden. The diners at the picnic tables stared.

Laura shifted in her seat, studying the group.

'You're not going to intervene, are you?' Redstone said.

'I'm not the police. No, what concerns me is that turning up in a rowdy group like this is a well-known trick for people who want to harm someone. Look, five of them are in their early twenties, but one is much older. The one with the striped shirt hanging over his jeans. He's the one to keep an eye on.'

'Are you saying they could be after me, or you?'

'It's possible.'

'How could they have known where we'd be?'

She pointed to his phone. 'That. I'm sure Clodagh could locate it if she wanted to.'

'Should we leave, then?'

'No. We're in a good defensive position here, and if they really are after us, they'd just follow and do their worst somewhere else. Let's watch and wait. They haven't actually done anything wrong, after all. Yet.'

Two of the young men pushed through the tables to the play area.

'Hey,' one of them shouted to the others. 'Let's play!' He turned to the children within the fence. 'Time to go, kids. Get lost.' He spread his arms, bared his teeth, and gave a wordless roar. Two of the children started to cry, and they all ran out.

A couple of men, who Redstone assumed were the children's fathers, rose from the picnic tables. Their partners pulled them back down. A couple of women rose and went into the pub. Laura lifted her phone and started filming.

'Why are you videoing them?' asked Redstone.

'I'm collecting evidence in case I have to take action which might merit another enquiry. And I'm sending it to the office live, so that they can identify anyone in our records.'

The other four men joined the first two inside the play area, and the six of them started to use the equipment. One climbed up the frame of the swing and hung from the bar, shouting that everyone should look at him, while two others stood on the swing seat. The frame broke, and the men fell down, calling out with glee. All six then climbed the frame supporting the slide, which also collapsed. Two then went to the see-saw and jumped up and down on it until it snapped.

A squat man in a cook's apron emerged from the pub.

'Hey!' he said. 'What the hell are you doing? Get out of there immediately. I'm calling the police.' He took a phone out of his pocket.

Two of the young men jumped over the low playground fence. One strode to the cook and grabbed the phone from him. The other glared at the diners, slowly turning his gaze from one table to the next.

'Nobody uses a phone here,' he said, pointing at a young woman who had picked up her phone, then at another who was typing on hers. 'Put the fucking things away.' Laura carried on filming.

'Hey, you,' he called to Laura. 'You fucking deaf? Gimme that.' He strode towards Redstone and Laura and leant over their table, hand outstretched. Laura tilted the phone to capture the image of his face. He grabbed for the phone, but she swayed her arm so that he missed.

Two other young men came over to the table. Laura put a restraining hand on Redstone's arm as he started to get up.

'Leave this to me,' she said quietly.

He sank back down, knowing she was right, while she stood up, back to the brick wall. She carried on filming.

'This video is being sent to a number of people in the security service,' she said in a clear, calm voice. 'Your faces have been registered, and facial recognition software is working as I speak. My advice is that you now pay the pub owner for the damage you've caused, apologize to everyone here, and leave.' She waved at the playground. 'Ten thousand pounds should cover it.' She passed the phone to Redstone, gesturing that he should continue filming.

All six of the group were now crowded on the other side of the table from Laura and Redstone. The young man who'd tried to take the phone turned to the others.

'Any of you believe that shit about the security service?' he said. 'No, nor do I.'

'What's your name?' asked Laura. 'Is it Ron? As in moron?'

He lunged forward across the table and tried to slap her. She pulled back so that he missed, grabbed his wrist as it went past, and the next thing Redstone knew was that the man's face had banged into the table. Laura crashed her elbow down on the back of his neck with scary ferocity. He went limp and slid to the ground.

The other five stood staring, and then one rushed round the table towards her. She swivelled, raised her leg and drove her heel into his knee. He howled a curse and bent over to grab his injured leg. She seized the back of his head with both hands and jerked his chin down sharply onto her own raised knee. His eyes rolled up and he collapsed.

Another of the attackers edged round the table on Redstone's side, trying to get at Laura's back. Redstone jumped out of his seat and shoved the young man with his shoulder. Laura whirled round and hooked the man's leg with her foot. As he fell sideways, she punched him hard on his right ear. The left side of his head banged into the brick wall. He slumped to the ground.

She spun back to face the remaining three. The older man reached behind him and drew a pistol from under his loose shirt, starting to aim at Redstone. As he was moving, Laura whipped out her own gun and shot him twice in the abdomen, the two loud cracks so close they almost merged into one. A woman screamed, and a child started to sob. The shot man dropped his gun, clutched his abdomen with a look of surprise as blood started to seep through his fingers, and collapsed forwards, thumping his head on the edge of the table.

The other two men raised their hands and backed away. Laura ran round the table towards them. They turned and sprinted to the gate. Sirens sounded in the distance. The men wrenched open the doors of the front black car and squirmed in. As the engine started, Laura raised her gun and shot the front tyre, which deflated with a bang.

A police car jammed to a halt. Two uniformed officers jumped out. One went to the black car, while another shouted at Laura to drop her weapon. She opened her jacket and pointed to her ID badge attached to the nylon holster strap. The officer stepped closer. Redstone jogged up to join them.

'I sent a code to summon an armed response team, but it's a bit late for that now,' she said to the officer. 'You need to get the paramedics here fast.' She gestured back to the table. 'A lot of bleeding going on there.'

Two more police cars screeched to a halt, doors opening as they stopped diagonally across the road. Six armed police officers ran into the pub's grounds. A sergeant stood back, surveyed the scene, and gave some orders. He walked over to Laura and Redstone.

'Ah!' he said. 'Laura Smith! And Dr Redstone. Great to see you again. Seems everything's under control here, and we're not needed.' He held out his hand, which Laura and then Redstone shook warmly. The officer from the first police car raised his eyebrows.

'Last time we met was last year, wasn't it,' Redstone said. 'When those thugs invaded my house. Well, it seems the person who recruited them is on my case again, but with different thugs on this occasion.'

'So I gather,' the sergeant said. 'Still no sightings of that person, as I understand it.'

'Afraid not,' said Laura. 'But we might get some clues when these vermin are interrogated. Especially the one I shot.'

'Surprised he's alive,' said the sergeant, gesturing at the table where the other of the first pair of officers was applying first aid. 'Very kind of you.'

'I had to aim down to avoid hitting any of the civilians if a round went through. Anyway, as I said, he might have something useful to tell us.'

The sergeant nodded. 'I've been told you've transmitted video of the whole shebang to Thames House,' he said. 'Can I see it, please?'

Laura gestured to Redstone, who passed her phone to the sergeant. He fiddled with it and then stood watching the video, with two of his colleagues peering over his shoulder.

'All seems crystal clear,' he said. 'If I can send a copy of this to my own phone, I see no reason why you two can't be on your way. We'll sort out the mess here.'

'Of course,' Laura said. 'Thanks.'

Redstone looked at her. His mind had gone blank.

'I don't know about you,' she said to him, 'but I'm longing for a drink.'

'Me too, but… Laura, we can't stay here. God knows what the other customers are thinking.'

'Anywhere else nearby?'

'There's a carvery place in a converted manor house back through the woods. I'll call and see if they can fit us in.'

*

'Not bad,' said Laura, dabbing at her lips.

'No,' Redstone said. 'My first time here. I'm surprised I was so hungry after all that excitement. Laura, you saved my life. You have my… undying gratitude.'

'Ho, ho. You did well yourself – kept your head, and acted at the right moment to deflect that thug, the one who came behind me. Not bad for a total amateur.' She smiled, then coughed and looked away.

Her phone rang. While she took the call, Redstone took the opportunity to text the twins, to tell them he and Laura were OK, in case they saw reports of what had happened and got worried.

Laura put her phone on the table.

'Some reactions to the Home Secretary's video, but nothing major. There's so much porn available online now that sex scenes featuring a middle-aged woman aren't a great draw. She'd taken the sting out of the whole affair by telling people in advance that the video existed. Good PR.'

Redstone blushed, thinking of who'd been responsible for that PR.

'What is it?' asked Laura. 'Have you seen the video? Is it particularly juicy?'

He shook his head. 'I can't… No.'

She stared at him. 'Oh well, moving on, the office wants you to be present when we interview the guy I shot. He's in Barnet Hospital, under police guard. They've already operated, and he's expected to be able to talk to us tomorrow.'

'Fine.'

'And I've saved the best bit till last. We've got the DNA result from the US. Remember you said we shouldn't assume the hair in Hitchcock's flat was hers – it could have been Clodagh's?'

'Yes. When you found a match with DNA left in the St Albans house.'

'Well, you were half right.' She sat back and grinned at him.

'What? Either it was Clodagh's or it wasn't.'

'Not necessarily.'

'What on earth does that mean?'

'It *was* Hitchcock's, but also half Clodagh's.'

'Are you saying Clodagh is Hitchcock's mother?'

'Got it in one.'

He gaped at her. 'That's… I was going to say that's ridiculous, but of course it isn't. So Clodagh gave birth to Valerie, if that was what she was called then, and must have quickly got her adopted by a couple called Hitchcock. And then carried on her campaign of bombing and general terror.'

'More or less right. My colleagues have looked into it. Clodagh dumped the baby Valerie with Birmingham social services. They arranged for her to be fostered by a couple called Hitchcock. But eventually the Hitchcocks decided they couldn't cope with her any longer, and she spent the rest of her childhood in care homes.'

'Ah' he said. 'Why would Clodagh dump Valerie but not do the same with her son Carter? In fact, she stayed with Carter all his life. She nurtured him so well that he became president.'

'Maybe it was to do with her immediate circumstances. Or her differing relationships with the two fathers.'

'Assuming there *were* two. Seems likely, I suppose, since she dumped the first baby but not the second.'

'Hard to think of someone being a terrorist and a mother, isn't it,' said Laura. 'But being a mother doesn't rule out being a fanatic.'

'I suppose not.' Redstone rubbed his chin. 'When we were colleagues in the Department of Energy, Valerie never talked about her childhood. I remember her getting quite ratty and defensive when I asked her where she grew up. But it doesn't follow that she knew who her mother was.'

'I wonder when she found out.'

'Maybe Clodagh traced her a couple of years ago, while she was plotting to come over and wreck Britain.'

'Yes, that would explain how Valerie shot from disgrace to power. Clodagh was pulling all the strings here by then, and getting her daughter to be Cabinet Secretary must have been a dream.'

'And now they're the dream team,' he said, 'if you're into clever, brutal terror.'

'Oh well, it doesn't affect what we're doing. We need to hunt them down whatever their relationship.'

'At least we're now pretty certain it is Clodagh who's behind the hacking,' said Redstone. 'And I've just remembered the thought I wanted to put to you this morning. Maybe we've been underestimating the scope of Clodagh's ambition. If you think about it, she's shown incredible patience over the years, building up her position of power in the US and then using it to get power over us, the British, so she could punish us for… for what we did in Northern Ireland, presumably. I guess she's not forgotten her IRA roots. And now she's back on the same track. It would explain—'

'Yes, right,' said Laura. 'It would explain the scale and persistence of the atrocities. Not only about one man, Michael Jones – it's about getting rid of his government and somehow installing herself in a powerful position again.'

'Or someone else, who she'd use as a puppet, as she did before.'

'It all makes sense, but I don't see how she could expect to regain power on her own. She'd need huge resources.'

'You mean like aid from an enemy state.'

'Exactly,' she said. 'And there's no sign of that.'

SUNDAY 13TH AUGUST

2 a.m. Redstone was woken by a jabbing pain beside his right eye. *Oh, not again.* He felt sick. He stumbled into the bathroom, squinting against the light, and found the medication. As he returned to bed, Laura opened the door and peered in.

'You OK?'

He winced. 'Migraine,' he whispered. 'Taken a tablet. Should go in an hour or so.'

'Anything I can do?' she asked. 'Glass of water?'

'Got one, thanks.'

She stood looking at him. He gave a weak smile.

*

He pushed open the kitchen door. Laura was outside, walking round the garden with Treacle darting in and out of the flower beds alongside her. He wandered out.

'How are you feeling?' Laura asked.

'Not too bad. Washed out. The medication's worked, but it leaves me feeling exhausted for hours. I wish we'd sorted out our migraine cream.'

'I'll make you a cup of tea. Eat what you can, and go back to bed. We're not due in the hospital till this afternoon. If you don't feel up to it by then, I'll get it put back.'

'I'll be all right by then,' he said.

*

Laura drew her battered Land Rover to a sharp halt in the hospital car park, and switched off the engine. Redstone's ears rang in the silence.

'Thank God that's over,' he said. 'Has it got any springs at all?'

'Mark,' she said, 'you can insult me, but any criticism of this vehicle will bring dire retribution. Let's go in.'

They were directed to a side ward in the surgical department. An armed police officer stood outside the door. McKay, sitting in a plastic chair against the wall, gestured to them to sit next to him.

'How is he?' Laura said.

'Expected to make a partial recovery. The other three will be discharged today, into police custody of course. It would have saved the taxpayer a lot of money if you'd killed all of them.'

Redstone stared at him, unsure whether he was joking. Half joking, he decided.

'Laura,' McKay said, 'you can't conduct the interrogation. You're too involved in the incident. The lawyer also argued that you, Mark, couldn't be present, for the same reason, but I disagreed. Of course, the real reason I want you here is your mind-reading ability. I'll interrogate the bastard myself with Mark to help as necessary.'

Laura shrugged. 'Understood. What do we know about him and the others so far?' she asked.

'A drugs gang based in Hatfield. Its clients include people living in St Albans. The older guy, the shooter, is the leader, known to be violent. Seems pretty clear that Hitchcock paid him to do the hit.'

'So Hitchcock's found a new way of recruiting thugs,' Laura said. 'We can expect her to use such people again. There are a lot of them.'

'I agree,' said McKay. 'You ready, Mark? The bastard's lawyer is sitting in there waiting for us. The doctors have allowed us ten minutes. Put your cap on.'

Redstone switched on the cap and tugged it onto his head. He felt no difference – he would have expected to pick up a faint background burble of thoughts when there were people around. He checked the switch, put it back on and pointed the peak at McKay. Nothing. He moved closer.

'What are you doing?' McKay said.

'The cap doesn't seem to be working.' He stood over McKay with his knees almost touching McKay's. Still nothing.

'Sorry to do this, but I need to put my head right next to yours,' he said, removing the cap and bending forward. Nothing. To his surprise, he missed the background burble. He felt sad and alone.

'The mind-reading – it's gone.'

'Bloody hell,' said McKay. 'Think it's gone permanently? I suppose you don't know.'

'No, I don't. I had a migraine last night – maybe this is an aftereffect.'

'Or maybe it's a sign your brain has reorganised itself in some way, and the ability is finished,' Laura said. Redstone thought there was a note of hope in her voice.

'Either way, you might as well go home,' McKay said. 'I'll do the interrogation alone. I don't expect to get anything of use, but I'll let you know if I do.'

MONDAY 14TH AUGUST

‘Looks as through you’ve got good news,’ Redstone said to the assembled Smoothaway team. ‘Unless you’re just a very happy bunch.’

‘That’s it,’ said David. ‘The latter. They wanted to show you what a wonderful Chief Scientist you’ve got.’ He paused for dramatic effect. ‘Oh, and we wanted to tell you about Project Smoothaway. Rosie?’

Rosie stood up and walked to the whiteboard on the office wall.

‘This was indeed David’s doing,’ she said. She picked up a marker and drew two chemical structures. ‘These are the components David thought might be dehydrating the membrane and causing the problem. What we’ve done is modify the first, like this.’ She drew a slightly different structure. ‘The result is the molecule carries its own water around with it, and is no longer greedy for water from the membrane. And we’ve swapped the second one for this.’ She drew another structure. ‘Same idea.’

‘What a good idea!’ said Redstone. ‘I like the modifications. But _’

‘You’re going to ask two questions. First, yes, the changes seem to do the trick. The nerve fibres remain intact. And second, the formulated product has the right consistency and all the other properties we need.’

‘What about safety?’ Redstone said. ‘Are there any data in the literature?’

‘I do respect a man who uses the plural with “data”,’ said David. ‘Yes, they’re both used in a couple of other medications, for the same reason as ours, I guess. Maybe I subconsciously registered that, some time ago. So the long and the short of it is that we seem to have a formulation which works in the lab.'

Redstone clapped. 'So we're ready to go to the next stages?'

'Yes, I'm in touch with Star Boston Pharma for in vivo testing and more safety work. And I'll start talks about clinical trials. Lots of potential for failure, so let's not get too excited.'

'I know you're right,' Redstone said, 'but I've got a good feeling. The product's not ingested, which reduces the risks. We understand each of the components…'

'Mark, I don't want to be a wet blanket, but we've only got lab experiments so far. All sorts of things happen when a real live person gets a medication, including one that's applied via the skin.'

'Yes, of course, but… Oh, you're right to be cautious. It should be me warning against over-optimism. But even so—'

'Don't worry, I accept we've achieved an important milestone. Joanne's getting some bubbly in as we speak. We should celebrate having got this far.'

'Great,' Redstone said. 'Well done, everyone. See you later, glasses in hand.'

After they'd left, he reflected on the meeting. It had felt odd to be surrounded by people without sensing the background murmur of their thoughts. Amazing how quickly one adapted to changes – after all, it was only five weeks ago that he'd first read Laura's mind. He considered himself someone happy with his own company, but it had been comforting to sense the company of others. Oh well, back to being alone. Like everyone else. Anyway, the news about Smoothaway was extremely cheering. If only he'd had some of the cream at home on Saturday night. After it had been tested and approved, of course.

Joanne put her head round the door.

'Number 10 on the phone, asking for your mobile number. Can I give it to them?'

'Don't see why not,' he said. 'Did they say why they want it?'

'No, but I expect you'll find out if I give it to them.'

'True.'

Minutes later his mobile rang. Number withheld.

'Hello?' he said cautiously.

'Hello Mark,' said a familiar voice. 'Michael here. Michael Jones.'

Redstone resisted an urge to stand up. 'Hello Prime… Michael. What can I do for you?'

'I wanted to know if you'd heard from Sophie in the last couple of days. Anne's getting worked up. We haven't heard from Rhiannon since Friday evening, and she and Anne speak every day.' Anne was Michael Jones's wife.

'I spoke to Sophie on Saturday morning,' Redstone said. 'She enthused about Rhiannon's house.'

'That's something, but Rhiannon isn't answering her mobile, which seems to be switched off, and hasn't returned any of our messages. Anne went round to Rhiannon's place first thing this morning, but nobody was there.'

'Strange. I haven't heard from Sophie in the last couple of days, but I wouldn't have expected to. Well… on reflection maybe I would, given what happened to me and Laura Smith. You've probably been briefed. It was in the press, without naming us, but I told Sophie it was us and we were OK.'

'Yes, I was briefed. Glad you're OK. I assume you mean you texted Sophie and she didn't respond.'

'That's right, though I didn't read anything into that at the time. I also texted her twin, Graham, and he did reply. I just didn't notice… Can I ring off, call her, and phone you back?'

'Please do.'

'I'll need your number. It came up as withheld, for obvious reasons.'

Feeling anxious, Redstone tried Sophie, but the call went straight through to voicemail. He left a message for Oskar in Brussels, and then called Graham in California.

'Hello?' said Graham's voice, thick with sleep.

'Hi, it's Dad. Sorry to call at an unearthly hour, but I'm having difficulty contacting Sophie. Have you heard from her recently?'

'Not for a week or so. Why, do you think she might be in some sort of trouble?'

'No idea, but her phone seems to be switched off, which isn't like her.'

'You're right, it isn't. Have you tried Oskar?'

'Yes, but got his voicemail. I'll try again.'

He rang Oskar, who answered immediately. He also hadn't heard from Sophie.

'I was about to call,' Oskar said. 'I can't raise her either. Mark, I'm worried.' Redstone told Oskar he'd get back to him.

He was now very anxious. He phoned Michael Jones and briefed him on the calls.

'Are you worried?' Jones asked.

'I am. I know they're both adults, so the police wouldn't normally be interested at this stage, but Rhiannon isn't a normal risk. Because she's your daughter. Are you going to get them to look into it? Or maybe the security service?'

'I think I have to. I need this to be handled sensitively, so I'll get Gavin McKay to come in and I'll talk it through with him. You want to be present?'

After he'd rung off, Redstone sat back, numb with fear. Was this down to Hitchcock and Clodagh?

Joanne came in.

'What's wrong?'

He told her. Her shocked reaction amplified his own concern.

‘Keep it to yourself,’ he said, ‘in case…’ He swallowed. ‘Well, anything to do with the Prime Minister’s family might be very sensitive.’

He returned to his seat and phoned Laura.

‘Sorry to say this, Mark, but I share your worries,’ she said. ‘I wonder if Hitchcock and Clodagh arranged the attack on you and me to distract the police while they were… doing whatever they were doing with Rhiannon and Sophie. Or maybe that’s being fanciful.’

‘You think they’ve kidnapped the two young women? Or might they…’ He wiped his brow.

‘I don’t think they would have harmed them at this stage. They need them unharmed if they’re to use them for blackmail.’

‘You mean blackmail Michael? Or me? Or both of us? Christ, Laura.’

‘Their previous attempts to make Michael Jones resign have failed, so I wouldn’t be surprised if they were targeting Rhiannon to use her as a new form of pressure on him. Maybe Sophie was caught up in it by accident. I can’t see why they’d want to blackmail you.’

‘Yes, but Hitchcock would do anything to harm me.’

‘I suppose that’s true, but then she wouldn’t have grabbed Rhiannon as well. Too risky, given who Rhiannon’s father is. They’d only go for Rhiannon if she was the primary target.’

‘Aren’t you overthinking this? And what if your theory is right – might they think Sophie’s… dispensable?’ He felt faint.

‘Let’s not get ahead of ourselves. They’re bound to contact Jones with their demands, if our guesswork’s correct, and then we’ll have a better idea of where things stand.’

Redstone tried to speak, but all that came out was a choked cough.

‘Mark, I’m truly sorry I’m not being more reassuring,’ Laura said. ‘I wish I could… I shouldn’t have said…’

'No, I need to hear a reasoned assessment. Don't apologise. You go and—'

Joanne put her head round the door. She'd been crying. 'You're asked to go to Number 10 now. I've ordered a taxi.'

'You heard that, Laura. Must go. We'll stay in touch.'

*

Redstone was ushered into the Prime Minister's study.

Jones walked in, followed by Gavin McKay. Jones looked awful – pale, stooped, shrunk.

'It *is* a kidnap,' Jones said, as they sat round the desk. 'Just received an email to my private account, nominally from Rhiannon's account.' He waved his phone. 'I'll read it out.' He cleared his throat.

'"Your last chance to free the British people from your pernicious self-aggrandising dictatorship. You have five days to resign." Then there's a photo of Rhiannon holding this morning's *Financial Times*, standing against what seems to be a dirty brick wall. Sophie's standing next to her. Both are, well, bedraggled.' He blinked and wiped his eyes. 'It continues. "Don't contact the police or the security services. We monitor them and will know if you disobey."'

He looked at McKay. 'Too late about contacting you, but I forbid you to tell any of your staff.' McKay looked back expressionlessly.

'Can I see the photo, please,' said Redstone, struggling to breathe normally, his voice quavering. Jones handed him the phone. The young women were dishevelled but to his relief there were no obvious signs of harm.

McKay gently took the phone, studied it, and gave it back to Jones.

'They can't expect the kidnap to go unnoticed,' he said. 'Several people already know the young women are missing. Mrs Jones for one, of course, and anyone she's told.' He turned to Redstone and raised an eyebrow.

'I've told Sophie's twin brother Graham in California, her partner Oskar in Brussels, my PA Joanne at London Bio, and your colleague Laura Smith,' said Redstone.

'Ah,' said McKay. 'So there's no point in not putting Laura on the case.'

'All right, I accept that,' said Jones. 'But she mustn't use any of MI5's resources. Or GCHQ's. I insist.'

McKay sat back in his chair. 'In other circumstances,' he said, 'we'd use our analysts to see what they could deduce from the photo, and GCHQ to see what they could work out from that email. Specifically, where it was sent from. Prime Minister, I'm not going to argue about whether the kidnappers can monitor MI5, though I don't believe it, but do you really believe they can find out what GCHQ are up to? Seems very unlikely.'

'I'm not prepared to take the risk,' Jones said. 'Look how skilful they've proved themselves on IT matters.'

'I know how we can solve this problem,' said Redstone. 'Get Michelle Clarke on the case. You know how good she is at this sort of thing. She's literally world-class. And she has no connection with GCHQ, except a bit of mutual antipathy.'

'I strongly support that idea,' said McKay.

'I can see its merits,' said Jones. 'I trust her.' He pressed a button on his desk, and almost immediately an aide knocked on the door and entered.

'Please get in touch with Professor Michelle Clarke at Cambridge University immediately, tell her I need her here as a matter of utmost urgency and also total secrecy, and arrange for her to be brought here by the fastest route possible.'

'I suggest you also tell her I'm involved,' Redstone said. 'Sorry, Michael, but for some reason she seems to be reassured when I'm around. Her daughter works for me, and…'

'That's fine,' said Jones, gesturing to the aide, who left the room. 'Meanwhile, you must tell everyone who already knows about the girls' disappearance to keep absolutely shtum about it. I'll tell Anne.'

'What are you going to do about the kidnappers' demands?' asked McKay. 'Because I have a suggestion.'

'Go ahead.'

'I suggest you wait till the kidnappers get in touch again, which they will – with a more specific threat, I'm afraid. Then announce you're taking a backseat temporarily because of a health problem. That'll give them something to think about and buy a bit of time.'

'Good suggestion.' He stood up and paced round the room. 'I chose not to appoint a deputy PM, but now I will. Tomorrow. Without telling her about the kidnap. She'll be alright. She owes me.'

'Can I have a copy of the email?' McKay asked. 'I'd like to study it myself, to see what I can deduce from it. And Laura Smith will need a copy.'

Jones stared at him. 'No offence, Gavin, but I'd rather not. For all I know your phone is the one the kidnappers have tapped somehow.' He turned to Redstone. 'Mark, they'll expect you to see it. I'll give you a copy. You're a scientist – you might be able to work something out from it. And you can show it to Laura Smith.'

Redstone refrained from pointing out he wasn't that type of scientist. But he might pick up something. 'Thanks. Best thing is to send it to me by WhatsApp.'

Jones passed Redstone his phone. 'Here you are. You do it.'

'Sorry to be blunt,' said Redstone, 'but so far this has all been about Rhiannon. Let's remember Sophie's as much at risk.' He cleared his throat. 'Maybe more, because she's not a bargaining chip in their blackmail of you, Michael, in the way Rhiannon is.'

Jones reddened. 'Of course I know it's not just about Rhiannon, but you can't expect—'

'You and I can talk about Sophie's situation outside,' said McKay to Redstone. 'The two cases are inextricably linked, and I recognize you have as much of a personal interest as Michael. As I'm sure he does.'

Jones nodded briefly.

*

McKay and Redstone sat side by side on a bench overlooking the lake in St James's Park.

'Sophie used to love looking at the pelicans when she was a little girl,' Redstone said.

'As she will when you sit here with her again, in the not-too-distant future,' McKay said. 'Mark, I had to bite my tongue in there.'

'What do you mean?'

'It's a well-established convention that ministers don't interfere with operational decisions by the security services or the police. And that includes the prime minister. On the other hand, we do take into account the wishes of parents in cases like this. So I see myself as not taking orders from Michael on how to conduct this case, but yes to listening to his wishes as a father. Now I want to know what your wishes are, as Sophie's father. Are *you* concerned that Clodagh might be able to eavesdrop on my organisation and GCHQ?'

'I suppose I am. Anyway, as you said, the two cases are inextricably linked. What's your advice?'

'My *decision* is that for the time being I will keep the MI5 machine out of it, but I'll also ensure that Laura gets all the support she needs in terms of equipment, planning, you name it, without giving her colleagues details of the case. And I'll not bring in the Met yet, because the police are much leakier than us. Are you happy to go along with that?'

'Yes. And thanks for being understanding, and fair.'

'Goes against the grain, but sometimes you have to drag these things out from where you've hidden them for years.'

*

'It's no good,' Redstone said to Joanne. 'I can't concentrate on anything except… you know. I keep imagining what she must be going through.'

'At least we know she's unhurt,' Joanne said.

'We think she was unhurt when the photo was taken, but who knows what those wicked people are capable of. No, that's wrong. We do know what they're capable of. They've done it. Killed, maimed… they've got no morals. They're driven by hate.'

Joanne started to cry. Her phone buzzed.

'It's Laura, downstairs at reception. I'll tell them to let her come up.'

Two minutes later, Laura came into the office. She hugged Joanne, who started to cry again.

'We'll sort it out,' she said, nodding to Redstone over Joanne's shoulder. 'Meanwhile, not a word to anyone. If people ask you what's wrong, say Mark's got a family problem and leave it at that.'

Laura and Redstone went into his office. She studied the photo on his phone.

'Let's blow it up,' she said. 'Send it to your PC.'

'Maybe you could use a different phrase from "blow it up" when talking about terrorists, but OK.'

She smiled. 'That's the spirit.'

She sat in front of his PC and manipulated the photo.

'The advantage of modern phones is that their cameras are so excellent. Look, I can enlarge this and still see lots of detail. What strikes you about this?'

He peered over her shoulder at an enlargement of the wall behind the young women.

'It's a brick wall. Old, or oldish. Rough, unfinished, as though it's somewhere unimportant.'

'You think the photo is indoors or outdoors?'

'Indoors. The lighting is wrong for it to be outdoors.'

'Right,' she said. 'I think we're looking at the cellar of a Victorian house. Well, a house old enough to have a cellar.'

'God, you're right,' he exclaimed, putting his hand on her shoulder. 'It's a natural place to hold a hostage. Hard to escape, and nobody outside the house could hear them shout…'

'If they've put in a modicum of soundproofing.'

'Yes. This wall could be on the side of the cellar away from the front or the neighbours. The others could be thick with soundproofing.'

'But there must be tens of thousands of houses with cellars in north London,' she said. 'And that's assuming Michelle's right in her suspicion about where the Octavia video was sent from. And it was no more than a suspicion, she said. We're going to need more.'

Redstone's shoulders slumped.

'Sorry, I've done it again,' she said. 'Upset you. Don't despair – we'll find a way of locating them. At some stage they're going to have to offer to release the girls in exchange for their demands, and that's when we'll be able to find a way. If not before, which is my hope and expectation.'

Redstone's phone buzzed – Michelle.

'I don't understand why you got me into this,' she said without any introductory niceties.

'Because… let's talk face to face. Can you come over to London Bio? Laura's here. You remember her from—'

'Yes, of course. OK. I'll take a taxi.'

*

Half an hour later the three of them were sitting round Redstone's table.

'The only worthwhile bit was the journey from Cambridge,' Michelle said. 'Police car with flashing blue lights to a field with a helicopter, helicopter to that barracks place by St James's Park, police car to Number 10. Exciting! Made me feel quite important. But when I got into the Prime Minister's study, it became obvious that the whole thing was a waste of time.'

'Oh, no,' Redstone said. 'You couldn't get any information from the email?'

'Of course I could, but so could you. Or anyone who knows how to google. And the result was predictable and useless.'

'What do you mean?'

'I got the IP address of the email, geolocated the origin, and – surprise, surprise – it was St Petersburg. Any decent cybercriminal would hide her tracks, and we know that Clodagh is more than decent.'

'Damn. You couldn't trace it back further than St Petersburg?'

'No. She'd taken care of that.'

'Maybe you can help us in another way,' said Laura. 'Did you see the photo the kidnappers had sent?'

'Yes. What about it?'

'We think it was taken in the cellar of an old house.'

'Interesting. Have you got the picture here? Can I study it?'

Redstone went to his PC, called up the picture and gestured to Michelle to sit at the computer. She examined it, typed a few words, studied the screen, and returned to the picture.

'I agree it's a cellar,' she said. 'Would you say all of these bricks are identical?'

Redstone and Laura peered over her shoulders.

'No,' said Redstone, 'they have natural variations.'

'Agreed,' said Laura.

'What you call natural variations means that they were made by hand rather than in a machine. That dates them to before about 1890. So this cellar was constructed before then. And if my thinking about the source of that rude video is right, in outer London.'

'All this is pretty speculative,' said Laura, 'but it's much more than we had before. Michelle, could you use your computer skills to make a list of older houses in outer London suburbs which have been let out in the last three months and which have cellars?'

Michelle sat back in the chair and studied her fingernails. She looked up.

'Hmm,' she said. 'I'd have to train the program to judge the age of a property from its appearance. I don't think estate agents usually give the age of their properties. Actually, while I'm doing that, I could train it to reject houses not made of yellow bricks. Do estate agents normally say if there's a cellar?'

'I'm pretty sure they do,' said Laura. 'It's a big selling point nowadays. They tend to call them basements rather than cellars.'

'Don't reject houses which appear not to be made of yellow bricks,' Redstone said. 'If you think about it, the main visible walls of many older houses are covered with render. You know, smooth, and painted cream or white. And the builders might have used yellow bricks in cellars of houses with red bricks on visible walls.'

'OK,' Michelle said. 'Simplest to start with outer north London houses which have been let out in the last three months and have a basement or cellar. Let's see how many that throws up.'

'What about older houses not in the outer suburbs?' said Redstone.

'We've got to start somewhere,' Laura said. 'If the outer north London angle doesn't work out, we'll think again.'

Michelle stood up, walked to the window and stared at the Georgian buildings on the other side of the street – now offices, but originally houses, with cellars.

‘Mark,’ Michelle said without turning round, ‘I know how you must be feeling. I was thinking how I’d feel if it was Rosie who’d been kidnapped. I’m going to do my best to help you locate these terrorists.’

Redstone felt tears pricking at his eyes. Coming from Michelle, this little speech was quite something. He wiped his eyes and started to thank her, but his voice caught, and he turned away. Laura put her arm around his shoulders. He picked up no trace of Laura’s thoughts, but it was obvious that both women cared for his plight. You didn’t always need to be literally a mind-reader – though when he’d possessed the ability it had removed the need for guesswork, deductions and reliance on instinct. He gave both women a weak smile.

‘Laura,’ he said, ‘I’ve been thinking about the fact that the kidnappers contacted Michael but not me. There’s all that bad history between me and Hitchcock. I’m sure she’d love to taunt me if she knew Sophie was my daughter. So maybe she doesn’t know. Maybe Sophie didn’t reveal her surname, or gave a false one.’

‘Sounds plausible.’

‘Then why would they not let her go?’ asked Michelle.

‘They could be keeping her as a means of pressurising Rhiannon,’ Laura said. ‘Like threatening to harm Sophie unless Rhiannon does what they ask. Anyway, if Sophie’s seen their faces and knows where they are they can’t release her till the whole thing is over and they’ve somehow escaped. Or I’ve killed them.’

‘Are you serious about killing them?’ Michelle asked. ‘I don’t always understand when people…’

‘Yes. And you can tell your computer the odds are heavily in favour of that outcome.’

*

Redstone phoned Graham with the bad news. Graham was almost speechless with shock. He said he'd take the first flight to London he could get a seat on. There might not be much he could do to help find Sophie, but he couldn't bear the thought of being so far away.

'Extra pairs of hands may well be useful,' Laura said.

Redstone then called Oskar, who, unlike Graham, had known that Sophie was staying with Rhiannon, and who Rhiannon was. He was distraught.

'I'm coming over to London,' he said. 'I can't stay here while she's in danger there. Don't worry about having to put me up – the Norwegian embassy arranges accommodation for visiting members of the Foreign Service.'

'So we've got two bright and highly motivated young men coming to help,' Laura said. 'We may need them, given we're not allowed to use MI5 or police resources.'

'I've no idea how many properties with cellars would have been let in north London suburbs in the last few months,' Redstone said. 'Might be thousands.'

'Nor have I. Let's wait and see. I guess Michelle will give us the first results tomorrow.'

TUESDAY 15TH AUGUST

'You look awful,' Laura said as she mopped her face with a towel. 'You should go for a morning run with me from now on. It helps take your mind off things. I'm going up for a shower.'

'It's not just Sophie's situation, though I hardly slept through worrying about her,' Redstone said. 'But soon after I finally got to sleep, I woke with another migraine. It took ages for the medication to work.'

'Oh, I'm so sorry. If it happens again, you should wake me.'

'Thanks, but there's no point. Nothing you can do. Better if at least one of us gets undisturbed sleep.'

'I suggest you finish your breakfast and go back to bed. I'll stay here on guard duty.'

*

Three hours later Redstone walked into the kitchen, feeling much refreshed. Laura was sitting at the table poring over several pages of A4.

'I used your printer,' she said. 'These are Michelle's first results. I had no idea how many houses get let each week. She says there are lots more to come, as she traces more single-branch estate agents.'

'Let's get to work,' he said. 'What do we do?'

'We google each one on our phones and decide if it might be the sort of place Clodagh and Hitchcock would have rented. Let's discard the lower-rent houses, which will make up the majority. Oh, and we'll have help soon – Oskar and Graham each rang to say they'd be arriving at Heathrow, coincidentally both at about noon. I suggested they try to meet and come here together.'

The doorbell chimed. Redstone went to the front door.

'Oh, hello Mark,' said Zena. 'I called on the off-chance that Sophie might be at home. But you are. You all right? You look… can I come in?'

'Well, I —'

'Thanks.' She pushed in and closed the door. 'Oh, you're here,' she said to Laura, who'd appeared in the hall. 'Hi. Mark, can we sit in the kitchen?' She walked through, pushing past Laura, who gave Redstone a quizzical glance. Redstone and Laura followed Zena to the kitchen table, which Laura quickly cleared of papers.

'It's about Sophie,' Zena said. 'I assume she's not here.'

'No, that's right,' Redstone said.

'It's very strange. We were exchanging texts last Saturday morning. She was at her new friend Rhiannon's. I'm sure you know that. She had to stop because there was someone at the door and Rhiannon wanted her. She said she'd text back soon, but she didn't. Then, about an hour later, or maybe it was more, I got a strange text. Didn't mean anything. I've been trying to contact her, but her phone seems to be switched off. Not like her at all. Is she OK?'

'Tell us about this text,' said Laura.

Zena looked at Redstone.

'Please,' he said.

'It's meaningless.' She picked up her phone and scrolled. 'Here.' She passed the phone to Redstone, who spelt out the text.

'n-s-4-n-e-5.'

'Do you ever communicate in code?' Laura asked.

'Why are—'

'Zena,' Redstone said, 'Sophie's been kidnapped. We're trying to trace her whereabouts. Laura is leading the hunt.'

'Oh my God,' Zena said. She turned to Laura. 'Of course, you're some sort of spook, aren't you. Is it because Rhiannon is the Prime

Minister's daughter? God, I hope she's alright. Mark, have you heard from her? Sophie, I mean.' She stood up and wrung her hands. 'This is awful. It's…'

'Calm down,' Redstone said. 'I'm sure you want to help, don't you?'

'Of course! What can I…'

'The first thing is we have to keep this secret. We mustn't give the kidnappers the slightest clue about what we know and who knows it. They're expert at tapping into phones, emails, messaging. You mustn't breathe a word, write anything, tell anyone on the phone, say anything on social media… get the picture?'

'Yes, yes. What about saying anything to Mum?'

'I think I'd better speak to her,' Redstone said. 'Now, back to Laura's question. Do you and Sophie ever communicate in code?'

'We're not kids anymore. I'm a grown woman.'

'Did you use codes when you were children, then?'

'Not that I remember. More the sort of thing that Graham did with his friends, I guess.'

'So if Sophie isn't using a code she thinks you might recognise,' said Laura, 'why would she be typing a meaningless message?'

'She's not the sort to type anything meaningless,' said Redstone.

'Right,' Zena said. 'I'm sure she meant something.'

Laura nibbled at her thumbnail, staring at Zena.

'I've got an idea,' she said. 'Zena, could you please type a text on your phone so I can see how you do it?'

'What do you mean? I do it like everyone else. What are you getting at?'

'What I'm getting at is that people of your generation use their phones in a different way from mine. Can you please do it, or do I have to go out and ask some random young woman in the street?'

'No need to get stroppy. Who shall I text?'

'Anyone. Doesn't matter.'

'I'll text Mum. What shall I say?'

'Doesn't matter, but make it fairly long.'

Zena gave a theatrical sigh and, holding her phone with both hands, sent a text, her thumbs flashing across the virtual keyboard.

'Satisfied?' she said.

'That was very helpful. So what you do is press the right keys almost by instinct, but look at the screen while you're typing.'

'Of course.'

'Could you please now repeat it with your eyes shut?'

'What?'

'Shut your eyes, then pick up the phone and text your mother again.'

'If you want.' Zena closed her eyes, groped on the table for the phone, picked it up, and started typing.

'This is ridiculous,' she said. 'I'm sure I'm producing garbage.'

'Open your eyes and tell us what you've typed.'

'Oh,' Zena said, 'I see. It's like what Sophie sent. She couldn't see what she was typing.'

'And could you have sent the second text to anyone other than Mary?' Laura asked.

'Not with my eyes shut. Had to be the last person I was texting. That's why Sophie texted me, isn't it? Is it some sort of cry for help?'

'Let's try to work out what she was trying to type,' Laura said. She picked up her own phone.

Redstone took his out of his pocket. 'Hang on,' he said, 'we'll need some paper and pens.' He ran up the stairs and returned with an A4 pad and a couple of ballpoints.

'Let's assume she was trying to type a word,' Laura said. 'If that's right, the numbers were a mistake, and should have been letters near them on the keyboard.'

'That works only if her phone has that type of keyboard,' Redstone said. 'Some don't have numbers and letters on the same display. I don't know what phone she uses.'

'I do,' said Zena. 'Same as mine. It does have both on the same screen.' She waved her phone at Redstone.

'Good,' said Laura. 'Let's see if my idea makes any sense. What's near 4?' She looked at her phone, but Zena said immediately 'e and r. And the letters near 5 are r and t.'

'So we're looking for a six-letter word which is blank, blank, e or r, blank, blank, r or t.'

'Too many options,' said Redstone. 'What sort of word might she have tried to send? Knowing her, it wouldn't be anything banal, like "help". It would be information.'

'Place name,' said Zena.

'But if she could see where they were, she could see to type,' said Redstone.

'Let's work on the assumption that somehow she knew where they were, but couldn't see to type,' Laura said. 'Maybe blindfolded but overheard something.'

'Satnav,' said Zena.

'Yes!' said Laura. 'Maybe they were in the back of a van, or in a car wearing blindfolds.'

'Wouldn't the kidnappers have taken their phones?' said Redstone.

'Good point.' Laura frowned. 'And yet we have evidence they didn't. I don't understand—'

'Sophie had two phones,' said Zena. 'A personal one and one her work gave her. Lots of international calls in her job. And she has to give out a phone number to all sorts of work contacts. They're each given a work phone so they can separate work calls from personal calls.'

'Of course!' said Redstone. 'They searched her, found the work phone, and didn't think to search further.'

'Probably hid her personal phone down her pants,' Zena said with a grin. He shook his head in disbelief she could find humour in the situation.

‘Zena,’ said Laura, ‘please tell us how long it was between the last text she sent before the kidnapping and the one that looks like code.’

Zena studied her phone. ‘Er… one hour fifty-five minutes.’

‘God, that’s a long time,’ said Redstone. ‘They must have been terrified. Imagine, sitting there, on the floor of a van, being bumped and thrown around, blindfolded…’ His voice broke.

Zena put her hand on his arm, tears welling.

‘Sophie’s tough and resourceful. She’ll have got through it.’

Laura looked up from her phone.

‘The timing fits with what we’ve been saying. Five minutes max for the kidnapping itself, then just under two hours to get out to the M25, drive round to the north, and drive into a north London suburb. Nothing for Sophie to report till they left the M25 and the satnav started to give road names.’

‘That’s where we suspect they are,’ Redstone said to Zena, gently removing her hand from his arm. ‘Outer north London.’

‘So we’re looking at the name of somewhere in outer north London,’ Laura said. ‘Six letters.’

‘Enfield,’ said Zena, studying her phone. ‘Oh no, that’s seven. Hendon. No, doesn’t fit with the number thingy. She tapped on her phone. ‘Pinner – no. Harrow – no. Bushey – no. Hampstead Garden Suburb – just joking.’ She grimaced. ‘Surprisingly few places with six letters.’ She flicked her finger across the phone’s screen. ‘Barnet – no. Running out of ideas here…’

‘What’s wrong with Barnet?’ asked Redstone.

‘The code is n-s-4-n-e-5. So the first and fourth letters must be the same. Oh, Christ, it *is* Barnet! She got the fourth and fifth letters right!’

‘And Sophie might recognise road names in Barnet,’ Redstone said. ‘It’s not far from here. Laura, did Michelle’s list include Barnet?’

Laura grabbed the pile of paper and started leafing through it.

‘I need to know what postcodes we’re talking about. She gives just the first line of the address, with a postcode. Anyway, the house we’re looking for might not be in Barnet itself – it might be nearby.’

‘And what did she mean by “Barnet”?’ Redstone said. ‘She couldn’t type things like High Barnet, or New Barnet, or East Barnet. Too difficult. She might even have meant the London Borough of Barnet, which is huge.’

‘You’re overthinking this,’ said Zena. ‘If one of us says let’s go to Barnet, the other knows she means High Barnet. If she’d meant East Barnet, say, she’d have tried to type an E before the Barnet word. Who produced that list? Can you get them to cut it down to houses in Barnet itself?’

‘They may not have ended up in Barnet, even if they drove through it,’ Laura said. ‘Let’s say houses within a two-mile radius of the centre of Barnet. I’ll get on to Michelle straight away. Or do you want to do it, Mark?’

‘No, you speak to Michelle. I’m thinking we’ll need people with some local knowledge when she produces the addresses, so I’ll ask Mary to help. You too, of course, Zena. Is Mary in?’

‘Yes, but she’s sleeping. You know, shiftwork.’ Zena consulted her watch. ‘Oh, she’ll be up now. And of course I’ll help.’

‘I’ll ring Mary, then. And when Graham and Oskar arrive, we’ll get Graham to join in, after he’s caught up on his sleep. I’m sure we can find Oskar something to do.’

‘Oh, Graham’s coming, is he?’ Zena said. ‘Of course. Haven’t seen him for ages.’

*

Redstone couldn’t bear to stay at home waiting for news from Michelle. He decided to go into the lab to take his mind off what might be happening to Sophie. Laura said it would be safe – she judged the threat to him was minimal while the terrorists were concentrating on Rhiannon. And perhaps Sophie.

'Sorry to say this,' said Joanne as he walked in, 'but I've seen you looking better. The stress must be awful. Any progress with finding Sophie?'

'We're waiting for the results of some more computer magic from Michelle. So I decided to come in rather than mope at home. Try to take my mind off…'

'Good. Oh, Rosie wanted a word.'

Minutes later Rosie edged into the office.

'It's not about science,' she said, 'it's… well, I may be putting two and two together and making five, but I'm concerned that something might have happened to Sophie.'

'I can't—'

'I'm sure there's a problem. Just looking at you and Joanne, the way you're behaving… And Mum's working flat out on something which she refuses to discuss, but I know she's been to see the Prime Minister, and Sophie told me she was going to spend time with his daughter, Rhiannon.'

Redstone squeezed his eyes shut, but tears leaked out.

'Mark,' Rosie said, 'I don't want to upset you further… But Sophie's my friend. I'm thinking the Prime Minister's been the terrorists' prime target, Sophie and his daughter were together, and…' She wiped away a tear herself. 'At the very least, can you tell me she's not…?'

'That's the trouble with you intelligent people,' Redstone said. 'You take facts and make sensible deductions from them.' He cleared his throat. 'Yes, Sophie and Rhiannon have been kidnapped by the terrorists who've been demanding Michael Jones goes.' His voice broke.

Rosie gasped. 'I sort of guessed it was something like that, but to hear it…'

‘I know. We think Sophie happened to be in the wrong place at the wrong time, and we suspect the terrorists don’t know who she is. Michelle and Laura are working flat out to locate where the young women are being held. Michelle thinks she’ll have some useful information by tomorrow – a short list of possible places. We’ll then narrow the list down to as few as possible.’

Rosie asked if she could help, but Redstone explained they needed local knowledge of the area where they suspected Sophie and Rhiannon were being held. He swore her to silence, though she could discuss the kidnap with Michelle and Joanne. She left with tears in her eyes.

He phoned McKay and explained that several people who knew Sophie had worked out what was going on.

‘The same must apply to Rhiannon,’ he said. ‘It doesn’t make sense that lots of people know but MI5 and the police are to be kept in the dark because the bloody kidnappers say so.’

‘I agree,’ said McKay. ‘And I’ve acted accordingly. I’ve told Jim Clothier what’s happened, and he’s preparing his team to use all the technical wizardry at our disposal, as soon as we’ve located the kidnappers and the girls. Once we’ve got the results from his staff, we’ll have a better understanding of which rescue technique to use. If it’s using minimal personnel, we’ll do it ourselves. But if it requires more force, we’ll bring in the Met.’

‘Have you told the Met what’s happened?’

‘Not about the kidnapping. They’re searching for Hitchcock and Clodagh anyway. They’re a leaky outfit, and I don’t see any advantage in saying any more to them at this stage, given the PM’s views.’

‘I suppose you’ve been kept up to speed on Michelle’s efforts and our latest breakthrough. Barnet.’

‘Yes, Laura keeps me briefed. I think we’ll identify the location in the next day or two.’

WEDNESDAY 16TH AUGUST

'Oh no, another migraine?' said Laura as Redstone stumbled into the kitchen, which was brightly lit against the heavy gloom outside. 'You look…'

'Yes,' he said. 'They're getting me down. I suppose it's the stress.'

A flash of lightning was followed by a huge clap of thunder. Large raindrops rattled against the windows.

'Or it could be the weather,' he said. 'The heat, and now this. You know, big changes in air pressure, ions in the atmosphere…'

'If you say so,' she said. 'But I still worry you could be experiencing a delayed reaction to that treatment we gave you. And that it's connected with your mind-reading.'

'Can't rule it out, I suppose.'

'Has the mind-reading come back at all? Gavin was pretty pissed off that you couldn't use it for the interrogation of that thug.'

He walked up to Laura and bent over so that his head was near hers.

'Think of a number,' he said.

'You know I don't like this, but… very well, just this once.'

'Total blank,' he said.

'Can't say I'm sorry. Unless you could have used it to help with the kidnap investigation, of course, though I can't see… How do you feel about it?'

'Mixed feelings. In many ways it's a relief, but I do feel more, well, isolated.'

'We discussed that,' she said. 'We're all isolated. Here, let's have a hug.'

He hugged her, awkwardly at first but then firmly and tenderly, feeling the pressure of her body melt away some of his tension. She leant back and looked into his eyes.

'We'll rescue Sophie. Don't worry. Should be hearing from Michelle soon.'

*

The printer rattled out Michelle's results.

'How many properties are there?' Redstone asked.

'Michelle said fifteen which seem to meet our criteria. Far fewer than I'd feared. Let's call in the troops, and then I'll explain what we're looking for.'

The front door opened, and Graham called out a greeting. Redstone rushed to hug him, but he raised a cautioning hand.

'I'm soaking,' he said, standing dripping in the hall. 'Didn't plan for weather like this. Have you kept any of my old clothes, Dad?'

'Yes, in your room. But you're a bit broader than you used to be. About the same size as me, I suppose. Look in my wardrobe and help yourself to anything you want.'

'Thanks. Oskar doesn't have any local knowledge, so he decided he'd just get in the way, and he's not coming at the moment.'

'How is Oskar?' asked Redstone. 'He must be worried sick, like the rest of us.'

'Yes, that's how he is. I suspect he wanted to be on his own.'

Ten minutes later the three of them, plus Mary and Zena, were sitting round the kitchen table.

'I'm going to tell you what we're looking for,' said Laura. 'First, we know that both women are wealthy and are used to a high standard of living. So we can rule out any property which isn't pretty expensive.'

'What if it's a large family house with lots of bedrooms?' Mary asked. 'That would be expensive.'

'Even if it seems much too big for just two people, don't discard it.'

Mary nodded.

'Second,' Laura said, 'we know it has a cellar made of those yellow bricks.'

'They're not really yellow, are they?' Zena said. 'More ochre.'

'True. It's just a term. Anyway, when you search for details on the internet, remember that the houses might be covered in painted render in any pictures you can find. You may have to rely on Google Street View or other pictures, because these houses are of course already let, and so we're unlikely to see anything on the estate agents' websites.'

'And, depending on the age of the property, the outside walls might be made of red brick, with only the hidden walls made of the cheaper yellow ones,' Redstone said. 'So let's look at all expensive houses which have or might have a basement.'

'Understood,' said Graham. 'But if they've disappeared from estate agents' websites, how did whatsername, Michelle, find out anything about them?'

'Michelle can work wonders with IT that the rest of us can't dream of,' said Redstone. 'I haven't a clue. Maybe that's why it took her what's a long time by her standards.'

'Third,' said Laura, 'the kidnappers would have been seeking a house that's as private as possible. You can't rule anything out on that basis, but we might be able to find one or more which are favourites because of that criterion. That's where your local knowledge comes in.' She handed out A4 sheets. 'I've marked four properties for each of you except Graham, who's got three. As soon as you find one that you think is a possibility, tell me, and I'll look into it myself, though of course I haven't got your local knowledge.'

The group picked up their phones and tablets, and started googling. Half an hour later, they were sitting back in their chairs looking at Laura.

'Hmm,' she said, 'less clearcut than I'd hoped. We can discard these six,' she waved her A4 sheet with red lines through some of the list, 'because they're quite small, but all of the others seem possible.'

'If you were doing the kidnapping, which would you choose?' asked Redstone.

'I like this one, 2 Southwold Crescent. Huge, detached property made of yellow brick, extensive grounds, woods on the opposite side of the road. But then there's also this one, and…' She shrugged.

'I prefer this one, 14 Henry Close,' he said. 'Smaller than the one you like, and semi-detached. But it's near the hospital, so there would be senior doctors and managers renting, when they've been posted to Barnet, while they're seeking a permanent house. Neighbours would be used to different people coming and going. And it's at the end of the road, with Green Belt fields further on.'

'Can't rule it out,' she said.

'What next, then?'

'What's next is my MI5 colleagues visit the estate agents who let these nine houses and find out what they can about who's renting them. I'll get on the phone now. Should have some results by late afternoon. Till then, we might as well disband. I'll let you know when we've found something.'

'I'll escape to the lab again, then,' Redstone said. 'Escape my thoughts and fears. Or try to.'

*

'What a contrast,' Joanne said as Redstone shook out his raincoat. 'Hot sunshine for weeks and then this.'

'Good for the garden,' Redstone said, on autopilot.

'What news about Sophie?'

'It looks like the team are closing in on where the girls are being held, but they're now waiting for the results of some more enquiries.

I've come in to take my mind off things, but also… I'd like to talk to David and Rosie, please.'

He stood at the window watching the rain stream down the glass. The gutters couldn't take the volume of water pouring into them – the street was flooding. A taxi edged past, leaving a strong wake. An intense white flash of lightning highlighted the scene, followed by a massive thunderclap which shook the window. The weather suited his mood. How was Sophie coping? He couldn't imagine how she must be feeling.

David and Rosie came in. He pushed away his thoughts about the kidnap and gestured to them to sit at the meeting table.

'You're not going to approve,' he said, 'but I've decided to try Smoothaway. I've been getting frequent bad migraines, which my usual medication isn't fully curing. And even that partial relief is at the cost of leaving me washed out.'

'But we—' Rosie said.

'I know the arguments against. Possible unknown side effects, dosage not yet sorted out, leaving the company open to legal action. On that last one, I've written a note saying you advised me against it, and I knowingly ignored your advice and used my position to get the cream.' He handed David a sheet of A4 paper.

'It hasn't even been tested on animals yet,' said David.

'I want to be a guinea pig.' He wished he could tell them he wasn't being a guinea pig for researchers into brain function, so it was only fair he acted as one for Smoothaway. 'There's a venerable history of scientists testing their own discoveries and inventions on themselves.'

'And in some cases, injuring or killing themselves by doing so,' David said.

'True, but we know more nowadays than they did. And it's not as if I'm proposing to go on a lengthy course of the cream. Anyway, life's a choice between real alternatives, and the alternative I face at the moment is frequent debilitating migraines.'

'I suppose we're not going to be able to dissuade you,' David said. 'What about the dosage? We'd normally start off very low and gradually work up.'

'What's your guess as to the amount of active ingredient we'll end up with in a recommended dose, if the cream passes the safety tests?'

David looked at Rosie. 'A hundred milligrams?'

'I was going to say a hundred and fifty,' she said, 'but I'd be happier with a hundred in this situation.'

'Have we got the apparatus to put the cream in a squeezable tube?' Redstone said.

'Yes,' David said. 'In that cupboard by the first fume hood on the right.' He waved in the direction of the big lab.

'Ah, I remember now. Good. How about making up a cream which contains fifty milligrams in each centimetre that I squeeze out of the tube? Then I can start low and work up if it's not having an effect.'

'I don't think you'd squeeze out only a centimetre if you're in pain in the middle of the night. I'd rather we went for twenty-five.'

'OK. Do you think it'll work if I apply it in two or three goes? I mean like one squeeze, doesn't work properly, another squeeze, still some symptoms, third squeeze, pain-free and nausea-free and… you know.'

'Don't see why not, but that would be one of the things the clinical trials would be examining.'

'Sorry, David,' Redstone said. 'I promise to make full notes after I've tried it.'

'You know you can't use it as a preventative measure?' Rosie said. 'It's a cure, not a prophylactic. So if you don't get a migraine, don't apply it.'

'Understood. Now, would you like me to make up the preparation, so that nobody can blame you for anything if my head falls off or whatever?'

'Certainly not,' Rosie said. 'If you're going to put yourself at risk, at least we want to be sure we know what it is that's causing the risk.'

David roared with laughter. Rosie looked surprised, then realised the implications of what she'd said and covered her face with her hands.

Redstone smiled. 'Don't worry, Rosie. You're right. My formulation skills weren't a patch on yours even in the distant past when I occasionally used them.'

'Thanks,' she said. 'I'll go and make up the cream. My best hope is that you don't get to use it because your migraines disappear, but if you do, good luck.'

*

'Watch the news,' McKay said on the phone. 'Michael Jones has received another threat. An email telling him to go now, with a picture of a severed finger. We've found the source of the picture – it's on the internet, so it's not one of the girls – but Michael's close to panicking, as you can imagine.'

'Jesus Christ,' Redstone said, 'are those foul women threatening to maim Sophie? I'll personally—'

'No, you won't,' McKay said. 'We've got professionals to do that. Don't worry – the government's announcement, that you're going to listen to, will give us more time. The kidnappers will have to decide how to react to it, because it'll seem like a partial victory. Meanwhile my people are coming up with helpful results from the estate agents. Laura will be fully briefed by about five o'clock, and she'll meet you at your house. I suggest you watch the announcement and then go back home to hear our results and the next steps. Or you could watch the news while you're travelling – shall I send a car?'

Redstone gazed out of the window at the rain beating down from the dark sky.

'Yes, thanks, a car would be good.'

He rang Graham to update him.

'I'm in the West End with Oskar, Dad,' Graham said. 'He's helping me buy some clothes suitable for this English weather. I'm going to stay here tonight in the posh flat they've given Oskar. We're a sort of mutual support mini-group. You'll have Laura for company, and she'll do a much better job of keeping you sane than I would.'

'OK. I'll call you about what MI5 have discovered.'

Half an hour later, the Mercedes was gliding up a hill in Highgate, passing huge posh houses deluged with rain, like the council estates the car had just passed. Redstone turned his attention back to his phone. Octavia Pitt had been elevated from deputy to acting prime minister, and was giving a press conference in the Cabinet Office. She was standing at a lectern, and the camera picked up Sue Abercrombie sitting a couple of meters to her left. He blushed as he remembered the last time he'd met Sue. Tavia must have appointed her to some advisory position.

The government press release had said that Michael Jones was stepping down temporarily for health reasons. Tavia was refusing to expand on what those reasons were, despite repeated questions from reporters. Redstone wondered how much she actually knew. McKay wouldn't have revealed what had happened, and he doubted that Jones had told her. He scrolled through what its new owner had just renamed Twitter. It was full of speculation, most of it wildly inaccurate. Some wiser heads were speculating that Jones had at last yielded to the pressure from the terrorists, but none had come up with the specifics. *Just a matter of time,* Redstone thought. Some skilful and dogged reporter would work it out. He was terrified they would also work out that Sophie had been with Rhiannon when she'd been kidnapped. If Hitchcock realised who Sophie was, God knew what she'd do to her to exact revenge on him.

Laura arrived at his house half an hour after he'd got in.

'Good news,' she said, waving a couple of printed A4 sheets. 'Seems my colleagues have come up trumps.'

'Go on.'

'Amazingly, four of the houses are being rented by Japanese banks to house executives and their families. And then two of the rest are being rented by families who've sold up somewhere and are between houses. Looking for a property in the area.'

'That leaves three,' Redstone said.

'Yes. One was rented by an American family. The estate agent had shown the husband and wife around. I did wonder when I heard the word American, but my colleague was sure it couldn't have been Clodagh and an accomplice – the woman was much too young. So that leaves two. The first one was rented by an agent on behalf of a US company. US records show the company's business as software development, but there are no traces of it doing any trading.'

'So you think that's our target.'

'I do. What's more, it's the house I selected when you asked me which I'd choose if I were a kidnapper, 2 Southwold Crescent.'

'What about the second one?'

'It's the one you liked,' she said. '14 Henry Close. Rented by a doctor, doubtless for the reason you gave – just been posted to Barnet Hospital.'

'And did your colleagues look into the doctor?'

'Yes. A consultant psychiatrist. She's currently trekking in the Andes with her wife.'

Redstone frowned. 'Does that mean they're uncontactable?'

'Yes, afraid so. But it doesn't follow that there's something fishy.'

'I accept that,' Redstone said, but if you were Clodagh and Hitchcock, and wanted to hide your true identity, which would you choose – an American software company, or an uncontactable psychiatrist and her wife? First one's a bit close to reality, don't you think? Could Clodagh have stolen and used the doctor's identity?'

'I see where you're coming from,' Laura said, 'but my gut feeling is still Southwold Crescent. The location is so suitable. With the woods over the road, and –'

'Are you saying the Henry Close house is unsuitable?'

'No, it's… OK. We'll investigate both. Shouldn't take long to eliminate one of them.'

'Good. So Sophie's probably in one of those two houses.' He felt sick. What had been somewhat abstract was now much more concrete. He could visualise her in the cellar of one of the houses, dirty, tied up, terrified… He swallowed.

'Once we know which it is, how do we get her out safely?'

'Our first step is to gather intelligence,' Laura said. 'I've spoken to Jim Clothier. He'll use drones with cameras sensitive to visible and infrared light. There will also be cameras and directional microphones installed in trees around the target houses. I'll text him now and tell him the houses we've chosen.'

She picked up her phone and typed rapidly. A minute later it pinged.

'He's starting the process. Henry Close first. They'll do more during the night. If it looks like the right house, tomorrow morning his people will put an assortment of tiny sensors through the wall of the cellar.'

'They can't do that! How can they drill holes without alerting Hitchcock and Clodagh, and any other thugs they have in the house? And how can they get to the other side of the cellar wall in the first place?'

'Don't worry, we have a planning protocol for this scenario. The internet will go down in a few houses along the street, and a BT

Openreach van will appear soon after. Two engineers will openly go from house to house to locate the problem. I imagine Hitchcock and co won't answer their door, at least in the first instance, but when the engineers get to the next house, the other semi-detached that's joined on, they'll find – that's find in inverted commas – the problem is in the cellar.'

'What happens if the occupants are out?'

'Do you think that would stop us getting in?' she said.

'Oh. Well, what happens if the occupants know something about the wiring in their house, and aren't fooled by your colleagues' tale?'

'If the worst comes to the worst, they'll tell the occupants a variant of the truth.'

'Right. But you still haven't said how they get these sensors through the wall without the kidnappers getting suspicious.'

'The sensors and their wires are as thin as a human hair. Jim has developed drills for these tiny holes which are so quiet and free of vibration that they're impossible to detect, even if you're in the same room. I've seen them. It's astonishing.'

'Thank God it's Jim,' Redstone said. 'I trust him. What are these sensors? What will they be sensing?'

'Sound, vision, infrared, firearms ammunition, explosives...'

'God. You think they might have explosives down there?'

'Clodagh was an IRA terrorist, after all. She made her name, her vicious brutal name, using explosives. It would be stupid to ignore the possibility.'

Redstone fell silent. He could imagine Clodagh blowing up the house rather than yielding the girls. Maybe she'd already fixed explosive jackets to Sophie and Rhiannon. He felt faint.

'Don't worry,' Laura said gently. She stepped towards him and hugged him tightly. 'We know what we're doing. We'll get them out safely.'

'Laura,' he said, 'I'm relying on you to prevent… prevent the worst happening. I'm going to do everything in my power to help, but I've got to be realistic – you're the one with the relevant skills.'

'And I have strong motivation,' she said.

He squared his shoulders. 'I must update Graham and Oskar. They'll be worried sick.'

'Of course. Say we think we've identified the house and are pouring resources into preparing for a successful rescue.'

*

The spattering of the rain against the windows was loud even through the striped drapes, which Clodagh insisted on keeping permanently closed. Valerie disliked the stuffy, old-fashioned décor, and found the gloom depressing.

Clodagh was sitting back in a heavy, winged armchair, her feet on a padded stool. She looked fit and well for a woman of seventy-five. Valerie hoped she'd inherited the relevant genes.

'I need to talk to you,' Valerie said, handing Clodagh a mug of tea. 'About our strategy.'

'Go on.'

'We've got Jones out of office. I know we failed to get him replaced by someone we can control, but at least we've achieved our main objective. So I have a proposal about—'

'Jones's removal is good, but you're underplaying what a disaster it was to lose control over Pitt. Any thoughts yet on how we can recover? How we can get back into a position where we can make the British establishment pay?'

'I know that's been our theme for the last couple of years, but—'

'More, for me,' Clodagh said. 'Much longer.'

'Right, but… We need to be realistic. We now need to limit our objectives. We can't win against the whole British establishment.

Jones, Smith and Redstone – they're our main targets. We're nearly there with Jones, and I've got a proposal about—'

'I do want the establishment to suffer.' Clodagh stared at the steaming mug. 'Not just those three.'

'But why? The Irish struggle is at least partly won. You can't live in the twentieth century for ever.'

'There's something I haven't told you.' Clodagh moved aside a small plastic box on the coffee table.

'Go on.'

'It goes back to when I was seventeen, in Belfast. I was working in a bakery as a shop assistant. And I did the accounts, as it happens, but that's irrelevant. British soldiers used to pass by and make suggestive signs.' She stared at the plastic box.

'And?'

'One day, a young officer with a posh voice came in.' She turned the plastic box round. 'I was on my own in the shop. He chatted to me, and suddenly… he grabbed me, dragged me into the alley behind the shop, and raped me.' Her eyes filled with tears. 'Nobody did anything about my screams.'

'Oh, Mum. I'm sorry—'

'I got pregnant, and my family disowned me.'

'Oh.' Valerie stopped. 'Oh… are you saying… was he my father?'

'Yes. I couldn't keep you, my darling. I'm so sorry. I left Belfast and came over to Birmingham. I joined a nationalist group there. I did try to keep you, but there was no way I could look after a baby.' She started crying.

Valerie stared at her. 'What was his name?'

Clodagh shook her head and continued to cry.

Valerie sat unmoving for a long moment. This was new information, but so what? It didn't make any difference, when all was said and done. She thought back to what had happened to her in the care home. Clodagh's story didn't change what Valerie had been forced to come to terms with, over the decades.

'It's all in the past,' she said. 'As far as I'm concerned, it's just another piece in the jigsaw. Let's move on.'

'Yes, it is in the past, but that officer represented the British state. In so many ways. Valerie, darling, I want to destroy these people, and I know you do too. We were doing so well last year, before Jones and his crew intervened. We must get back on track.'

'I'm just trying to be realistic. As I was saying, I've got an idea about how we can make the best—'

'Sweetheart, it's ironic that we lost control of Pitt just before she took over as prime minister, but I'm sure we can recover. We'll find another stooge.'

She picked up the plastic box and toyed with it.

'For heaven's sake, be careful with that,' Valerie said. 'It might go off.'

'Don't worry. Your Russian friends know what they're doing when it comes to this sort of thing.'

'Mum, I understand where you're coming from. I do. But I'm worried that if we keep hold of Jones's daughter and her friend, it won't be long before we're traced. MI5 and the police won't give up till they find the girls.'

'What are you saying? We simply hand the girls back?'

'No, I'm not. I've got another plan. Listen.'

THURSDAY 17TH TO FRIDAY 18TH AUGUST

'Another bad night?' Laura said as Redstone slumped into a kitchen chair.

'Yes, I couldn't sleep. For worry. What news?'

'The Henry Close house is empty. They're not there.'

'Oh, God.' His shoulders slumped. 'My guess was wrong.'

'Afraid so,' she said. 'Jim's equipment didn't pick up any signals indicating there was anyone in the house, so to make sure, his people went in. No sign of anyone having been there for weeks.'

'So…'

'So Jim's moved his team and their equipment over to Southwold Crescent. We should get their first results in a few hours.'

'I wish I'd kept my mouth shut,' he said. 'I've cost the girls yet more hours in the cellar, wherever it is. I'll never forgive myself if it turns out that something awful happened during that time.'

'You didn't make the decision,' she said, 'I did. What's done is done. I doubt that there's been any significant development overnight in the house, wherever it is.'

Redstone bowed his head. She was just trying to reassure him. He felt powerless. He *was* powerless. But so was Sophie, of course. He must remain strong for her.

'I can't stay here waiting,' he said. 'I'm going for a walk. Can you please phone me when you get some news?'

'Of course,' she said. 'But it'll be some time. Don't rush. At least have a cup of tea first.'

*

Redstone thumped down onto a park bench. The sky was gloomy and threatening, and there was nobody else nearby. He looked at his watch yet again – only an hour and ten minutes since he'd left home. He checked his phone had a signal. How was Sophie feeling right now? What had they done to her?

He reckoned it'd take another hour to complete his circular walk back to the house. Laura would think it reasonable that he'd returned by then. He stood up.

*

'No news yet,' Laura said. 'You look exhausted. Sit down and I'll make you a coffee.'

As she put the kettle on, her phone rang. She snatched it from the counter.

'It's Jim. I'll put it on speaker.'

'Mixed news,' Clothier's voice said, surprisingly un-tinny.

'What?' Redstone said.

'The house is big and complicated. It has a couple of outbuildings. It's detached, unlike the Henry Close place, and surrounded by open spaces. We can't get near on any side without the risk of being spotted. So some of our tools are useless. But our directional microphones and infrared scanners have convinced us there's someone inside.'

'No information on the cellar?' Laura said.

'Afraid not.'

'What next, then?'

'The house has several outside doors, and I think that one at the side leads down to the cellar and was originally used by men delivering coal. There are residual black stains on the nearby bricks. I'd like to get some apparatus attached to and inserted through that door – in particular a micro camera and sniffers.'

'Couldn't you have got up to the door and done that during the night?' said Redstone.

'By the time we got to Southwold Crescent it was dawn, but anyway—'

'Christ, it's my fault. I should never have suggested Henry Close. I won't forgive myself if—'

'No, Mark,' Clothier said, 'it wouldn't have made any difference. We couldn't have gone in last night. There's a security lamp over the cellar door. In fact, there are several security lamps round the property. Bright buggers.'

'So how—'

'So what I have in mind is to produce a power cut tonight after dark. Cover the whole local area to allay any suspicions. And then we'll be able to get to work on the door.'

'Right,' Laura said. 'I'll set it up with the power company. The process of getting their agreement will take several hours, so I need to get on with it. I'll also make other preparations in case it turns out we need to effect rapid entry.'

'Good,' Clothier said. 'Mark, we have to be patient, I'm afraid. I know it must be awful for you. I'll get back to you as soon as we know more.' He rang off.

'So I have to go into the office,' Laura said. 'I'll arrange for security cover here before I go.'

'Maybe I'll go and lie down for a bit,' Redstone said. 'I can't do anything to help Sophie, and I can't concentrate on anything else.'

'Yes, have a rest. You're under a hell of a lot of stress. Did you get another migraine last night?'

'No, not a trace. I don't understand why I've been getting them sometimes and not others. I had my tube of Smoothaway ready on the bedside table, but it's still there, unopened.'

'You sound almost disappointed,' she said.

'I suppose I am. Bizarre, to be disappointed at not getting a migraine.'

Redstone's phone rang – Graham. Redstone told him that there was some way to go before MI5 was in a position to confirm that they'd located the right house. Graham said he and Oskar were leaving Oskar's flat now to come over, so they'd be there in an hour.

'Good,' said Laura. 'I like having them around. When I've finished at Thames House, I'm going to base myself here, if that's OK with you. It's convenient for the kidnap site, if it does turn out to be 2 Southwold Crescent.'

'Of course it's OK. It's more than OK. I love having you here. It's just so awful that what's brought you back are these terrible circumstances.'

'I know,' she said. She looked away. 'Actually I prefer being here to being in my place. Somehow, you're less alone in a suburban house than I am in a central London flat.'

'I can see that,' he said. Was Laura signalling a change of heart about having left? Doubtful. It was the current special circumstances. No point in getting his hopes up.

Joanne rang. 'Any news?'

He told her the hunt was closing in.

'I'm praying for Sophie and Rhiannon,' she said. 'I'm sure they'll be fine. Anyway, I called because you're in demand again. The new prime minister wants to see you.'

'Octavia Pitt? Why on earth…?'

'The aide wouldn't say. What shall I tell them? You can't refuse, can you.'

'Suppose not. Did they give a time?'

'11:30.'

'I'll think about it and ring you back,' he said. He put his phone down and turned to Laura.

'I heard that,' she said. 'What would she want? I hope she hasn't been told the details of what's going on. Tell you what, I'll call Gavin McKay and see if he knows why she wants you to go to Number 10.' She picked up her phone, dialled, and spoke briefly.

‘He’s not available, but his PA assures me Gavin hasn’t told Tavia anything about the kidnap. I know her, and if she says that, it’s true.’

‘Do you think there’ll be any developments on the kidnap between now and early this afternoon?’ he asked.

‘Only in the sense of our getting everything ready for Jim’s intelligence gathering and a rescue mission. You won’t miss anything here if you go to Downing Street for a short meeting. I’ll text you with any news.’

He rang Joanne.

‘Please tell them I’ll come, but they’ll need to send a car to pick me up from here and return me as soon as the meeting’s finished. And I’ll want to go in the back entrance despite not having a pass. No publicity. Oh, and please tell David and Rosie I didn’t get a migraine last night, so I haven’t used the Smoothaway.’

*

Redstone was shown into the White Room at Number 10. This was where visiting statesmen and women posed for photos with the prime minister of the day. It was also in this room that he and Michael Jones had revealed, to the previous prime minister, evidence of Hitchcock’s blackmailing. Prime ministers liked using this room – it reeked of prestige and power.

The double doors opened, and in walked Tavia, with Sue Abercrombie a step behind.

‘Hello Mark,’ Tavia said, ‘many thanks for coming in.’ She shook his hand. ‘I understand you know Sue.’ Sue smiled at him from behind Tavia’s back.

‘Yes,’ Redstone said, ‘we have met.’

‘Sue’s now one of my special advisers,’ Tavia said. ‘Please sit down. I’ve asked you here to pick your brains.’

They sat in the grouped white brocade seats.

'I'm faced with a serious issue,' Tavia said, 'and Sue advises me that you might be able to help. This is the problem. There's evidence that Michael Jones may be in a terrible situation which could lead to a major security leak.'

Redstone blanched. What did they know, and how did they know it? He kept silent.

'Michael has said he stepped aside for health reasons,' Tavia continued. 'But nobody around here knows anything about a health condition.'

'Could be the stress,' Redstone said.

'Of course we can't rule that out. But we wondered if the terrorists were using new tactics to achieve their ends. Like kidnapping a member of his family.'

Redstone felt the blood drain from his face. What was she going to say next? What could he say without giving something away? He stayed silent.

'His daughter Rhiannon seems to have disappeared off everyone's radar,' Sue said. 'You might be asking what's that got to do with you, but I suspect you're not, and with Tavia's permission I'll explain why.'

'Go ahead,' said Tavia.

'I've looked at the Number 10 logs of visitors to the Prime Minister, and phone calls from him, over the last couple of weeks,' Sue said. 'You're on both lists, and you stand out as not having any obvious connection with his party or the big current policy issues.'

'I can't argue with any of that,' Redstone said. 'As you know, Michael and I have shared history and a good relationship on a personal level. He wanted to chat.'

'That's great. I suppose it explains why he visited your lab on the first of August without any prior arrangements, and before that – right at the start of the terrorist campaign – he called you round to his office following a bigger meeting with Tavia and others.'

'Correct,' Tavia said.

'Yes, it does explain that,' he said. 'I've no idea what you're leading to, but none of what you described was underhand or devious or… or whatever it is you suspect. It was to do with our personal relationship.'

'That's what I assumed,' Sue said. 'When you and I last met, you mentioned that your daughter Sophie was coming over from Brussels for a short holiday. I've found out that Rhiannon has been offered a job in Brussels. I'm thinking the two of them got together. Maybe you suggested to Mr Jones that Sophie could show Rhiannon the ropes in Brussels.'

'I—'

'And Mark, to be honest, you look awful. I mean you look as though you're under tremendous strain.'

Tavia leant forward. 'So we're putting two and two together, Mark,' she said. 'We suspect Rhiannon has been kidnapped by the terrorists, to put pressure on Michael. And my fear is that the terrorists have done that in order to pressurise him to give very high-level secrets to a foreign power.'

'And Sophie was taken too,' Sue said. 'Maybe she was with Rhiannon at the time and was just caught up in it.'

'Sorry,' he said, shaking his head, 'I can't say anything about any of that. You should ask Michael directly, and if he won't tell you I suggest you respect his decision.'

'Not as simple as that,' Tavia said. 'The security of the state is involved. That makes it very much my business.'

'Then ask the security services,' he said.

'I've learnt that the right thing to do is get information from more than one source. You get a better picture.'

He knew she hadn't got any information on the kidnap from Gavin. She wasn't going to get it from him.

'Look,' he said, 'for the sake of argument, let's suppose Sue's on the right track. The last thing anyone would want is that the kidnappers would get wind of what the security services know and plan. Do you accept that?' He realised he was verging on being rude. Or maybe he'd already crossed the line. 'Acting Prime Minister,' he added, trying to soften his tone.

'I'm sure you're not saying your acting prime minister can't be trusted with secret information.' Tavia said.

'I'm saying that, as a general rule, the fewer people who know the sort of thing you're suggesting, the safer the victims would be. In Sue's scenario I'm sure you'd have the welfare of the two young women as a top priority.'

'You're still ignoring my responsibilities for the security of the state.'

'I'm not – it's not my role to brief you on this sort of thing.'

Tavia glanced at Sue, who nodded.

'Very well,' Tavia said to Redstone, 'I can see we're not going to get any further. We can draw our own conclusions. Let's leave it there. Sue will escort you downstairs.' She stood, shook his hand, and marched out. Sue lingered behind.

'I'm terribly sorry if that was upsetting,' she said, taking his arm and leading him to the staircase. 'There is a genuine security concern. Prime ministers get told the most secret material – you'd be amazed. Would be a gold mine to the Russians, or Iran, or China… whoever is ultimately behind the terrorists. And of course, in addition to that, Tavia wants to know as much as possible about… let's say her prospects.' They descended past the pictures of previous prime ministers adorning the wall.

They reached the hallway. 'Maybe when everything's resolved we'll be able to get together and share reminiscences of this awful time,' she said.

He stared at her.

She gave a wry smile. 'Being insensitive, aren't I. Sorry. I'm sure it'll work out well.' She kissed him on the cheek and hurried away. He reeled back – he'd caught a flash of her thoughts as she'd kissed him. Affection for him, conviction her story about the kidnapping was right, thinking about how to use it. His mind-reading ability had returned. Why was it coming and going? And was that connected to the spate of migraines? Something strange was happening inside his head, obviously.

*

When he arrived back home, he found Laura, Graham and Oskar seated round the kitchen table.

'No more news from Southwold Crescent yet,' Laura said. 'What happened in Number 10?'

Redstone gave them an account of the meeting. 'Do you think there's anything in the theory about a foreign power?' he asked Laura.

'It's possible one is involved behind the scenes,' she said. 'But we know who the actual terrorists are. And their motives are personal. Anyway, it wouldn't affect our plans even if, say, Russia is providing some sort of background support.'

'Yes.' He hadn't considered the possibility that an enemy state was involved. They could be providing all sorts of resources – weapons, explosives, manpower. But it seemed that Laura and her colleagues had already factored that into their planning. Back to his major worry.

'I'm concerned that Tavia or Sue, probably Sue, will leak information which will lead to Hitchcock realising who Sophie is,' he said. 'I mean that she's my daughter. Sue is first and foremost a reporter. She'll want to report. A story like this could make her reputation.'

'And Octavia might see some political advantage in leaking something which makes Michael Jones seem weak, vulnerable and capable of being manipulated by terrorists,' Laura said.

'This is awful,' said Graham. 'What can we do about it?'

'I'll call Gavin McKay,' Laura said.

Ten minutes later she put her phone down.

'He says he's going to speak to Octavia and Sue urgently, and tell them that if anything happens to the girls as a result of leaks from Number 10, he personally will let the media know who was responsible, and he'll use phrases like "blood on their hands".'

'Oh, God,' said Oskar, 'does he think they'll… harm Sophie?'

'He doesn't know any more about that than the rest of us,' Laura said. 'He just wants to scare Number 10. He went on to say he'll tell his staff to press on with the investigation at maximum speed, not that they're dawdling anyway, and as soon as we have enough intel we'll swing into action.'

'Intel?' Oskar said.

'Intelligence, information,' Laura explained. 'To mount a successful rescue, we need as much knowledge as we can get. But of course we have to weigh that against the need to act urgently.'

Oskar went pale.

'Don't worry,' she said, 'we're trained to deal with this sort of thing.'

Oskar and Graham decided to go for a walk in an attempt to calm themselves. As soon as they were out of the door, Laura grabbed Redstone's arm.

'Another development,' she said. 'I couldn't tell you in front of the others. Michael Jones has received another message. It included a photo of the girls in the cellar, holding a copy of yesterday's paper. The terrorists will release the girls in exchange for you and me.'

'What?' He paled and slumped into a chair. 'What are we going to do?'

'I've talked it through with Gavin, who of course has also talked it through with Michael. The first point is that we can't trust the terrorists. Maybe I should stop using that word and simply say Clodagh and Hitchcock, as it's increasingly clear it's them. In this case I'm sure it's Hitchcock, who wants you and me in revenge for the events of last year. And before.'

'And what would she do? Kill us?'

'She'd try.'

'Would she accept just me? I'd give my life for Sophie.'

'Forget that. They don't know we're so close to locating them and freeing the girls. Our strategy is to play for time. Michael is going to tell them he'd like to agree, but he has to find a way of tricking you and me into the deal, and he'll come back to them as soon as possible.'

'Very well.' He ran his fingers through his hair. 'Laura, when we do get Clodagh and Hitchcock, what are you going to do? What I mean is… take them alive?'

'I've had a very off-the-record discussion with Gavin about that too. Clodagh presents a real problem. We have no firm evidence she was behind the terror, including the mass killings on the trains. And although she's been exposed as an escaped IRA terrorist, she was the mother of the US president. So the Americans will want us to extradite her to them.'

'But…'

'The point is you can't extradite a dead body,' she said.

'Ah. And Hitchcock?'

'I'm to conclude the unfinished business Gavin and I set out to do last year.'

'Good.'

Laura put her hand on his shoulder. 'Look at it this way. It's good news. The girls are alive and unharmed, and Clodagh and Hitchcock will keep them that way for the time being.'

'Yes,' he said. 'Christ, what a lot to absorb. And I was going to tell *you* something private, though it pales into insignificance beside your news.'

'What?'

'It's come back.'

'What? Your migraine?'

'No, the mind-reading.'

She stepped back. 'Oh. Does that mean you're reading my—'

'No. I'd have to be even closer unless I was wearing the cap. In fact, come to think of it, it might be weaker than it was before. I didn't detect anything till Sue gave me a peck on the cheek on her way out of this morning's meeting, and even then, it was only fleeting.'

'Oh, she kissed you, did she? I didn't realise you were that close.'

He reddened. 'We're not… look, there are more important issues here. First, what I said before about my fears for what Sue might do – that was based to some extent on what I picked up during the peck. She was convinced her story was accurate and was thinking about how to use it.'

She stared at him.

'Yes, that was useful. And anyway, it's none of my business who you kiss, or…'

'It would be if you and I were together again. Which is what I'd like. Love.'

'Really? I… Let's get on with the important issues, as you put it. You implied there were others.'

'One other. Could the ability be of use when you rescue the girls?'

'Ah. Might be. Could be useful to know what the kidnappers have in mind. Depends on what range you get with the cap on.'

'Let's try, then.' He rushed upstairs and returned with the cap.

'We should try without the cap, first,' he said. 'Think of a number, and I'll gradually get nearer you till I pick it up.'

She stood still. He took baby steps towards her, but only when they were toe to toe did he pick up what she was thinking.

'Number 2 Southwold Crescent,' he said.

'That's right. But as I remember, last time you could pick it up further away than that.'

'Yes, from about three feet.'

‘Better try it with the cap. If it’s just a short distance, it’s unlikely to be of much use in a… a rapid confrontation.’

He switched the cap on, placed it on his head and moved close to her.

‘The signal’s stronger than when I wasn’t wearing it,’ he said, ‘but still weaker than it was originally.’ He frowned. ‘I wonder if Jim Clothier could amplify the signal a bit more than what the gubbins in this cap can do. I’ll ring him.’

He phoned Clothier.

‘Hello Mark. I was about to contact Laura.’

‘Hold on,’ Redstone said, ‘I’ll put you on speaker.’

Clothier said they’d sent a sniffer dog into the garden. It had wandered around the patios and the drive at the side of the house and then returned to its handler in the woods opposite. The handler was sure the dog’s behaviour indicated the presence of explosives somewhere on the property.

‘Not unexpected,’ Laura said.

Redstone slumped back in his chair, shocked and unable to say anything coherent.

‘Listen, Jim,’ said Laura, ‘Mark’s mind-reading ability has come back, but not as strong as before. There’s a chance it might be valuable when we mount the rescue. Is there anything you can do to improve the cap’s sensitivity? Live information on the enemy’s plans is always worth having during an operation, but I can’t have Mark too near the action, so he’d have to be able to pick up thoughts from at least, say, ten feet.’

‘Hmm,’ Clothier said. ‘You haven’t given me much time, have you? Fortunately, I did some work on this when we made the cap. The answer is that we can’t make anything more powerful that could still be hidden in a baseball cap. But I could increase the sensitivity if I made some more complex gear. At a cost of high selectivity and it being obvious to an observer.’

‘What do you mean by selectivity?’

'Ability to pick up thoughts from only one person at a time, and only when the apparatus is pointing at that person.'

'Anything that might help,' Redstone said.

'Righto. I'll go back to Thames House and assemble the kit. My colleagues don't need me here at the moment.'

*

'I saw a dog wandering around the garden,' said Hitchcock, 'sniffing everywhere for quite a time till its owner called it from the woods over the road. Seemed odd. Nothing's happened since, but even so…'

'So what?' said Clodagh.

'I'm getting nervous. We need a plan B if they don't react quickly to your message.'

*

Redstone, Clothier and Laura sat in the back of a tall Transit van parked in a side street two hundred metres away from the target house. It was 3 a.m. Rain was drumming on the roof. The sign on the side of the van read *JC Hydraulics – 24-hour service*, and bore a phone number and website address which were fake. Clothier had told him that he'd chosen wording which sounded technical and important but was meaningless.

'Sorry we had to ruin it with these detectors,' Clothier said, holding up a bulbous cap with two metal antennae fixed to the peak, one on each side.

Redstone took it.

'These look like pieces of coat-hanger wire, with end bits soldered on,' he said.

'That's because they are. The idea is that with two detectors we can tune the device to be more directional and sensitive than the original cap. We can use the minute differences between the two signals. Modern electronics are good at using minute differences.'

Redstone hefted the cap. 'Quite heavy,' he said. 'I suppose that's because of those modern electronics, as you put it.'

'No. It's because we've enhanced the coils which sit on your skull.'

'What about this cable?' Redstone lifted a length of wire, coiled like an extended spring, dangling from the back of the cap.

'That plugs into this.' Clothier stood and held up a khaki gilet studded with many bulbous pockets. 'It contains the main electronics, and the power supply. It's the sort of thing worn by people who like huntin', shootin' and fishin'. These pockets are where they keep their cartridges, their devices for prising animal rights activists out of horses' hooves, and their peasant pluckers.'

'Pheasant pluckers,' said Redstone.

'I don't care what those pluckers pluck,' said Clothier. Laura burst into laughter, and Redstone grinned despite the tense situation.

'It's a bit Heath Robinson,' Clothier said, 'because we had so little time. Just enough to nip out and buy these elegant items of clothing. Incidentally, if you ever want a hat, there's this fantastic little shop near Victoria—'

'Let's get on with it,' Redstone said. 'I need to try it out.' He took the gilet, put it on, and was just about to put the cap on his head when Clothier stopped him and pointed at the rain streaming down the back windows of the van.

'One more thing. This goes over the cap. Need to keep the electronics dry in this weather.' He handed Redstone a large elasticated transparent plastic cap.

'Is that what hotels give you to protect your hair in the shower?' asked Laura.

'No, those are too small and flimsy. We use these at home to slip over plates or bowls of leftovers before we put them in the fridge. Bloody useful.'

Redstone fitted the plastic over the cap and gingerly placed the contraption on his head. He plugged the connecting wire into a socket on the shoulder of the gilet.

'Was your primary aim to make me look ridiculous?' he said.

'No, that's merely a welcome side effect.'

'Just the sight of you will cow the terrorists into submission,' Laura said.

'If only,' said Redstone. With Clothier's guidance he found the on/off switch and activated the device.

'Don't point it at me,' Laura said seriously.

'Try me,' said Clothier, moving to the end of the van. Redstone moved to the other end and faced Clothier.

'You're worrying about getting through the cellar door undetected,' he said.

'Right,' Clothier said. 'But not worrying more than I always do before a venture like this. Let's try a longer distance. I'll get out of the van and walk about ten feet from the back doors. You stay here in case someone comes by. We don't want anyone to see you wearing that thing.'

He put up the hood on his anorak and climbed out, hunched against the beating rain. He strode three steps away from the van and turned to face the open doors.

'You're wondering what Laura is planning for breaking into the house if it turns out the girls are there,' Redstone called out.

'Right,' Clothier said. He climbed back into the van and shook the rain off his coat. 'Seems it's working fine. So, Laura, what *are* your plans?'

Redstone automatically turned towards Laura. *He's got to be right back, well out of harm's way,* she was thinking. *Called on only if absolutely necessary.* She was picturing herself questioning Clodagh, and Redstone telling her what Clodagh was thinking.

He felt a huge sense of relief. He hadn't realised how nervous he was about being in the rescue operation. He took off the cap.

'... decided yet,' Laura was saying to Clothier. 'Depends on what you find. The Met team are concerned because the house is so complex. We'd like to get into the house undetected, before we start any violent action, so while the lights are off, we'll ask you for a quick technical survey to find where the occupants are.'

'Of course we're not yet sure the terrorists and the girls are here,' Clothier said. 'What if they're not?'

'We'll move on to another house on the list.'

'Aren't you confident this is the right place?' said Redstone. 'It's so well-suited to their needs.'

'Pretty confident,' she said, 'not least because the dog sniffed explosives, but I'm always prepared for a plan to go wrong. Don't worry. We will rescue them.' She looked at her watch. 'Five minutes before the lights go out. Let's switch on the monitors.'

*

They sat on a narrow bench on the side wall of the van. There were two screens on the opposite wall. The right-hand screen was blank, but the left-hand screen showed a clear picture of the right side of the house, which was illuminated by the security lamps. Redstone focused on the faded dark brown cellar door, set in a dirty brick wall.

Suddenly, the security lights went out and the picture changed. It took a few seconds for Redstone to realise it was the same scene, but in skeletal white lines on a black background.

'Night vision lens,' Clothier said.

The other screen clicked on, showing a similar image, changing as the camera appeared to be approaching the door.

‘Head camera on one of our officers,’ Clothier said.

The head camera scene became difficult to interpret as hands and tools moved in and out of the picture. The other screen showed three officers crouched round the door.

Five minutes later the head camera screen went blank and then showed a jerky picture of steps and a wooden structure, which Redstone couldn’t quite interpret.

‘Damn,’ Clothier said. ‘This is the picture from the probe they’ve inserted. It seems that the door leads to a sort of vestibule with a few steps down to a trapdoor. I suppose the trapdoor leads to the coal cellar itself, and is opened from the inside. No way we can get to the trapdoor without breaking open the outer door. That’s bound to make some noise. What’s your decision, Laura?’

‘Don’t do it,’ she said without hesitation. ‘Getting inside covertly is more important. If it’s the right house, we’re fairly confident the girls will be in the cellar unharmed. Where’s the plan of the house?’

‘I can put it on the screen,’ Clothier said. He typed on a keyboard. A photo of an architect’s plan appeared on the right-hand screen.

‘I’ve agreed with the Met commander that there are two options for a silent entry,’ Laura said. She pointed. ‘Here and here. Which one we use depends on where the two women are sleeping. Can you now get your staff to use your equipment to find out where they are?’

‘Sure.’ He spoke on his phone. ‘They’ll tell us in ten minutes.’

Laura rang the police commander and told him to get ready. She turned to Redstone.

‘Listen, Mark. We have a simple key objective for this operation – rescue the girls unharmed. We’re going to do that by what I judge to be the most effective means, which involves silence for as long as possible followed by actions which may be fast, shocking and violent. You’re going to be well in the background, present only in case I need your ability. You mustn’t move unless I call you, and if

I do you mustn't let qualms or shock cause you to hesitate. Understood?'

'Yes.' This was one of the reasons why MI5 had recruited Laura – for her special forces experience.

'The bomb squad is on standby, and—'

A wave of fury hit him. 'Laura,' he said, 'don't hesitate to kill Hitchcock and Clodagh. Do it with my blessing.'

'We'll do what's appropriate,' she said. 'Listen. I hadn't quite finished briefing you. We'll be supported in the rescue operation by a small group of Met counter-terrorist officers. Make sure you don't get in their way.'

'Sorry. Of course.'

'Jim,' she said, 'could you please check they're ready? Mark, let's put our kit on.'

'More kit?' said Redstone.

She went to the front of the van, picked up a plastic crate, and brought it over.

'First thing is this flak jacket.' She handed him a short padded sleeveless black vest. 'Slip it over your head and fasten it with the Velcro at the sides. It goes under Jim's gilet.'

'I'm going to be boiling in all this,' he said.

'Warfare is uncomfortable. This is warfare. Now these.' She gave him a pair of large, padded headphones and some goggles with thick rims.

'Why do I—'

'We may have to use stun grenades, also called flashbangs. They disorient people. Your kit lets light through the goggles and sound through the earphones until the grenade goes off, when it reacts immediately to stop the wearer being affected.'

'OK.'

'Now I'll put my own kit on,' Laura said. 'A bit different from yours in that I wear a helmet with the equipment built in. Oh, I forgot to say – there's a microphone built into the headphones, so you'll be able to talk to me. Now turn round, the pair of you. I'm getting changed.'

A minute later she said they could turn back. She was dressed in black, including the helmet. Redstone thought she looked sexy, and then felt guilty and amazed at himself for thinking such a thing at a time like this.

'Right,' Clothier said. 'We've located signs of life in this bedroom,' he pointed on the screen, 'but nowhere else. Of course we can't see below ground-level, but it seems unlikely that Clodagh or Hitchcock are in the cellar, so I suppose they're both in the same bedroom. Seems odd, but…'

'Or we've got the wrong house,' Redstone said.

'I'm going to work on the assumption that this is the right one,' Laura said. 'So this is how we're going to do it.'

*

Redstone and Laura stood side by side in the trees across from 2 Southwold Crescent. Big raindrops were splashing on the ground.

'Now,' Redstone heard her say, through the headphones.

'Received,' a male voice replied.

'That's the house alarm out of action,' she said to Redstone.

'How did they—'

'Jim can explain tomorrow. Let's go.'

They crossed the road and met a group of five helmeted black-clad officers in the front garden of the house. One pointed to the gravelled drive on the left of the house, put a finger to his lips, beckoned the group to follow, and tiptoed across the front lawn. He pointed to a narrow grass strip at the edge of the gravel. The group followed him, stepping silently in single file along the side of the house. Laura was behind the leader, and Redstone brought up the rear. He could hardly see the ground in the dark and rain, so he copied the steps of the officer ahead. They passed a door with pebbled glass windows and reached the end of the house's side wall.

The file turned right, and tiptoed across the back of the house. The leader held up a hand outside a pair of big French windows. The group bunched behind the leader, who manipulated a pick in the lock of the left door. After what seemed an eternity, the lock gave a soft click. The officer sprayed the hinges with oil, and eased the French window open. It creaked slightly. They stood stock still and waited, but there was no sound from inside.

Laura took the lead officer's position by the French window. She slowly pushed aside a heavy curtain and stepped inside. It was totally dark. She switched on a dim penlight and beckoned the others. Redstone was last into the large, carpeted room, furnished with heavy armchairs, a sofa and some occasional tables. Laura whispered in his headphones that he should wait by the door in the opposite wall until she called him.

Laura and the officers crept out of the door into a panelled hall. Redstone stayed in the doorway and watched them fan out and edge through other doors leading off the hall. Within a couple of minutes each had returned, indicating the room they'd explored was empty. Laura whispered that they were now going upstairs. Redstone should follow, but stay at the top of the stairs, while the rest of them would go to the door at the left end of the landing. That bedroom was where Clothier's team believed the terrorists were.

Laura led the way. The group crowded behind her. She flung the door open and crashed in, the officers storming after.

'Armed police!' they shouted discordantly, in shocking contrast to the previous silence. 'Stay where you are!'

A couple of seconds passed. In his headphones, Redstone heard Laura say, 'Mark, come in now.'

He rushed into the room. An officer was shining a big torch at Clodagh, who was half out of bed, staring at the group. Suddenly she jerked over to the bedside table and grabbed a small plastic box.

'She's going to detonate a bomb!' Redstone shouted.

Two sharp cracks in his earphones. Clodagh's face disintegrated as she fell sideways, banging into the bedside table. An officer ran for the plastic box, now on the carpet.

'Everyone out, now!' Laura said urgently, using her pistol to wave the officers to the door. 'She pressed the button! Now, now! The explosives may be on a timer.'

'What about the girls?' Redstone shouted as he joined the group galloping down the stairs, their helmet lights bouncing.

'I'm going to find the cellar and get them out,' Laura called over the communications system. 'For God's sake get out of the house! This isn't your scene.'

He ripped off his headphones, ignored her instruction, and followed her as she flung open a door in the hall and rushed down a flight of concrete stairs. She tugged at a plain wooden door.

'Hell!' she said. 'Locked.' She pointed her pistol at a shallow angle to the door, and shot at the lock. A loud bang, splinters of wood flew from the door and the doorpost, and the door edged open. She kicked it wide and rushed in, Redstone at her heels. They were in a utility room – boiler, washing machine, dryer. A plastic sack sat in the centre of the floor. A wire snaked from its mouth to a small phone, sitting on a high shelf. No sign of the girls. Redstone scanned the room but couldn't pick up any trace of their thoughts.

'Oh, Christ,' he said. 'Where are they?'

Laura rushed through an arch at the far end of the cellar and came back after a few seconds.

'Empty except for junk. They're not here. Out, fast!'

He raced up the steps, through the hall and sitting room, and into the garden.

'Bomb in the basement!' Laura shouted over the communications system as she followed close behind him.

The security lights sprang to life, almost blinding him. He felt on the edge of panic. Had they killed Sophie? An officer grabbed his arm and pulled him away from the house. They jogged over to the other officers, who were grouped in the grounds at the far end of the drive, in front of the double doors of a large yellow brick building with two garage doors.

Help! he heard, or perhaps only felt Sophie call.

'They're in the garage!' he shouted.

At the back.

He ran along the garage wall to a side door, which was secured with a heavy padlock. He looked around wildly.

An officer ran up with a garden spade. Holding the shaft above his head, he hammered the blade down on the hasp. The padlock and hasp fell to the ground with a clunk. Redstone pushed open the door. There were Sophie and Rhiannon, cowering in front of stacked garden furniture in a high, square room with narrow windows just below the roof beams. He rushed in.

'Dad!' Sophie rushed into his arms. He felt her overwhelming relief and love, and hugged her fiercely. His tension drained away.

'You're safe now,' he said, removing his cap before it attracted attention. He gestured to Rhiannon. 'Come and join the hug.'

Laura ran into the room. She kicked aside a tray of paper plates and cups, moved a bundle of blankets with her foot, and peered into the stack of chairs and tables. She turned round and rushed to a rucksack in the corner behind the door. She pulled it open and peered inside.

'This is another bomb!' she said. 'Out, now!'

'Well,' Sophie said, 'it's—'

'Now!' Laura said sharply. She jabbed her finger towards the door and spoke into her helmet microphone.

'Come on,' Redstone said, pulling Sophie. 'And you, Rhiannon. Can you both run?'

'Yes, Dad, but—'

'Come on!'

They ran down the drive and into the road. Laura caught them up. The police officers were close behind.

'Round to the van,' Laura said. They jogged down the road and round the corner. The streetlights were on, and the sky was beginning to lighten with the first traces of dawn. The rain had stopped.

Clothier stood next to the van. 'Bomb squad getting geared up,' he said, gesturing to more vans further down the road, blue lights flashing.

'Tell them the bomb in the cellar has a mobile phone trigger,' said Laura, 'but the one in the garage is different. A small box connected to the detonator. I think Clodagh tried to activate it, but it didn't work. Maybe a fault. Could go off at any time.'

'Will do.' He turned to go, but stopped. 'I take it you didn't locate Hitchcock,' he said.

'No.'

'If she's escaped, she could activate the mobile phone trigger whenever she chooses. I'll warn the bomb squad.' He ran down the road.

'Dad, Laura,' said Sophie, 'I've been trying to tell you. We took the battery out of that plastic box at the top of the rucksack.'

'What?' said Redstone. 'You're mad! It could have been wired to go off if the box was opened!'

'We thought of that. Once we got the screws out, we opened it just a crack and peered inside. The lid wasn't attached to anything, and there wasn't anything pressing against it. We had a lengthy discussion about what to do. We decided opening it was less risky than leaving it. The kidnappers could have exploded it at any time.'

'What did you find inside the box?' said Laura.

'One of those rectangular nine-volt batteries and a small circuit board with some stuff wired to it. We put the battery in the oily mess in the bag inside the rucksack. To hide it. There were big nails in there too.'

'Well done,' Laura said. 'I'll tell the bomb squad.' She ran down the road and spoke to Clothier and three men who were donning camouflaged armour.

'You are a cool pair,' Redstone said to the young women. He put his arms round them both and hugged them tightly. Rhiannon burst into tears, deep sobs racking her body. Sophie started to cry softly.

'Let it out,' he said. 'It's all over now.'

Laura returned.

'What do you think happened to Hitchcock?' Redstone asked her.

'I imagine she slipped out when the lights went off. Maybe she heard Jim's team, and used the kitchen door. The one we passed in the dark. But I don't suppose we'll ever know.'

'Are you saying the kidnappers are still out there?' Rhiannon said, her voice cracking. 'How many were there?'

'Probably two,' Laura said. One is dead, but I think the other has escaped. Don't worry. You're safe.' She stroked Rhiannon's arm. 'You'll be guarded from now on.' She took Rhiannon's and Sophie's hands. 'We need to get you two to hospital. You have to be checked over, and you'll need some psychological help.'

'We need a shower and clean clothes before anything else,' Sophie said. 'Sorry, I must smell awful.' She started crying. 'Oh, Dad, we were so scared. She wore a horrible clown mask. We had to use a bucket. Laura, are you sure we're safe?'

'Absolutely,' Laura said. 'Can you tell us anything about who they were?'

'No. We only saw one woman. We thought she was middle-aged. She didn't say anything. It was all pointing and gesturing, and waving a gun.'

'What about when she took the photos?'

'She just pointed. So you got the photos. We had to stand against the inside wall. I hoped the bricks might give you a clue that it was part of a garage. Well, we thought it was a Victorian coach house that had been converted to a garage.'

'The pair of you are heroes,' Laura said. 'You've done bloody brilliantly. Tell me – how did you get the screws out of the lid?'

'Yes, that was the most difficult bit. Tiny screws, fingernails no good.' She gave a weak smile. 'But you'd be able to do it, while Dad wouldn't.'

'Ah,' Laura said. 'Yes, that's what I would have done.'

'What on earth are you talking about?' Redstone said.

'What do we wear that you don't?' Sophie said.

'Oh. What, with those annoying little hooks and eyes?'

'Exactly.'

The bomb squad soldiers, armoured in protective gear, came up the road. As they walked past, a huge explosion banged and roared in Redstone's ears and lit up the sky above the house. A blast of dusty hot air hit his face.

'Get in!' shouted Laura, pushing the Sophie and Rhiannon. They clambered up into the van. Rubble pinged and rattled on the van roof.

A second explosion sounded, not so fierce. The young women crouched on the van floor, arms protecting their heads.

'First one was the cellar,' Laura said, 'and I suppose the second the garage, set off by hot debris. Better stay here for a minute or two.'

'So the phone trigger was activated?' Redstone said.

'Guess so.'

'Why would they do that?' Rhiannon said. 'What sort of people are they?'

'Destroying evidence, I guess.' She gave Redstone a warning look. He kept his mouth shut. Sophie stared at them.

'I'm going to be sick,' she said, stumbling to the door.

SATURDAY 19TH AUGUST

Throbbing pain in his right temple, nausea, generally feeling awful. Redstone heaved himself out of bed, and was about to stumble to the bathroom for his migraine medication when he remembered the tube of Smoothaway on the bedside table. The pain was getting more intense and spreading down the right side of his head. He switched on the lamp and screwed his eyes shut at the light. Was it four centimetres? He half-opened one eye and squeezed out some cream, knowing he wasn't thinking clearly.

He gently rubbed the Smoothaway into his temple. No effect. How long should he wait before adding more? If it didn't work quickly, there was little chance of the cream being successful – it wouldn't have a significant advantage over existing treatments. He'd give it two minutes. The clock read 5:46. He'd wait until 5:48.

Two minutes later, he thought the symptoms might have eased a little, but he wasn't sure. He'd experienced no ill effects, so he might as well add a bit more cream. He squeezed out another two centimetres and massaged it into his temple. He felt pleased with the way he was handling this. Delighted, actually. He stood up and grinned. The pain had pretty well gone, as had the other symptoms. No, it had totally gone. Amazing! What a triumph! He strode to the window, drew back the curtains and breathed deeply. The sky was light and cloudless. He threw open the bedroom door and hurried into Graham's room, at the back of the house, so he could see the sun rising over the trees at the far end of the garden. Lucky that Graham had gone back to Oskar's flat.

What a gorgeous sight! The sky was painted with low bands of red orange, the air was crystal clear after yesterday's heavy rain, and the wet grass and leaves were sparkling in the dawn sunlight. Sophie and Rhiannon were safe. And Smoothaway worked.

Laura appeared behind him, wearing a short nightdress.

'What's going on?' she said. 'Unlike you to be up so early.'

'It's great to be alive, and even greater now you're here. God, you look lovely.' He pulled her to him and hugged her. 'Oh, I haven't a clue what you're thinking. The challenge of finding out makes this morning greater still.'

She put the flats of her hands against his chest, leant back and looked into his face.

'You're saying the mind-reading has gone again?'

'Yes, but let's not worry about that.' He stroked her back.

'You don't seem to be drunk, but… are you on some drug?'

'Of course not. I had a migraine, and it's disappeared. Such a wonderful feeling! It's so… so *good* to be without those symptoms. And there are all the successes of yesterday…'

'Did you use your new cream?' she asked.

'Yes, there's that too. It worked like a dream!' He pulled her back to him and kissed her on the mouth. After a moment she responded. He released her and pulled her by the hand back into his bedroom, smiling broadly. She didn't resist.

*

They lay in each other's arms.

'You realise you'll have to report this side effect,' she said.

'What are you talking about?'

'Your cream. Smoothaway. I know one example doesn't count statistically but it seems to induce… well, euphoria. Not that I'm complaining. Quite the contrary.'

'Nah, it's not the cream, it's the good stuff that's happened, all come together.'

'I don't think so. You'd better do an experiment – use it again tomorrow, even if you don't have a migraine. If it's safe to do so.'

'Fine. I don't see a problem in doing that. In fact, I'm scientifically obliged to do it.' He snorted with suppressed laughter.

She laughed because he was laughing.

'Your mind-reading still gone?'

'Totally. Stop worrying about it. I'm not.'

'It must be connected to your migraines. Something's happening inside that brain of yours. I'm not worrying about the ability having gone. I didn't like the intrusion.'

'Sorry,' he said cheerfully.

'You realise I could go home now. No need to protect you anymore.'

'One problem with that.'

'Oh?'

'I won't let you go.' He tightened his arms round her and kissed her.

'Well, that's good, because I've decided to stay. If that's OK with you.'

'I think I can cope with it,' he said, kissing her again. 'What about the boredom of living in this suburban hellhole with this suburban plodder?'

'Oh, that.' She tossed her head. 'I've realised I can't have everything. I can get my excitement from my job. And I like your posh shower, and Treacle, and the friendly neighbours. And you're not so bad yourself.'

*

'Well, Valerie,' the FSB agent said, pulling up his chair, 'this is a first.'

‘What do you mean?’ said Hitchcock. She looked around the small café. It could have been anywhere in Europe, except for the Cyrillic writing.

‘First time I’ve debriefed anyone with the same name,’ he said. ‘Though I admit we spell it differently. I’m Valery with a Y.’

She set her mouth in a hard line. ‘I suppose you’re trying to put me at my ease. Don’t worry. I’ve felt safe ever since Heathrow.’

‘Good.’ He beckoned the waitress and spoke in Russian. As she walked away, he tilted his chair back and scanned Hitchcock.

‘Now take me through what happened at the end. The British are saying the American was killed in the blast.’

‘Yes. Once we’d lost our leverage over Pitt, I didn’t see any future in pursuing her grandiose plans. And I thought her strategy of mass violence was unsubtle and counterproductive.’

‘And her money?’

‘What do you mean?’ she said.

‘The money in her offshore accounts. Had you got her to give you access to it?’

She blinked. ‘That was a secondary issue.’

His face remained impassive. ‘Your losing control of Pitt is irrelevant, isn’t it,’ he said. ‘She’s going back to the Home Office, now Jones’s daughter’s been rescued. Jones will be prime minister again. So even if you still controlled Pitt, you would have no more influence over the British government than you did at the start of your campaign.’

‘There’s an English saying – “If at first you don’t succeed, try, try again”.’

‘I prefer to say, “try a different strategy”,’ he said.

The waitress brought coffee and a bottle of vodka.

‘And on Jones’s daughter,’ Valery said. ‘If the blast killed the American, why didn’t it also kill her?’

'The important thing is that all the evidence was destroyed. I did hope to get her and some key British officers as well, but the rescue was faster than I'd expected.'

He took a drink of coffee.

'Let's look at the big picture,' he said. 'Tell me if any of this is wrong: you collaborated with the American last year, before you were expelled from the Cabinet Secretary job she'd got you into. When she was exposed as an IRA terrorist, you hid her in your home. You both kept a very low profile for several months.'

'Yes, we wanted the fuss about the temporary regime to die down.'

'Temporary regime is one way of describing the US takeover of the UK's government, I suppose. Skipping forward to this summer, you helped the American organise the train crashes and the other acts. And your motive was to get back into power when Pitt replaced Jones as prime minister. Hers were more complex.'

'That's right. She wanted revenge for things that happened in her early life.'

'Quite so. Carrying on, you say the British authorities have no reason to suspect that you were involved in what they describe as the terrorism. No reason and no evidence. They're seeking you only for your failed blackmail of Pitt. Right so far?'

'Yes,' she said, 'but even that—'

'And the young women you kidnapped can't identify you, and you've destroyed the physical evidence linking you with the kidnap. So you're in the clear.'

'Yes.'

'There's nothing you've not told us? No personal agenda?'

'Of course not.'

He stared at her.

'What?' she said.

He gave a thin smile. 'So you still want to go ahead with the operation.'

'Definitely.'

'Well then, let's drink to a productive relationship in the future.' He poured two generous measures.

'Bit early for me,' she said.

He raised his glass. 'Drink up – I insist.'

A YEAR LATER

Redstone and Laura walked from the car park to the entrance of 'Amaze,' the upmarket restaurant which Mary and Zena had opened on the outskirts of Barnet.

'This is so not my scene,' Laura said.

'You'll be fine. Maybe we should have applied some Smoothaway.'

'I wish.'

'Come in, come in,' said Mary, kissing their cheeks. They stepped into the restaurant, a spacious room divided into several sections, all open to the centre, but screened from each other by low partitions of differing designs. Each section was subtly decorated in a manner suggesting a theme from a film.

Zena, in a clingy long dress with a slit down one side, came to Mary's side. Mary moved away to the next guests.

'Am I allowed a kiss?' she said to Redstone.

'Only because it'll make the other customers jealous.' He gave her a peck on the cheek. 'You look great.'

'Thanks,' she said. 'It's all a show to attract the customers. Not too different from the theatre.'

'But different from nursing, for Mary,' Laura said.

'Back to Mum's roots. I'll escort you to your table.' She waved her hand round the room. 'Laura, you're an intelligence officer. See if you can work out which is your table.'

'Could be the one with the Prime Minister, Sophie, Graham… Is the film *It's a Wonderful Life*?'

'Well done.' She took Laura's arm. 'Let me escort you. By the way, you look pretty stunning yourself. If I were that way inclined…'

Michael Jones and his wife, Anne, stood to greet them.

'Anne,' Jones said, 'this is Laura, who I've told you about and to whom we owe so much. You know Mark, of course. Laura, my wife, Anne.'

Handshaking ensued.

'So, Michael,' Redstone said, 'you promised – no speeches.'

'But I'm a politician. You can't trust a word I say.' He beckoned Mary over, turned to face the rest of the party, and coughed loudly.

'Hello everyone. I promised Mark that I wouldn't give a speech.'

'Hooray!' said Rhiannon. 'Hear, hear,' said the others.

'I'm ignoring my daughter, as usual. We're here to celebrate the anniversary of the brilliant rescue by this brilliant woman,' he gestured to Laura, 'aided by this brilliant man and various other brilliant people, including my friend Michelle' – he gave a small bow to Michelle, who looked startled – 'and Mary and Zena, founders of this super restaurant. So let's drink to… to the rescuers!'

Mary gestured to a waiter to fill their glasses. There was a disorganised round of congratulatory calls and glass clinking, followed by chatter and chair scraping. The group settled down to their meal. The volume of the chatter increased.

'What's the latest on your magic cream, Dad?' Graham called, leaning over Oskar.

'It's now definitely repurposed as a psychiatric drug for depression. Just has to pass the remaining tests.'

'How do you feel about that?'

'Mixed feelings. I still hanker after a cream to cure migraines.'

'I thought it does both.'

'Yes, but it seems it's addictive, so it can't be sold over the counter, and the side effects – well, what would have been side effects – mean it won't be prescribed over existing migraine treatments.'

'Mmm, the side effects,' said Laura. Redstone was almost sure she'd winked at him.

*

Valery handed Hitchcock a large brown envelope.

'It's all there,' he said. 'Top quality – indistinguishable from genuine articles. We used the identity of a girl born in the same year as you. She went missing in Central America in her gap year. Now no living relatives.'

Hitchcock tipped the contents onto the table.

'You're good to go.' Valery said.

She shuffled through the papers and picked up the passport. She opened it and stared at the photo page.

'Amazing, isn't it?' he said. 'He's one of the world's leading plastic surgeons.' He looked her in the eye. 'Even your own mother wouldn't recognize you.'

THE END

AUTHOR'S NOTE

The characters in this novel are fictional. Some of the described technology can be done now, some may be doable in the near future, and some…?

ACKNOWLEDGEMENTS

Thanks to my wife, Viv Finer; my sister, Susan Joslin; and my friend Robert Hedges. They each gave thoughtful, insightful advice on how to improve early drafts. Thanks also to Becky Stradwick for her outstanding professional editorial suggestions, to Rocko Spigolon for his excellent cover design, and to Richard Blandford, my copy editor. And I'm most grateful to Daniel Jaeggi for explaining how hackers work and outlining the IT systems of modern trains.

Finally, thanks to you, the reader. I hope you enjoyed this novel. If you did, I'd be grateful if you'd post a review on Amazon, to guide others to a book they might enjoy.

And if you did like *Dead Personal,* you'll also enjoy my first two Redstone thrillers – *Killing Power* and *State of Resistance.*

ABOUT THE AUTHOR

Elliot and his wife live in London. They have two sons, three grandchildren and two cats. His career has included spells as a research scientist, a senior civil servant, and the CEO of a company serving the chemical industry. He enjoys reading, writing, gardening and creative DIY.

Elliot recently realised he has aphantasia - he has no mind's eye.

Find out more, and give feedback, at **www.elliotfiner.com**

KILLING POWER by ELLIOT FINER

Mark Redstone's life is on an upward turn. It has taken years for him to rally from the body blow of his wife's murder, but his biotechnology company has seen recent success, and he's even noticing the opposite sex again.

Out of the blue he receives a phone call – from the country's top official – that changes everything.

He is tasked with an assignment: to investigate a plot involving Britain's nuclear reactors that, if unresolved, could devastate the country. And his means for doing this is a ground-breaking scientific discovery which gives him amazing abilities.

Working with Laura Smith, a tough MI5 agent, Redstone embarks on a mission to save the country's energy supply and bring those responsible to justice...

...and to use his new skill to mete out justice of his own.

This fast-paced story blends thriller, science fiction and romance to keep the reader turning the pages towards the exhilarating conclusion.

STATE OF RESISTANCE by ELLIOT FINER

US President Turner Cardew has made failing Britain an American colony, governed by a puppet regime and occupied by US forces. But his administration is further damaging the UK, rather than helping it recover. No-one can figure out why.

Mark Redstone's biotechnology company is his life, but faces ruin by the regime's corrupt top British official, who is pursuing a personal vendetta against Redstone.

Desperate to save his company, Redstone fights back with the help of Laura Smith, who's been fired from MI5, and Michelle Clarke, an expert in artificial intelligence. One lonely man, two very different women.

They join a clandestine group working to restore independence. Their struggle is dogged by deceit and violence.

State of Resistance is an imaginative political thriller, interlaced with a story of developing love. A reader of the first Redstone thriller, Killing Power, wrote 'I was immediately hooked on this book and couldn't put it down. I am hoping there will be a sequel from this fine writer.' State of Resistance is that sequel.

Printed in Great Britain
by Amazon

45025756R00199